ANATHEMA

K.A. Tucker

Meg —
Chase your dreams
K. A. Tuck
XOXO

Papoti Books

Library and Archives Canada Cataloguing in Publication

Tucker, K. A. (Kathleen A.), 1978-

Anathema / K.A. Tucker.

Issued also in electronic format.

ISBN 978-0-9869155-0-5

I. Title.

PS8639.U325A66 2011 jC813'.6 C2011-903186-8

Editing by Marg Gilks

Cover design by Extended Imagery/Carl Graves

Printed in the U.S.A

v1

Published by Papoti Books

www.papotibooks.com

To Lia and Sadie, for being.
To Paul, for reading a girl's book...twice.
To my friends and family, for their endless support.

Prologue

"Trust me," Sofie whispered, her delicate hands sliding up Nathan's chest to slip behind his neck.

"And if you're wrong...?" Nathan began but, unable to finish the sentence, his voice trailed off.

"I'm not wrong!" she snapped.

He pulled away and moved to stand before a nearby window, his arms crossed over his chest.

"Let me prove it to you." She glided over to his side, and lifted a finger to push a stray lock of chestnut brown hair off his forehead.

But Nathan ignored the affectionate gesture, focused now on the bustling nightlife beyond the walls of his chateau. Rarely did he envy humans. Tonight, though, as he watched horse–drawn carriages roll along Paris's cobblestone streets, carrying passengers on their way home from frivolous celebrations and too much wine, his jaw tightened with jealousy. Why couldn't his problems be so trivial?

He saw a man stumble out of a tavern and fall to the ground in a drunken heap, directly in the path of two draft horses, and his eyes widened. The idea of witnessing a man trampled to death lifted his spirits. That human's problem would rival his own...He gripped the window frame in anticipation, watching the beasts' mammoth hooves trotting toward the man's limp body, seconds away from squashing his head as if it were a ripe melon. At the last moment, two men grabbed the drunk by the heels and dragged him to safety. The horses continued on, undisturbed. *Damn those good Samaritans.*

Nathan scanned the streets for another person in a predicament worse than his own, knowing the chances were slim. His attention landed on a young couple in the midst of a lovers' quarrel, one that quickly escalated from shrieks and hand gestures to a swift knee to the man's groin. The growing crowd of spectators around the couple erupted in laughter as the young man crumpled to the ground, writhing in pain. Despite the situation, Nathan chuckled, aware that his redheaded spitfire may react in the same fashion momentarily.

Sighing heavily, Nathan dropped his eyes to the oak tree beneath his window, its leaves a rich golden hue with the change of season. It was to be Sofie's burial spot.

That day couldn't be today, though. He wasn't ready.

Nathan shook his head. "No...I cannot bear the risk."

Sofie didn't respond immediately. When she did, it was with the sharpness of a well–honed blade. "Fine." The silk layers of her evening gown rustled noisily as she stalked toward the door.

Before she reached it, Nathan was across the room, his hand barring her exit. "Please don't ask it of anyone else," he pleaded. He knew the request was useless, though. She stared back at him, her olive green eyes blazing in defiance, her intentions clear. She would find someone—someone who didn't care whether she survived. He couldn't allow that.

Another heavy sigh, this one in surrender. "You're impossible, woman," he whispered, shutting his eyes. There was no hint of anger in his tone.

Sofie's throaty laughter filled the room. Victorious, she stretched up to lay an intense kiss on his lips. A farewell kiss, if this failed …

Taking her hands in his, he pulled her to the center of the room where the kerosene lamp burned, the only source of light in the spacious master bedroom.

"No," she protested, scowling, as he reached for it.

"I'm not compromising on this," he answered firmly.

After a second of deliberation, Sofie nodded, relenting—knowing better than to press him further, knowing she had won the war. She lifted her hands to pull her loose hair up off her neck.

Nathan shut his eyes, mentally preparing himself. He trusted her abilities. If anyone could solve this problem, it was his Sofie.

But if she was wrong ...

He opened his eyes to see Sofie's dazzling, confident smile. How he would do anything to see that smile for eternity!

In one fluid motion he extinguished the lamp, plunging the room into darkness.

੨

Sofie's chest heaved as she inhaled deeply, trying to regulate her pounding heart. She had worked tirelessly for this moment, to allow for this possibility—pushing her mind to the brink of sanity, drawing on her skill until she'd drained every ounce of energy.

It was finally happening.

Or was it? Anticipation turned to panic as the seconds stretched to minutes with no signals from Nathan. She stood in silence, her eyes searching the darkness in vain, fighting against the urge to speak out, to plead with him. What if he had changed his mind? What if he had left the room? What if—

Pain. All concern vanished.

Sofie regained consciousness on the bedroom floor. The room was still absolutely dark, yet her eyes darted wildly around, taking in every picture, every fabric pattern, every crack in the ceiling as if sun streamed through the windows. Exhilaration flooded through her.

With only a thought, she was on her feet and standing in front of a mirror. She gasped at the reflection. The eyes staring back were no longer her lackluster olive but a mystical pale mint. Her hand flew to her neck. No puncture marks. Not even a scratch. The only evidence was some dried blood on skin that was now creamy and pale. A slow sigh escaped her lips as the crushing fear of failure lifted from her chest.

It had worked.

She began giggling.

"What in God's name are you so happy about?" a voice boomed. Her head whipped around. Mortimer stood in the doorway, a look of sheer horror splayed across his face. "Do you realize what you've done?" he yelled, slamming his fist against the solid wood door. Splinters flew from the blow.

Sofie twisted her mouth in annoyance. "What are you talking about? It worked!"

"You call *that* success?" He gestured to Sofie's left, his eyebrows raised mockingly.

She turned curious eyes to follow his hand. Her stomach dropped when she saw the body lying motionless beside the bed. "Nathan!"

She flew across the room with inhuman speed, dropping to her knees to clutch Nathan's beautiful face, needing to see his rich chocolate–brown eyes gazing adoringly at her. She released a sharp gasp when she saw the vacuous gray of death staring back at her.

"I don't understand," she whispered, tears welling in her eyes.

"You have no idea what you've done to us," Mortimer answered through gritted teeth. It was obvious that Nathan's death was the least of his concerns.

1. Sofie

"See you tomorrow, Betty," I called out to the shelter's evening receptionist as I passed the front desk. The plump, middle–aged woman responded with a gentle smile and a quick nod before turning her attention back to the homeless man standing beside her.

I held out my hand as I stepped onto the dimly lit sidewalk, testing for rain, expecting it. A relentless, bone–chilling drizzle had laid siege to Portland for the month of September—the kind of gloomy, wet weather that made a person dream of hibernating under a heavy blanket until spring.

To my pleased surprise, my hand encountered not a drop—no rain yet, anyway. I tucked my umbrella under my arm and began walking toward Congress Street, a nightly ritual after finishing my volunteer shift at the shelter. There was something therapeutic about wandering through the city's Art District, admiring the hopes and dreams of local artists on display. More importantly, it dragged out the inevitable trip home before curfew. I was never in a rush to get back to my foster home.

Half a block up, I found a scruffy old man lying across the sidewalk ahead of me. "Evening, Eddie!" I called, smiling gently. Eddie split his time between the shelter and a nearby alley. "I'll bet Betty can find you a nice, warm bed tonight."

Eddie clambered to his knees with surprising agility and, seizing the corners of my navy raincoat with his grimy hands, began a recital of complete gibberish, his fervor increasing exponentially as he rambled on. "Oh, chocolate pools flatter my wretchedness. Yours is the face of an angel, complete with heaven's cream and a halo of spun gold. You are a goddess!"

There were random moments of lucidity with Eddie, days where we could chat normally about trivialities like the weather and local politics. Other days I found him perched on a makeshift pedestal, ranting about giant beasts lurking in the shadows. Then there were days—like today, as he made my dull brown eyes, pallid complexion, and blonde hair sound like gifts from the gods—when he was a whole new kind of crazy.

"No, Eddie. I'm not your goddess, but thanks...I'm flattered." I gently patted his hand.

Three drops of water landed in quick succession on my nose, then the rain began to fall. *Drat.* "Do you need an umbrella?" I eyed the roof of Eddie's home in the alleyway behind him—a cardboard box cleverly shielded by the four umbrellas I had provided for him over the last two weeks.

Eddie responded with his familiar vacant stare, placid eyes indicating he was now there only in physical form. Reaching down, I gently tugged at his arm. His body resisted, as unyielding as a concrete statue. I knew it was hopeless. "Oh, Eddie," I sighed. "You're going to catch pneumonia if you stay out here." I popped open my own umbrella and wrapped its handle within his hands, hoping it would keep him dry until his mind returned and moved his body indoors.

Wrapping my arms tightly around my chest, I set off at a brisk walk. I could handle a little rain. As if Mother Nature were privy to my thoughts, the sky suddenly opened up and the light drizzle evolved into a monsoon, pouring buckets of water onto my head. I began running blindly, seeking shelter.

Guilt welled in the pit of my stomach as I ran, picturing Eddie sitting on the sidewalk with one measly little umbrella to protect him. *I should go check on him. Maybe the cold rain snapped him out of his daze, and I can convince him to stay at the shelter tonight. Yes, that's the right thing to do. It's only a few blocks back, if I turn around now—*

My shin collided with something solid. I stumbled, executing an awkward cartwheel before crashing facedown in a puddle on the concrete sidewalk.

How long I lay in heap on the sidewalk, disoriented, faintly aware of rain permeating my clothes through to my skin, I couldn't say. I regained my senses when I couldn't hear drops pelting the sidewalk anymore. Crawling to my knees, I wiped the mucky water off my cheek and checked for blood. None. No scrapes or cuts. My shin didn't appear to be broken or even hurting, though it should by all accounts be shattered. Maybe I'd earned a bruise at least. Otherwise, miraculously, I was fine.

The victim of my inattentiveness was not so lucky. I groaned, my hands flying to my forehead in dismay as I appraised what looked to have been a lovely and expensive stained–glass object, now scattered in dozens of pieces. I leaned over to begin collecting the shards.

"You'll cut yourself," a woman's silky voice called in a French accent.

I looked up. A stunning redhead stood in a doorway, regarding me with eyes that were the most peculiar shade of pale mint green—so pale, they appeared inhuman. *She has a good point,* I realized as I regarded the jagged piece of glass in my hand. "But I can't just leave it here. Someone may hurt themselves on it."

"And what do you plan on doing with all the pieces?" she asked, lifting a brow in query.

"I don't know...glue them back together?" I said with the certainty of a gas station attendant asked to perform solo brain surgery.

The woman smirked. "I bought that lantern in France. It's one of a kind and it certainly can't be glued back together," she informed me, her tone cool, yet serene.

Oh no. This was hers. "I'm so sorry. There was so much rain! I was distracted and I just...hit it. I'm so sorry. I'll pay you for it."

"You have ten thousand dollars?" Those haunting eyes gazed down at my rain–soaked department store clothes with amusement.

I felt the blood drain from my face. "No, but—" The ground swayed, and I tasted bitter bile forming in the back of my throat. I didn't have ten thousand dollars. I had exactly forty–seven dollars in my bank account and no job.

She regarded me silently, her expression unreadable. Finally she spoke. "I'm Sofie. What's your name?"

I hesitated, swallowing. "Evangeline."

"Evangeline …" My name sounded so elegant, rolling off her tongue. "Please, come in and warm up with something hot. On the house, of course. I insist." She reached out with a delicate–looking hand to help me to my feet. "Leave all of this. I'll clean it up later."

Confused by her kindness, I accepted, following her like a disoriented puppy.

A soft buzz of conversation and jazz music enveloped me as I stepped into the warm café. A stone fireplace was the source of that heat, a blaze of fierce orange flames dancing on its hearth.

"Welcome to Newt's Brew," Sofie said as she led me past sharply–dressed patrons lounging in upholstered chairs of varying style and pattern as they sipped lazily from colorful mugs. "Here, sit." She pointed to a stool by the counter. "Hot chocolate?"

I nodded.

"I also offer lattes, cappuccinos, espresso, herbal teas—anything at all, if you would prefer something else. And of course, the most supremely delectable pastries," she added, noticing my eyes bulge as I observed the array of sweets in the display case behind the counter.

"Hot chocolate would be wonderful, thanks," I said, curiosity pulling my eyes away to scan the place—all dark hardwoods, rich fabrics, and ornate moldings.

Sofie went behind the counter and tossed me a large towel. "You look like a drowned cat." Her accent made the statement sound exotic.

I glimpsed my reflection in a mirror on the wall behind her, and had to agree. I spent the next few minutes quietly drying my long hair, wishing I could strip out of my wet clothes and curl up by the fire.

"Follow me, please," Sofie said, heading over to the fireplace. "Would you mind?" she asked the couple sitting in the seats directly in front of it, as she gestured at me.

"Oh no, that's okay!" I quickly countered, embarrassed, but the couple was already up and on their way out the door, all smiles.

Sofie motioned to one of the chairs.

"You really didn't need to do that," I said, guilt creasing my forehead.

She waved my protests away, her other hand pointing insistently toward the chair.

Accepting with a sheepish smile, I sank into the chair, my wet jeans clinging uncomfortably, then closed my eyes as my body absorbed the heat.

Moments later I heard something being set on the table beside me and opened my eyes. A mug of hot chocolate mounded high with whipped cream sat there; Sofie had settled in the seat across from me. I stared at her in awe. No one, aside from my own mother, had ever shown a quarter of the compassion that this stunning woman was doling out so freely and unwarranted to a girl who had just broken one of her valuable possessions.

"So, how do you propose to pay me back for my lantern?"

Her words yanked me back to reality. My gaze dropped to floor, and that pungent bile crept up to touch my taste buds again. The simple act of breathing became difficult. *Great question.* How was I going to come up with *ten thousand dollars*? Though I'd tried hard to find a job in the last four months, the rejections were always the same: experience needed. And I was fresh from high school graduation—no experience here.

The silence dragged on as I studied the flames. Finally I braved Sofie's gaze again. She was leaning back in her chair with the poise and style of a super model, her fitted black dress accentuating her curves and highlighting her creamy pale skin.

She spoke before I could. "You know, many people would say that it's my fault for putting something so expensive out on the sidewalk. It was bound to get broken," she offered, still with no emotion.

My mouth opened to respond but no words came out. That thought hadn't crossed my mind. The excuse would certainly get me off the hook, but I knew my conscience would never accept it, instead pricking me endlessly like a sliver in my clothes. "No. You're nice, offering me an excuse, but I broke it and I should pay for it...somehow."

An oppressive weight settled on my chest and I sent my eyes to roam the room again. The tables were covered with dirty mugs waiting to be picked up and I could see that the wet floor was in desperate need of a mop. It dawned on me—I hadn't seen anyone serving customers. "I could work here?" I blurted without thinking. A vivid image of me in my Sketchers and faded jeans, tripping over a chair leg and scalding a customer with a tray of hot drinks, popped into my mind. I quickly amended my suggestion. "I could wash dishes, clear tables, run errands—whatever you need. All day, seven days a week. Whatever you need. It may take a while for me to earn the money ..." *More like forever.*

Those cool, pale eyes studied me silently, revealing nothing.

"I don't know. Maybe it's a stupid idea." I bit down on my thumbnail.

She ignored that. "Yes, I believe I can find something for you here. Can you start tomorrow night at six?"

"Seriously?" I exclaimed, unable to hide my shock.

She nodded, once.

As I glanced around the place, a thrill stirred in my stomach. *What would I be doing?* I didn't care. "Okay. Yes. Thank you." I made a mental note to call the shelter to let them know I wouldn't be coming in for the next few...years.

"Wonderful." Sofie rose and walked over to the counter. She grabbed a pen from behind the counter and scrawled something on a sheet of paper, then returned and handed it to me. "Please fill this out. I've marked your starting pay at the top." I saw the slightest smile touch Sofie's plump lips—the first one that night. "Some say I pay too well."

I looked down at the elegant writing at the top of the job application, and gasped.

CB

My watch read ten minutes to six when I pushed through the heavy wooden door of Newt's Brew the next evening, my nerves performing a full circus production in the pit of my stomach. I'd sat up in bed most of the previous night, replaying the inexplicable evening in my head countless times. Half of me was sick to my stomach knowing I wouldn't be registering for college before my fiftieth birthday, given the debt I had so clumsily acquired. But the other half wondered how I had managed to go from landing my first job in a trendy cafe to a salary that could only be described as ridiculous.

Newt's Brew was empty. Not one customer idled with a cup of coffee. No buzz of conversation in the air. Maybe it was still early, I decided. Sofie stood behind the counter, her back to me, intent on something in her hands. "Hi Sofie!" I called in a bubbly voice.

"Good evening, Evangeline," she responded without turning, with that same reserved air I was coming to recognize as a usual aspect of her personality.

My chest tightened. *What if she regrets hiring me?* "Tell me what I can do," I urged, sprinting around the counter to face Sofie. Clad in a provocative, knee–length indigo–blue dress that accentuated her waspish hourglass figure, she was opening a trash bag. I tugged self–consciously on the bottom of my shirt. After spending the entire day in front of my closet, fussing over my mediocre wardrobe, I had finally settled on my nicest pair of dark blue jeans and a gray and black striped shirt, certain that I would still look like a hobo off the street next to the worst–dressed customer in this place.

"These all need to go," she said, waving a hand dismissively at the display of desserts.

I picked up a silver platter and sniffed a slice of apple pie. It *smelled* fine.

"Help yourself, if you're hungry," she offered, bending to tuck the bag into the trash can.

"Are you getting a new batch in?"

She shook her head. "I have to close Newt's. I have some unfinished business in New York."

Close? My smile faltered. "Oh...For how long?"

"A few weeks, at least. Maybe more."

My smile fell completely. "Well...is there anything I can do to help? I

have ten thousand dollars' worth of hours to put in for you, don't forget."
A small, uncomfortable giggle escaped me. I'd happily forget that part.

"This place is pretty much ready for closing," Sofie answered, moving to the sink to rinse her hands.

"Okay. Well, I'll be here when you get back, I guess."

We spent the next minutes in awkward silence as I scraped chocolate sauce off a plate, feeling as if an internal bubble had just been popped. *Why am I so disappointed? So I'll have to wait a few weeks to begin paying off my gigantic debt. So what?*

Because it wasn't just about the money, I realized. I *wanted* to work here—to meet new people, to talk to them, to have them actually respond to me. To befriend Sofie...I stole a glance toward her back. *She's so interesting. So cool.*

"Unless you want to come with me to New York?" Sofie asked suddenly, turning to meet my gaze.

The plate slipped from my hands and clattered noisily against the tile floor. I felt my eyes bulging. *Go to New York City with her?*

"You don't have to. I could use your help, though," she added.

"I...I don't—" I stammered, my heart beginning to race. *Me in New York?* I had never been beyond Portland's suburbs.

"You wouldn't have to worry about accommodations or meals." Sofie leaned down to pick the plate up off the floor.

"It's a wonderful offer, Sofie," I began, picturing myself surrounded by skyscrapers and the bustling city life. My stomach spasmed with excitement. *This is crazy—isn't it? Would a sane person say yes to this? I barely know the woman!* Granted, I had smashed her property and she in turn had graciously invited me in for cocoa and a high-paying job—hardly the signs of a serial killer. And this was a job, after all. People traveled all the time for jobs, I rationalized.

"Consider your debt to me squared away after this trip," she added. "You'll have earned it."

My jaw dropped, and my shoulders lifted as if relieved of an oppressive weight—and they had been. *I won't owe her anything? But...that means she won't be obligated to have me work here.* I bit my lip, glancing around the empty café with a twinge of regret.

"Of course, if you want to continue working at Newt's, you're welcome to," Sofie added as if reading my mind.

The offer was turning richer with every second that I dithered. I didn't know what to do. I wished I could ask my mother for advice. "Wow. You're hard to refuse," I began, smiling nervously.

"What's there to refuse?" Sofie reached out, a cordless phone in her hand. "Tell you what: if your parents are okay with it, then you know it's a good idea, right?"

I hesitated for a few seconds but eventually accepted the phone and dialed home.

My foster mom picked up on the second ring. "Hello?"

"Uh, hi, Shelley?"

"Yes, Evangeline. What would you like?" she asked in her typical polite but detached tone. She was never unkind, nor was she overly friendly. She was just there. All of my foster families had been the same. I was used to it. Sometimes I wondered if they were government–designed robots disguised as foster parents—programmed to conform to the law but incapable of exhibiting emotion.

"Um, well, I got a job yesterday, down at a café in the Art District," I began. This was the most I had spoken to her in days.

"That's nice." Silence.

"And my new boss just asked me to go to New York to help her with some business. Would that be okay with you?" I held my breath.

"You turn eighteen tomorrow. You can legally do what you want."

I was amazed that she'd remembered my birthday. Clearly she had no plans to celebrate it. Not a shocker. I normally went full–fledged hermit on my birthday anyway, burrowing under a blanket with a bag of popcorn and a mittful of Disney classics. "Okay, well, I may go then. I'm not sure when I'll be back, though."

"Have fun." I heard the phone click before I could say another word.

"Well?" Sofie asked.

I stared at the dead receiver in my hand. How representative of my life. In the five years since my mother's death, my existence had become like a one–way conversation with the world—a solitary life spent drifting through homes and schools, all but invisible to those around me.

Until now. Sofie had noticed me.

"I think I'd like to come to New York with you, if that's alright." *Am I really doing this?*

"Wonderful!" Sofie said, revealing a rare spike of excitement.

"Yes, great." I smiled nervously, half expecting men in white coats to storm through the door. "So, when are we leaving?"

Sofie reached under the counter, retrieving a purse and coat. She walked toward the door, her stilettos clicking sharply against the wood floor. "Now," she called to me, flicking off the light switch. I stared, waiting for her to elaborate. "Don't doddle!" she added, suddenly urgent.

I joined her at the front door and we stepped out just as a black sedan pulled up to the curb. "You're kidding," I exclaimed, my nerves stirring my bladder.

"Hop in!" she instructed, opening the door for me.

"But...I should pack some things …"

She waved away my concerns. "Don't worry about any of that."

I stood there, baffled. *Don't worry about clean underwear and a toothbrush?*

A sharp edge in Sofie's voice brooked no argument. "Get in the car, Evangeline! The plane is waiting."

2. The Gift

My hands fidgeted in my lap as I surveyed the bright and airy cabin of Sofie's friend's private jet for the umpteenth time. We were about two–thirds of the way to New York and I was on my third glass of red wine. I had politely declined when the flight attendant first offered, admitting I was underage. But Sofie rolled her eyes dramatically and ordered the woman to disregard my silliness and keep my glass half full at all times.

I had protested then. Now, feeling the alcohol–induced relaxation seeping through my body, I silently thanked them for ignoring me. Easing back into my chair, I pressed a button on the side of my armrest and watched with fascination as a footstool magically rose from the floor.

"Finally...you'd think we were escorting you to an enema," Sofie muttered, glancing up from her magazine.

"Sorry." I offered a sheepish smile. "I'm a little nervous of flying." I was lying, of course. Flying didn't bother me—that part was exciting. The fact that twenty–four hours ago this woman was a complete stranger and now I was flying to New York with her—without so much as an extra pair of underwear and for God knows how long—had me frazzled.

Sofie, on the other hand, was totally relaxed, stretched out in one of the ivory leather lounge chairs across from me, her long, slender legs crossed at the ankles; she could easily be posing for the cover of a

Lifestyles of the Rich and Famous magazine.

"So this friend of yours who owns this plane...what does he do?" I asked.

"Oh, Viggo has his hands in everyone's pocket," Sofie answered cryptically, setting down her magazine to root through her purse. "Here. " She handed me a long, narrow wooden box. "As a thank you for coming. Also, I noticed on your application that your birthday is tomorrow, so...happy birthday."

I gaped at her, speechless.

"It's nothing extravagant," she added.

"I …" I stared down at the box. After a long moment, I opened it. A heart–shaped, black glass pendant the size of a quarter nestled inside. I lifted it gingerly, running a thumb over its smooth surface; it felt much like a highly polished stone. "You really didn't need to—" I stopped to swallow the lump in my throat.

"Here, let me put it on you," she offered, moving to sit next to me and lifting the silver chain to affix it around my neck. The pendant settled against my chest. "Shoot," she murmured.

I glanced over my shoulder to see her frowning. "What?"

"Oh, something's wrong with the clasp," she replied. I could feel her examining it. "It won't open without breaking. Do me a favor and leave it on for now."

"Of course!" I answered, my hand cupping the smooth stone to admire it. I'd gladly wear it forever.

Sofie shifted back to her chair, watching me with a curious expression. "It looks nice," she finally offered with a strained smile that never reached her eyes.

"Thank you. It's beautiful," I said, looking down at it. There was a precious quality to its simplicity. I wondered when she'd had the chance to get it, since we'd gone directly from Newt's to the airport. I opened my mouth to ask, but Sofie had already turned her attention back to her magazine.

I turned to gaze out the small window beside me. We were descending through the clouds. I expected to see a billion lights below soon, welcoming us to our destination, escorting me into a new and unknown chapter in my life. But for now, the flashing lights on the plane's wings were alone in the sky, beacons serving as both protection and guidance.

A hollow feeling blossomed in my chest as I realized that warning lights like those could have saved my mother's life. It had been five years since the night she'd been run down by a car. An eternity for me. The police investigation had been short and inconclusive, suggesting that the driver hadn't seen her. There were no tire marks to imply otherwise. Scared, drunk, oblivious—whatever the reason, the driver never stayed, leaving my mother's shattered body on the pavement and me a broken–hearted orphan.

I closed my eyes and imagined forcing that terrible hollowness into a bottle and corking it tightly. That's how I had learned to deal with the loss of my mother. It usually worked. This time, though, the empty void expanded, pushing against my rib cage, constricting my lungs, becoming a stabbing ache in my heart. *Deep breaths, Evangeline.* I inhaled and exhaled slowly, waiting for the pain to dissipate. It didn't. It only intensified with each new breath, as each beat of my heart came harder and faster. Blood rushed to my head, the sound in my ears overpowering the roar of the jet engines.

What's happening to me? My eyes darted wildly around the plane's interior. The walls and floor wavered. I knew it had nothing to do with the pilot's flying skills.

And then my heart stopped beating altogether. Just like that. I couldn't even manage a gasp. My right hand flew to my chest while my left groped through the air for help, for Sofie. It only lasted for a second or two, then my heart thumped once, twice. Three times. And then it was beating again.

A cool hand rested against mine. "Feeling okay?" Sofie asked, leaning in to peer at my face, her brow furrowed with worry.

"Yes. Just felt a little funny for a sec. Must be my nerves," I assured her, adding with a nervous grin, "or the wine."

"Are you sure?"

I nodded, smiling reassuringly.

The copilot poked his head out from the cockpit to announce that we would be landing shortly. My body jerked in response as the seat reverted to a stiff, upright position. Exactly how it should be for a safe landing. Sofie's gentle laughter filled the cabin.

Everything else was forgotten.

 C3

"We're staying here," Sofie announced as our sleek black town car turned into a driveway off Fifth Avenue. I looked out at a luxurious five–storey building illuminated theatrically by exterior lights shining upward, high-lighting the grooves and ridges and other rich details of its architecture. The car idled quietly, waiting for a heavy iron garage door to glide open before pulling into the dimly lit tunnel beyond. It ended at a second garage door that didn't open until the first was firmly shut.

"I guess we'll be safe here," I murmured.

Sofie offered only a small smile before turning her minty eyes for-ward, her jaw tense. She seemed nervous.

The second door opened and the car pulled forward. My eyes widened in amazement. "Wow. This is …"

We were in an enclosed courtyard filled with lush gardens bisected by winding walkways. Giant coach lanterns illuminated five storeys of bal-conies climbing the four walls—there had to be a hundred of them, each adorned with a wrought–iron windowbox overflowing with flowers in vibrant sunset hues.

A throat cleared. I turned to find the car door wide open and a white–haired man in a three–piece suit patiently waiting, his hand out-stretched.

"Sorry!" I scurried across the seat to accept his hand. My feet landed on cobblestones as I slid out.

"Good evening, Miss Evangeline," the man said in a rich British accent as he executed a formal bow. "I am Leonardo, the butler. Please inform me if you require anything at all during your stay."

I nodded dumbly, awed as much by him as I was by my surroundings. It was warm in here—balmy, compared to the frigid temperature outside.

I took a few steps forward and knelt to touch a velvety rose petal. "I didn't think roses could bloom this late."

"They don't, normally. Look up," Sofie said. "See the dome?"

I tipped my head back and squinted at the dark night sky above us, finally noticing the web of black lines holding the glass panes between them in an intricate pattern. The giant courtyard was an atrium.

"Feel free to tour the gardens," Leonardo offered, smiling encouragement.

I hesitated only a second before returning the smile and taking off down one of the paths like a child investigating a secret garden. Until tonight, a place like this had only existed in fairytales filled with royal palaces and princesses. Now, as I strolled along the cobblestone path, inhaling the heady scents of lavender and mint, it was real. And I was living in it.

Something white in the center of the atrium caught my eye. Drawn to it, I stopped before a large statue—a sculpture of a woman in a flowing gown, arms reaching toward the sky, hands awkwardly clasped together as if offering up a gift to the heavens.

"Spectacular, isn't she? Truly one of a kind," a male voice called in an unusual accent. I jumped, startled, as an attractive blonde man of about thirty in a pinstriped suit approached along the path. "The smoothest white marble imaginable. Go on, touch it!" he said in a commanding tone.

I obliged almost mechanically, leaning forward to slide my fingertips along the statue's toes. They were icy cold. "Very smooth," I agreed, straightening. Blood instantly rushed to my head. The ground began to sway. I closed my eyes, vaguely aware of a strong hand grabbing my arm and moving me.

When the dizziness disappeared, I found myself sitting at a bistro table near the statue. Sofie, Leonardo, and the blonde man stood around me, concerned expressions on their faces. *What's wrong with me lately?* I felt my cheeks grow hot. "Must be the flight. Or the wine. I'm sorry." I smiled sheepishly. When Sofie's distressed expression didn't fade, I added, "This atrium is spectacular," hoping to redirect their attention.

The blonde man's sparkling cobalt–blue eyes roamed over the gardens, a proud smile stretching his lips. "Isn't it, though? I hate the long, cold winters but I love this city too much to move to a warmer climate. This atrium is the perfect compromise."

"Yes, the gas company agrees whole–heartedly. The fool keeps them in business, heating this place," a man muttered darkly behind me in a thick French accent. I turned to see a tall, broad–shouldered man with chestnut brown hair and black eyes marching toward us. He was dressed as sharply as the blonde.

"You ridicule, yet you have no trouble taking full advantage," the blonde retorted with a deep scowl, pointing toward the bistro table. When his attention fell back to me, his face lit up again. "Welcome to our home, Evangeline! I'm Sofie's friend, Viggo. That grouch there is Mortimer." Viggo draped his arm casually around my shoulder as if he were a long–time friend. My shoulders tensed in response, unaccustomed to the closeness. Luckily, if he noticed, he didn't seem bothered.

This entire place is theirs? Wide–eyed, I scanned the multitude of bal-conies again. "Thank you for letting me stay here."

"Oh, Sofie warned us that you were a darling, with such manners," Viggo said, smiling. "I hope it didn't take too much convincing to get you here."

Mortimer chuckled deeply. "Sofie could convince a troll to abandon his bridge if she set her mind to it."

Viggo threw an unimpressed glare at Mortimer before turning back to me. "But you are far from a troll, my beautiful Evangeline." He laughed, his eyes twinkling as he pulled me out of my chair and squeezed me in a fatherly side–hug.

It was how I had always imagined my father would embrace me, if I had known him. My dad had never been in the picture, deciding father-hood was too daunting the second he learned of his seventeen–year–old girlfriend's pregnancy. Oddly enough, he had no concerns about scaling treacherous cliffs. It was a freak mountain climbing accident—not the cries of a little girl—that had killed him.

My face flared with heat at Viggo's brazen compliment. "Give her room to breathe, Viggo," Sofie warned. "She's been two seconds away from a mild coronary the entire trip here."

Viggo chuckled. "Come. Let's show you to your room. You must be exhausted. This way."

I turned to follow him. And gasped.

Four beasts stood in a row ten feet away from me, their unsettling, beady yellow eyes studying me with suspicion. I call them beasts because they were simply too large to be anything else. Their cropped, pointy ears were level with my shoulders—and at five foot nine, I was by no means considered short. Their muscular bodies, covered in glossy black fur, were easily triple my weight.

One of them sauntered forward, its talon–like claws clicking against the cobblestones with each step. It halted in front of Mortimer for a sniff and a pat, its gaze never leaving mine.

"Evangeline, meet Maximus, Sebastian, Charleston, and Remington. My fiercely loyal and protective guard dogs." Mortimer gave the dog a playful shove before pulling its head affectionately into his chest.

"What kind of dogs are they?" I asked warily, edging back to stand behind Viggo.

"Oh, they're...a unique strain. No others exist in the world."

"Because their mother was a horse?" I mumbled under my breath.

Mortimer's laughter reverberated throughout the atrium. It was deep and menacing and left me unsettled. "I agree, they are much larger than we had expected—and they consume the equivalent of a horse."

My hand flew to my mouth.

"Don't be worried about offending us, dear Evangeline," Viggo said, patting my back, chuckling.

"You don't like my dogs?" Mortimer's eyes narrowed.

"Oh, no! I'm just...shocked by their size." I stepped forward and reached up to stiffly pat the top of a head. I didn't know whose. They all looked the same.

Mortimer laughed again, obviously aware of my discomfort. "You will learn to appreciate their companionship, I promise," he called over his shoulder as he walked down the path toward a set of double red doors embedded in one of the walls.

I peered at the four pairs of eyes gazing back at me, unconvinced.

CR

I received the grand tour of their home, or parts of it, because a full tour would have lasted into the wee hours of the night. Viggo explained the extensive renovations while we wove through the countless rooms and marbled hallways, including the construction of an atrium where one had never existed.

"We could have built an identical home from the ground up for one–eighth of the cost," Mortimer complained. "But Viggo had to have *this* location and what Viggo wants, Viggo gets."

Viggo only winked in response.

So they lived together. That meant they were more than platonic friends—although, listening to their interaction, I never in a million years would have guessed it.

We ended the tour on the top floor. Viggo pushed open a set of double doors, and threw his arms wide. "Your suite, mademoiselle."

To the left of me was a king–sized four–poster bed, dressed in layers of feathery pillows and opulent bedding, all in a mixture of white and silvery gray. Circular glass tables on either side of the bed held crystal lamps and fresh bouquets of ivory calla lilies, and a crystal chandelier sparkled above it all. To my right, a white velvet chaise waited beside an oversized fireplace. A watercolor of a young girl picking wild flowers hung over the marble mantel. The softly–hued image stirred familiarity within me, though I couldn't place it.

"Leonardo stocked your room with clothing, toiletries, and the like," Viggo said, placing a firm hand on my back to prod me toward a door in the opposite wall. With the turn of a knob and the flick of a switch, I found myself standing in a walk–in closet filled with a department store–worth of clothing and shoes. "Everything your little heart may require for your stay," he added with a smile.

My jaw dropped. *All for me?*

"Yes, it's for you. It should fit perfectly. All new and—" His eyes narrowed as something caught his attention. He walked over and reached into a basket to pull out a lacy pink thong. "Oh, you old devil, Leonardo." He grinned.

If there was a competition over whose face turned a harsher shade of red—Leonardo's or mine—I couldn't say who would win.

Leonardo gruffly cleared his throat. "Martha was in charge of those...items," he answered curtly. Spinning on his heels, he marched out of the room.

"I should be more careful or I'll give the old man a heart attack," Viggo murmured, casually tossing the frilly thing back into the basket and walking out.

I followed, still shocked by their generosity. *At least that solves my underwear issue ...*

"It's late. You likely need your rest," Mortimer exclaimed after releasing an obviously phony yawn.

"Please help yourself to anything in the kitchen, should you get hungry. Our staff made sure the fridge was fully stocked," Viggo added, patting my back.

They all turned to leave.

I panicked. "Wait!" Three sets of piercing eyes turned to regard me curiously. "What if I get lost?"

Viggo threw his head back and howled with laughter. "Oh, you are precious, aren't you!" He pinched my cheek.

"Maximus will guide you," Mortimer answered, trying to keep his amusement from showing.

I turned to find that the massive animal had crept in behind me. I eyed the beast skeptically.

"Don't worry, he knows this place well." Viggo chuckled.

Maximus stared at me with oddly perceptive eyes for a moment and then, letting out an unimpressed groan, he flopped down beside the fireplace.

Sofie was the last to leave. She gave me a small, apologetic smile. "I'm sorry. Those two can be...overwhelming."

I shook my head, giggling "They're nice. And extremely generous."

Sofie bit her bottom lip, suddenly pensive. "I'm just down the hall if you need me."

"No worries. I have a tour guide, remember?"

Sofie glanced over at the big beast, her eyes narrowing to slits. "Well, if you need anything, I'm there."

"You're kidding, right? What more could I possibly need?" I waved to the luxurious suite. "I could die a happy girl here, tonight."

Sofie's face contorted in horror for a second before she schooled it to her normally reserved expression. "Well, good night then." With another icy gaze at the giant mass of canine muscle, she was gone, walking briskly down the hall.

"Well, I guess it's just you and me, Maximus. Max."

Max groaned and stood. He walked over to stand beside the bed and lifted one paw to the mattress, patting it several times as if instructing me to get in.

I laughed, my fear of him melting away. He didn't look so threatening after all. "Are you trying to tell me something?" I glanced at the bedside clock. A quarter to midnight, and I was wired. There was no way I'd get any sleep tonight. *But I may as well get comfortable,* I decided, heading to the closet to find some pajamas.

Now that I didn't have an audience, I could shamelessly investigate the plethora of clothes. My hands eagerly sorted through racks upon racks of stylish clothes, all with designer tags still attached—*Fendi, Burberry, Versace, Vera Wang*—names I recognized from fashion magazines but never imagined wearing. An entire wall housed shoes; I counted thirty pairs. *Thirty!* From runners to boots with three inch–high heels, and everything in between. On another wall hung dozens of wire baskets filled with socks, pajamas, and intimates—including the infamous thong.

As I rifled through the pile of cozy flannel separates—my typical choice—my eye caught white lace trim. Curious, I pulled out a gray two–piece set. I rubbed the material between my fingers, reveling in the softness. "Why not?" I muttered, stripping down to try on the slinky outfit. I looked in a mirror. Half my chest was exposed, the tank top's plunging neckline bordering on obscene. "What do you think, Max? Too sexy?"

He pushed past me and, walking over to the basket of pajamas, stuck his muzzle into it. He resurfaced with a pair of fuzzy pink Tigger–printed flannels between his teeth.

"Yes, Max, that is more me." I chuckled wryly. "The old me. This," I twirled, "is the new me. The adventurous, confident Evangeline." My life was full of new beginnings. "I think I'll stay in it. I'm not going out in public anyway," I threw over my shoulder, leaving the closet.

Max followed, groaning.

Next I checked out the ensuite bathroom—an outrageously large, spa–like room constructed in white marble and crystal. The counter held dozens of creams and soaps and the equivalent of an entire drugstore cosmetics aisle, including some metal tools that in my opinion belonged in a serial killer's torture kit.

Max nosed through the door and sauntered over to nuzzle my neck affectionately. I giggled. His nuzzles turned to shoves as he herded me out into the bedroom and toward my bed, his sheer size easily overpowering me.

I sighed, scratching his ear affectionately. "I'm not tired yet, Max." My eyes wandered around my luxurious suite, taking in every detail from the bed frame to the doorknobs. "They sure do have a lot of money, don't they ..." I slid my fingertips along the sculpted mantel, likely worth enough to pay for my first year of college.

My eyes lifted to the watercolor and that same twinge of familiarity stirred. The little girl was in a park, with a swing set and red and white striped monkey bars in the distant background. Leaning in, I read the signature in the bottom right corner. My eyes widened in shock. "Sofie painted this?" *Could it be?* Yes, I supposed it could. I knew absolutely nothing about her.

A gigantic yawn escaped me. *Maybe I will sleep tonight, after all.* "Okay, Max. You win. Now I'm ready to sleep."

I crawled into the giant bed and burrowed under the luxuriously soft duvet, suddenly exhausted. Max hovered beside my bed, watching keenly. "Night, Max," I said through a yawn, reaching out to pat his nose. My other hand clasped Sofie's pendant, imagining heat radiating from it.

ଔ

I must have blinked a dozen times before my pupils adjusted to the dark. It was either late dusk or early dawn, I couldn't tell which. Trees towered over me, soaring skyward to form a canopy so expansive that I could barely glimpse the moonlit sky beyond. I was surrounded by forest. *Where am I?*

3. Drowning

From the corner of my eye, I saw a person standing motionless nearby. I turned my head to look. Not a person, a statue—the white woman from Viggo and Mortimer's atrium. I frowned. *Hadn't Viggo called her one of a kind?*

Something burned hot against my chest, like an ember scorching my skin. Looking down, I realized it was my pendant. Only it wasn't the cold, glassy black heart Sofie had given me. It had come alive, glowing with a swirling current of orange and crimson. I lifted the pendant off my chest by its chain; no burns marred the skin underneath. *It must be like a mood ring, only it gets hot with color changes. Someone's discovered a way to revive that dreadful fad.*

A faint breeze caressed my body. I shivered in response and wrapped my arms tightly around my bare arms. *Bare?* Glancing down, I groaned. I was in my pajamas, the revealing gray ones. *I can't believe I left the house in this!* Peering farther down, I saw exposed toes. *Perfect. No shoes either. Did I sleepwalk out of Mortimer and Viggo's place?*

I sat up and checked the shadows, grumbling, "Where is that bloody mutt?" The big black dog hadn't followed me. I pushed to my feet and took a step forward, the cold, damp moss of the forest floor tickling my bare skin. A twig snapped beneath my weight—so slight a sound that it should have gone unnoticed but instead echoed like a thunderclap in the eerie silence. Nothing moved. Nothing seemed alive.

My stomach knotted up in panic. I inched back toward the statue to wait for rescue. My teeth began chattering, the chilly night air uncomfortable, even with my blazing pendant as a source of heat. *I may freeze to death out here,* I realized. *Maybe this statue is the frozen result of another girl wandering into the woods, never to be heard from again.*

I finally accepted that I had to seek out help. I stepped hesitantly forward, my feet barely registering the cold from the ground anymore. I wandered into the mass of bushes and ferns surrounding the clearing where the statue stood, my face periodically caressed by a stray leaf as I pushed branches out of my path. I kept moving, stumbling over roots as the darkness deepened within the dense thicket, beginning to feel as if I were being swallowed whole.

"I'm from Maine and I have zero basic survival skills," I admitted sourly to myself. "That will change. As soon as I get back, I'm signing up for the first Wilderness for Dummies class I can find." *And a psychiatrist.*

My ears caught a faint and distant sound. I held my breath, listening intently. *Laughter?* It was so far away, and barely audible...It couldn't be. *My mind must be playing tricks on me.* I took several more steps then froze, praying I wasn't hallucinating. Seconds ticked by. *There!* This time, I heard a clear howl of mirth in the distance. *People!*

I took off like an arrow, abandoning my usual caution, tearing recklessly through the thick undergrowth toward the sound. Branches and leaves whipped against my body but I barely noticed, too busy holding my breath. *Do I shout out to them? Let them know I'm coming?* I opted for keeping silent, concentrating on not running headfirst into any of the mammoth tree trunks. I figured they'd see the glow from my necklace anyway, now blazing with brilliant light like a beacon in a thick fog.

I finally broke free of the bushes to find a moonlit river, maybe twenty feet wide, stretching out in front of me. I had to grab the trunk of a small tree growing at its edge to stop myself from tumbling in. Momentary panic clenched my stomach. *How am I going to cross this?* It wasn't a huge river but it was October. The water would be icy cold.

Boisterous male laughter rang out. I turned toward it and saw, maybe a hundred feet away on the other side of the river, my soon–to–be rescuers standing with their backs to me. I exhaled and then breathed in slowly, sweet relief filling my lungs. I was going to be okay.

There were three of them and they were keenly focused on a large object at their feet. Something was extremely funny because they were practically doubled over in laughter. They obviously hadn't noticed me yet—astonishing, given the noise I had surely generated while streaking through the forest like a wild boar.

I opened my mouth to holler but a sound other than laughter clamped my mouth shut, the short hairs on the back of my neck standing on end. It had come from a female, and it wasn't laughter. All three men crouched down around whatever was by their feet. *What are they doing?* I squinted, concentrating hard on the object.

It moved.

A chill of realization slid down my spine. It wasn't an object. It was a person.

"I'll visit, I promise," I heard a male voice bellow as one of them hoisted the person's body up and tossed it toward the center of the river. A large rectangular object followed closely after, entering the river with a big splash.

The blood coursing through my veins turned icy as I stood there, my eyes wide with terror. I waited for the body to resurface, a kick or a splash—some sign of life, some clue that this was a prank.

It finally sank in. I was witnessing murder. Someone was drowning right before my eyes. These people weren't going to save me. Once they noticed I was here, they'd hunt me down and toss me in to join their first victim, to hide all evidence. All they had to do was turn around.

My hand flew to my pendant, trying to mask the pulsating glow. I dropped noiselessly to the ground and slithered commando style into a thick mass of ferns until I was adequately concealed but still able to observe the killers. They loitered on the edge of the river, chattering and laughing like a bunch of teenagers while their victim drowned.

Feeling marginally safe for the moment, I turned my attention to the person in the water. It had to be the female. Was she alive when she was tossed in? She hadn't struggled or even uttered a sound. If she was alive, surely she could only hold her breath for three, four minutes, tops, if I had learned anything from high school Biology class. *One...two...three...*I began counting seconds in my head but couldn't get past *five.* The sound of my pounding heart kept making me lose count. The more I focused on slowing it, the more furious the beating became.

The group's casual chatter died down and they turned and began scanning the forest. My chest tightened in alarm as three pairs of eyes landed on the very bush I was hiding under. *Oh God, they can see me. They're going to drown me too.* My body went rigid. Would they go through the trouble of crossing the river to get to me? Of course they would. I was a witness to their evil crime.

I waited for splashes, for that menacing laugh, for a hand to wrench me from my hiding spot. I gritted my teeth as the burn of my pendant intensified, certain that it was searing my skin. Thankfully it was buried under my body, otherwise there'd be a bright red flare to guide the murderers over.

Leave! Leave! an insistent voice screamed inside my head.

My palms were damp, my knuckles had turned white, and a full–scale panic attack was imminent when the group dismissed whatever had caught their attention and disappeared into the woods in the opposite direction. I allowed myself the smallest sigh of relief, afraid anything louder would echo across the water.

As soon as I judged they were out of earshot, I crept out from under my bush and darted toward the riverbank. I silently waded into the water, now too fueled with adrenaline to notice its chill. I was sure I was too late. I was sure I was swimming out to find only death—if I could even find her in the river's murk—but I swam out anyway.

Taking a deep, resigned breath, I dove under. Blonde, wavy hair billowed softly beneath me. She was there, motionless, at the bottom of the river.

I resurfaced, grief washing over me. I was too late.

Be more certain, my conscience whispered. I stalled. *Swim to her now,* it insisted. It was right. I couldn't ignore it. So I took another deep breath and under I went, propelling myself down to the riverbed in seconds to face her. She had been a pretty girl of maybe sixteen, with a dainty button nose and delicate, high cheekbones. Her eyes were closed, tightened in a way that suggested she was alive and in pain, but her lips—large, plump, pink lips—were parted to allow water into her lungs.

I was sure she was dead, and yet...My hand slowly reached toward her shoulder. I jabbed her with my index finger.

Green eyes shot open, focusing on me.

I gasped. Water flooded into my mouth and throat, pushing down into my lungs. I had to get to the surface, breathe—now. Flailing my arms and legs wildly, I clawed my way to the surface to cough up the frigid river water.

She's alive! Why doesn't she swim up? I wondered while I choked. It didn't matter, I had to help her. I dove back down and grabbed her forearm. Both her hands floated up in unison, bound by a silvery cord. I'd have to untie that later—no time now. I hooked my arm around her waist and kicked forcefully, attempting to tow her up.

She wouldn't budge. Something was weighing her down.

I let go of her waist and swam farther down to find a large concrete block resting on the riverbed, fastened to her ankle with more silvery cord. It had to weigh at least three hundred pounds. *That's* what they threw in after her, I realized, though I didn't know how any one human being could have hoisted it and tossed it in with the ease I had witnessed.

The cord was fastened to her ankle in an intricate knot. It would take me hours to unravel, if I could even loosen it. Hours she didn't have. I reached down and, with one hand on either side of the knot to test the tautness, I tugged lightly. My eyes widened in shock when the silvery rope pulled apart like cotton candy. I didn't waste time dwelling on the small miracle. I reached up and pulled at her wrist bindings to find they came apart as easily.

She was free. Hooking my arm around the girl's waist again, I pulled her to the rivers' surface.

"You're going to be fine," I whispered hoarsely, my breathing ragged, one arm gripping her tightly while I used the other to paddle us to shore. She didn't struggle, or speak, or even gasp for air. *I'm too late. I took too long.*

By the time we reached the nearest bank, I was on the verge of unconsciousness. I dragged her to safety, then collapsed with my cheek in the cool mud, where I would have willingly stayed for hours.

"You're breathing. You're gasping for air," someone said in a raspy voice. It wasn't offensive or ugly in the least. It had that inflection that men find sexy.

I pulled my face out of the mud to see my would–be drowning victim sitting calmly in the mud, unscathed. My shock reenergized me, reviving my exhausted body. I sat up to stare at her.

She repeated herself.

"I'm sorry, I'm not a strong swimmer," I said.

She wore a curious expression as she studied me with big, almond–shaped green eyes. This girl was pretty when I thought she was dead; now that she was alive, I could see that she was drop–dead gorgeous. She had the creamy pale skin and dimpled cheeks of an angel, reminding me of one of those cheerleaders—the bubbly, popular kind. "Was the rope difficult to untie?" she asked softly.

I shook my head. "It practically crumbled in my hands. Why didn't you break free?"

"I couldn't," she replied simply.

My body shuddered violently then, succumbing to the frigid temperature of the water and the air. A peculiar look flashed in the girl's eyes— eagerness, shock—a mixture, perhaps. She seemed unaffected by the cold air though her clothes were dripping wet. More importantly, she was too relaxed for someone who had just been dumped into a river to die. *She must be in shock.*

Her eyes darted to the darkness under the trees. "We need to leave right now, before they come back. This way." She was on her feet instantly.

The idea of facing murderers had me jumping up to follow her. I hadn't taken two steps, though, when I lost my footing under the slick mud, and fell.

CR

For the second time that night, I woke up in a strange place. My head throbbed. Reaching up, I winced as my fingers grazed a sizeable goose egg behind my right temple. *How did I*...Memories of the night flashed through my mind then—the statue, icy water, the girl with the emerald eyes. She'd been drowning and I rescued her. Sort of.

A comfortable heat warmed my back. Rolling over with difficulty, I found myself lying beside a large firepit. I spent a few moments staring at the flames as they flickered in a captivating dance.

"Are you too hot?" a raspy voice asked.

I recognized the owner as my near–drowning victim. Rolling onto my back, I found her sitting cross–legged on the ground behind my head, peering down at me with eyes that sparkled like emeralds in the firelight.

"What's your name?" she asked, casually twirling a strand of wildly curly blonde hair—now dry and jutting out in all directions like shiny, fat springs. The curls reminded me of Medusa's head of snakes.

I scrambled to sit up but swooned, my head throbbing.

"Don't rush," she said, patting my back as I lay in a heap on the ground, my forehead against a stone. "At least you're dry. And clean. I think I got all the mud off you. I can't believe you went into that water. Do you know what's in there?" She rambled on, though I couldn't focus on her words; I was too busy trying not to vomit.

Once the spinning subsided, I slowly pushed myself up to sit in front of her. *God, she looks like an angel. Except for her clothes.* They were shabby and dark and frayed by what looked like decades of wear—clothes one would expect to find on a homeless person. I hadn't noticed them before.

She frowned. "How's your head?"

I didn't answer, too busy investigating the stone walls, low ceiling, and general eeriness around me. We were in a cave.

"I think there's something wrong with her," Medusa–girl whispered to someone behind me.

I turned. A man in his early twenties towered over us, several large chunks of wood in his arms. He had the same large, beautiful green eyes as Medusa–girl, only a different shade of green—jade instead of emerald, and more intense. His long slender nose and pronounced cheekbones were almost femininely pretty, but those features were well balanced by a masculine square jaw and unkempt chestnut brown hair, neither too long nor too short.

I gawked openly at him, unable to peel my attention away, until I noticed his jaw clench. I quickly averted my gaze to my hands.

Cool, sinister laughter echoed through the cave then, sending a shiver down my spine. Searching the darkness for the owner, I saw a woman suddenly materialize out of nothingness, her seductive, confident gait triggering images of a wild cat stalking its prey. She stopped beside the young man, tossing her thick mane of raven black hair over her shoulder before gazing down at me with a detached air and lemon–yellow eyes, too light to ever be mistaken for hazel.

I was staring into those eyes, mesmerized, wondering if they were authentic or colored contacts, when more voices spoke.

"What's with the fire?" a male voice asked, its owner walking through the cave entrance. He stopped beside the firepit, a surprised look on his face as his charcoal–gray eyes landed on me. "Who's this?" Except for his pale complexion, he fit the stereotype of a surfer with his shaggy, golden blonde hair, lean, muscular build, and boyish, carefree grin, which he was proudly displaying for me now.

Yet another set of piercing eyes landed on me then—large, catlike, violet eyes—as a woman stepped in beside him. His girlfriend, by the way he immediately draped his arm around her shoulder and planted a kiss on her heart–shaped face. She pushed a strand of long, caramel–brown hair off her brow.

I suddenly understood what it felt like to be a gangly, awkward twelve–year–old with braces and frizzy orange hair, stumbling into a group of inhumanly beautiful *adults*. They were utterly flawless, free of the usual suspects—the crooked teeth, the deviated nose, the disproportionately set eyes. Their faces were perfectly symmetrical and universally desirable, their hair impeccably groomed, their skin soft–looking; even their fingernails were manicured. Everything about them was perfect. Everything except their ratty clothes.

"Who is she?" Surfer Guy asked again.

"Dunno. She bumped her head and now she's a mute," the dark–haired one murmured, the corners of her broad, cherry red mouth curving into a condescending smirk.

My drowning victim tried again. "What's your name?"

"Evangeline," I finally croaked, trembling.

She nodded once. "I'm Amelie. This is Fiona, Bishop, and over there is my brother, Caden. And that's Rachel."

I cleared my throat. "It's nice to meet you." *Is it really? Stupid response, Evangeline.*

"Evangeline," Amelie said calmly, "don't worry. We won't hurt you. What were you doing out in the woods?"

"I don't...remember," I stammered.

"Where did you come from?" the girl named Fiona asked. Her voice had an appealing huskiness to it.

"Manhattan...?" Their blank looks confirmed it meant nothing to them. *How did I wander so far from Viggo and Mortimer's place?*

"What do you remember?" Amelie asked softly.

"Not much. I went to sleep in my bed and woke up in a forest, beside a statue. I heard those people by the river and I went to find them. They laughed a bit and then threw you in, and I hid under a bush...I was sure you were dead," I added.

The guy named Bishop roared with laughter for some strange reason.

"Thank you again for...helping me out of that predicament," Amelie said, a strange smile touching her lips.

That's a blasé way to thank someone for saving your life.

"The statue was of a woman reaching up to the sky?" the beautiful guy with the firewood—Caden—asked.

I nodded. They were all silent then, exchanging cryptic glances.

In a flash, Caden was crouching down beside me, so unexpectedly that I flinched, startled. He leaned in close, staring intently at my chest. My half–naked chest, I realized. I instinctively crossed my arms over my torso, my hot face turning every shade of humiliation from rose to egg-plant, I was sure. With everything else going on, I had forgotten about my clothing—or lack thereof. He raised his eyes, his brow furrowed in confusion for a moment. Then his jade eyes went wide with comprehension. "Your necklace—I was looking at the charm," he explained, raising his hands in surrender.

"I wasn't!" I heard Bishop call from behind him, followed by a loud smack—presumably Fiona's response to his lewdness.

"Can I please see it? The pendant," Caden asked gently.

"Um, yeah, sure...I guess." I reached up to unclasp the chain, then remembered Sofie's request to leave it on. "I can't take it off. The clasp is broken and I don't want to lose it." He nodded once. I grabbed the chain and pulled it as far out from my half–exposed chest as possible, the glowing red heart swinging back and forth thanks to my trembling hand.

Caden slid in closer to me.

I swallowed, my chest tightening with anxiety at his proximity, my heart beginning to hammer my chest again. I noticed his eyes flit curiously to my face for a second and I thought I detected the slight crook of a smile, but his face smoothed before I could be sure.

His hand reached out to grasp the pendant. A burst of red light flashed brightly. He recoiled. Leaning back to squat on his heels, he placed his chin in his hands.

"What is it?" Rachel asked crisply. I glanced over to see her standing with arms crossed, scowling.

Caden, a pensive expression on his face, ignored her. "Where'd you get that?"

"It was a gift."

"Recent?"

I nodded.

"From whom?"

"Sofie. Um, I mean...my boss."

Caden continued studying it in silence, his eyes shifting back and forth. "You'll have to thank Sofie. I think it saved your life."

I glanced down at the radiant heart and an unpleasant chill ran down my spine. "What do you mean?" I stammered.

Caden opened his mouth to answer, but Bishop sprang to his feet, cursing vehemently as his eyes darted to the cave entrance. "They've tracked us here," he growled, his jovial tone of moments ago gone.

"Damn it, Amelie!" Rachel cursed.

"Oh, shut it!" Amelie threw a withering glare in Rachel's direction. It didn't phase the dark beauty in the least.

"Must be the fire," Fiona whispered.

"How much time?" Caden asked, his eyes locked on mine, his voice now hard and determined.

Bishop inhaled deeply. "Maybe two minutes...I can't believe I missed their scent," he hissed through gritted teeth.

Scent? I inhaled deeply but my nostrils filled with nothing but smoke.

"There. I can sense them...three of them. They'll be here soon," Rachel confirmed.

Three...there'd been three people by the river. Three murderers. I wondered if it was the same group.

In the next second I was flying across the cave, cradled in Caden's strong arms. Setting me on my feet, he gently pushed me into a small alcove. Standing within it, I couldn't see two–thirds of the cave. *They're hiding me,* I realized.

Caden's hand lifted my chin, tilting my head back far enough that my eyes met his. He stared at me so fixedly that I began squirming, trying to turn away. "No, don't," he whispered calmly, holding my chin securely between his thumb and forefinger.

The tension slid from my body as I fell deeper and deeper into those infinite pools of jade, my focus becoming cloudy, my thoughts muddled.

Caden's voice whispered, slow and deliberate, "You need to stay hidden and remain calm. Don't speak. Don't make a single sound." His words strung together, swirling around inside my head, repeating over and over. I nodded involuntarily. With a satisfied nod, Caden removed his hand from my chin and turned to face the cave entrance.

I stood staring at his broad, muscular back, imagining my fingers running through his hair, barely noticing the burning against my chest as my pendant blazed ...

The temporary fog in my brain lifted. I began tapping my fingers against my thighs in response to my growing panic. "What do they want?" I finally whispered.

Caden's head whipped around, his eyebrows furrowed in confusion as he searched my face, until his gaze landed on my pendant. "Interesting …" he mumbled to himself. He paused. "They want Amelie. They're the ones who put her in the river. But you...when they find out about you …" His eyes left the pendant and returned to my face.

He didn't need to finish his sentence. I caught the drift. "Because I helped Amelie?"

His eyes narrowed. "You don't know where you are—who we are?"

"We're in a cave and you're...homeless people?" I said. *Oh, stupid, Evangeline. That was so insensitive.*

"Just stay hidden and don't say anything. I'll keep you safe, I promise," Caden whispered, smiling down at me reassuringly. Or sympathetically, because I sounded like an imbecile.

I couldn't resist asking, "What's going to happen?"

"Would you shut up? Unless you want to die tonight, little girl," Rachel hissed through clenched teeth. She had edged to the back wall of the cave and was now watching us keenly.

I blanched at the threat, my heart doubling its pace.

Caden reached out, his hands cupping my chin. Again I sensed a gravitational pull toward those deep pools, only it wasn't nearly as strong as before. "You have to calm down. Now."

I took a deep breath. I focused on his soothing voice, the intensity of his eyes. Although my heart kept racing, its thunderous pounding dulled to an irritating thud.

Caden put his finger to his lips in a hushing motion. I nodded. He turned back to the cave entrance, his feet shifting position ever so slightly.

I felt something boring into the side of my face. Glancing over, I saw Rachel glaring at me sadistically, those yellow eyes lit with some private enjoyment. I cowered within my alcove, wishing I could turn into a chameleon and blend into the rock. The pendant, tightly grasped in my hand now, continued to burn hot against my skin.

4. Dead Is Dead

So silent was their approach that I was unaware anyone had entered the cave until I heard a new voice. "Why, hello again, Amelie! We didn't expect to see you mobile so soon." The man's tone oozed false kindness.

Impulsively, I peeked out from behind Caden to catch a glimpse of the speaker, figuring the shadows and the glare from the fire would be sufficient cover. All I saw was the back of a snow–white head before Caden's body subtly leaned back, forcing me into full hiding again.

"Jethro," Amelie responded, her tone icy. "I warned you, I don't like that river. Too murky."

"Yes, I recall...I'm curious about how you escaped, and so quickly!" Jethro's voice grew louder and I heard footsteps as the man walked farther into the cave.

"Oh, it's my little secret," she responded glibly, as if joking with a friend instead of the man who'd tried to kill her.

"I'm sure we can get it out of you." Jethro's voice indicated a smile but his words were full of malice. "I'm surprised to see another highly esteemed Council member here...Rachel," he said in greeting.

My eyes darted to Rachel. She nodded once, undaunted and still exuding confidence; she wasn't afraid of Jethro.

"And your brother is uncharacteristically quiet this evening, skulking in the back corner like that. Are you hiding something?"

I pressed further against the wall until the jutting stone hurt my back.

"Only his infatuation with me." Rachel swooped over and wrapped her arms seductively around Caden's waist, skimming her lips across the side of his neck.

So they're together, I realized. Despite the urgency of the situation, bitter disappointment coursed through me.

Caden didn't acknowledge Rachel's affection, though. "Did you think you could walk in here after what you did to my sister?" he said through gritted teeth.

Jethro's laughter echoed through the cave. I recognized that sound. I had believed it to be my salvation, earlier that night. Now that laugh made me want to swallow my tongue in fear.

"That sounds like a threat. Amusing."

The footsteps moved away from us. I had no urge to peek again.

"Quite silly of you to start a fire. Someone may accidently trip and fall into it. That would be a much more permanent ending than sitting at the bottom of the river," Jethro mused.

A silent warning to Amelie, though I didn't see how drowning had a different outcome than burning. *Dead is dead.*

"You know, it was interesting earlier, out by the river," Jethro said, his voice falsely casual, "after we chucked you in. We—all of us—sensed a true rarity. A *human* heartbeat, of all things."

What? My face twisted with confusion.

"It must have been wishful thinking, of course...but it brought back fond memories. I remember ripping one of those tasty morsels right out of a chest once, so quickly that the little thing continued pulsing in my palm. I even showed it to the terrified lemming I had snatched it from before she collapsed to the ground. How I would do *anything* to hold one of those again ..." Jethro sighed wistfully.

As if my poor heart had heard the threat, it began thrashing against my chest, likely trying to grow legs so it could break free and run away before this psychopath could get his hands on it.

"There it is again—that heartbeat!" Jethro exclaimed in a hiss. "Do you hear that?"

My stomach lurched. Was he referring to *my* heartbeat? A hand squeezed my thigh in warning. Glancing down, I saw it was Caden's hand, covertly reaching back, attempting to calm me. Unfortunately his touch pushed my heart further into overdrive until I was sure it would explode; it was a thunderous, repetitive boom against my eardrums. The cave, Caden, everything began to swirl. I leaned against the wall for support, begging my knees not to buckle.

Unevenly paced footsteps moved toward us, slowly edging in, taunting. Rachel's arms slid away from Caden, who shifted. I knew they were preparing to react.

My hands groped forward in desperation, my fingers digging into Caden's back. Clenching my teeth together, I fought the urge to let out a blood–curdling shriek.

What happened next came in a flash. Rachel was no longer beside Caden. She was slamming into the opposite wall, the rock crumbling from the impact, surely every bone in her perfect body shattering. I didn't see her collapse to the ground, though; the demon who now stood in her place had my full attention.

I couldn't decide which was more sinister—those cold white eyes with their web of tiny blue veins staring down at me, or the creature's face, so contorted that it pulled his skin back severely against his facial bones. His long hair, also stark white, was tied back in a ponytail that only emphasized the tautness of his skin. He was like some monster out of a horror film, only a hundred times more hideous because he was real. *Demon,* sprang into my mind—*something straight from hell.*

As hard as I struggled to turn away from that repulsive face, it held me riveted. The blood drained from my own face, and my body trembled uncontrollably. I felt as vulnerable as a mouse cornered by a hungry snake.

A strange expression passed over the demon's face. It took me a moment to identify it as shock. "Where did you find her?" it hissed, and I recognized the voice as Jethro's.

"It doesn't matter," Caden responded levelly.

I glimpsed a springy curl as Amelie edged in behind Jethro, shifting her weight, ready to react to the impending explosion—an explosion over me, and I hadn't the first clue why.

"Oh, but it does! She could lead us to more...I need to bring her to the Council."

"And how do you suppose you'll do that?"

Jethro laughed wickedly. "Do you actually think you'll walk out of here alive with her?"

"Do *you*?" Caden growled. He leaned back to shield me with his body just as Jethro lunged forward.

I didn't see anything else. I curled up in my hollow, my face buried in my shoulder. Growls and shrieks filled the cave. Ghastly sounds—bones crunching, flesh tearing—sucked the breath out of my lungs. Caden was no longer protecting me. Now, exposed, I was an easy target. I winced, waiting for a hand to wrench me out of my hiding place and rip my heart out.

But instead, the ferocious brawl died down to an eerie silence and I heard Amelie's voice murmuring in the distance. Still afraid to breathe, I lifted my head to peek out around the corner—in time to see a white object sail through the air and land in the fire.

Jethro's head.

Those alarming white eyes stared intently at me from the flames as if still alive. A body followed, quivering violently.

If anyone else remained in the cave, I didn't notice. Because, for the second time in one night, everything went dark.

ଔ

I woke up as my head slammed into something hard. Cringing, I opened my eyes to see the legs of a white chaise and a shaggy cream rug beside a fireplace. I recognized that chaise, that fireplace. I had fallen out of bed in the guest room at Viggo and Mortimer's.

"Oh, thank God!" I exclaimed, crawling back into bed and dropping onto the plush pillows. I winced in pain. Reaching up, I found a bump already forming on the side of my head. *That was quick.* But even the throbbing injury couldn't outweigh my relief. *It was all just a dream.* A horribly bad dream.

Something wet nuzzled against my ear. I turned toward it and saw Max's enormous black nose. I grinned, scratching his chin. He proceeded to sniff me, head to toe. "Okay, enough Max!" I giggled when he licked my feet.

Today was my birthday and I was in paradise. *This*, I knew, was real. A huge smile stretched across my face.

The clock on the nightstand read ten–thirty. *I slept in!* I bolted out of bed and ran for the shower. After all, Sofie had brought me to New York to work off my ten thousand dollar debt to her and here I was, lazing around.

As I stood in the giant tiled shower stall, allowing the numerous jets to drench my body in warmth, my thoughts wandered back to my dream. Oddly enough, I could recall every moment with complete clarity—the forest...the laughter...rescuing Amelie...Caden...Jethro's head in the fire. I shuddered with that last memory, swiftly replacing it with much more pleasant thoughts—those few brief moments of closeness with Caden. Butterflies fluttered in my stomach. I immediately felt ridiculous. *It's not like he exists, you moron.* It wouldn't matter if he did. He had Rachel. Beautiful, seductive, confident Rachel. I groaned, leaning my forehead against the iridescent cream tile. *Even my subconscious is against me.*

A short time later I entered the kitchen to find Sofie sitting gracefully on a stool in the kitchen, magazine in hand. As usual, she looked impeccable in a pair of skinny blue jeans and a patterned black and white shirt. In my new stylish gray jeans and loose–fitting pink sweater, I didn't feel completely inadequate next to her. Only marginally.

"I'm so sorry!" I blurted. "I never sleep in—it must have been that comfy bed."

Sofie looked up, relief flashing across her face. "That's quite alright." Her eyes darted to Max.

"He's way smarter than I gave him credit for."

Max glared at me in response, as if understanding.

"Good dog," I murmured, scratching his chin.

Seemingly mollified, he ambled over to a bearskin rug by the stone hearth and hunkered down with his brothers.

"She's awake! Finally," Mortimer grumbled as he entered the kitchen dressed in a charcoal suit, a folded newspaper under one arm. If he'd seemed a little annoyed yesterday, today he was downright irritable. *Maybe he's not a morning person.*

I dropped my head in shame and was about to apologize again when Viggo walked in, instantly lifting the dark cloud that Mortimer had brought. "Happy birthday! What are you craving this morning, my darling—waffles; pancakes; steak and eggs? It's been an eternity since I've cooked for someone," Viggo offered, snatching up a cast iron pan and flipping it effortlessly around in the air.

I glanced at Mortimer, wondering if he wasn't "someone."

"Oh, he doesn't like my cooking. Says it's too bland," Viggo explained, giving Mortimer a secretive wink. Mortimer rolled his eyes with annoyance.

"Coffee would be great, but only if you have a pot made already," I said.

"But of course, mademoiselle! Anything for you. Leonardo?" Viggo snapped his fingers. The gentle old man suddenly appeared, shuffling over to an elaborate machine on the counter.

"And I'll have whatever you're having," I added. "No needed to go to any extra trouble."

"Oh, we've already eaten," Viggo said, flashing a pearly white smile. "Speaking of which," he yanked the newspaper out of Mortimer's grasp, "Sofie, did you see that article on the quadruple homicide in this morning's newspaper? Japanese mob. They likely deserved it; however...a little excessive, wouldn't you agree?" He smiled knowingly at her. *He must be a lawyer. Bizarre segue, though. Why would he—*

"Besides," Mortimer interjected, throwing his partner a look of unimpressed shock, "Viggo wouldn't be cooking. The pan is for theatrical effect. He's a complete buffoon in the kitchen. He almost burnt it down once and has since been banished."

"Sadly, that is true," Viggo admitted, pouting.

I giggled, looking around the state-of-the-art kitchen. Surely it had to be any chef's dream, with its industrial–sized stainless steel appliances and stone countertops.

"Here you are, dear," Leonardo said, gently placing a mug of hot coffee in front of me. "And while you're deciding on breakfast—" His other hand magically produced a double–helping slice of chocolate cake, slathered with chocolate icing and colorful sprinkles.

Nostalgia slapped me across the face, pulling me back to my childhood. My mother used to serve me the same breakfast on my birthdays, sprinkles and all. It had been one of many traditions that died with her.

Until now.

"I guessed at the flavor. And the sprinkles," Leonardo quickly admitted. "That's what you kids are eating these days, right?"

I nodded, unable to speak.

"Lucky guess," Mortimer said, fixing Sofie with an unreadable stare.

Sofie sipped her tea, the corners of her mouth turned up in a devious smile.

"How are you feeling, Evangeline? Did you sleep well?" Viggo asked.

I faltered, instinctively touching the sizeable bump near my temple. "Yes I did. Thanks."

"That wasn't a convincing response. We can provide you with a different room or bed if you'd like," Viggo offered, concerned.

"Oh no, the room and the bed are perfect! It's...well, it's silly. I had a dream. More a nightmare."

Mortimer stiffened in his seat. "What about?" His gruff voice was suddenly two octaves higher than usual.

"It was nothing, really. I was in the woods and there was a drowning. An attempted drowning."

"Details, please. I'm somewhat of a dream interpreter," Viggo said. He leaned against the counter, resting his strong, square jaw in the palm of his hand. "From the beginning—don't leave anything out. You never know what's important."

"Alright, I guess," I agreed, suddenly self–conscious as the three of them stared intently at me. Even Max perked his ears. I began describing the forest and the river and quickly found myself pulled back into the stark reality of the night. They interrupted frequently with questions.

"You saw that same statue in your dream?" Sofie asked.

I nodded.

"And this...Jethro—he could hear your heartbeat?" she continued.

"Only when it was pounding, I think."

"That silver rope—that sounds horrendous!" Viggo said when I described the flimsy cord that had somehow effectively bound Amelie.

"Describe these people again," Mortimer instructed, his expression grim.

I described the group a second time, careful not to emphasize my pathetic infatuation with Caden, though I'd have been curious to hear Viggo's interpretation of that part.

"And you're sure no one...hurt you in any way?" Mortimer probed.

I shook my head, and remembered the pendant. "Caden said this necklace saved my life somehow. I don't know...it was bizarre."

Viggo eyed the pendant. "Did it do anything strange?"

"Yes! It shimmered in a reddish–orange color. Like a sunset. And it was hot. Does that mean anything?"

"It means you had quite the dream. And you remember it with such clarity, you'd think it was real," Mortimer answered, smirking. "How is that bump?" He reached over, his hand roughly stroking the side of my head. I flinched. "Ah—that's a nasty welt. But you should be all right. We'll get you a helmet to sleep in."

He turned away. "Sofie, you and I have some business to attend to. Max, why don't you take Evangeline out to the atrium?" Mortimer's voice had turned unnaturally light and airy, as if he were hiding something.

"Of course, Mortimer," Sofie said, responding with a sweet smile. Their eyes exchanged a silent message.

5. Veronique

"Do you know what Sofie needs me to do, Max?" I asked the giant beast as we strolled along a path in the atrium, my arm hanging over his back. "No, of course you don't. I don't either, but so far, this trip has been one giant fairy tale." I stooped to pick a sprig of lavender and inhaled deeply, relishing its comforting fragrance. "It's got to end sometime soon, I suppose. I'm going to miss you, though, Max." I played with one of his cropped ears. He groaned in response, giving me a quick lick on the cheek. *Such a deceiving appearance for a big suck.*

We stopped in front of the white woman. I gazed up at the statue's face, her expression a mixture of tranquility and anticipation. "Exactly how I feel right now," I mumbled to her, sighing.

Evangeline, someone whispered faintly.

I turned to look for the source. I couldn't see anyone. "Did you hear that?" I asked Max, frowning. He began tapping his front paws against the stone, clearly excited. "What are you so happy about?" I asked, confusion deepening my frown.

Evangeline.

"There!" My head whipped around, eyes searching. "Did you hear—"

A loud crash preceded angry shouts.

"One hundred and twenty years, you unreliable witch! You seem to forget. How much longer?" Mortimer's voice boomed.

"I've told you what I know!" Sofie shrieked in response.

Silence.

And then I heard doors creak open to my left. "Evangeline? Could you be a doll and come here, please, for a moment?" Viggo's voice called.

"Coming!" I scurried toward his voice, playing the short exchange between Mortimer and Sofie over in my head. *I wonder what that was about? And why would he call her a witch?* He was brusque, but he seemed too sophisticated to resort to petty name–calling.

I found Viggo holding open a French door, smiling. "Come, join us in the library."

Nodding politely, I stepped inside. Sofie and Mortimer sat on opposite ends of a cocoa–hued tucked–leather couch, talking casually, as if they hadn't just been screaming obscenities at each other a moment ago.

The library was dim, but lamps of various sizes and heights scattered throughout the room gave it a cozy atmosphere. A giant ebony grand piano filled one corner while a full wall of mahogany bookshelves filled another, reaching all the way up to the soaring two–storey ceiling. In between was a fireplace with a large oil painting above it.

"Hard to avoid, isn't she?" Viggo asked, walking over to admire the piece.

I followed him. It was a portrait of a young woman with plump auburn curls tumbling midway down her back and framing a heart–shaped face in which olive green eyes twinkled. Her smile for the painter was mysterious, and revealed sizeable dimples that reminded me of Sofie.

"This was Sofie's sister, Veronique."

Was Sofie's sister. Past tense. I hazarded a glance at Sofie, only to see her staring at the portrait of her sister with admiration.

"She was a real beauty, Veronique was," Mortimer said, adding, "It's funny, how different two sisters can be from each other."

Sofie's lips pursed.

"When was this painting done?" I asked, gazing at the woman's vintage–looking sapphire–blue dress that nearly exposed her breasts. They were accentuated nicely with a black heart–shaped pendant identical to mine. Instinctively, I reached up to touch the one around my neck.

"So what do you have planned for today, ladies?" Viggo asked abruptly.

My eyes darted to Sofie; I was wondering the same thing. Her jaw tightened.

Before anyone answered, Viggo spoke again. "Well, that doesn't sound like fun! Why don't you two go out and do some shopping?"

"Unfortunately I have several errands I have to run," Sofie answered briskly.

Viggo ignored her, pulling a cherry red purse from a drawer and tossing it to me. "Just a gift from us. Prada. Not available in stores yet. I believe some women have clawed eyes out for one of those."

"Thanks. You've already given me too much," I stammered, looking down at the bag. It was fat and heavy. *Full of something.* I glanced questioningly at Sofie, only to see her glaring at Viggo, her eyes narrowed suspiciously.

"Open it!" Viggo ordered, winking. I hesitated. "Go on!"

I pulled the zipper. Like a Jack in a Box, out popped money—bundles of bills with multiple zeros on their faces. My legs buckled. I grabbed the back of a chair for support before I keeled over.

"Are you feeling alright?" Viggo was by my side in seconds, his hand on my shoulder.

"Yes," I stammered, "it's just...you're much too generous."

"Oh, nonsense. We're billionaires! We have wads of cash lying around this place," Viggo boasted casually.

"Yes. This is nothing—loose change, for us. Take it and have some fun. We insist," Mortimer added, standing.

"We'll just steal more when we're running low," Viggo said, chuckling.

Sofie stood up abruptly, her face and voice a mask of calm. "Evangeline, why don't you go grab your coat. It's chilly out." She didn't glance in my direction as she spoke, her pale eyes glued to Viggo's face. Something was very wrong.

"We can go another time, Sofie, if you have other things you need to do. It's okay," I said.

An uncomfortably long pause ensued, Viggo and Sofie exchanging silent looks. Then she suddenly turned to me, a brilliant smile on her face. "Nothing is more important than taking you out shopping on your birthday. Now go, get ready!"

I turned to Viggo and Mortimer. "I don't know what to say but thank you—again."

"Anything for such a sweet girl, my darling," Viggo said, winking a second time.

Max—always by my side—took that as his cue. He was back on duty, leading me up to my room with my ridiculous stash of money. *Was I greedy to accept it? But how could I say no?* They had practically forced it on me. Well, I didn't have to spend it. I would leave it in the nightstand when we left for Maine. A maid would eventually find it. *An early Christmas bonus for her.*

CR

Our black town car pulled out of the tunnel around two that afternoon with Leo at the wheel and Max whining by the gate, eliciting an exasperated look from Sofie.

As we turned onto a busy street, Sofie pointed to a massive forest on its other side. "That's Central Park, right there."

I'd been too overwhelmed to notice it the night we arrived. "Wow, it's so big," I murmured.

"Maybe we'll go one day this week. Drop us off at Saks, will you?" Sofie instructed Leo.

"I can't believe Viggo and Mortimer, with the money. They're so nice," I said.

"Yes, it would appear that way, wouldn't it?" Sofie said through clenched teeth. Then she sighed loudly and, as if that simple act released a mountain of tension, a broad smile splashed across her beautiful face and the fire went out. "Let's go spend all their hard-earned money."

The car dropped us off and I followed her into Saks like a seven-year-old tailing her mother. "Fifth Avenue is the most expensive street in the world for shopping," Sofie announced. And then she transformed into a human wrecking ball, weaving through the place without caution, casually yanking clothes off the racks and tossing them at me. "Try these on. And I want to see all of them," she demanded, the look in her eyes brooking no argument. Not that I would argue. I'd gladly play her dress-up doll if that's what she wanted.

Two sales ladies descended upon us, eyes alight with the possibility of large commissions, but froze in their tracks with one venomous look from Sofie. I guessed she wasn't in the mood for help.

With my arms buried under clothes, we headed back to the fitting room, where I spent the next half an hour modeling for Sofie.

"I always dreamed of doing this with a daughter," Sofie sighed, helping me with the zipper of a black evening gown.

"You still can. You're young."

Sofie laughed sadly. "There was a time when I dearly longed for two little girls—my dolls."

It was my first glimpse of Sofie as something other than my confident and beautiful boss. By briefly sharing such a personal dream, she became human to me. I desperately needed to see more. "You still have plenty of time, Sofie." She smirked but said nothing. "You just haven't met the right guy yet," I continued, defaulting to the universal explanation all females had firmly committed to memory by their early tween years.

Sofie's lips pursed. "I did. The perfect guy." She finished with the zipper and turned me to get a look.

"What happened?"

"It didn't...end well." She glanced at my pendant before scooping up a pile of clothes and walking toward the cash register.

I paid for my purchase with my birthday money, holding my breath as I counted out and laid thousand dollar bills on the counter. We stepped out of the store to find Leo waiting with the car.

"Let's drop these bags off in the car and—" Sofie stopped in mid-sentence, her eyes suddenly scanning the street, an apprehensive grimace marring her beautiful face.

"What's wrong?"

She didn't respond, still searching.

"Sofie?"

"This way. Lots of shops to hit still!" she said abruptly, pounding the trunk door twice with her hand. It popped open in response. She tossed her bags in, then turned to stalk toward the next retail victim.

Hurricane Sofie whipped through three more posh stores on a spiteful mission to exhaust every last cent of Viggo and Mortimer's money. I noticed her glance out the window several times with that same cautious gleam in her eye but each time I asked, she shrugged it off.

"I really don't need any more clothes, Sofie," I said as we stood in front of the fifth clothing store, my arms laden with bags. And I meant it. Between what we'd just purchased and the full closet back at Viggo and Mortimer's, I had enough clothing to last me a lifetime. Growing up, my mother never had enough money for more than a pair of Wranglers and tennis shoes at one time. My foster families were required to ensure I had an adequate selection of clean, hole–free clothing, but there was never enough money to indulge in a pair of designer jeans, let alone go hog wild. This was beyond excessive.

"You're right," she said, her brow furrowing in thought. A devilish smile spread her lips. "Follow me."

I remained clueless of her intentions until I saw the Harry Winston sign. Jewelry. I groaned.

Marching in, she headed straight for a counter and turned to me. "Pick something out, Evangeline," she demanded.

I swallowed, gazing down at the display cases full of sparkling jewels. "I don't need—"

"Okay, this one." She pointed to a diamond bracelet. The clerk rushed to pull it out. "Wrist," Sofie ordered.

I obliged. The clerk slipped on the bracelet. I turned my arm slowly, watching the light reflect off the countless stones. It was stunning. "How much is it?" I asked. When the clerk told me I choked, my eyes bugging out of my head in shock. "Get it off! Please!"

"We'll buy it," Sofie announced.

"Sofie! I don't need a bracelet! That could pay for college!" My stomach churned as the words left my mouth, the truth of it distressing. It would take me a lifetime to save that kind of money.

She ignored me, wrenching my purse from my arm and pulling out a wad of money. The clerk behind the counter raised an eyebrow but remained quiet, likely calculating his commission. Sofie calmly counted out bills—a thick pile of them—with the ease of someone paying for her weekly groceries.

"Thank you!" she said, smiling at the clerk. "Okay, we're done." She handed me the box holding the bracelet.

I stared at her, flabbergasted, wondering what this wild woman had done with the reserved, graceful Sofie I had met only days ago.

Surprise flashed in her minty eyes then, and she sighed. "I must seem a little erratic today," she murmured, smiling sheepishly. "I'm sorry. It's just...you deserve a hundred times more than anything Viggo and Mortimer could ever buy you."

I frowned. "I don't understand—"

She cut me off, grabbing hold of my arm. "Come on." She led me out the door. I clutched the box with the bracelet to my chest with my free hand, visions of a mugger waiting to pounce and steal it playing through my head.

"Where to now?" Sofie asked.

"Why don't we just window shop for a bit?" I suggested. *You've won! You've punished Viggo and Mortimer for whatever they did to you.*

But Sofie hadn't even heard me. She was busy scanning the pedestrians and cars along Fifth Avenue yet again. Wearing that look again.

"What's wrong, Sofie?"

Silence. I watched quietly as her expression turned from suspicion to comprehension to fury.

"Come," she suddenly said, hooking onto my arm and tugging me forward. "I'm tired. It's time to go home." She practically threw me into the car. "Home. Now," she ordered Leonardo. The wheels squealed as we cut into traffic and raced off, earning several angry blasts from horns.

CR

"Leonardo, please help Evangeline with her things," Sofie called out over her shoulder, marching through the red doors at Viggo and Mortimer's expansive abode. "Viggo!" I heard her yell.

Max galloped over to stand by my side while I stared after Sofie, my head still spinning from the chaotic afternoon with her. I turned to see Leonardo struggling with countless shopping bags, not at all ruffled by Sofie's dark mood. "I can do that." I ran over, grabbing the bags out of his hands.

The sound of glass breaking and Sofie's shrill voice stopped me in my tracks. "Someone's watching us!" she screamed. Silence followed, presumably while Viggo tried to calm her. It didn't work. "Do you think this is another one of your games? Do you realize what's at stake?"

"Come, Miss Evangeline. You must be hungry." Leonardo grabbed my arm. He pulled me into the building with more strength than I expected from the old man. Max followed, practically glued to my hip.

"What's going on, Leonardo?" I whispered, but the old man didn't answer. Maybe he didn't hear me. I opened my mouth to repeat the question but decided against it. I was probably better off not knowing.

∝

I sat quietly at the counter as Magda, the heavy Russian cook, placed a bowl of stew in front of me. "You eat now," she commanded in broken English.

"Thank you."

She nodded once, unsmiling, and marched back to the stove to stir the contents of a giant pot.

Despite Sofie's screams and my growing agitation, I was famished; I dove in with reckless abandon, shoveling a spoon filled with gravy and a chunk of meat into my mouth.

"Oh, good! You've found food!"

Startled, I dropped my fork. It clattered loudly against my plate.

"So sorry to scare, darling," Viggo apologized, placing a cool hand on my shoulder. "Did you have fun today?"

I nodded, my mouth full.

"We have a special surprise for you," Viggo continued. "When you're finished, go get dressed. There's a dress hanging on the door of your closet. We leave at seven o'clock. Meet in the atrium." With that, Viggo vanished, leaving me chewing my stew, and very curious.

❧

"What were you thinking, Viggo?" I mumbled, standing in front of a full–length mirror in my room, studying the clingy green satin dress. Pivoting slightly, I watched as the satin separated to reveal my upper thigh. As if that weren't risqué enough, the dress was completely backless, exposing my pale white skin. A *lot* of pale white skin, all the more obvious next to the vibrant jade hue of the dress.

That color...it brought me back to Caden's piercing jade eyes. I closed my eyes then, trying to recall the intensity of them, the way my skin tingled under their gaze. How vulnerable I'd felt with his tall, muscular body towering over me. If only he were real.

Silly girl. I gave my head a shake back to reality and took one last long look at myself. The plunging neckline left little to the imagination but at least it served as the ideal frame for my pendant. Grabbing a white fur stole, I headed out the door.

The trip down the long hall gave me ample opportunity to improve my walking skills in the matching jade three–inch heels. Realizing that walking in these things was a hundred times harder than it looked—and it looked impossible—I settled on trying not to look like a gorilla on stilts as I made my way to the atrium.

Sofie was waiting for me in a black strapless evening dress. I couldn't help gawking as she glided ghost–like toward me, the soft layers of chiffon swaying with her movements, looking every bit the actress on a red carpet. "You look like …" Sofie began before dropping off. "Someone I knew," she finished with a wistful smile, her eyes twinkling as she reached out to me.

"Now that's how a woman of your natural beauty ought to dress," Viggo called. Blushing, I turned to see him skipping down the steps two at a time, clad in a black tuxedo. "Sofie," he acknowledged with a nod and a smile, which she returned. I guessed they had reconciled. "Shall we?" Viggo said, offering his arm. I accepted, giggling shyly.

"Where's Mortimer?" I asked tentatively as we walked through the garden.

"Oh, he has a previous engagement so it'll just be us three," Viggo answered, smiling.

My shoulders dropped in relief. I didn't know why, but I was nervous around Viggo's somber partner. Viggo was just so much more easygoing and friendly.

We reached the other side of the garden to find Leonardo holding open the door of a Rolls Royce. He inclined his head. "Miss Evangeline."

"Thank you." I slid awkwardly into the car, trying to keep all the slits and gaps of my dress in place. Viggo and Sofie took a seat on either side of me, sandwiching me in the middle. In seconds we were pulling into the exit tunnel, passing Max and the other dogs sitting on their haunches, guarding their fortress.

CR

"Seriously?" I exclaimed in a rare burst of childlike gaiety as the Rolls pulled up to the curb in front of the theater.

Viggo laughed as he slipped out of the car in one fluid motion, then offered me his hand. Even Sofie's smile looked giddy in response to my reaction.

"*Romeo and Juliet* was my mother's favorite story," I said, gazing up at the marquee. In truth, it had been a staple in my bedtime routine, growing up. My mother, the hopeless romantic, referred to it as a fairy tale. It wasn't until years later that I learned fairy tales didn't usually end with the main characters dying.

"Then you're in for a treat," Viggo said as we walked toward heavy, ornately carved bronze doors.

"You look like a hunchback. Stop skulking and stand up straight," Sofie murmured, looping her arm in mine.

Viggo immediately grabbed the other one, pulling me closer to him. Sofie tightened her grip. I was beginning to feel like the rope in a tug–of–war as we made our way into the lavishly decorated theater.

The lobby was vacant.

"We're late!" I cried.

"Impossible." Viggo smiled, winking mysteriously.

A lanky usher dressed in an intricately beaded suit appeared to personally guide us to our seats, a box near the stage.

"So this is what a theater looks like," I murmured, taking in the splendid green, blue, and gold decor. Five levels of box seats adorned with fleur–des–lis and gold–plated cherubs wrapped three walls of the theater, overlooking a deep orchestra pit and floor seating before a curtained stage. I looked up to see a giant mural painted in vibrant hues on the ceiling.

"If you ever have the chance, visit the Theatre of the Estates in Prague. This place was designed with it in mind," Viggo said.

If I ever get to visit Europe, I thought wistfully, but I kept quiet. I'd likely be on the jet there tomorrow if I sounded at all deprived.

The lights dimmed as soon as we sat down, indicating that the show was about to begin. It was as if they had waited for our arrival. The audience hushed as the conductor stood, baton raised. He was so close—close enough that I could poke him with a stick if I wanted to!

Butterflies fluttered in my stomach. This was my first *real* play in a *real* theater with *real* actors. I fanned through the pages of the program, curious who the actors were, expecting not to recognize any names. And I didn't, except for one. It jumped out immediately—the producer.

Viggo. No last name. Just Viggo.

"Is this...you?" I asked, pointing out the name.

He chuckled. "I like to dabble in the arts. This theme holds a special place in my...heart."

"What exactly does 'producer' mean?"

"It means he told somebody what he wanted and threw obscene amounts of money at them to do it," Sofie replied cynically. "He's good at that."

Viggo chuckled but I thought I sensed contempt. "I built this theater and I wrote the play."

My eyes widened in amazement. *He's a lawyer and a playwright!*

The curtain parted, and the heart–wrenching story of Romeo and Juliet, the star–crossed lovers, doomed from the beginning by their opposing family ties, began as I remembered. The actors sobbed and moaned dramatically. The orchestra played soft music with perfectly balanced undertones of melancholy and longing. It was exactly as I had always pictured the story in my head. Right up until Juliet, traveling along a wooded trail alone at night for some unknown reason, was dragged out of her coach and bitten in the neck by a male attacker.

"I don't remember this part," I whispered, my brow furrowing.

Both Viggo and Sofie burst out laughing, earning a hush from the woman in the box next to us. "Sorry," Sofie offered politely. She tapped the program where it said "an adaptation."

"Oh...that's what that meant," I mumbled.

They laughed again, receiving another warning in the form of a sharp hiss from the same woman. Sofie turned to regard her. I couldn't see her face but whatever look she gave must have had the desired effect, because the woman shrank into her seat, practically disappearing from view for the rest of the show. I was beginning to see another side to Sofie's reserved, charming demeanor.

From there, the play took on a much darker, more seductive tone. Juliet, now a vampire, was torn between her absolute love for Romeo and her newfound urge to kill him whenever he was near. Romeo longed to join her in the world of the undead but because of a curse was unable. The story was full of scheming, supernatural strength and mind–bending tricks and, by the end of the play, their feuding families were the least of their problems. The story finished with Juliet accidently killing Romeo and then jumping into a fire to end her eternal misery.

"So, how did you like it?" Viggo asked, stretching out in the car on our way home.

"Amazing. Disturbing. Heartbreaking. An interesting 'adaptation.' Bravo, Viggo!" I ended with a scholarly clap, giggling. "How did you come up with the idea?"

"Oh, I have a deep fascination with vampires. They're such misunderstood creatures, don't you agree?" he said, his voice somber.

I paused. "Well, I doubt they'd be like that...you know, beautiful and emotional. Aren't they supposed to be evil, blood–crazy creatures with stained, dirty nails and vile breath? You know—bats and coffins?"

"What a terrible misconception," Viggo said, shaking his head furiously, his brow furrowed. "In my opinion," he added.

"But they kill people; we're like giant drinking boxes."

"Well, they need to survive! I don't suppose pigs and cows look too fondly at humans. It's the same thing! A little earlier in the food preparation process perhaps," Viggo rationalized.

"Hmm." He had a point, I guess.

"And imagine what it would be like to have heightened senses and super–human strength."

"That would be pretty cool," I agreed. "What do you think, Sofie?"

She hadn't joined in the conversation, instead gazing listlessly out at the streetlights. "It would be lonely," she answered now, her voice flat. "Everyone around you dies and you live forever."

"Well, that's why you'd turn those you loved, so you could be with them. Right?" I said.

Sofie turned to give me a tight–lipped smile. "It sounds so simple, doesn't it?"

"Unless you can't turn them for some reason," Viggo added, sadness dragging at his features. "Because of a curse."

"Right...and then all the super powers wouldn't change the reality that you're the loneliest creature in the world," I whispered. "That would be awful."

Viggo's mouth curved up in a half–smile and he patted my hand affectionately. "Yes, it would. No one deserves to live like that, don't you agree? So lonely?"

I nodded, thinking about my own solitary existence. *Am I that obvious?*

Sofie turned back to gaze out her side window. The rest of the car ride was silent.

CR

It was close to midnight by the time I staggered to my room, Max on my heels. I sluggishly kicked off my heels and flopped onto the bed, exhausted from a day of decadence. Even with all the fighting between Sofie and her friends, I could easily get used to living my days in their world.

I briefly considered pulling my weary body up to undress and get ready for bed, but I drifted off to asleep before I could act on it, faintly aware of a burning heat against the skin of my chest.

6. Déjà Vu

This feels too familiar.

The same statue stood beside me. The same trees towered over me. The same twilight challenged my eyes. The only thing worse than last night's dream would be last night's dream repeating itself.

I looked down to see my jade green evening gown. That was different, at least. My pendant had come alive again, burning hot and shining a brilliant orange–red.

"We've been waiting for you," a low voice called from the darkness.

My body went rigid. My eyes scanned the trees for the speaker. I sagged in relief as a woman with an angelic face and springy curls stepped out from the shadows. Amelie. This was a different dream.

"We're alone," Amelie confirmed when she noticed my eyes checking the trees for the others. "Sorry about last time...we didn't have much choice. Though I can't say I didn't enjoy part of it." She grinned sheepishly. "You are...an apparition of sorts. I'll explain later, but we need to get away from here." She stepped forward, then hesitated. "Sorry about this."

I frowned. "About what?"

I regained consciousness as my bare feet hit stone. Full darkness had descended and I couldn't see a thing. "Amelie?" I whispered.

"Sorry," Amelie said again.

"What did you do to me?"

"Nothing, really. It was just easier if I didn't have to explain things yet. Besides, it would have taken all night at your pace," Amelie said, evading my question. "Plus you probably would have tripped and knocked yourself out on a tree root again."

"I'm not *that* slow," I muttered, reaching up to touch the bump on my head from the previous night. I had excelled at track in high school. *The perfect loner's sport.*

Amelie laughed. "You are, next to me. Besides, I'd like to see you run through the woods and up a mountain in *that*," her eyes appraised my dress.

I pursed my lips, conceding to her logic.

"Come on, let's build you a fire. You're shivering." She grabbed my hand and began leading me through the darkness.

"How can you see anything?" I asked incredulously.

"I have great eyesight," she answered simply. "Stay right there."

"Where am I gonna go?" I mumbled, wrapping my arms around my chest.

I heard a harsh scraping sound, like stone striking metal, then a flame suddenly appeared. I watched as it floated through the darkness, sparking other flames as it moved until dozens of little fires lit the space around me.

The torchlight revealed we were in another cave, this one much larger than the one last night—its ceiling invisible from where I stood. It was empty except for a few cast iron park benches arranged around a circle of stones. A perfectly-formed teepee of wood, dried grass, and miscellaneous shreddings was piled within. A firepit. A new one, given the lack of ash. On the other side of the cave, three tunnel openings led into oblivion.

"You'll be safe here for the time being," Amelie offered, walking up to me with a torch in her hand, as I surveyed the place.

"Cozy." I hugged myself tightly.

"Right. A fire." Amelie strolled over to hold her torch to the teepee. In seconds a roaring fire was blazing. "You'll need to come closer to feel the heat," she said, giggling cheerily.

I walked over to sit on one of the benches. A worn piece of metal lay where the wooden slats of a normal park bench seat had rotted away. I awkwardly sat down, trying to avoid the sharp corners on the metal, afraid of tearing my dress or cutting myself.

Amelie slid in easily beside me, seemingly unconcerned about injury. "I love your dress." She reached out and lightly touched the silky material with her fingertips.

"Thanks. I was wearing this tonight when I fell asleep," I responded. And then it hit me and I began laughing.

"Why is that funny?" Amelie asked, confused.

"Because I'm worried about tearing my dress on this bench!"

She frowned. "As you should be—it's a pretty dress."

"No, you don't understand. I'm dreaming. This cave, this fire, you— it's fake. I know that, and yet here I am, worried about my dress!"

"You think you're dreaming," Amelie said slowly.

"No. I *know* I'm dreaming. Last night I went to sleep, dreamed about you guys, then woke up in my bed—right after you threw that man's headless body into the fire." I shuddered.

"*Last* night...?" Amelie repeated, looking perplexed. "Maybe you did wake up in your own bed but, here, you disappeared into thin air. And it wasn't last night. You've been gone for over a month." Her tone and her expression were so convincing that it was a struggle not to believe her.

A puff of wind cooled my shoulder. I turned to see Bishop and Fiona sitting on the next bench; the unexpected and freakishly quiet entry made me jump.

"Finally!" Bishop said by way of greeting, his charcoal eyes twinkling. "You took your time coming back."

"Where are they?" Amelie asked them quietly.

Bishop shrugged, a serious look flickering over his face. "Hopefully Rachel will prove useful."

All three turned to me now, dismissing their secret concern.

"So, how does it work?" Bishop asked eagerly.

I frowned.

"Evangeline was just telling me how she thinks this is all a dream and we are figments of her imagination," Amelie said, her eyebrows raised.

Bishop roared with laughter. "You think you're dreaming?"

Fiona cuffed him sharply upside the head, the slap echoing through the cave. It didn't appear to hurt him in the least, though he looked unimpressed. "You'll swear it's a nightmare, soon enough," he muttered, standing up and stalking out of the cave.

"Ignore him, he has an odd sense of humor," Fiona apologized in that smoky voice, offering me a pleasant smile.

"So why are you dressed up?" Amelie said, chucking another log into the fire.

"I was about to ask," Fiona murmured, adding, "It's gorgeous!" Her long, slender fingers reached out and caressed the material, as Amelie had. "It's been so long …"

I glanced at their frayed clothing but averted my gaze politely. They both laughed.

"We look homeless, don't we?" Amelie said, holding the corners of her tattered shirt up with beautifully manicured nails. It didn't make any sense. *But of course—this is a dream!*

"Isn't Evangeline lovely?" Amelie suddenly asked someone behind me.

I turned my head to see Caden standing a few feet away, his piercing green eyes on me. My heart skipped a few beats. "Hi," I managed to sputter, feeling heat creep up my neck to engulf my cheeks.

"You're wearing slightly more than last time," he observed, his mouth curving in a tiny smile. "What's the occasion?"

I felt a second wave of embarrassment flare, remembering that obscene outfit. Now here I was, barely covered again. "My birthday."

"Oh, I love birthdays! How old are you now?" Amelie asked gleefully.

"Eighteen."

"To be eighteen again," she sang dramatically, tilting her head back, her eyes closing as she reminisced.

I frowned, looking at her childish face. *She's not a day over sixteen, is she?*

She clapped her hands together in small, quick taps, a mischievous grin on her face. "Oh, goody! You don't believe me! How old do you *think* I am?"

I blinked. "I don't know...nineteen?"

"Nope! Guess again!" Amelie exclaimed, her face bright with amusement.

"Okay...um, twenty?"

She shook her head, giggling wildly.

This didn't seem like much of a game. "I give up!"

"Well...I'm not exactly sure. But, if we've been keeping accurate track of time, I'd say I'm about 752, give or take a decade."

I frowned, biting my lower lip. "I don't get it."

"We're sorry, Evangeline. This isn't as much fun for you as it is for Amelie," Fiona apologized, her face softening with a sympathetic smile.

"Humans never did find this game fun," Amelie said with a pout, her springy curls bobbing.

Humans? I stared blankly at her.

"Haven't you figured it out yet? What we are?" she asked.

I glanced at the others' solemn expressions. *If they aren't humans, what could they be?* It hit me then. I started laughing. "Of course! You're vampires!" Viggo's twisted adaptation was still fresh in my mind, and now in my dreams.

"We won't hurt you, I promise!" Amelie said earnestly, dropping to her knees in front of me to hold my hands. "We just want to be friends." Her eyes darted to Caden, who was watching me with a concerned expression. I noticed Bishop beside him; he must have snuck back in at some point.

"Of course! You are," I was on my feet now, replaying Viggo's conversation, "beautiful, emotional creatures. Misunderstood." I paced around the fire. "And you want to be friends, right? With quiet, meek Evangeline, who has no friends. People don't even notice me. But you—" my arm swept around the circle in rare dramatic flair "—all you want to do is protect me." I paused. "So this is how things manifest into dreams," I mused, more to myself. The events from the day were merging with my...what? Deep inner fears of loneliness, perhaps? Forcing them to the surface in this fantasy of super–powered beings.

I stopped pacing in front of Caden. "And you." I walked up to him. "Of course you're in my dream. No guy has ever even so much as blinked in my direction. And here you are, so perfect, and beautiful, and sweet ..." Caden's eyes widened in surprise. "When I see you, I want to ..." I didn't know how to finish the sentence.

Luckily I didn't have to, as Rachel suddenly appeared out of thin air to wrap possessive arms around Caden's waist. His arm quickly found its place around her shoulder, albeit stiffly.

A vile bitterness bubbled up in me. "And of course you're dating the gorgeous but trashy girlfriend that I could never compete with. Typical. Is this what you like?" I blurted at Caden, gesturing callously at Rachel. "She's not a very nice person, you know."

Bishop's head fell back and he barked laughter.

"Clearly I've missed an interesting conversation," Rachel said, smiling haughtily at me. Her voice didn't carry the same hostility as the previous night. It was sickly sweet and therefore no more pleasant. "And I would love to hear the rest of this tirade of yours. However, we have visitors that I wasn't able to deter. Eight of them."

"Great! Invite them in!" I said, throwing my hands up in the air. "Another one of those monsters, maybe? Is that supposed to represent my ugly inner demon?"

Rachel turned to Caden, grimacing. "Has she lost it?"

"Let's play it cool," Caden suggested, ignoring both of us.

"And maybe we should get her out of here," Fiona added, eyeing me warily.

Caden's hand—silky smooth and on the cool side—latched onto mine, sending a frisson through my body. He tugged me after him, running toward one of the tunnels and pulling me with him into the blackness.

I ran blindly, unable to see in the darkness, until my foot snagged on something hard and I stumbled, smashing my shoulder against the wall. I yelped in pain.

"Quiet!" Caden hissed, but followed that with an apology.

"How can you see?" I grated through my teeth, rubbing at the burning pain in my shoulder.

He didn't answer. Instead, he hoisted me up by one arm and continued running. My pain instantly vanished, as if his closeness had injected me with a shot of morphine.

Finally he stopped running and set me down gently. He shoved something soft into my hands. "Put those on," Caden instructed in a whisper.

"Put what on?"

He mumbled something incoherent. Seconds later a flickering torch illuminated a tiny, low-ceilinged cave. "Change, please," he whispered urgently, turning to face the exit. I could sense the apprehension in his voice. It was all too familiar from the other night.

I looked down at my hands, which held a ratty pair of pants and a shirt similar to what Amelie and Fiona wore. *They're disguising me. Okay, I'll play along.* I pulled on the pants. Unclasping my dress's neck strap, I let the dress drop noiselessly to the ground, wishing it had allowed for a bra.

I had my arms through the sleeves of the shirt and was about to pull it over my head when Caden's body suddenly crushed mine against the cave wall, his arms wrapping around me in a tight embrace.

"Just go along," he whispered in my ear, close enough that his bottom lip grazed my earlobe, sending ticklish shivers through my body.

And then he was kissing me.

I had only ever kissed a boy once in my life—a chubby, awkward fourteen-year-old named Stewart who was staying in the same foster home as me. The kiss had been the result of a lost bet. It had been a dreadful, open-mouthed fish kiss and I was sure he would swallow my tongue whole. Even I—unseasoned in the make-out department—recognized that Stewart wasn't going to get far with the ladies without vast improvement. This kiss was *nothing* like that. It began soft and inviting, only to intensify into urgency. Caden knew what he was doing.

Please don't wake up right now! I pleaded with my subconscious, enjoying this too much.

"Who's back here?" a voice called.

Caden's grip around me tightened. His lips slid off mine as he guided my face into his strong, broad chest, away from the voice. I was relieved that my half–dressed body was well hidden against his.

"Do you mind? We're busy," Caden spat toward the voice.

"Indeed," another voice said. "We're looking for Jethro. These are his caves. You wouldn't happen to know where he's disappeared to?" The lilt in his voice screamed suspicion.

"Don't know. This place was vacant when we stumbled across it a few weeks ago," Caden replied, his tone icy.

"That's odd...Jethro's occupied these mountains since the war. I'm surprised he would abandon them."

War? My palms began sweating at the mention of Jethro, the image of those cold, spidery eyes clear in my memory.

"What can I say? I guess they needed a change," Caden answered, turning to caress my cheek with his cold nose, feigning ignorance. Another shiver ran through my body.

"What's with all the torches around here?" a second male voice said. "You planning on burning someone?"

I tensed up. Caden's arms gripped my body more securely. A warning squeeze.

"We like firelight. Now beat it, unless you wanna watch," Caden said, his lips now running along the side of my neck, as if he were dismissing the two men. My knees buckled but he was prepared for my reaction, holding me upright.

"What's that?" one of them suddenly hissed.

Caden pivoted smoothly, turning so I was completely hidden from them.

The dress, I thought, panicking. I scanned the cave floor but couldn't see any green satin.

"It's called foreplay. If you don't know what comes next, I suggest you go find someone to teach you. The Council has a bunch of prepubescent girls to practice on." Caden smirked, acting nonchalant, trying to steer them away from whatever they had noticed. It didn't work.

"It looked like a wound."

My eyes instinctively darted to the raw, reddened skin on my shoulder where I'd hit the cave wall. *Why would that matter?*

"You must be seeing things." Caden's voice was light and humorous.

There was a pause. I thought his efforts had paid off. They may have, had the sounds from a violent commotion not drifted in from the main room just then.

"Don't—" Caden growled, but he didn't have a chance to finish before being wrenched from me and launched across the room.

A tall man took three quick strides to stand in front of me, his hand reaching out to roughly grip my arm as he inspected my shoulder. His steely blue eyes searched my face, stopping briefly at the light sheen of sweat on my forehead before locking with my own terrified eyes. With his short, strawberry–blonde hair and chiseled face, I would have considered him attractive had he not been looking at me predatorily.

He let out a low whistle. "I'm seeing it but surely I don't believe it." He inhaled deeply. "I can't *smell* it." He paused in thought. "Where have you been hiding, little one?"

I bit my lip and remained silent, though I doubt I could have formed two words, had I wanted to.

"Don't hurt her," Caden grunted. "She can lead us to more."

I glanced over to see him pinned beneath an ape–like fellow with no neck, the kind who spends more time in the gym than sleeping.

"Oh, I would never hurt you, *trust me*," the man crooned innocently to me, his voice so soothing that my body intuitively relaxed, *wanting* to trust him. He reached up to grip my chin with his thumb and index finger, effortlessly pushing my head back until I couldn't see anything but the cave ceiling.

I sensed him leaning in. *Oh God, he's going to kiss me. And then probably rape me.* I cringed.

And then I felt pain. Sharp, stabbing pain as something pierced my exposed neck. My mouth opened to scream but only a gurgle escaped. I struggled to break free, swinging my arms in defense, but every move sent jolts of acute pain through my body, as if I were snagged on a barbwire fence. I stopped fighting.

The ceiling began spinning as dizziness set in and my body slackened. Soon my arms hung limply at my sides. The pain finally dulled to an uncomfortable pressure. Only then did I sense the extreme burning sensation against my chest.

"Stop. Please," I heard Caden plead.

"You'll kill her before we find out where she's been hiding," someone else—it had to be the ape man—warned.

The pressure continued.

"Hey!" the ape man shouted more sharply a few moments later.

The pressure subsided as my attacker stopped whatever he was doing to me. He held my body up as my head lolled back. I didn't have the strength to lift it anymore.

"Strange. Her blood doesn't taste like anything," I heard my attacker say, followed by, "She'll cooperate more as one of us." His voice seemed distant, even though he was standing right next to me.

Everything seemed distant.

And then I felt that uncomfortable pressure again. This time a new sensation came with it, like an inoculation pumping something into me to snake through my veins. It carried a warm, numbing tingle through my limbs. *What can it be...poison?*

Something sharp and blistering hot suddenly stabbed me in the chest. I moaned feebly, all I could muster. Seconds later I was falling; my body hit the ground like a rag doll at the same time that I heard a skin–peeling shriek. *Was that me screaming? No, it came from beside me. Caden!*

I struggled to turn my head. My attacker was convulsing on the cave floor like an epileptic.

"You alright?" a voice called.

Another screech sounded. The cave plunged into complete darkness.

∞

I faded in and out of consciousness, unable to move, my breathing strained and irregular. I had no idea how much time had passed since the lights went out—seconds? Hours? Only silence and darkness surrounded me.

"Caden?" I finally whispered, my voice feeble.

"Shhh...it's over," a deep, soothing voice murmured. Something cool stroked my cheek. A hand, I think. I felt my body shift slightly and then I was being cradled in arms—warm, protective arms. Caden's arms.

"What...happened?" I asked.

"It's okay. You're going to be okay," Caden said, his hand tenderly cupping my chin, followed quietly by, "Please be okay." His thumb caressed the corner of my mouth.

"I'm...cold."

"Here. Let me help you." There was a gentle tugging as something slid over my head—my shirt. *Oh, right. I was only half-dressed. Why was I only...oh right.*

"Sorry about earlier. You were too slow. It was the only thing I could think of," he apologized softly.

My lips crooked into a tiny smile as I recalled that incredible kiss. The smile only lasted until I remembered the excruciating pain that had followed.

"There's a hole...in my chest...It was on fire," I croaked.

Caden's hands fumbled with my shirt, his fingertips gently inspecting me, careful not to expose or touch anything inappropriate. It sent a quiver through my limp, weak carcass of a body. My heart began to wallop against my chest wall, as if in its last-ditch effort before handing in its resignation.

"No holes. No fire," Caden confirmed gently.

"What did he...do to me?" I panted, tears welling up in my eyes. Something about blood and the taste, I remembered that much.

"You're okay," he said again.

"I can't see. Am I blind?"

I heard Amelie's voice then. "What happened?"

"Light, please," Caden requested softly and in the next instant a torch was burning again. Caden looked down at me, worry tarnishing those perfect jade eyes. Rolling my head slightly, I saw ape man lying facedown on the ground, another torch jutting out of his back. My attacker lay motionless where I had seen him last, his glassy, unfocused eyes assuring me he was dead.

"Where's Rachel?" Caden quietly asked Amelie.

"Dealing with the last of them," Amelie responded levelly, her concerned eyes never leaving me.

Caden turned back to gaze down at me. Despite everything, I sighed. I could happily stay like that forever.

He leaned forward, his mouth against my ear. "Don't tell her. Rachel can't find out. Please."

I nodded feebly.

"Take her for me," he whispered to Amelie.

I felt a slight jostle and then Amelie was in Caden's place as my cradler.

Caden left, dragging the ape man with him.

I lay in silence, mulling over his plea. Of course Rachel couldn't find out about the kiss. It would hurt her even if it hadn't meant anything. *If she had a heart underneath that prickly exterior. Highly unlikely.* What would she do if she found out? I didn't want to find out. She seemed like the vicious, jealous type.

"...and it killed him?" I heard Rachel saying in her typical detached voice as she strolled in, Caden and Bishop behind her.

Bishop grabbed my attacker's leg and began dragging him away, mumbling, "Let's just make sure." He glanced at me as he passed by, the same worried look on his face that Caden and Amelie wore.

"Are you okay?" Fiona asked, crouching down beside me.

"I will be...when I wake up from this nightmare," I whispered. *I keep forgetting this isn't real ...*

She gave me a reassuring smile—a smile that slid from her face when she glanced up at Amelie. "Do you think she'll change?" she whispered.

Change? Does she mean back into my dress?

Amelie shrugged.

They both looked back down at me again.

Amelie's hand grazed my throat. "It's so bizarre—all this blood and it could be mud, for all I care," she murmured, adding, "thank God."

What blood?

"It's the pendant. It must be masking it," Caden said.

Rachel crouched down to inspect my throat. "It doesn't want her to become one of us." Those eyes stared at me, in deep thought. "How did they figure it out?"

"A scrape on her shoulder," Caden was quick to answer.

Her eyes slid to my shoulder. She frowned. "Where? I don't see it. How could they see it?" she asked slowly.

"I'm as shocked as you." The lie rolled off Caden's tongue as effortlessly as if it were the truth.

I averted my eyes guiltily. As much as I disliked Rachel, I hated lying. More importantly, I was terrible at it.

Her eyes narrowed. "Do you believe us now?"

Believe...What am I supposed to believe again? I couldn't remember.

"I wonder what her blood tastes like," she murmured, eyeing me curiously.

"Leave her alone. She needs rest," Fiona growled, magically producing a cool, wet cloth. She began gently patting my neck.

As if her words had given a signal, I drifted off to sleep.

CR

I stared vacantly at the plaster swirls on the ceiling above my bed in Viggo and Mortimer's room, my body cold and stiff. *Why do I feel so weak? Am I getting sick? No.* I'd had plenty of colds and flu bugs. This didn't feel like any of those.

Max whined, resting his head on my chest, giving my neck a few gentle licks. "Hey boy," I whispered, struggling to lift my hand to scratch his head.

The clock indicated noon. I'd slept in. Again. I forced my body to sit up, fighting the overpowering urge to curl back up under the covers. I couldn't do that. Sofie needed me. Moaning loudly, I dragged the cozy duvet off my body and gave my eyes a good rub with the heels of my hands to help focus.

*Huh...*The last thing I remembered was lying down in that gorgeous green satin gown. *When did I put on these old sweats?*

7. Crazy?

I staggered to the bathroom in a daze, my eyes barely cracked. Shrugging off the mysterious sweats without giving them another thought, I stepped into the shower stall. I intentionally turned the faucet to cold and let frigid water stream down my body until it was borderline torturous, hoping that would wake me up. It helped, marginally.

Fumbling with the tap, I leaned my forehead against the tile, reveling in warmth, waiting to come alive.

My shoulder began to sting. Peering down at a sizeable scrape on my shoulder, I cringed. *Where did I get that?* I wondered, wracking my brain.

The cave.

Caden.

The attack.

It hit me like a speeding train—a wave of recognition as everything from the night suddenly pulsed into my head at once, the flood of memories overwhelming.

I pushed on the glass door and stumbled out of the shower, dropping to the cold tile floor before faintness could drive me down.

But, that had been *a dream.*

The attack.

My hand trembled as it reached for my throat. I sensed the wounds as soon as my fingertips grazed the area. Working up the courage to stand and face the mirror, I immediately spotted two distinct round marks across my jugular.

Bite marks.

I stared at my reflection as if expecting it to talk back to me, to provide some rational explanation, something other than the obvious.

That I had lost my mind.

There has to be a reasonable explanation. My brain churned frantically, searching for a thread of logic to grasp. *Maybe I changed before going to bed last night and I just don't remember. I did bump my head on the bedpost, after all. I could have amnesia.* That I had incorporated these old sweats into my dream was coincidence. Though I didn't know where the clothes came from. *Leonardo wouldn't have bought these for me. One of the maids must have accidently left her laundry in my room.*

What about the scrape on my shoulder, how could I explain that? *I must have banged my shoulder on something in the middle of the night. Maybe I was on my way to the bathroom. That could do it.* And the bite marks on my neck? *Max must have bit me. He has fangs. I knew that dog was odd. But why would he bite me? Why would anyone bite me?*

A vampire would bite me …

A tornado of explanations whirled around inside my head, none of them plausible, all of them creating more questions than answers.

A trick. Maybe this is a prank. A game. Vampires. Vampires and games. Sofie's screams from the other day rang in my memory: "Do you think this is another one of your games?" she had said to Viggo.

My eyes widened suddenly as I put two and two together. *Could they be drugging me and dropping me off across the street, in Central Park?* Caden, Amelie, and the others could be hired actors. That would explain their movie star looks and their perfect nails and their well–groomed hair. Viggo and Mortimer had more than enough money to pull it off. And they had been so interested in hearing about my "dream" yesterday morning.

Even considering this as a possibility bordered on insane but I was growing more fond of the idea by the second.

Yes. It made sense. It explained why I was in and out of consciousness so much. Not normally a fainter, I was unconscious all the time lately. Being drugged could do that, couldn't it?

By the time I dressed—in a turtleneck sweater to hide the bite marks—I was convinced that I had to do some research. I couldn't accuse them without concrete proof.

If I could just run across the street to the park, maybe I'd find it.

℘

I pushed through the double doors to the atrium in time to witness Sofie deliver a vicious slap to Mortimer's cheek.

"Evangeline! There you are," Sofie said, turning to smile at me as if everything was fine.

What is going on between these two?

"Evangeline," Mortimer greeted in a gruff voice before spinning on his heels and walking briskly toward the statue.

Viggo sat at the bistro table beside it, quietly reading a newspaper. He looked up. "There you are! Come, Evangeline."

I practically ran down the path toward them, until I realized what I was doing and deliberately slowed to a saunter. What if they had nothing to do with this? Maybe it *was* all in my head. *Is this what a paranoid schizophrenic feels like?*

A mysterious expression flickered across Mortimer's face. "Are you feeling alright?"

My stomach tightened. "Yes. Why?" I lied as calmly as I could.

"You look stiff. And your face is much paler than usual." His eyes darted to Max, narrowing suspiciously.

"Oh, no, I'm fine. Just tired. Must have been from all the excitement yesterday," I said, striving to make my voice light as possible. It came out sounding strangled.

"How did you sleep?" Viggo asked from behind his newspaper.

I paused for a moment, searching for a standard answer. "Like a baby." *Lie number two.*

"No bizarre dreams again?" he asked, his attention still half-buried in his newspaper. He seemed indifferent today. *Could he be feigning indifference?*

"Nope." My hands hurt. I glanced down to see them clenched into fists by my sides, so tight that my knuckles had turned white. I forced them to relax, my fingers unwinding painfully, as if crippled.

"Well, you're probably well rested then," Viggo said.

Can they tell I'm lying? I wondered. They both seemed more bored than culprits in an elaborate rouse.

Sofie's stilettos clicked against the cobblestones behind me as she approached. "I have some business to tend to and I'll be away for the afternoon. I'm sorry to leave you alone."

Perfect. "That's okay. I was thinking I could take Max for a walk to the park."

Mortimer's baritone laughter filled the atrium. "Maximus isn't the kind of dog you take out for a walk," he said, shaking his head in amusement.

"Besides," Viggo added, "there's supposed to be a protest outside, and those fanatics are known to get violent. You don't want to get mixed up with them. You're better off staying here. There's plenty to do, darling—Leonardo can show you around. We have a lovely indoor pool and games room, as well as a sauna, a gym, a movie theater—whatever you like. And if we don't have it, Leonardo will get it."

I nodded. *Drat.* So much for my reconnaissance mission. *How else can I gather some information?*

The Internet.

"You wouldn't happen to have a computer that I could use?" I asked politely. *Please don't ask why.*

"Of course! Maximus, please show Evangeline the way to my study," Viggo ordered, confident the giant dog understood him perfectly. He stood, folding his paper under his arm. "We have some things to tend to. We'll see you later." He nodded to Mortimer and they headed toward the house.

Mortimer stopped. "Sofie, are you coming? Now?"

She hesitated, her jaw tightening. "See you later, Evangeline." She followed them, disappearing through the red doors.

I was left standing alone with four giant dogs, feeling less confident about my conspiracy theory.

Ten minutes later I was in Viggo's brightly lit study, a second floor room overlooking the street through barred windows. I peered out. No picket signs.

Sitting down in the oversized leather office chair, I launched my investigation. First, I Googled Viggo and Mortimer. I didn't have their last names but I figured that, given their vast fortune and high–profile location, there had to be some information on a "Viggo and Mortimer"—a successful business, a generous donation, anything.

I found nothing relevant—not one article about the affluent New York couple, no mention of Viggo through his ties to the play. It was as if they didn't exist. That wasn't possible. Everyone who was anyone existed in cyber world.

Strange.

I shifted my focus to Central Park—the perfect location for their game, being nearby and enormous. Searching the park's website, I found listings for plenty of statues but nothing specific for the white woman. And no caves. It had to be in that park, though.

"Damn it!" I leaned back, my hands locked behind my head. *I must be doing this wrong.* I wasn't getting anywhere, penned up in this palace.

Max leaned forward and bumped his gigantic wet nose against my arm. "Do you know what's going on around here?" I asked him. He groaned in answer. I sighed, roughly scratching behind his ear. "Sorry, I don't speak canine, Max."

Chewing my bottom lip, I considered my options. Or lack thereof.

"How scary could those protesters really be?" I reached for the keyboard again, typing in "protesters" and "Manhattan" and "October." The first search result showed an image of gray–haired seniors with walkers and signs demanding health care reform. "Oh, come on! Them? Seriously?" I exclaimed. It didn't make any sense. I scanned the next five or six results and found nothing that fit the fanatical protester profile.

And then it hit me. Perhaps this was all part of the game, keeping me locked up in their fortress so I couldn't go out and uncover their plot. It was a disturbing idea, but it made more sense than a bunch of maniacal geriatrics getting violent for cheaper drugs.

I had no choice. I needed to escape.

Rushing to my room to grab my jacket, mitts, and purse—and praying no one saw me—I convinced myself that I was doing the responsible thing by sneaking out. If this was all a big game, I'd be free of these lunatics. If it wasn't and I was hallucinating, then I had bigger issues than protesters. I just had to get out without anyone noticing me. It was a good thing this place was the size of a shopping mall.

"Evangeline! There you are," Leonardo called out as I stepped into the atrium. His elderly eyes zoned in on my coat.

Busted. "I was cold," I lied.

"I can turn the temperature up, if you wish."

"No, that's alright. I'm good now."

He nodded. "Okay. Well, would you like me to put a movie on for you in the theater? Or perhaps you're hungry. We could see what Martha has on the stove."

"I think maybe I'll just sit out here for awhile," I said.

"Great. Why don't we take a seat over here," he suggested, heading toward the bistro table.

Leonardo wasn't going anywhere. He had obviously been assigned babysitter duty. He pulled out a chair for me which I accepted, smiling politely. We sat across from each other in awkward silence.

I decided I may as well get some information out of him. "What is Sofie fighting with Viggo and Mortimer about?"

Leonardo held his hand up to inspect his fingernails. "Oh? I didn't know they were fighting."

"Well...I saw Sofie hit Mortimer earlier today. And yesterday, the screaming ..."

"Hmmm. I'm sure it's nothing." He smiled warmly at me.

That confirmed it. He was either senile or covering for his employers. More uncomfortable silence.

"You seem fidgety. Is everything alright?" Leonardo finally asked, eyeing my hands, which were strumming aggressively against the table.

No, everything is not alright. You're hampering my investigation. How was I going to get away? "I'm not feeling well," I blurted, an idea sparking in my brain.

"Oh. Would you like some Tylenol?" He stood.

"Tylenol doesn't sit well on my stomach," I lied.

"Well, I'm sure one of the maids has some Advil or Aspirin," Leonardo offered.

I shook my head, stalling. "No...what I really need is...Midol."

"What's that?"

"Um...it's for...female problems." My cheeks heated.

"Oh. Hmm...okay," Leonardo said, his eyes dropping to the cobblestones. "I'll go ask the maids." He started toward the red door, moving slower than usual. I suspected he wouldn't be in a rush to fill that request—a proper elderly gentleman polling young female maids for PMS pills.

"Sorry, Leonardo," I whispered, then forced the guilt of my deception aside to race toward the gate. I remembered an ominous–looking solid door beside the car entrance. It had to be the exit to the street, though it appeared more appropriate for a bank vault. I'm sure they needed the best security here, with all their wads of cash lying around.

*If I can just get to it before anyone comes out...*I was twenty feet from the door when Max's massive black body appeared in front of it, the other hounds flanking him to create a formidable barrier. A low warning growl rumbled in Max's throat as I approached. It was deep and threatening and if I hadn't already developed a certain level of trust and fondness for this dog, I would likely have dropped dead from terror right then and there.

I veered to the right, attempting to sneak around the canine wall. They all shifted their bodies, blocking my path.

"Max? What are you doing? I need to get out," I whispered, glancing anxiously over my shoulder for Leonardo.

Max whined.

Why would they do this? Unless ... 'Max, were you *ordered* to keep me here?"

Another whine and a bow of his head, as if he were nodding. Yes, it was clear he had been. I was imprisoned. Leonardo was the warden and these dogs were the guards.

I had to get out, and fast, but with well over a thousand pounds of ferocious muscle forming a barricade, this was going to be tricky. I needed a distraction. What would distract a dog? *Something to chase.*

"Look! A kitty, over there! Go fetch!" I whispered excitedly, pointing to the other side of the atrium.

None of them budged. Their eyes didn't even shift.

"Right. You're smarter than that. I forgot," I muttered.

I reached forward and pushed against Max. Nothing. I leaned in, putting all of my hundred and twenty–odd pounds against him. It was like trying to move a concrete wall. I groaned in frustration. These dogs were more well–trained than Jake, the only dog I had ever really known. That golden retriever's sole purpose in life was chasing his tail and trying to steal thawing meat off the counter.

An idea hit me—a desperate one. I dashed up the stairs and into the house, heading toward the kitchen. Luckily it wasn't too far from the atrium so I found it easily enough on my own.

Magda was chopping up vegetables when I entered. "Hi, Magda," I called gaily, trying not to arouse any suspicions. She glanced up to acknowledge me with a polite nod, then returned her focus to her carrots. "I'm just going to grab a snack," I said, heading casually toward the commercial–sized fridge. She nodded again without looking up, likely having no idea what I had said. That was fine with me.

I pulled open one of the doors. *Bingo! Meat.* And it wasn't hard to find, considering one entire side of the fridge was stocked with it. Why did they need so much? *Doesn't matter,* I decided, reaching in to grab a zip lock bag before peeking around the door. Magda was now tending a simmering pot, her back to me. I closed the fridge door softly and hurried out before she could turn around. I'd have a hard time explaining what I was doing with eight raw steaks in any language.

When I returned to the atrium, Max and the others were still standing in the same positions as before, like statues. Thankfully Leonardo wasn't back yet. *This has to work.*

"Look what I found for you!" I exclaimed, holding up the bag of bloody meat. I didn't think they'd mind that it was raw. Jake had never been too picky.

This time my method of distraction worked. Unfortunately, a little too well. All four dogs erupted in a chorus of vicious snarls and deep growls, revealing razor–sharp fangs—much more pronounced than I remembered. Muscles rippled with tension as they began stomping and pawing at the ground with their hooked claws, clearly torn between holding their positions and springing.

The bag dropped from my hand, spilling blood onto the cobblestones as I scrambled back, terrified. *Brilliant idea, Evangeline. Forget protesters. Leonardo's going to come back to find your mangled body in the atrium. And then he's going to have a heart attack and die.*

I locked eyes with Max, pleading silently with him. It seemed to work, as he settled down, his fierce snarls turning to snorts.

The other three were still focused on the raw meat and frothing at the mouth. Max let out a ferocious growl and, turning, snapped at the dog to his left, his teeth tearing a chunk out of the dog's ear. With a yelp, the three dogs stiffened immediately, resuming their guard. The meat was instantly forgotten.

I stepped forward cautiously, deciding my last–ditch effort would be a show of confidence. "Okay, Max, you're either with me or against me. You choose!" I commanded with as much conviction as I could muster, throwing in, "I'll never forget this moment," for good measure.

Those perceptive yellow eyes gazed into mine as if judging the truth of my words. We remained frozen like that—eyes in a deadlock—for so long that I was ready to give up. Then Max suddenly covered my cheek with a lick. He stepped to one side, allowing a small space for me to fit through.

I gasped. "Thank you!" Planting a quick kiss on his snout, I darted past, ready to throw the door open.

Until I saw the keypad.

"Damn it!" I cried, pounding once on the door. Tears welled in my eyes as defeat swept over me. There was no way out. I was in Alcatraz.

*Six...two...one...*a distant deep voice whispered. I recognized the voice from the other day. Only this time it was speaking in numbers. Seven numbers, repeating over and over.

On impulse, I punched the numbers into the keypad. My eyes widened in shock when I heard the lock release. *How?*

It didn't matter right now. I was free.

8. Reconnaissance

I studied the throngs of people as I crossed Fifth Avenue. There wasn't a single person who could ever be mistaken for a protester. That seemed to favor my conspiracy theory.

I passed through one of the park gates and stopped to take in the gardens and paths of the famous landmark, exhaling heavily. *Where do I begin?* The aroma of a hot dog cart wafted my way. My stomach growled. *Start with lunch.*

Foot long and Coke in hand, I searched out a park bench and gingerly sat down, recalling the sharp metal seats of the benches around the fire the night before. This bench's wooden seat was intact, definitely not one of their props. I scanned the other benches in the area to confirm that all of their seats were also wooden. *I'm like Nancy Drew,* I thought proudly as I took a big bite of my hot dog. A gob of mustard dripped onto my lap. *A slovenly version.*

I couldn't help but feel discouraged, sitting there. It didn't *feel* like the same forest. I didn't remember autumn foliage. But it had been dark and, if they were drugging me, I couldn't trust my instincts, I rationalized. Still, something didn't add up.

I scrutinized the people hurrying along the various paths and sidewalks around me, hoping to catch a bubbly blonde skipping by. Or better yet, Caden. My heart began to race at the thought.

It was sunny but the gusting wind carried a bite, enough to warrant a thick jacket and mitts. My hands—ungloved while I handled my messy lunch—were turning red.

"So many people about, all in a rush, aren't there?" a petite, elderly woman in a blue wool peacoat remarked as she slowly eased herself down beside me on the bench, a bag of dried bread in her frail, wrinkled hands.

I smiled politely at her. "People prefer the warm weather."

"And you? What are you doing out on a day like this?" she asked, turning to face me as she leisurely tossed a few pieces of bread out to some eagerly waiting pigeons. She had to be in her late eighties, judging by her heavily creased face and her stark white, curly bob. Oddly though, her eyes were not clouded and bland with age but an intense hazel, speckled with dark green flecks.

Looking for evidence that I'm being drugged and dropped off in Central Park at night, I replied mentally. She'd likely keel over dead if I shared that. "Oh, just taking in the sights. I'm visiting from Maine," I said instead, drawing a big gulp of soda through my straw.

"Oh, isn't that lovely," she replied. A typical old lady response.

We spent the next twenty minutes idly chatting about the differences between Portland and New York as the old lady fed the hungry birds and I finished my lunch. She was a sweet, grandmotherly type, eager to ramble on about her ten grandchildren and three great–grandchildren.

With the last chunks of bread devoured by the scavengers, she rose. "Well, it was nice to meet you …"

"Evangeline."

"Evangeline. What a lovely name. Evangeline, I must be heading home now. It's too cold out here for these old bones."

"Goodbye," I said, smiling.

"Are you going home now too?"

"Yeah, probably," I said, crumpling up my hot dog wrapper. "I don't think I'll find what I was looking for."

"Oh? And what was that?"

I hesitated. "A statue."

She paused. "Anything in particular, dear?" she asked, her eyes squinting in query.

I described the white woman in detail to her. Those unusual hazel eyes widened. "Yes! I know the one you're talking about. Just take the paths through Shakespeare Garden and you'll find it."

"Really? Thank you!" I said, feeling a mixture of distress and relief.

With that, she shuffled away, moving surprisingly quick for such an old lady.

I followed her directions and soon found myself deep within the park, surrounded by trees of all varieties, their leaves turning the colors of autumn. I was surprised how wooded and quiet it was with the city bustle so close by. It still didn't look like my dream, but …

On and on I walked, searching. I wondered if Leonardo had discovered that I had snuck out yet. I hoped he wasn't too worried. *If I could just find this statue soon, I'd have the proof I need,* I thought. *It has to be around here somewhere.*

Leaves rustled, stopping me dead. My head whipped toward the noise and I saw a stout, round–faced man walking a scruffy gray mutt of medium size. He had well–groomed, salt–and–pepper hair and a tidy mustache, and he was smartly dressed in a blue tweed coat and a matching plaid wool cap. *A perfectly respectable–looking gentleman,* I concluded, relaxing.

The dog's front legs were practically off the ground as it pulled its owner toward me. When it reached me, the mutt sniffed my pant leg, let out a low growl, then lunged upward, snapping at my arm.

"Badger! Sit!" the man yelled, tugging the dog back sharply before its fangs could sink into my skin. Badger sat back on his haunches.

If only Max were here, I thought spitefully, glaring down at him. *You'd be shaking in your hairy paws.*

"I apologize, miss. Badger has issues with other dogs. He must have caught the scent of one on your clothing. He's seeking therapy," the man joked in a gentle voice, patting the dog's head. I noticed a small tattoo of an angled cross on the fleshy part of his thumb.

I laughed along with him, keeping one eye on the mutt's ugly face.

"Are you lost? You look lost," he inquired.

"Oh, I'm looking for a statue that's supposed to be around here …" I described the statue, hoping he could redirect me.

"Oh yes. This way," the man said, smiling as he began moving off the path.

That's right! There hadn't been a path the night before. *That*, I would remember. I followed him with renewed excitement.

"Are you a tourist?" he asked.

"Is it that obvious?" I said, giggling.

"What brought you to the city?" he asked, veering into a more densely wooded area.

"Visiting friends." *Friends who paid someone to bite me and make me think I'm crazy.*

He held a branch back for me to pass. "Friends…hmm…and have you known these friends long?"

"No." I frowned. *Why would he ask that?*

"But you're visiting them?" His eyes darted to our left, as if searching for something. Or someone.

Warning bells began sounding in my head. *Get out of here.* "Thanks for your help. I think I need to get home," I squeaked.

It was too late, I realized, as I turned to see two scruffy men closing in behind me, one holding a gun.

9. Attacked

The two thugs smiled crookedly at me, one of them revealing a brown tooth. A pretty, young, round–faced woman of perhaps twenty–five, with shoulder–length auburn hair and rosy cheeks, stepped out from behind them.

Cold sweat trickled down my back as panic set in. *I'm such an idiot!* I was trapped and it was my own fault. I was that stupid, gullible girl from Maine, wandering through Central Park. *A big, shiny target for any lowlife.* My eyes darted about, frantically searching for an escape route. There wasn't one. Either by flying bullet or flying mutt, I'd be stopped.

I swallowed. "I have money. Lots of money. Here, you can have it all," I quavered, thrusting my purse forward.

No one made any move toward it.

"Evangeline, correct?" the man with the dog asked.

A chill ran down my spine as I ran our brief conversation through my head. *I hadn't given my name, had I?*

He chuckled. "You really should be more careful, sharing information with strangers. Even sweet old ladies. Looks can be deceiving." His smile sent a chill through me.

I managed a small gasp, shocked that the bird–feeding lady could be in league with them.

"When we saw you leave the leech house alone, we were intrigued. So we followed you here." I remained silent but my bewilderment at their "leech" reference to Viggo and Mortimer's place must have been evident, because the round–faced man cocked an eyebrow. "So they've kept their secret from you...interesting. They're very good at it, aren't they? And there aren't as many telltale signs as the stories would have you believe." He paused. "I can't believe they allowed you out on your own, though...Why are you with them?"

I swallowed hard several times, struggling to form words. "I'm just visiting...I don't know what they've done to upset you, but I have nothing to do with it." I started trembling.

"On the contrary, we believe you have everything to do with it," the woman interjected, her voice cold and detached. "You are here with Sofie, correct?"

I blinked. *How do they know so much?*

The woman closed the distance between us. Those eyes...hazel eyes with dark green flecks, like the old lady's eyes. *She must be a granddaughter.* A grandmother–granddaughter criminal team—that *had* to be a first.

The woman paced around me slowly, like a cat circling its prey. "You're human; I would know, otherwise."

I fought hard to stave off tears. "I don't know what you're talking about."

"Perhaps you don't; it wouldn't surprise me that Sofie didn't inform you of her designs for you. She's cunning, that one," she mused. Her eyes darted to my pendant and she reached up, but her hand hovered over the stone, not touching it. "Incredible," she murmured. Her mouth crooked in a smile of realization. "Do you know what she's done to you?"

I noticed her eyes flicker toward the bushes; they narrowed suspiciously, and she started backing away. "So sorry, if you are indeed guilt-less," she said in a rush, nodding to the man with the gun.

He answered by raising the weapon to point at my chest.

I heard the click of the trigger.

Once, I had wondered what a bullet would feel like, tearing into my flesh and organs. I expected it would involve a considerable amount of pain. I didn't expect that the impact would send my body flying as if hit by a train.

But it did. The next thing I knew, I was lying on my back some distance away, with a crushing weight in my chest. The bullet must have punctured my lung because I couldn't inhale. *This is what drowning in your own blood must feel like.* I hoped it wouldn't take too long. It was painful.

I was lying on a cushion of brittle leaves, staring up at the overcast sky as I made my peace with God, when the tightness in my chest began to subside. I found I could inhale again—small breaths at first, then increasingly normal ones. Maybe I would be okay. If I could get to a hospital. If I could get away from here.

I closed my eyes and remained still, feigning death until I was sure they were gone.

A wet nose poked against my cheek. *Badger, checking to see if I'm dead yet.* That mutt would surely give me away, I realized, fighting panic. I kept my eyes closed, trying to calm myself.

Another, more forceful nudge against my cheek— followed by a familiar whine. I dared to peek through one eye to see Max's large snout. He was lying beside me. Three other massive black bodies surrounded us, on guard. I breathed a huge sigh of relief. The dogs must have scared off everyone.

"Oh, thank you, Max!" Propping myself up on one elbow, I reached over to stroke Max's shoulder. I felt something warm and slick. I pulled my hand back, gasping when I saw the blood.

Examining Max's fur, I found the tiny hole where a bullet had entered. The bullet that was meant for me, I realized then, checking my chest to see that I was unscathed. Well, almost unscathed. Max nosed my left hand, growling. It was covered in my own blood from a deep gash across my palm. *I must have cut it on a rock when I fell. When Max crashed into me to take the bullet.*

"I have no idea how you guys found me, but let's get out of here before they come back," I whispered, staggering to my feet.

My stomach lurched.

No one had left.

They wouldn't be going anywhere, except in body bags.

Body parts were strewn everywhere, heads practically decapitated, necks torn wide open. And blood—pools of it. So much blood that it stained the forest floor bright crimson. I spotted Badger's head lying three feet away from me, his lifeless eyes staring vacantly up at the sky, his tongue lolling out. His body was nowhere in sight.

The trees began whirling around me. I was unconscious before my body hit the ground.

❧

Sitting on the leather couch in the library, I watched in silence as a diminutive, elderly woman cleaned and stitched the three–inch gash on the palm of my hand with skilled precision, her slender fingers weaving the needle in and out of my flesh. It should have been painful. Instead, I felt nothing.

I recall stirring only once after seeing the corpses, to find myself cradled in Leonardo's gentle arms. When I came to again, I was lying on a sheet on the hardwood floor in Viggo and Mortimer's library, a maid hovering over me with a set of blood–free clothes, adamant that I remove mine immediately. Once changed, I watched her toss the stained outfit and the sheet into the lit fireplace. Slightly dramatic, in my opinion, but the clothes were ruined so it didn't matter.

The grandfather clock gonged. It was four in the afternoon.

"Leonardo, where is everyone?" I asked.

"They'll be here soon," he responded calmly, placing another log in the fireplace.

"Do they know what happened?"

Leonardo sighed. "Oh, yes…they know."

"Are they angry?"

His eyebrows arched severely, but he said nothing. I'd take that as a yes.

"What about Max?" I suddenly remembered.

Leonardo glanced over, frowning.

"The gun shot…he was shot," I elaborated.

He opened his mouth to speak, then paused to choose his words. "So you were aware of that." He chuckled. "Don't you worry about that brute."

"How did he find me?"

"You'll need to ask him," Leonardo answered with a secretive smile.

My brow puckered as I tried to make sense of that. I couldn't. "How did *you* find me?"

"Thank you for your services," he said to the old woman as she finished wrapping my hand in gauze, ignoring my question.

In response, she shoved two tiny blue pills—presumably painkillers—into my mouth, then packed up her medical tools and disappeared without uttering a word.

"Hopefully those don't upset your stomach," Leonardo murmured with a hint of annoyance, handing me a glass of water.

I averted my eyes, feeling my face heat.

Leonardo eased himself to his knees beside me and surveyed the carpet and furniture from various angles, a clear spray bottle and rag in hand. He then began scouring the operating area.

"Let me do that," I offered.

"That's quite alright, Evangeline. I may be old, but I'm not completely useless."

"No, I didn't mean—" I stammered, "I just thought...it's my blood. I should clean it up."

"Well, that's a remarkably courteous way of looking at the situation, though not surprising. You're a remarkably courteous young woman, aren't you?"

I felt myself blush. "And you're not old."

"Yes, I am," he responded, chuckling. "Seventy–eight, to be exact."

A few more minutes passed. "You're very meticulous," I observed.

He offered no response as he struggled to stand.

"Leonardo …" I began hesitantly.

"Call me Leo if you wish. Leonardo is such a mouthful."

"Okay...Leo." An inconsequential question suddenly popped into my head. "Hey, why do you have such an Italian name when you're so...British?"

He chuckled. "My father was Italian and I grew up in England."

"Oh."

"Was that your burning question?"

I shook my head. "Should I be worried about anything?"

He sighed, gave me another strange smile, then walked over to throw the rag into the fireplace. I sensed that was the only reply I would get.

My eyes roamed aimlessly around the library, landing on the painting above the mantel. On the black pendant. "Why is Sofie's sister's picture on the wall?"

"Do you normally ask so many questions?"

"Sorry," I mumbled, flushing.

Leo chuckled, glancing up at the portrait. "I believe she was a lady friend."

"Lady friend...oh, you mean girlfriend?"

A rare smirk appeared on Leo's face. "Yes, girlfriend, you young folk would call her."

I smiled sheepishly. "Whose?"

He pursed his lips. "Can't say, really."

"So when did Viggo and Mortimer—" I stopped abruptly. *'When did they switch teams?' God, Evangeline. Be a little more tactful.*

"When did Viggo and Mortimer what?" Leo probed.

I searched for the appropriate words. "Begin their relationship?"

He repeated my question to himself, confused. Then, suddenly, his face lit up and he erupted in raucous laughter. I widened my eyes, startled by the unexpected reaction.

"Viggo and Mortimer are no couple. I wouldn't even call them friends. Partners in a common interest, one may say."

I struggled to translate his words as he stoked the fire. *What a cryptic old butler.*

"Although I suppose I can see how someone on the outside may mistake their relationship," he continued. "They live together, spend all their time together, and squabble like an old married couple."

"Who squabbles like an old married couple?" a deep voice boomed.

I spun around to see Viggo and Mortimer strolling into the library. *But where's Max?* I held my breath, waiting for the dogs to trot in behind them. They were never too far away. When none of them did, my stomach tightened another notch. What if the police had them? They'd destroy them for that massacre, even if they did save my life.

"Where's Max?" I asked as the two men took up positions before me, arms crossed over their chests. Viggo's face displayed the same placid expression as usual. In stark contrast, Mortimer's was primed to throw daggers. I couldn't help shrinking guiltily onto the couch, feeling less like an eighteen–year–old adult guest and more like a naughty six–year–old in need of a spanking.

"Busy," Mortimer said.

"How's the hand?" Viggo asked, eyeing my bandages, a strange grin on his face.

"A bit sore."

An uncomfortable silence followed. "So...were those the protesters you were warning me about?" I asked awkwardly.

"You could say that," Viggo replied.

Another long pause. "How much trouble are the dogs in?"

"None. It's been taken care of," Viggo answered as if referring to a minor bill needing payment.

"What does that mean?" I asked warily.

"It's cleaned up. No evidence. No witnesses."

A chill ran down my spine. "But, it was broad daylight in a major park. And there was so much blood."

"So...?" Viggo shrugged, unconcerned.

"So ..." I faltered. "Aren't you afraid you'll be accessories to murder? The police would understand, wouldn't they? Wouldn't it be easier to report it?" I pictured a full–scale S.W.A.T. team crashing through the gate and pinning the lot of us—the gentle old butler included—to the ground.

"It would have been easier if you had *obeyed* us," Mortimer answered through clenched teeth.

I cowered further into the couch.

"Mortimer, please," Viggo said, patting the air in a soothing gesture.

"I'm sure Evangeline has an excellent reason for defying us." His raised eyebrow indicated he was expecting the explanation right then and there.

Did I tell them the truth? Did I accuse them? I had gained no proof through my adventure. Only more questions.

"Are you going to explain yourself, or sit there and fidget all afternoon?" Mortimer said, drumming his fingers loudly on a console table.

"Well...I didn't think I was disobeying. It was just a suggestion, wasn't it?" I finally answered in a meek voice.

Mortimer's fist slammed down on the table, sending a lamp flying and me cowering.

The library door exploded open and four giant black bodies barreled through. The dogs. In seconds they were circling the couch where I sat, their hackles raised and growling a warning at Mortimer.

If the wall of fangs and froth intimidated him, Mortimer didn't let on; he stared Max down, looking ready to lunge himself.

Sofie ran into the room.

"I thought you had him under control." Viggo's voice was calm but I sensed the underlying contempt.

"You try controlling that beast." Her eyes fell on me. She took several quick steps forward then froze, glancing uncertainly at Viggo.

"It's okay, Max," I said, reaching up to stroke his side, trying to calm him. I examined his shoulder for the wound. Nothing. I must have mixed up the sides. I checked the other shoulder. Nothing. No wound, no bandage, no dried blood. I screwed my face up. Yes, he had been shot. I remembered. "I saw the bullet wound. His blood was all over my hand," I said out loud.

No one answered. I looked up to see worried glances passing between them.

"Leo. Tell them you saw it too," I pleaded, frowning my confusion.

Leo shrugged noncommittally, his eyes darting to Mortimer. He ducked his head and exited without a word.

"It happened, didn't it?" I cried as tears welled in my eyes, blurring my vision.

"Do you believe it happened?" Viggo asked calmly.

I looked at each of them in turn, at their blank faces. Maybe it hadn't happened. *Is this what a schizophrenic feels like, skating through delusions and reality so seamlessly that it's impossible to discern which is which?* I raised my hand to see the bandage. I felt the throbbing ache of my gash, a result of the attack. No, this had to be real.

"I warned you two," Sofie said softly, her eyes never leaving me.

"Well, go ahead then, Sofie. Tell her what you've done. See if that doesn't terrify her, you self–righteous witch," Mortimer answered, smiling smugly at her.

What is he talking about?

In the next instant Sofie was standing where Mortimer had been and he was airborne, his tall, muscular body flying through the air and slamming into a wall twenty feet away. Glass rained down as the impact from his body shattered a mirror into countless pieces.

I gaped at Sofie, who—with her delicate arms and her lithe frame—had thrown Mortimer across the room right before my eyes. It was impossible. It couldn't have happened.

Mortimer pushed to his feet and strolled back, brushing glass from his jacket sleeves. "My, you've gotten strong, Sofie. Who have you been snacking on?" He paused only a foot away from her, looming, their eyes communicating silently.

What did he say? My stomach dropped with the realization that this was beyond hallucination. This was a full–scale delusion. There was no conspiracy, no one was tricking me. I had lost my mind. "None of this is real. The bullet, Sofie's lip, my hand, the bites ..." I rambled, picturing straitjackets and padded cells with tiny peepholes and seemingly normal people having intellectual conversations with empty chairs. Maybe I could share Eddie's alley with him. I was his goddess, after all.

"What bites?" Mortimer suddenly said, eyes narrowed.

"No bites. They're not real. I thought they were real but they're not," I rambled absently, yanking the collar of my shirt down. "See? Nothing."

Sofie gasped.

10. Truth

"**Y**ou lying bitch!" Mortimer snarled. He flew at Sofie, sending her crashing into a glass side table, which shattered.

"And you!" Mortimer turned his furious eyes to Max. "Traitor!"

Max responded with a short but fierce snarl.

"I didn't know this would happen!" Sofie shrieked, on her feet in seconds and lunging at Mortimer's neck with a jagged chunk of glass in her hand, intent on decapitating him.

Mortimer barely avoided the swipe at his jugular, taking a nick on his shoulder instead. Catching her arm in mid–swing on her second attempt, he snapped her forearm with a sickening crack. He followed with a backhand that split her bottom lip wide open.

Arm dangling and blood pouring from her lip, she grimaced in pain. "Is that all you've got?" she grated, taunting him.

Mortimer's dark eyes flashed with rage. He was going to kill her. I couldn't watch. I buried my face in Max's body, my hands digging into his fur, bracing myself for the blood–curdling screams.

I heard Viggo's serene voice instead. "Everyone, calm down please."

Peeking out from behind Max, I saw Viggo standing between the two of them, his arms outstretched. "You have some explaining to do, Sofie," he said calmly.

I dared look at her. And gasped. Her lip was as beautiful and unharmed as ever, except for a patch of smeared blood which she now dabbed at with a cloth, using the arm that should be hanging limp at her side.

"Please stop fighting. You're terrifying Evangeline. She's already been through enough today!"

All three turned to regard me. "And I suppose you have some questions," Viggo said, smiling gently. He took a step toward me.

Max growled.

Viggo raised his hands in surrender and backed up to sit in one of the armchairs. "But us first. Why did you sneak off to the park?"

I gaped at Sofie's uninjured lip a moment longer. "I was looking for an explanation for the bites."

"And how does Central Park offer that explanation?" Viggo asked.

Here we go. "I thought you two were drugging me, taking me into the park, and paying a bunch of people to pretend they're vampires." There. It was out there.

Viggo's jaw dropped, his face twisting in a mixture of horror and insult.

"Why on earth would we do that?" Mortimer stared at me in disbelief.

"I don't know...you're bored? Viggo is fascinated with vampires and I overheard you guys fighting the other day about a game. Anyway, I figured if I could find the statue in the woods, then I would have proof."

"How would the statue prove that? You're not making any sense, my dear Evangeline," Viggo exclaimed in frustration.

I sighed. "I had another dream last night."

"And what happened?"

I told them about waking up beside the statue again, about the cave, and the attack. "And I woke up with these." I gestured to my neck.

"And did you find proof of this trick you suspect us of?" Mortimer asked, eyebrow raised.

I shook my head, dropping my gaze to my hands. I could feel their eyes boring into me, waiting for me to speak. "Am I going crazy?" I finally asked.

Viggo changed the topic. "These people who attacked you. How did you come across them?"

"They cornered me while I was looking for the statue. Four of them," I answered, explaining how a seemingly sweet old lady set the trap.

"Four of them," Mortimer repeated, his expression unreadable.

I nodded. "Three men and a woman. And a dog." I shuddered, remembering the mutt's decapitated head.

"A woman?" Sofie asked, glancing at Viggo.

I nodded.

"And did they tell you who they were or what they wanted?"

I hesitated. "It didn't seem random. They knew you—all of you. They said they've been watching you." I looked at Sofie. She had known. Yesterday, shopping. She had sensed it somehow.

"What exactly did they say?" Viggo asked.

"Something about this necklace, about me being human, about Sofie doing something to me. You being...leeches?"

Viggo tisked, shaking his head in disdain. He rose and walked over to rest his arm on the mantel. "Well, I guess we can't keep this from you any longer." Viggo gazed up at the painting of Sofie's sister. "No, Evangeline. You are not crazy, or hallucinating, though what I'm about to tell you will not help convince you of that." He paused to clear his throat. "'Vampire' has such a stigma to it, wouldn't you agree?" he said casually, followed by a resigned sigh. "I am over two thousand years old. I'm the oldest surviving vampire on earth. Mortimer is just shy of nine hundred."

My stomach tightened into a tight ball. If I wasn't crazy, then I was surrounded by a bunch of people who were.

"Sofie, you are—what now, a hundred and forty–eight? Is that right? I wouldn't want to age you. I know how sensitive females are," Mortimer sneered.

Sofie rolled her eyes in annoyance, but nodded.

"You're all...vampires," I repeated, listening to the words come out of my mouth.

"Now Sofie, you're not being completely honest," Mortimer mocked.

Sofie glared at him before turning to me. "I was born a sorceress."

"Sorceress...like witch?" I asked.

"An extremely powerful one," Mortimer emphasized.

"Oh, Mortimer, you flatter me," Sofie answered sarcastically before turning back to me with that haunted look on her face. She lifted her hand and a tiny flame rose from her index finger, out of thin air.

My eyes went wide. Without thinking, I slid off the couch and pushed past Max to inspect it closer, intrigued. Lifting my hand to it, I flinched as the heat scalded my skin. It was real.

With a burst of excitement, Viggo skipped over to the grand piano. Picking it up with one hand, he launched it across the room. It crashed into a concrete column and splintered, the sound deafening. "Need more proof?" He was instantly standing in front of me. Grabbing an empty glass, he crushed it with his hand. I cringed as he held his hand out, expecting to see blood. Instead, tiny shards of glass scattered out of his pristine, uninjured palm.

"A song and dance now, if you please, court jester!" Sofie tittered, mockingly clapping her hands.

Viggo bowed. "It's been so long since we've had to prove ourselves. It's exhilarating!"

I gaped at him. *How is this possible? Vampires don't exist. They're just another scary tale.* "But...no. Sofie, I've *seen* you out in the sun, and ..." I stammered.

Viggo laughed. "Oh, don't believe any of that. The majority of it is pure poppycock. We're not allergic to crosses and garlic, we can come in and out of your house as we please, there are no coffins under this roof— I could go on for hours with all the nonsense."

My eyes bulged as a thought hit me. Backing away quickly, I practically fell onto the couch. "What about people? Do you...drink blood?"

Viggo's face grew more serious. "We want to be completely honest with you, my dear Evangeline. No lying. So ..." He paused. "There are those of us who do feed on humans, impulsively and without remorse. However, Mortimer and I have made it our mission to eliminate that type of vampire from this world. I think we've done quite well."

"So you don't?"

He exhaled. "Only in desperate situations and only on the worst criminals—child rapists and murders; bottom–feeders, bane to all humans."

The fascination with criminals...He wasn't a lawyer or a detective. He was merely scouting out his meals. I shuddered and looked at Sofie and Mortimer. Both remained quiet, their faces expressionless, though I sensed distress in Sofie's eyes.

"We are not those terrible creatures the stories paint us to be, I swear it! Have I been anything but generous and kind to you since the moment you met me?"

I paused, then shook my head. "And sitting here with me...and my blood—that isn't hard for you?" I asked hesitantly, afraid that reminding them I was human would have adverse side effects.

"Darling Evangeline! We would never harm you!" Viggo cried, distress contorting his face. "And we're experienced enough that we can control ourselves. Now, being in a room with free–flowing blood is a tad trickier...but we always manage."

So Leo obviously knew who his employers were, I gathered, recalling his meticulous cleanup. It also meant he wasn't a vampire.

The silence in the room grew beyond the awkward stage as I absorbed what they were telling me. Viggo watched me with the look of a dejected animal begging for love and acceptance.

Finally I spoke. "Wow, that's quite the secret."

"That's not the half of it," Mortimer grumbled, studying his manicured fingernails.

"Are you afraid? Please say you're not," Viggo pleaded.

"I'm okay," I said, swallowing my fear. *More like petrified.*

"The thing is...we need your help, Evangeline," Viggo said.

That took me aback. "How? With what? And what does all this have to do with my dream and the bite marks on my neck?"

Viggo's expression turned grim. He sat back down in the armchair. "For one hundred and twenty years, our venom has been useless."

"I don't underst—" I began, frowning.

"We can't turn humans anymore," Mortimer said abruptly, sitting down in a chair beside Viggo.

"And that's a bad thing?" I said without thinking. I caught Mortimer's glower.

"If we can't create one of us, we're left watching the ones we love grow old and die." Viggo looked up at the portrait.

Had he watched Sofie's sister die? I wondered. *Had she been his lady friend?*

"It becomes too painful to get close to anyone, knowing the misery and loss will just repeat itself over and over again for eternity. It's such a lonely life." Viggo sighed. "Can you imagine that, Evangeline?"

I shuddered. I had spent five years utterly alone. It was a dismal, dark place to be. But eternity?

"Please say you'll help us," Viggo begged.

"I...of course, I'll help you if I can …"

"Oh, thank you, Evangeline. Thank you! I knew you would understand," Viggo said, elated.

"But how?"

"This is the terrible part about it." Viggo's face fell in despair, and he turned to scowl at Sofie. "Unbeknownst to us, that witch has cursed you!"

Cursed? My eyes shifted to Sofie, who sat in her chair, looking ready to explode. "What is he talking about, Sofie?" I asked warily.

Sofie's jaw clenched. "I didn't mean to—"

Mortimer cut her off. "Sofie is the reason for our problem. She played with magic for her own selfish gains and we are all now victims of the results."

I glanced back at Sofie to see her minty green eyes alight with fire, but she said nothing.

"You've probably been wondering why things have been...tense...between us these past few days," Viggo said. "It's because Mortimer and I are so angry with her for what she's done to you."

"What did she do, exactly?" I asked slowly, again looking at Sofie. Her eyes were focused intently on a spot on the Persian rug.

"Sofie, please explain," Viggo urged, adding, "Only what's necessary. No need to confuse the girl."

Sofie swallowed. When she began speaking, her voice was emotionless, as if she spoke by rote. "You are the primary channel for an incantation that will solve our venom issue. That necklace and the two identical statues—the one in the atrium and the one in your...*dream*," Sofie hesitated on that last word, "they're all conduits."

"Conduits for what?" I asked, glancing down at the pendant. Her gift.

"These dreams you're having...they aren't dreams, Evangeline. *It* decided the best way to fix our problem was to search the universes for another world like Earth, one where vampires exist and their venom is intact."

"Who decided?"

"The spell."

I frowned.

"It's all hocus–pocus," Viggo murmured. "Don't worry. We don't understand it either."

Sofie ignored him. "You're being transported to another world—one that is identical to ours."

"And there are vampires there as well?"

She nodded. "It seems you've found some already."

My stomach dropped. "They're...vampires?" I whispered, my face twisting in shock. "*All* of them?" *My Caden is a vampire?* He was so sweet, so kind, so beautiful. I couldn't believe it. I didn't want to. I hesitated before asking, "How is my going over there supposed to fix this problem for you?"

"Sofie told us that you would be transformed into a vampire and come back with the ability to convert humans," Mortimer answered flatly.

"That's not what I said!" Sofie yelled.

I barely heard her. Mortimer's words were like an electric shock coursing through my body. "I'm supposed to be a vampire?" I whispered, my eyes wide.

"I wanted to tell you, Evangeline! She—" Viggo glared at Sofie "—swore me to secrecy. Said she'd hurt you if we told you!"

I bolted off the couch and pushed past Max, having heard all I could handle. *The pendant.* I looked down at the precious gift Sofie had given me only days earlier. I needed it *off*, away from me—forgotten. As if it never existed. My hand flew to the chain and I yanked it hard enough to snap the clasp, just as Sofie shrieked, "No!"

Before I could take another step, I crumpled to the floor, excruciating pain surging through my body, running along every nerve to my fingertips, seeping down into the core of my bones. I gasped, unable to breathe, or scream, or see, the intensity crippling. I was sure I would die. I *wanted* to die.

And then the pain vanished as instantly as it had begun. My eyelids fluttered open and I saw Sofie leaning over me, fumbling with something around my neck. "There, it's fixed," she murmured to no one in particular. Her pale green eyes lifted to mine then, full of anguish. "I'm so sorry, Evangeline," she whispered, "but please don't take this necklace off again, or you will die."

11. Cursed

Sofie's warning rang in my ears as she scooped my limp body into her arms as if I were a frail child. She carried me back to the couch I had stormed away from and set me down gently. I wanted to fight back, to resist her help, but I couldn't even lift my hand.

"What just happened?" I asked, my voice hollow.

"Sofie's curse, darling. I'm so sorry. Witches can be such wicked creatures," I heard Viggo murmur.

I rolled my head to regard Sofie. The distress in her eyes appeared genuine. But I knew better than to believe it now.

I turned back to stare vacantly at the coffered ceiling. Seconds strung into minutes as energy slowly returned to my limbs. My jagged breathing competed with the crackling of the fire as the only sound in the room.

Physically, the hurt had vanished. There were no residual aches or pains, no scars to serve as evidence. It was as if had never happened. Emotionally, though, the injury was as real as if Sofie had held a hot branding iron to my chest. The fantasy I had unwittingly created in my head, where I was finally welcomed and accepted—even loved—had instantly crumbled to dust. Of course there was an ulterior motive. Of course Sofie wasn't doing all of this because she enjoyed my company.

I am such an idiot.

Still too weak to fight gravity, my hand slid up over my stomach to touch the pendant, to feel the smooth stone rolling under my fingertips. It was no longer mere jewelry. I could sense the chain coiled around my neck as surely as if it were a tight noose. Closing my eyes, I pictured Sofie ready to kick the stool out from under me.

"Here. Sit up and have some water," Viggo said, offering me his hand and then a glass.

"So what happens now?" I asked, accepting both with a small smile of thanks.

"The spell is unclear," Sofie said softly. "I can't see beyond you transporting to this world. It's like getting an instruction manual with a large chunk missing from it. I *assumed* it would involve you being transformed into one of us. You would then have the venom to create more of our kind here. But clearly, based on what happened last night, I was wrong."

"You put a spell on me and you don't even know how it works?"

"Isn't it terrible? Again, Evangeline: we had no control over what she was doing," Viggo said.

A low, feral sound came from Sofie but with one sharp glare from Mortimer, her face went expressionless again. "The pendant rejected the venom. It's protecting you in this other world—masking your heartbeat, changing the taste of your blood."

"And *how* are we supposed to know how it'll work?" I demanded, hearing the bitterness in my voice.

"Sofie is trying to—" Viggo began.

"I know what you need to do now," Sofie interjected.

"Oh, really." Mortimer's voice was hard, suspicious. "How convenient that you finally know something."

Sofie ignored him. "You need to bring one of them back. The pendant will tell you how, exactly. It's sentient. It will communicate with you."

I peered down at the pendant, muttering, "So I'm going to start hearing voices?"

"I'm not sure," Sofie said, adding, "You will know when it happens."

Her candor didn't ease my anxiety. I dropped my gaze to the floor, focusing on a knot in the hardwood. The stabbing pain of Sofie's betrayal had begun to fade, replaced by an all too familiar emptiness that slowly crept through my body. It was the numbness of loss—loss of an illusion of friendship I had quickly accepted as reality. I *was* delusional, after all.

And humiliated. Here I was, unwittingly the butt of a secret—a pawn, greedily accepting the gifts they showered upon me, turning a blind eye to the fighting and screaming.

The disturbing fact was, I now had an explanation for the bites and the old sweat clothes—albeit an insane one—and that brought me some small comfort.

"Is there anything else I need to know?" I wasn't sure I could handle anymore.

"No," Mortimer answered abruptly.

Another growl from Max.

I swallowed. "What if I want to go home?"

"This is your home for now," Viggo answered calmly. "It's for the best. For your safety, until this is all sorted out."

The thought of leaving these walls—my elegantly wallpapered and decorated prison walls—brought me back to the attack. "Who were those people in the park?"

"No one you need to worry about." Viggo smiled gently. "They won't bother you anymore."

No, of course not. They've been stuffed into bags by now. I shuddered.

"You probably need some time to yourself," Sofie suggested.

I was glad for the dismissal, wanting to get as far away from her as possible—as far as my prison bars would allow. I left the library without glancing in her direction, picking up speed until I was sprinting to my room.

Throwing open my bedroom door, I yelped in surprise. Sofie stood in front of the fireplace, her back to me, studying her painting.

"How did you—" I didn't bother finishing. *Just further proof that she isn't human.*

Max nudged me into the room as he barged through the door behind me. Once in, he sauntered over to my bedside and sat down, no longer the frothing, protective guard dog. I guess he didn't see Sofie as a threat to me. So much for canine intuition.

"We understand this is a lot to absorb," she said, turning to walk toward me, her face an emblem of sadness. For a second a pang of sorrow pulled at my heart. But then I remembered what she had done to me and that grief dissolved. It was all a masquerade. None of it was genuine.

She reached up to place a hand on my shoulder. I recoiled. Slowly dropping her arm, she sighed, her expression going blank. "It's best to keep some things to yourself for now, until you know them more. Don't tell them why you're there or anything about the necklace. And keep out of trouble. You could easily have died last night, if that vampire hadn't controlled himself."

"He said my blood didn't taste right...or human...something like that," I mumbled, remembering the attacker's words, suddenly finding them offensive. There was nothing wrong with my blood. But something else dawned on me. "Wait. What if he hadn't? What if the vampire hadn't tried to convert me and kept draining me of all my blood? I'd be dead—weren't you worried that would happen?"

Sofie pursed her lips. "It didn't happen so there's no use worrying about it. And anyway, the spell is irreversible."

"Right." I moved away until my back hit the wall, trying to distance myself from her—the evil vampire sorceress.

"Well, alright then. Be safe tonight." She moved as if to head out the door. But in the next instant she was beside me, gripping my arm tightly. "Don't trust any of our kind, including Viggo," she whispered, the words coming in a rush, "and don't do what the pendant tells you to, yet."

And then she vanished, leaving me thinking I may have imagined her words.

Was she trying to pit me against Viggo and Mortimer now, too? Why? She was the one who had tricked me—cursed me. I obviously knew not to trust her. But Viggo—who was as blameless in all of this as I was— was asking for my help.

Is this even happening? I wondered as I walked toward my bed. Maybe *this* was the dream that I'd wake up from soon. I pinched my arm but only winced at the pain. *This is real. Vampires exist. Witches exist. Viggo and Mortimer are vampires. Sofie is a vampire sorceress. The giant dog lying down on the other side of the room is...I don't know what he is.*

The three of them, fawning over me, a socially awkward stranger with no friends, giving me gifts and kindness...I should have known something was not right. I sighed. I wasn't Nancy Drew—not unless Nancy Drew was blind and deaf.

An awful numbness was taking over. I'm sure anger was there, buried deep under a blanket of shock and confusion, but it was all rolled up and somehow encapsulated within the numbness. I never understood why anyone described it as a lack of feeling when, to me, there was definitely a sensation with being "numb"; not one I could describe, except to say it felt *wrong*.

A glance out the window showed night looming. If I could force myself to stay awake for the night, maybe Sofie's curse wouldn't work. But if not, if I did get pulled into this dream world that I now knew wasn't a dream world, I had to prepare myself. They were vampires. They might bite me and drain me of my blood. Except that they hadn't done anything like that yet. They had protected me. When I was lying in Caden's arms, bleeding profusely, he could easily have finished me off, but he didn't. None of them had. The more I tried, the harder it was to picture Amelie, with her bouncy curls and childlike smile, being murderous. Or Caden...perfect Caden. They couldn't be bad. They had to be like Viggo and Mortimer—good vampires.

☙

It was pitch black this time. I couldn't see any shadows, any outlines, anything at all. I sucked in a deep breath, trying to calm myself.

"Hold on," a male voice called out. A light appeared to my left. I turned to see Caden anchoring a burning torch into a wall bracket. Even with my spirit drained from the day's revelations, my heart still skipped a beat at the sight of him, and I knew it wasn't out of fear. The possibility that he was a vampire was trivial. That he was no longer a figment of my imagination, that I was standing in front of him...*that* made me jittery.

Oh my God. I had all but professed my undying love to him the last time I was here, when I thought it was a dream. *Right before I insulted his taste in women.*

Blood rushed to my head along with my mortification. The room began to spin. I reached out, searching for a support, and my hand grazed something cool and smooth and hard. I turned to see the statue. The conduit.

"Is that—" I began, but my voice ended in a croak when Caden appeared in front of me, gingerly reaching for my bandaged hand.

"What happened?" His face twisted with worry.

"Oh, nothing. It's okay," I stammered, melting with the feel of my hand cradled in his. His vampire hand. Without thinking, I yanked my hand away.

When I hazarded a look up, I found his jade green eyes watching me. He nodded slightly, a strange expression on his face, as if acknowledging something. *He knows...he knows that I know.*

We stared at each other for a long, silent moment. Then he thrust a set of clothes into my uninjured hand. "You should put these on, in case we have more visitors," he said quietly.

I glanced down to see the same type of nondescript sweats I'd put on the other night. Heat crawled up my neck as I recalled the last time Caden had handed me clothes. It was right before he kissed me. I had made out with a vampire. And enjoyed it, immensely.

"Is this the same statue as in the woods?" I asked hoarsely, turning to point at the statue, desperate to change the topic. I looked back to find myself talking to an empty cave.

I fumbled slowly with the clothes, my injured hand awkward. I hadn't bothered undressing earlier that evening, opting to cuddle with Max until the blaze of the pendant and the fatigue set in, the warning sign that Sofie's curse was about to take me. I had held onto Max tightly, begging him to come with me, to protect me.

But it hadn't worked and here I stood, alone. Alone in a cave full of bloodthirsty vampires. Were they really bloodthirsty, though?

Now wearing my disguise, I retrieved the torch and followed the sound of distant voices. I found the group circling a fire in the same giant cave as the previous night. Four faces turned to smile at me. Four beautiful faces. I looked around; Rachel was nowhere to be seen. Relief washed over me.

Okay, try to act normal. Small talk. "Is that my statue back there?"

Amelie nodded. "It was Caden's idea to bring it here so we wouldn't have to sit down in the valley, waiting for you. It worked! Clever." Amelie's springy curls bobbed as she turned her head to smile proudly at her brother. "We replaced your statue in the woods with an imitation that Fiona created, in case someone wanders out there."

"It looks more like a fat, drunk ogre, but it should work—from a distance," Fiona said with a nervous giggle.

Amelie walked over, reaching out to take my hand, her brow furrowed in concern as Caden's had been. "What happened?"

"Minor mishap," I said, consciously not pulling away this time.

"So...do you still think you're dreaming?" Fiona asked.

By her tone, I could tell she knew the answer. Caden had told them. There was no point lying. I gave them a small smile and shook my head.

"Come, sit," Amelie said, taking my other hand and pulling me to a bench.

I sat down, ever aware of Caden's attentive eyes studying me from across the fire. "Where's Rachel?" I asked.

"Not here, thank God," I heard Amelie murmur under her breath, followed by, "She's watching over the fake statue. We all took shifts down there in case the switch didn't work and you showed up down there. She'll be back soon." There was no mistaking the contempt in her voice.

I glanced at Caden to check the effect of his sister's tone but his face showed no emotion, his eyes still intently focused on me. *Probably wondering what my blood tastes like.*

"What happened, exactly, to make you believe us?" Fiona asked.

"You mean, besides these?" I reached up and lightly touched the bite marks on my neck.

They all cringed. "Still hurt?" Bishop asked, unusually serious.

I shook my head. "It would seem that I'm surrounded by vampires, giant unkillable dogs, and a vampire–witch who put a curse on me." I suddenly began laughing, finding my predicament comical now that I had said it out loud for the first time.

"Why?" Caden asked, his eyes widening.

"I don't know. Apparently Sofie was messing around with magic and fried their venom. Now they can't 'breed.'" I shuddered. "I'm supposed to come here and find a way to fix it."

Silence filled the cave.

"You're handling this well," Fiona said softly.

"I'm glad it looks that way," I answered, staring down at the fire.

"Are you afraid?" Caden asked quietly.

"Yes, terrified," I answered truthfully, looking up into those beautiful, vibrant green eyes. *Good vampire. Definitely has to be a good vampire.*

"And you *understand* what *we* are?" he asked, his jaw taut. He hadn't enjoyed asking that question.

"You're...like Viggo and Mortimer and Sofie?"

He nodded once. "Viggo and Mortimer...yes."

I swallowed the giant lump blocking my throat. *Well, there's no denying it now.*

"But Sofie...not quite. You said she was also a sorceress?"

I nodded.

"Interesting." Caden's eyes flickered to his sister's but their expressions were unreadable.

"Why?"

"Because sorceresses can't become vampires. It's impossible. The venom kills them."

So Sofie was still lying to me. I should have known.

"In my experience, humans tend to freak out and run the other way, crossing themselves in prayer repeatedly when they find themselves in the company of a vampire. They don't willingly share a campfire with four of them." Amelie's tone was light, but her eyes were earnest, as if she expected me to turn and run at any second.

"I still might, but right now it's too cold," I said, a small smile on my lips.

Laughter filled the cave.

"We won't hurt you," Amelie said softly.

Could I believe her? Looking at that angelic face and kind smile, there wasn't a part of me that felt I was in peril. Then again, I had felt safe with Sofie. My sense of self–preservation wasn't exactly top–quality. "Well, I figured you guys were the good kind."

"What?" Caden's voice rose, his face screwing up.

"Viggo told me most of the stuff about you guys is myth."

"And you believed him?" I didn't miss the scorn in his tone.

"Caden," Amelie warned.

"You're so sure we won't attack you?" Caden continued, on his feet and pacing now.

"Caden," Amelie said through clenched teeth.

I glanced warily at her. "Well, you didn't attack me yesterday and you can't get much closer than that, so …"

Caden's eyes widened in surprise.

"After I was bitten, I mean. With all the blood!" I stammered, realizing that it sounded like I was referring to everything leading up to it.

Bishop barked out laughter. "We don't have time for that right now. You can test it out again later," he said, followed by, "and I *don't* mean after you were bitten."

I felt my face blaze, likely a hideous shade of beet red. *Why* would Caden tell him? Or maybe Bishop was reading my mind. Maybe that wasn't a myth. *Oh God, I hope Caden can't read my mind.*

Caden gave Bishop a shove in response, sending him flying into the cave wall. Chunks of rock crumbled to the ground as Bishop's back made impact but the blonde vampire simply stood up and brushed himself off, smiling broadly, proud of the ribbing. It was such a pleasant smile that I cringed when it disappeared, his face twisting up in disgust.

I found out why when an unwelcomed voice sang out at the cave entrance, "What's got you so upset, my love?"

"Oh good, you're back," Amelie answered dryly.

Rachel glowered at her. "You're lucky Caden feels an odd sense of obligation to you, otherwise I'd—"

"Look who's back!" Caden said, pointing in my direction.

Rachel turned to glance at me, her smile falling short of genuine, before turning to bestow a loving gaze on Caden. "It seems your scheme with the statue switch worked," she purred, forcing him onto the bench and climbing onto his lap. She planted an inappropriately long kiss on his lips.

I averted my gaze, not because of the uncomfortable public show of affection but because the twinge of jealousy pained me a thousand times more than my injured hand or even the bite from the night before.

It went on, even as Bishop cleared his throat loudly and Amelie let out an exasperated sigh. I had to find some way to peel Rachel off Caden. "Sofie said the pendant is magical," I blurted, ignoring Sofie's warnings. "It gets me here and it protects my human traits, like the scent of my blood and my heartbeat. It takes time to adjust sometimes, though."

It worked. Rachel stopped mauling Caden. "Like when you get all flustered and red near my Caden?" she asked sweetly. My face felt like it had burst into flames as a renewed surge of humiliation struck. "Seems it hasn't adjusted yet." She giggled viciously.

"How does it work?" Amelie quickly asked.

"Um...I don't know. Every night my necklace begins to burn and I fall asleep. Then I wake up the next morning back in my bed."

"The time in between your visits is weeks here," Fiona commented, frowning.

"And if one of us were to put that necklace on, I wonder what would happen," Rachel murmured, eyeing my pendant keenly.

Memories of excruciating pain had me shaking my head with panic. "No, I'm sorry. It can't come off, not even for a second, or I'll die."

"Only the quickest of seconds ..." Rachel said, off Caden's lap and standing over me in an instant, a hand clamped over the chain.

"Leave it alone," Caden said, appearing beside her. His hand closed over hers, stopping her from yanking the chain off and killing me.

Her left eyebrow arched severely. He replied with a hard stare of his own.

I turned to look at Amelie. Her eyes were locked on the two of them;

she looked ready to spring.

After a few tense seconds, Caden's shoulders visibly relaxed. He wrapped his free arm affectionately around Rachel. "If she dies, we'll have to wait for this sorceress to send another one."

I flinched. I was replaceable, like a goldfish.

But his callous words worked. Rachel's icy glare melted into adoring eyes and a childlike giggle. Then those snake eyes turned to me. "So you can bring us back with you?"

I opened my mouth to answer, but Sofie's warning rang loudly in my mind: *Don't trust our kind.* My instincts told me to heed the warning and, though those instincts had proven to be equivalent to those of a lobotomy patient, I decided to listen. I looked straight into those yellow eyes and I shook my head. It was easy to lie to her. Enjoyable, actually.

My lie prompted crestfallen expressions, which didn't make sense. I looked around at their faces. "Why would you want to come back with me?"

Something unspoken passed between them, conveyed only with a look.

"Because you're the only one left," Fiona answered quietly.

I frowned. "Only what left?"

"Human."

My jaw dropped.

Amelie sighed heavily. "Where do we begin? In our world— Ratheus—humans are extinct. You have been for seven hundred years."

I swallowed hard, unable to blink. "Why?...How?"

"We caused it," Caden answered coldly, having moved away from me to stand on the other side of the fire. "We killed them, every last one."

12. Extinction

A shiver ran down my spine. *That's why Jethro reacted the way he did when he saw me.* Now it made sense.

"Not us, specifically. Our species—vampires," Bishop clarified, the last word coming softly.

"We did our share, though," Caden said, turning to pace, head lowered.

"Why?" I heard myself croak.

"Vampires were no more than a myth for thousands of years, characters in horror movies. But then drained bodies with bite marks started showing up, left out for display. There was a new generation of our kind—one that didn't care, that wanted people to be afraid. The humans fought back in the only way they knew how: war. One that escalated so quickly, it was too late to reverse the effects, by the time we found out. Vampires converted humans by the hundreds to build their army. Humans killed any vampire they could catch. They even killed other humans, if there was any doubt as to what they were."

"So your kind can be killed?" I asked, my folklore facts not yet up to speed.

"It's hard, but yes. With nuclear warfare, everything within the blast radius will die, including vampires. The radiation did nothing to us, but it was deadly to the humans. Between the blasts and the radiation, few humans survived; most of the world was destroyed within a few months."

I asked into the silence, "How did you get away?"

"There was this large island in the middle of the ocean, thousands of miles from anything else. It was inhabited by people, but not overly developed—a Third World country; under the radar, so to speak. Many of us fled here, betting that it would survive. We were right. We brought humans with us, to breed. But humans take too long to reproduce and their blood is too tempting. They didn't last long."

"So now you live off animals? Like Viggo and Mortimer?"

A cynical smile touched Caden's lips. "Just like them. But we're starving—always starving—without human blood. Some of our kind experimented with feeding off other vampires. It mutated them into something altogether evil. You saw it...Jethro."

I shuddered, those white, veiny eyes flashing in my mind. "How many of you are left?"

"A lot less than there used to be. There's this self-formed Council composed of the strongest and oldest of our kind. They decided the population needed shrinking. We," he gestured at the others, "hid well and survived. Since then, for over seven hundred years, they've been searching for a secret human civilization, hoping some survived somewhere in the world. But we know there aren't any left. Deep down, we all know that. No human can survive in this world."

I noted the present tense, and his silent message. I was human. I couldn't survive here.

Caden's next words confirmed it. "There is no 'good and bad' of our kind. We're all bad."

"Caden!" Bishop warned.

"And if the Council got hold of you," Caden continued, ignoring him. "They'll do anything to get to this world of yours, to have a new crop of humans to feed off. It isn't safe to be around us."

"Stop saying 'we' and 'us,' Caden. We aren't like *those demons*," Amelie said, throwing a withering glare in Rachel's direction.

"I'm here, aren't I? And I've helped you so far, haven't I?" Rachel retorted haughtily.

"Us or yourself?" Fiona muttered.

"You're a Council member," I said slowly. "So was Jethro," I added, recalling his greeting the other night.

"Yes, and I killed him. For you. So you can trust me." Again, that sickly sweet smile that made my skin crawl. Hearing those two words, the same two words the vampire uttered before he sank his teeth into my neck, had the opposite effect. I had never trusted anyone less.

Here I was, a one–way ticket to survival for some lucky vampire. If I could bring back only one of them, how would I tell them? Or could I bring more than one? I had no idea! And, save for Rachel, how would I choose between the others? Would they make me choose?

Grateful I had listened to Sofie's warning, I said quickly, "Well, none of them can come back with me." I forced down the lump that rose in my throat with the lie. "No one can."

Amelie put her hands on mine. "It's okay, Evangeline. We're not like them."

"So...you don't want to come back with me?"

"Oh no, we do," Amelie answered firmly. "But not to feed off humans."

"Then why?"

She paused. "To feel like we're alive, instead of just ..."

"Existing," Fiona finished for her.

"And we'd never hurt you to get there," Amelie added. "But we, the *four* of us, are in the minority here." *Another dig at Rachel.*

Rachel grinned back viciously. "You're such a convincing liar, Amelie, that I almost bought it."

With a growl, Amelie flew across the cave to land on top of Rachel, claw–like fingers raking at her neck, drawing blood. Rachel answered with a swift kick and an equally vicious shriek, intentionally launching Amelie toward the fire. Luckily Fiona was there to catch her before she could land in it. Caden's arms wrapped around Rachel's body in the next second, holding her tightly to him, trying to restrain her.

"Are you insane? I'm stronger than all of you put together!" she shrieked, her face turning demonic with rage.

"Go get some air. I'll be out in a minute," Caden murmured, his hand softly caressing Rachel's cheek. I noticed his jaw was clenched, though. "Please," he added through gritted teeth.

Rachel snorted and, whirling, stormed out of the cave.

"Are you an idiot?" Caden hissed.

Amelie glared at him. "You brought this on us. *Fix it*," she responded.

Caden's face softened, as if Amelie had reminded him of something he had forgotten. He turned to me, his eyes full of concern. "Are you okay?"

No, I wasn't okay. They had just confirmed that my original fears were true—or mostly true: I was in danger. I'd be hunted if this Council found out about me. But I nodded.

Those beautiful eyes hardened. "You shouldn't be. Don't be a fool, Evangeline. Whatever this Viggo told you is likely a lie. That's what our kind does—we lie. We deceive. We are evil." His tone, cold and detached, threw the words like a sharp slap across my face. He was so different from the previous two nights.

"Caden!" Bishop boomed.

I nodded, silent.

Fiona threw an exasperated glare at Caden and came over to pull me off the bench. "Come on. Let's go for a walk. This mountain is honeycombed with neat caves." She linked her arm through mine.

"Wait up," Amelie called from behind us, doing an impossible leap into the air to grab a torch.

I looked back once as we left the cavern. Caden stood by the fire, those jade eyes regarding me without expression.

I could feel the weight of the mountain above us as we strolled down a long tunnel, the torch casting eerie shadows beyond jutting stalagmites and scattered stones.

"Well, at least the pendant will protect you while you're here," Fiona assured me. "We can't sense your blood. It's as if you're one of us."

And what if they could smell my blood? Is that all that's keeping them from bit-

ing me? "How did you figure out I was human, then?" I asked aloud.

"You were holding your breath underwater," Amelie answered matter-of-factly. "We don't breathe, so we don't need to hold our breath. Then you went and knocked yourself unconscious on that tree root, and—well, we're not clumsy and we're never unconscious."

"Not even when you sleep?" I asked.

Fiona laughed. "Sleep is needed to rest and rejuvenate the body. We never tire so we never sleep."

Made sense, I guess. I wondered what it was like not to sleep.

"Sometimes we meditate, though, and we get so deeply into it that it seems like we're sleeping," Fiona added.

"So, tell us about yourself, Evangeline!" Amelie said in a musical lilt. It was as if the near–death skirmish with Rachel five minutes before had never even happened.

"Um...there's not really much to tell. I'm pretty vanilla."

"Oh, come on. Sure there is. Tell us *everything*! What're your hobbies, your passions, your pet peeves? What do you like to do? Who is 'Evangeline'?" she said with theatrical flair.

I laughed. "You'd make a great actress."

Amelie grinned. "I thought so too! I was going to be an actress, a famous Broadway one. But then this happened." She gestured to her mouth, baring white teeth and hissing like a cat. It should have frightened me, but it was comical. I laughed. "Anyway, after that, I was...distracted by other things. Now, there's not exactly an opportunity." She shrugged. "It doesn't matter. Obscurity is key. You can't exactly be famous when you're a vampire. After all, you can only explain your youthful appearance with plastic surgery for so long," Amelie babbled, then waved her hand rapidly to and fro. "But enough about me. We want to know *everything* about you!"

I didn't know where to begin. No one had ever asked me to summarize my existence so directly. No one ever asked me much about myself at all anymore. I switched schools so frequently that no one noticed when I came or left. It was as if I didn't exist.

"Amelie's excited, if you can't tell," Fiona said, chuckling. "We haven't met someone we've liked in seven hundred years."

'Someone we've liked.' Are they just staying that?

"Start with something easy. Your family."

I faltered. "I live with a foster family. They're kind of strange. I don't really know them, to be honest."

"And your parents?"

"Gone." I offered a small smile.

Sensing my discomfort, they changed gears. "Do you have a boyfriend?"

I shook my head. No boyfriend. Ever. Not even an interested party.

"Okay, tell us about your friends. What's your best friend's name?"

"Oh...um ..." I faltered again. "It's tough to say ..." *No it's not. It's easy. You have no friends. You're a leper.* The truth was, I used to have friends, but they vanished after my mother's death. I blamed myself for unintentionally alienating them while dealing with my loss. The few times I had attempted to start conversations and cultivate friendships since then had failed, the intended participants unresponsive. It wasn't until I began volunteering at the shelters that I achieved some level of human interaction. And then there had been Sofie ...

A hollow ache filled my heart as I remembered the high expectations I'd set, the night I met her and the days following, until the moment I learned her true intentions.

Luckily, Fiona's voice interrupted my pity party. "Okay, let's start with an easy question." Fiona glanced at Amelie. "What's your favorite flower?"

I smiled wistfully. Finally, one I could answer. "Daisies."

Amelie's eyebrows rose. "Really? They're so plain."

"I prefer 'simple and elegant.'"

Amelie thought about that. "Yeah, maybe." She skipped gaily down the path.

"Favorite music?" Fiona asked.

"Jazz. I know ..." I said, grinning when I saw Amelie turn around to give me a baffled look. "But it reminds me of my mother."

She smiled wistfully, her thoughts wandering somewhere for the moment. "Fair enough. Favorite food?"

"Anything in a pie."

And so it went as we walked, Fiona and Amelie drilling me on every trivial detail they could think of. It was the conversation of normal girls getting to know each other—albeit quiz–like—not two vampires and a cursed soul.

"You know who loves reading as well?" Amelia asked as I mentioned my unhealthy obsession with books. "Caden. There could be a train wreck two feet away and his eyes wouldn't have lifted from the page."

"Really?" My heart skipped a beat at that tidbit of information. I was hungry for more—as much as possible. "So...he doesn't like reading anymore?" I asked casually.

"Oh, I'm sure he does, but there aren't any books to read," Amelie responded.

"Evangeline, you don't understand. This world...it's like living in medieval times, only worse. We're moving in reverse. Nothing's left—no books, no phones, no computers, no electricity, no cars, no music. Bishop would kill for music. I used to sing to him. Apparently I've ruined classic rock," Fiona said, a grim smile on her face.

"I'd kill for a long, hot shower...literally," Amelie added.

My foot caught a pebble then and I listened to it skip along the ground. This world was sounding more dreadful by the minute. And here I was, feeling sorry for myself and my five–star prison waiting back home.

We turned a sharp corner in the tunnel and Fiona held up a hand. "Stay here," she instructed before disappearing into the darkness.

"What's she doing?" I whispered to Amelie.

She turned to smile at me, her green eyes twinkling with excitement. "You'll see."

Flame after flame suddenly appeared as if on an automatic remote, illuminating Fiona as she moved quickly around, lighting torches. When dozens were lit, when they cast enough light on the area, I gasped, all thoughts of prison and curses vanishing as my eyes glimpsed paradise.

"At least we have this," Amelie sighed.

Directly ahead of us, a waterfall at least thirty feet high quietly tumbled down a wall of rock into a small lake, the water glistening invitingly in the torchlight. Several large boulders rose from the surface of the lake, creating private little alcoves. Steam rose off the water's surface. The entire scene looked man–made, so perfect in design and so out of place, deep within this cave, that I half expected palm trees and ferns.

"What is it?" I heard my awed voice ask.

"Don't know, but it's beautiful, isn't it?" Fiona crouched down to test the water with her hand.

I could only nod in agreement.

"Go swimming if you want," Amelie offered.

"You have bathing suits?" I asked in surprise.

She laughed. "It's just us girls here."

"Maybe later," I said, glancing back at the cave entrance. I wouldn't risk being caught naked in front of Caden again. I had already filled my quota the other night.

"Fiona and Bishop practically live in here." Amelie smirked, winking devilishly at the crouching vampire, who returned the wink.

"No wonder Jethro's had designs on this mountain for seven hundred years," Fiona quipped, laughing as she rolled off her feet to turn up the torn ends of her pants and dip her legs into the pool. Amelie mimicked her and reached her hand out to me, beckoning me to join them.

I happily obliged, sitting down between them to take off my sneakers and socks before sliding my feet into the warm, soothing water. "It's like bathwater," I murmured.

"I know. We can't explain it," Fiona said.

"It's definitely warmer than that river you found me in, right?" Amelie said, kicking the water playfully to splash me.

"Why did Jethro want to drown you, anyway?" I asked.

"Oh, he wasn't trying to drown me," she answered matter–of–factly.

"He tied a cinder block to your ankles and dropped you in the river and he *wasn't* trying to drown you?" I asked skeptically.

"We can't drown, Evangeline, remember?"

"Oh, right. I forgot. Sorry. It's going to take some time to get used to all this." *I'm never going to be used to this.*

Amelie continued. "We can starve, though. The stuff they tied around my wrists and ankles is called 'Merth.' It saps all of our energy. And it hurts. My God! Like a thousand tiny razor blades, cutting into our skin."

I grimaced.

"Exactly. No vampire can touch it. Well, except for mutants like Jethro. When they mutate, they become immune. It falls apart under a human's touch though, as you noticed."

"Oh. So why did Jethro want to starve you, then?" I amended.

"He was teaching me a lesson for killing a grizzly in his territory."

My gaze dropped to Amelie's slender frame, trying to picture the diminutive thing wrestling a ferocious grizzly bear with her bare hands. It was impossible; I just couldn't see it. There was nothing intimidating about her, aside from her outlandishly beautiful face.

All of them—save for Rachel—seemed so normal. *So human.* Had I witnessed one of them tearing Jethro and his friends up, or if I had seen Caden skewer and torch the ape man, maybe I wouldn't be so comfortable right now. But I hadn't seen it. I'd only seen the aftermath and in my mind, the two didn't connect. Even with Caden's grave warning and his change in attitude toward me, I wasn't afraid of them. Except Rachel. Was my intuition *that* pathetic? Or were they tricking me?

"Are you guys using your powers on me?" I blurted.

They both laughed. "No, we wouldn't do that. But we don't blame you for being paranoid. Besides, we can't," Amelie said.

"So that's a myth?"

"Oh no, it's not. But it won't work on you. We think it's because of your necklace. Caden tried the first night, before Jethro came, to keep you quiet, remember? But you started yammering away again." Amelie's hand opened and closed like a yapping mouth, teasing me.

I thought back to that night, tucked into the alcove with Caden...those deep pools that were his eyes, pulling me in. I remembered, alright.

"I know; it's hard not to like me," Amelie said, throwing her arm around my shoulder. "I'm extremely charming."

"And so modest," Fiona murmured, dipping her hand into the water to splash Amelie. Smiling, she put her hand on my arm. "Don't worry.

We'll keep you safe. Nothing will happen to you." Her smile suddenly faded as her eyes dropped to my pendant.

"What's wrong?" I asked, a second before I noticed the constant burning against my chest begin to fade. I looked down in time to see the fire in my pendant blink out, leaving the heart its original dull black.

Fiona quickly slid away from me, pulling her hand back as if I'd just admitted that I had a communicable disease. Amelie's arm dropped from my shoulder as well, but it was to grasp my hand tightly in hers.

"Let go of her," a voice shouted behind us. I turned to see Caden rush in, Rachel on his heels.

"It might work," Amelie murmured.

She's trying to come back with me, I realized.

"That's not the issue, Amelie," Caden yelled.

"I won't hurt her," she snapped.

"You have no way of knowing that."

I didn't hear the rest of the argument.

13. Bribery

The first thing I saw was the clock on the bedside table. Two in the afternoon. The second thing was Max's giant snout, welcoming me with a rub against my cheek.

Amelie.

I rolled over to find the other side of my bed was empty. It hadn't worked. I exhaled slowly, feeling a twinge of disappointment. *If only it could be that easy.*

"What happened last night?"

I yelped in surprise at the sound of Sofie's voice, and bolted upright. She was standing at the end of my bed, along with Viggo and Mortimer.

"You're a jumpy girl, aren't you?" Mortimer observed, smirking.

"Do you blame her, with everything that's happened to her?" Viggo retorted.

"What happened last night?" Sofie repeated, ignoring them.

"Nothing."

"Did you learn anything new?" she continued.

"Yes...they're all vampires," I sneered, hoping that being unpleasant would give me some level of satisfaction. It didn't.

Viggo smiled warmly. "You're still angry with Sofie. We understand." He walked over to sit on the edge of my bed, reaching for my hand.

Max growled.

"Okay, okay, I understand, Max. You're worried about her." He smiled soothingly at the dog and placed his hands in his lap. "Tell us about your night. And why are you wearing those dreadful rags?"

I eyed him suspiciously. *Is Caden right? Am I a naïve fool, falling for the act of a psychopath in disguise?*

Glancing down, I saw the dark clothes Caden had given me to protect me from the army of vampires ready to tear me apart. "All the humans are gone. Extinct. Killed by vampires over seven hundred years ago," I said flatly. "Apparently they have more bad vampires than good."

"What?" Viggo's brow furrowed. "Tell us everything."

When I finished recapping the war on Ratheus, Mortimer and Sofie's expressions were beyond grim. Only Viggo smiled. "Well, this is good news!" he exclaimed.

My brow furrowed. "How is this good news?"

"They'll be more than willing to help you get out of there! What does this world look like?"

"I don't know. I didn't see much of it. They're hiding me in this mountain cave with this amazing oasis that you can swim in, except they don't have bathing suits because they don't have anything. No electricity, no books, no nice clothes—"

Mortimer interrupted my rambling. "So they're all seven hundred years old?"

I nodded. "At least. And there's a council of vampires who dictate everything. They're thousands of years old. They'll kill me if they get hold of me, according to Caden."

"Oh, this Caden is smart. It's best you stay away from them. We don't want one of them coming back here."

Is Caden smart enough to see through your mask, Viggo?

"What's wrong, Viggo, feeling threatened by someone older than you?" Sofie said, smiling haughtily.

He responded with a tight-lipped smile of his own.

Leo entered silently then, carrying a steaming cup of coffee for me. I wanted to throw my arms around the sweet old butler.

"Did the necklace tell you anything?"

I shook my head, my eyes darting briefly to Sofie as I took a sip from the mug, remembering her warning.

"That's too bad," Viggo said.

"What does she need to do?" Mortimer demanded of Sofie.

She thought for a moment. "Not sure. This makes things a little more complicated. She may only be able to bring one back, so how can she choose …"

"I don't care if the rest of them rot alone there, as long as one comes back." Mortimer's teeth were clenched in anger.

"Mortimer!" Viggo chastised. "A little compassion!"

Sofie spoke quickly. "She can bring them some things—an act of kindness, given their predicament. Maybe they'll be more inclined to keep her safe."

Bribery.

Mortimer's eyes narrowed in suspicion. "I thought you said things can't transfer."

"I said *living* things," Sofie replied in a condescending tone. "People. But I have an idea that might work."

"Wonderful, Sofie," Viggo said. "The first one you've had in a while...Why don't you get on that right away? There's money in the library desk."

Sofie forced a smile. "Of course, Viggo. I just need to get an idea of sizes and needs from Evangeline."

ॐ

Several hours later, I slid my arms through the straps of an over-stuffed mountain bag. It was the same height as me and likely equaled my weight, making it impossible for me to walk while wearing it. Sofie, with her inhuman strength, effortlessly propped it up against the bed frame so it wouldn't topple over as she adjusted all the straps.

"What's in here?"

"Just some things for your friends."

"To bribe them?"

She glanced up at me. "It doesn't matter why. Think about how happy they'll be when you give it to them."

Like how happy I was to come to New York and get showered with gifts, only to find out that I'm cursed? "And what happens when I bring one back? Do they just have to bite someone and you'll be happy?"

"Something like that," she murmured. "There, I think those should hold." She gently patted the straps.

A thought crossed my mind. "Did you pack blood? Human blood?" *I can't believe I'm asking that.*

With lips pursed, she shook her head.

"Why not?"

"It's for the best."

What would it do to them? I wondered.

She turned and leaned back against the bed so she was sitting beside me. "Human blood tends to overpower all of our senses and logic. After seven hundred years, they've likely learned to compartmentalize that hunger, even think that they've forgotten it. They don't need to be reminded. It would be cruel. And I don't want them distracted from keeping you safe."

I tried to adjust my position but couldn't. The bag may as well have had bricks in it. "I don't know how those Sherpas walk up mountains with these things strapped to their backs," I mumbled, earning a soft chuckle from Sofie. "Do you think this will work?"

She nodded. "Think so."

"What's in here?"

"Just some clothes for the girls and—"

"For all of them?" I silently hoped she had forgotten about Rachel.

"Oh, that's right. Which one is it you don't like, again? Rachel?"" she asked, smiling secretively.

My eyes narrowed. I hadn't told her. "Get out of my head!"

She chuckled. "I can't read your mind, just your mood," she answered casually. "There was a spark of anger before, when you mentioned Rachel. I'm sensing jealousy right now. Perhaps something to do with this Caden?"

I dropped my gaze, flushing. *Am I that obvious?*

She chuckled again but then her expression grew solemn. "Just remember, that necklace disguises your human traits, but it doesn't make you indestructible. She can still kill you."

It was finally time I asked. "Sofie, how does this spell work?"

She heaved a loud sigh. "It's complicated." She glanced over and saw my frustration. "I'll explain the basics." She stretched her legs out in front of her. "There are two kinds of spells. Little, easy spells that you can learn and do anytime, anywhere—start fires, disguise yourself, that kind of stuff. But then there are other spells, where you're directly altering fate—life and death. That's a Causal Enchantment spell."

"Is that what you cast on me?"

She nodded. "Those spells draw on energies from the earth—everything from the atmosphere to inert materials you use every day. They also draw on the emotions of the spell–casters, even if those feelings are deeply buried. Arguably, these emotions are what form the end result of the spell. The spell itself, though ethereal, becomes a life force as it weaves these other sources together. It is set when it decides on the most suitable response to the spell–caster's dilemma and imprints the knowledge within his or her mind."

I tried picturing something intangible weaving other intangible things into an invisible blanket that would send me to another universe. It sounded like something a group of hippies on acid might have long debates over.

"So, when you cast the spell on me, you didn't know it would send me to this other world?"

She paused, glancing at Max, who lay by my feet. She nodded. "Something like that. But that's all I can tell you."

We sat in silence for a long time. When I glanced at the clock, it was almost midnight.

"You'll be going soon," Sofie confirmed. "At twelve, every night."

My stomach started churning, partly anxious about what was waiting and partly excited to see them again—to see Caden, even if he thought I was a complete moron. "Is there anything else I should know?"

She looked suspiciously at Max. "Why don't you go see the others?"

He groaned in response and rolled onto his side, making it clear he had no intention of moving.

"Damn mutt," she muttered under her breath.

"Why don't you like Max?" I asked, wondering what could spawn such hatred for a dog.

"He betrayed me once," she said, eyeing him. "Though he did redeem himself recently by saving you. But I still don't trust him."

"Betrayed...like, bit you?" *How does a dog betray anyone?*

She chuckled, shaking her head. She glanced at the clock and at Max again before deciding something. She turned to me and whispered so low I almost didn't hear, "If you find Merth, bring it back. As much as possible. But don't mention it to Viggo or Mortimer."

I nodded, curiosity drawing my brows together. *What could she possibly do with it? It's dangerous to her, isn't it?* I didn't bother asking. I figured she'd lie anyway.

☙

I squealed in surprise as the weight of the hefty mountain bag yanked me backward. I landed on my back, my arms and legs flailing wildly, at least two feet above the hard cave floor. "It worked!" I cried out.

Sofie had made sure the harness fit snuggly. Shifting my weight around, I quickly confirmed that no amount of wiggling was going to break me free. So I settled on lying there in the dark, helpless, waiting for rescue like a turtle flipped onto its shell.

A low chuckle sounded in the darkness, sending a shiver down my spine.

"Hello?" I called warily, my voice cracking.

There was a pause, then a loud strike. The cave flooded with torchlight. My heart skipped a beat when I saw Caden's dimpled smile; another shiver ran down my spine.

Caden approached slowly, shaking his head in disbelief. "Would you like some help?" he asked innocently, towering over me, his green eyes twinkling.

He's different today. More playful and much, much more relaxed. "No, I'm comfortable. I think I'll stay like this today," I answered calmly. Inside, I was as giddy as a thirteen–year–old at a boy band pop concert.

He crouched to inspect the numerous buckles and clasps. "Ticklish?" he asked, arching his eyebrow.

"Oh, please don't," I moaned, dreading that level of torturous embarrassment. My current predicament was bad enough.

He laughed softly, then deep concentration tensed his face as he fumbled with the straps. It gave me the opportunity to shamelessly study his face. It didn't seem real; more sculpted to perfection—his jawline impeccably defined, his lips tinted a lush shade of rose. I resisted the urge to reach up and touch his cheek, to confirm that his skin was skin and not porcelain.

"You're early," he murmured. "We didn't expect you for a few more weeks."

When he was finished untying me, he jumped lithely to his feet and offered his hand. I timidly accepted. He pulled me up and straight into a hug, sliding his hands tenderly around my waist and clasping them against the small of my back. Startled by the affection, I didn't know how to react. So I awkwardly reached up and placed my hands on his shoulders, fully aware that my body was as rigid as a plank of wood. He responded by curling his arms farther around me, tightening his grip to bring me closer to him. I could feel his firm chest against my own. He was strong—entirely muscle—and yet there was a warmth and softness that I hadn't expected. I think I'd expected something cold and dead, and he was the furthest thing from it.

I started to relax, assuring myself that he couldn't know how I felt about him; otherwise he'd never hug me so intimately.

"My favorite human!" Bishop called suddenly, snapping me out of my daze. A vision of Rachel's wicked yellow eyes and cruel smile flashed inside my head then, making me shove Caden away in fear. Bishop ruffled my hair as he passed by.

Seconds later, Fiona and Amelie came flying in, knocking me over with the ferocity of their hugs.

I glanced over at Caden to see a flicker of disappointment in his eyes. My heart sank.

"Ooh, what's this?" Amelie said, and she and Fiona began ransacking the bag like toddlers under a Christmas tree, pulling out individual parcels with names scrawled on them in Sofie's flowery handwriting. The guys stood behind them, shaking their heads and laughing. *Where's Rachel?* My eyes casually roamed the cave. *Probably lurking in the shadows. Or out slaughtering Bambi's children.*

Fiona pulled out some racy black underwear that she stealthily tucked under her arm, a reserved smile on her face.

"What's that?" Bishop asked. Fiona smoothly diverted his attention to a pile of men's clothing and soon both guys were rifling eagerly through their packages.

I sat back against the wall, pleased I could help them in some way, that I had the means. Well, Mortimer and Viggo did.

"Are you planning on staying a while?" Amelie said, pulling out an air mattress.

I frowned. "Is that for me?"

"It's not for us."

Right, they don't sleep. "I don't know. Sofie packed the—" My words ended in a gasp as Caden pulled his old ratty shirt over his head, exposing a perfectly rippled stomach and sculpted chest. He had a new sky blue crewneck over his head in seconds, but not before I had ample opportunity to stare at him like a pervert, a weird, unfamiliar sensation stirring deep within me.

Fingers snapped in front of my face, breaking my trance. Bishop. I instinctively reached up to my gaping mouth, sure that a gob of drool was trailing over my bottom lip. *Please don't tease me,* I prayed.

"Come on, let's go, before the daylight runs out!" Bishop exclaimed.

"Where?"

He playfully tucked me under one of his powerful arms like a football. "To kill some time."

‹∂

The way they had described Ratheus—desolate, medieval, decayed—I was expecting a world right out of *Terminator,* minus the cyborgs. So to say I was pleasantly surprised when we stepped outside would be the understatement of the century.

Standing on the edge of a plateau–like ledge, I saw that we were deep within a gorge in the mountains, the sky beyond a vibrant blue dotted with fluffy white clouds. A broad, densely wooded valley stretched out below, the lush green leaves of the trees signifying a warm climate. I could just make out a river snaking through the forest, dappled sunlight sparkling off its surface like a thousand tiny rolling diamonds. A crown of snow–capped peaks towered in the distance, protecting the valley from the outside world. It was more of a bowl than a valley.

Enthralled by those daunting peaks, I stepped forward without paying any notice to where I was until the ground suddenly disappeared from under my feet. A split second later a hand grabbed my arm and yanked me back. I glanced down at the tree tops several hundred feet below and realized I had unwittingly strolled off a cliff. Whipping around, I suctioned myself to the closest thing available. It turned out to be Caden's torso.

"Have humans learned to fly in your world?" He chuckled, then slid an arm gently around my back and half carried, half dragged me away from the edge. The others didn't even attempt to hide their amusement.

"You're safe now, Evangeline," Fiona said, chuckling.

I reluctantly unmolded myself from Caden, awkwardness taking over where paralyzing fear had left off. "Sorry," I mumbled, peering up at him, hoping he didn't think I had done that with the intention of copping a feel or something equally perverted.

The corners of his mouth curved up into a smile. He didn't seem bothered.

"Let's go!" Amelie urged gleefully. At some point between Bishop scooping me up and me stepping off the cliff, she had changed out of her old clothes and into a pair of jeans and a casual top. They all had, including Bishop, who was adjusting his striped gray and green shirt.

"You guys look...normal," I said, grinning.

Amelie hugged herself. "This shirt is *so* soft. Like furry puppies...Thank you!" She instantly appeared in front of me to plant an affectionate kiss on my cheek before skipping along a natural path that curled down the side of the mountain, her silvery blonde curls bouncing.

"Does it look anything like your world?" Caden asked.

"Yes. I mean, I think so," I answered, following the rest of them down the path. It was steep and full of loose rocks and altogether treacherous. "I've never seen mountains this big before, but I'm sure they exist." I was having a hard time not stumbling while keeping up with their fast, care- less pace.

"You'd better stick close to her, Caden. She's liable to tumble right off the side of the mountain," Fiona warned in that smoky voice of hers, adding, "And we can't turn into bats and catch you."

I grinned, shuddering. "Good. I hate those things."

"You know what the best part about today is?" Bishop suddenly asked in a low, somber voice. He paused dramatically before yelling, "Rachel's gone!" His voice boomed through the valley like a thunderclap. He took off, tearing down the path like a suicidal maniac, laughing hysterically. Fiona and Amelie trailed behind him, disappearing within seconds, leav- ing me alone with Caden.

I peered up from the corner of my eye, expecting to see a scowl of anger or annoyance with Bishop's blatant contempt for his girlfriend. Instead, I saw a smile. "So...where is she?" I asked. *Please say gone she's for- ever!*

The smile tightened. "Some sort of tournament she needed to judge." *Is that disappointment or relief in his voice?* I couldn't tell.

We walked quietly along the rocky path, Caden content to match my snail's pace as I cautiously stepped around the loose stones. Several times the stones slid under the weight of my foot, sending me skidding. Caden was always there to grab me and pull me back up.

"I'm sorry I'm so slow. I'm not normally this clumsy," I mumbled nervously.

"Don't worry. Just because we can run down rocky cliffs doesn't mean we expect you to."

The farther into the valley we went, the warmer the air became and the greener our surroundings. Now that I was looking upon the forest in daylight, I had to chuckle. There was no way anyone could mistake this place for Central Park, with its strange trees towering over us, some soaring well over a hundred feet with trunks at least two arm–lengths thick. It looked more like a primeval rainforest, untouched by anything but time. The floor was lush and green, blanketed with giant ferns and protruding tree roots coated in bright green moss and toadstools. Here and there, the trees allowed enough dappled sunlight in to nourish the tiny purple and white wildflowers scattering the forest floor, but otherwise it was shady and damp under the canopy.

I smiled as a butterfly fluttered past us on its way to one of those drifts of wildflowers, its vibrant yellow and orange wings contrasting beautifully with the verdant green backdrop. A family of crickets sang out happily somewhere in the depths of the woods. It was purely serene— hardly a world crawling with bloodthirsty monsters waiting to drink my blood.

I wondered what *did* live here. "What sort of wildlife is there?"

Silence answered. I turned. And froze.

Caden was gone. My eyes darted about, nervously scanning the woods. "Caden!" I called in a harsh whisper, then held my breath, listening. Nothing. "Caden!" again, this time the desperation in my voice unmistakable.

A branch cracked. "Oh, thank God—" I began, turning.

An enormous black panther stood beside a tree a mere five feet away, the head of a snake locked in its jaws. It placed a paw on the snake's body and then, with a sharp twist of its neck, it ripped the snake's head off and tossed it aside. The snake's body—at least six feet long—dropped to the ground, twitching.

The panther's attention now moved to me, its ocher eyes regarding me with interest. Or hunger.

I let out a squeak, scampering several steps back before common sense prevailed and I froze. The cat, its freakishly great height and build matching Max's, lowered its head and sniffed the ground, seemingly unconcerned by my presence. I knew better than to relax, though. There were razor–sharp teeth under that soft, unperturbed muzzle.

I watched in horror as the panther shifted its weight from side to side, then quietly edged in. It moved in close enough that its snout grazed my chest, stopping on my pendant. It let out a low snarl, its lip curling to display a lethal set of fangs.

And I thought I'd die by a vampire bite. I wondered if there was any point in running. *Would running make the kill more pleasurable for it?* Untestable— my muscles were locked with terror.

"It's okay, I'm here." I felt an arm wrap protectively around my shoulder and Caden pulled my rigid body close to him.

I let out a small gasp of relief. "What do we do?" I whispered, trying not to move my lips, my focus glued on the beast giving me a sniff–down.

"Just stay still."

"Or what?"

"This is Scout."

"It has a name?" My eyes widened.

Caden chuckled. "Yeah. Like it?"

"Depends on if it's going to maul me."

"No. He's my pet."

"What do you mean?"

"Bishop and I have a small army of animals to guard the mountains and warn us of any visitors. Better protection."

The panther named Scout lifted his head to peer into my eyes, his face only inches away. I shrank back against Caden.

"Don't move. He's just curious. He won't react if you don't surprise him. He knows you're scared."

I averted my eyes to the left, focusing on a branch as the giant cat inspected me, unable to bring myself to look him in the eye for fear of screaming. He finally dropped his head to sniff my shoes. Caden kept his arm around my shoulder, holding me tightly to him.

"How is he yours?" I whispered

"I bit him. He belongs to me. I'm his master."

I frowned. "So, what does that make him? A werecat?"

"We call them werebeasts. They're a bit different from human vampires. They crave flesh more than blood. They're immortal and they heal quickly, like us. But they become freakishly big, usually doubling in size."

"Like Max," I said, thinking of my giant canine friend. That's what he was. A werebeast.

I felt Caden nod. "They're a protector, bound to the person who transformed them."

"That means Max has a master." It had to be Mortimer. He had introduced him as *his* guard dog.

"Yeah, probably. The cool thing is, I can communicate with Scout from anywhere in the valley."

"How?"

"Telepathically. We can talk back and forth to each other in our heads. He reports in to me."

"Reports in to you ..." I gasped. "Son of a—"

At my unexpected outburst, Scout took three lightning–quick steps back, snarling menacingly.

"Easy, boy," Caden cooed, sliding in to stand between the panther and me. When the cat finally quieted, he turned to look at me. "What is it?"

"What if Max is Mortimer's spy? He's always tailing me, sniffing me and stuff." *He's just following orders. He doesn't really care about me after all.*

"Makes sense," Caden murmured in agreement. "I warned you, didn't I?"

"But, why?" I twisted my face up in confusion, my hands going to my forehead. "To protect me from Sofie? Max doesn't seem too concerned when she's around. Viggo, though...he gets that dog riled up ..." *They're hiding something. But what?* "I'm such an idiot," I mumbled.

"No; you couldn't have known."

"I should have. You're right. I am a naïve fool."

Caden sighed. "They probably...found your weakness—whatever it is—and exploited it, sucking you into their world, making you trust them. That's what our kind is good at—manipulation."

My weakness? What could Sofie have...My loneliness. That was it. That was my weakness. She used human companionship to lure me in, to make me want to be around her. And I—a lonely, helpless puppy looking for friendship—lapped it up. But how had she figured that out so quickly? Was she that perceptive, or was I that obvious—that pathetic?

I glanced around. Scout had disappeared.

"He's gone. You can relax," Caden said, smiling wryly.

Off to guard the forest for me. Too bad I couldn't bring him back with me. Then the dogs would have a cat to chase.

"Please don't disappear like that again," I begged Caden.

"I'm sorry." His gaze showed sincerity. "He wasn't supposed to get that close—but then that snake made a move on you...I was just getting these." He held out a bunch of daisies. "They grow up high, in the meadows."

My jaw dropped. No one had ever given me flowers before, let alone scaled a mountain to pick them freestyle. "These...they're beautiful." I stammered, taking the daisies. *How long has it been since I held a daisy?* Forever, it seemed. I brought them to my nose to inhale the natural bouquet.

That scent...so familiar. It reminded me of something, but what...*My childhood? Summer?*

The park. Red and white striped monkey bars.

I gasped.

14. Daisies and Deceit

Before I knew what was happening, Caden was easing me to the ground, my legs having given out on me. "What's wrong?"

My mouth opened but it took a few tries to form any words and when I did, they came out in rapid spurts and stammers. "I couldn't...I couldn't have been more than four. The playground near our old apartment. Red and white–striped monkey bars. The old kind."

"What playground?"

"The one in Sofie's painting!"

Caden crouched down in front of me, cupping my chin gently with his hands. "Evangeline, slow down. You're rambling. Start from the beginning."

I took a deep breath, suddenly overwhelmed with nausea. I swallowed a few times before I could speak. "Sofie painted a picture and hung it in my room at Viggo and Mortimer's. It's a picture of a little girl picking daisies in a playground." I paused. "I knew there was something familiar about it ..." I locked eyes with him. "It was me! Sofie's been watching me since I was four years old!"

Caden sighed heavily, pivoting to sit on the ground beside me. "I wonder why?"

I shrugged. My whole body felt numb from the shock. "It means she's lying. She told me she didn't mean for this to happen to me, but she did. She's been planning it for fourteen years!"

He thought for a moment. "Or she's leaving important details out."

"Not telling me more than I need to know," I murmured. It was exactly what she'd told me to do. "I wonder if Viggo knows. If he does, he hasn't let on. Maybe he didn't want to freak me out."

"Maybe," Caden said softly, though his tone suggested doubt. "Why would she paint that picture, though? It's as if she wanted to you find out."

"Some sort of sick joke?"

He shrugged. "Or some other reason. I don't know what's going on, but I guarantee you there's a lot more to it than any of them are letting on. It's what I've been trying to tell you."

I nodded, committing that to memory. I'd have to question everything from now on.

Caden leaned in, his shoulder nudging mine affectionately. "You going to be okay? You look a little pale."

Nausea surged through my body again. "I feel...like I just found out I've been standing naked in a room full of people with magnifying glasses for years." I shuddered. "I can't trust anyone."

"No. No one," he said with cold certainty.

"Even the dog is against me," I mumbled, picking tiny leaves off a fern branch and tossing them aside.

"Assume you're only ever getting half the truth—if any."

I hesitated, terrified of the answer. "Even from Amelie and Fiona and Bishop...and you?"

"Yes," he said quickly. "I mean," he looked off in the distance, frowning, "we *want* you to trust us, but we don't expect you to do so blindly. We hope we'll earn it one day."

I already trust you, I whispered to him in my thoughts.

He turned and locked eyes with me for a moment, his expression unreadable. He opened his mouth as if to speak, then quickly clamped it shut. Grabbing my hand, he pull me up. "Come on. Let's keep walking, if you're up to it."

"As long as there are no more lurking animals. I'm feeling pretty frag-ile right now." Fragile, but unbroken, somehow—though by all counts I should have fallen apart. Any normal person would have by now, would-n't they?

Caden reached down to pick up the daisies I'd scattered when I real-ized the extent of Sofie's treachery. "Sorry, I shouldn't have."

"No!" I exclaimed, grabbing the flowers out of his hand and inhaling their scent again, welcoming the fond memories that flooded back with it. My mother's laughter as she chased me through the park..."Thanks for these." I smiled timidly. "I love daisies."

Caden picked up a pebble and casually threw it into the trees, no doubt hitting some impossible target I couldn't see. "I know." He laughed at my bewilderment.

"We'd better get to the others before they empty the stream." He began walking briskly down the path, calling over his shoulder, "Hurry up, pokey!"

I trailed quietly, alternating my attention between the perfect, agile body ahead and the daisies in my hand before saying, "So Fiona and Amelie obviously told you a few things about me."

"Obviously."

"What else did they tell you?" I asked, wracking my brain to remem-ber the conversation.

He responded by casually tossing out his own question. "So you've never even had one boyfriend?"

Ugh. They told him that? I felt my face flush at the thought of them dis-cussing my pathetic social life. *So he must have figured out there's something wrong with me.*

"I never would have guessed it, based on the other night ..." He glanced back, and I saw the corner of his mouth curving in a smirk.

The other night? What's he— My eyes bulged as I realized he was talking about the night of the attack. I opened my mouth to respond several times, always faltering, lost for words. Even the pendant's powerful magic couldn't have masked my blazing cheeks. Mercifully, Caden kept his eyes ahead.

We wandered deep within the valley forest, where the trees blocked out most of the sunlight. In the few places where the thick canopy granted the sun access, shafts of light beamed down over the area like spotlights, the contrast between the deep shadows and the sunrays creating a mystical setting.

An enormous, knotty tree root jutted at least six feet from the ground, blocking our path. I hooked my foot into a nook and started climbing, but Caden's hands grabbed my waist and yanked me back down. "Where are you going?" He laughed, and in the next instant, we were sailing over to the other side.

"I thought you couldn't fly," I said sarcastically, releasing the mouthful of air I had sucked in.

"That was a jump." He chuckled and continued walking.

We found the others sitting on a pile of rocks beside a narrow, murky river that wove through the trees. Fluorescent green algae rested like a camouflage on its surface, bright against the inky water and the dark forest.

"So we're going to...fish?" I asked, eyeing the metal rod Bishop held. Three more lay beside him, nestled among some ferns. *This is what vampires do to kill time?*

Caden smirked. "You sound surprised."

"I thought your diet consisted of...liquid."

"They're for Bishop's pet. Are you any good?"

"I don't know; I've never tried. But I don't see myself as much of the 'angler and hunter' type," I answered.

Caden laughed, picking up a rod. "You could be a natural cave woman."

"Maybe." *I doubt it.* Seeing anything with more than two legs scurry past made my skin crawl so I didn't expect a flapping, slimy fish impaled on a hook would bring about a different reaction. I crouched by the riverbank and laid my flowers beside it with their stems dipped in the murky water.

"Whoa! Not too close," Caden exclaimed, leaning over to pull me back. "There are things in this water you don't want to...disturb."

A shiver ran down my back as I studied at the calm river. "Like snakes?"

Bishop answered. "Snakes, crocodiles, piranhas—I'm surprised you didn't meet one of them the night you went in for Amelie."

"But you didn't," Caden reminded me, seeing my eyes widen. He threw a look of exasperation Bishop's way.

"Here you go, Eve," Bishop said, smirking as he handed me a rod.

My mother used to call me that.

"I found these babies in a vault a few hundred years ago and I've been hoarding them ever since. I knew I'd have a reason to keep them!"

I stood awkwardly holding the rod. "Okay...what do I do now?" I inspected the metal contraption at the end of the long pole. *A reel,* Caden informed me.

"Well, first, you put one of these on." Bishop picked something up off the ground beside him and grabbed my free hand. He placed a six–inch leech into my palm. It began wiggling and I shrieked, shaking the slimy thing off my hand. "Poor little fella." Bishop stooped down to pick the disgusting thing up. Grabbing the end of my line, he jabbed the barbed hook through its body several times. It writhed furiously, trying to escape.

I screwed up my face in disgust.

Bishop snickered. "You're such a girl."

Fiona glanced over. "Bishop, seriously, you are so juvenile some-times." She rolled her eyes at me. "Sorry."

Bishop squatted beside Caden, who already had a line in the water. Caden chuckled. "So *those* leeches are terrifying."

"Not terrifying, repulsive. Two *entirely* different things," I clarified, bending down to wipe the leech gunk off my hand on some leaves. I straightened and regarded my rod. "Okay, I'm in need of a lesson."

Caden seemed happy to oblige, using his own rod to demonstrate how to cast and reel in.

"Looks simple enough," I said and got ready to cast. My bandaged hand made things difficult.

Caden held up his hands. "Wait."

I froze, assuming his vampire senses noticed something in the water.

"Wait...hold on...okay, now! And put your whole body into it," he commanded.

I complied with his instructions, swinging the rod back over my right shoulder before casting forward with all my strength. But my hook lodged in something behind me, at the same time that a howl of protest made me whirl.

Bishop stood wincing, the sharp metal barb through his left earlobe. I gasped, tears welling. "I'm so sorry!"

Beside me, Caden and Fiona were doubled over in laughter. Caden straightened and strolled over to inspect the hook. "Nice catch!" he called back to me, winking.

I rushed forward with the intention of begging forgiveness but stopped short, cringing, as Bishop yanked the hook out of his ear, tearing a sizeable chunk of flesh out with it. I expected blood to start gushing but the wound immediately closed up, leaving his ear looking unscathed.

"Pay more attention next time!" Caden lectured Bishop, giving him a whack on his back.

"Fiona was distracting me with—" Bishop stopped, realizing he was the dupe in a joint effort by Caden and her. "You'll pay for that later, woman," he threatened Fiona, though he was grinning when he said it. "My new shirt's ruined now!" He rubbed the sleeve where a few drops of blood had landed.

I stood there, wide–eyed with both amazement and horror.

"Don't worry, Bishop's fine," Caden said, strolling over to gently squeeze my shoulder. "It's next to impossible to catch one of us unaware like that. Impressive."

"What was Fiona distracting him with?" I asked, frowning. But then I saw the devilish smile she gave him and his answering grin, and I had a good idea what it was. I turned away, flushing.

Caden cast his hook into the water and seated himself on a boulder. I followed suit, glancing around to check for snakes. "So how long have they been together?"

"They met during the war. Bishop had just been turned and he was lost. It's not a natural process, the transition to what we are. He likely would have been killed in the war, had Fiona not taken to him. She took him under her wing, helped him. They've been together ever since."

"Wow. Seven hundred years? That's a long time to be with one person."

Caden smirked. "For a human, yes. Human desires change with age. People outgrow one another. It's different with us. Every day with Fiona feels like the first day Bishop met her—the sparks, butterflies, all that."

"Butterflies...I thought that was a chick thing," I muttered.

"No, definitely not," Caden murmured, glancing peculiarly at me before turning back to his rod.

"What about you and Amelie? Were you...turned in the war?"

Caden shook his head. "An attack about forty years before the war." He paused. "I was twenty-four. Amelie was twenty-one. Our parents ran a horse ranch, thoroughbreds—The Jennings Resort for Horses, some called it. One night we heard this awful sound coming from the barn. My father grabbed his shotgun, expecting to scare off some thieves. When we hadn't heard from him for too long, I grabbed another gun and headed out. Amelie and our mother followed with flashlights. We got to one of the barns and ..." Caden's voice fell; he stared out at the placid water. "There were rumors of strange things happening at cattle and horse farms but nothing could have prepared us...Every horse in that barn was dead, their throats torn out, blood sprayed over the walls, the hay—everything. Mom and Amelie ran to get the police while I checked out the other barns, looking for my father ..." Caden's voice drifted off and he sat for a moment, deep in thought. "I found him lying beside one of his prize-winning stallions. And that's where *they* found me—I never even saw a face."

I noticed the tip of his fishing rod dip, but Caden didn't seem too concerned.

"They decided Amelie and I were too appealing to waste—we'd make good additions." His voice was edged with bitterness.

"I'm so sorry, Caden," I said softly. And I was. It pained me to know that he and Amelie had suffered so.

He gazed down at his hands, a haunted smile on his face. "Do you realize that's the first time I've ever heard those words from anyone?"

My heart sank. I wanted to wrap my arms around him, to comfort him, to take his grief away.

I glanced over to the others as Amelie leapt into the air, squealing with excitement about the fish dangling at the end of her hook.

"So...Caden Jennings," I said aloud. *Evangeline Jennings,* the voice in my head said. I shook my head, feeling foolish.

He sighed. "In another time, yes. Amelie is all that's left of my family. At least we found Bishop and Fiona."

What about Rachel?

I noticed that the pile of fish had grown quickly as we talked. There was enough there to supply a supermarket. "So Bishop's pet is going to eat all of those?" I nodded at the silvery mound. "How big is this pet, exactly?"

The end of my rod dipped, followed by a second, then a third tug—the last one sharp. "I think I caught something!" I whispered, as if speaking too loud would let the fish know he was ensnared on a sharp hook. *Like he's not already well aware of that.*

"Reel it in!" Caden exclaimed. As if in response, the tugging became fierce and frantic. It was all I could do to grip the rod in my injured hand. Caden reached around me and placed his hands over mine, helping me wind the reel. "Almost," he murmured, his mouth close enough that his voice tickled my ear.

I'm going to pass out, I thought, feeling a strange excitement ripple through my body. By the time the line was out of the water, I was too busy trying to stop my hands from trembling under his to notice a fish three times the size of the others dangling off my hook.

"Big Brown's gonna love that one!" Bishop hollered.

"Who's Big Brown?" I croaked, allowing myself to release the breath I'd unknowingly held during the entire ordeal.

"He is," Bishop said, jerking his chin toward someone behind me.

I turned, expecting to see another cat. Instead, a grizzly bear with fur the color of milk chocolate lumbered toward us, equivalent in size to a young elephant I'd once seen at the Portland Zoo. It was eyeing the prize at the end of my rod—or me; I wasn't exactly sure which yet. My mouth opened to scream but no sound came out.

"It's okay," Caden whispered calmly, pulling me closer to him, his other arm slowly wrapping protectively around me. "No sudden movements and it'll be okay."

I couldn't move if I wanted to. Caden's arms were like a vise. "He's big," I managed to whisper. Big enough to slice me into six pieces with one swing of his paw. The ground shook as the bear neared us. I tasted bile in my throat. "I'm going to be sick," I groaned, wanting to give Caden some warning. I turned my face, praying he was out of range. I'd rather be torn apart by this beast than puke on Caden.

Big Brown stooped to sniff the fish on my line and then, with one lightning–quick chomp, bit the thing right off the line and swallowed it whole—hook, leech, and all. He continued on to the pile of fish behind Amelie and devoured it in mere seconds. No one moved.

With that pile done, he ambled over to stand in front of Bishop, stooping so that their eyes were level. After a minute–long menacing stare–down, Big Brown simply turned and barreled away, disappearing within seconds.

"No signs of anyone coming," Bishop said. "He can tell you're not one of us," he added, looking at me.

"So he's like Scout. And Max," I confirmed.

"Yes, only less predictable," Caden answered, his arms dropping from their protective embrace around me.

I took that as my signal to slide away from him, to allow for the appropriate amount of space. I began inching away.

"You seem cold. If you're warmer next to me, you should stay put."

I bit my lower lip. Before catching the fish, I had been contemplating taking off my pink fleece hoody. Even in the shadows of the trees, the air was muggy. "I *am* a bit cold," I lied, faking a shiver. Caden turned his attention back to the river, a knowing smirk on his face. *Could he tell I'm lying?* "So...*that's* Big Brown," I said, changing the topic.

Caden chuckled. "It'll take some time before he lets you rub his belly."

"And he eats fish? He'll need a lot more than that pile."

"That's just it. He's a bottomless pit. I think he's devoured half the deer population around here in a few weeks; we'll be fighting with him over food soon enough. Bishop didn't know what he was getting himself into. He should have stuck with wolves; even a cougar would have been a wiser choice. This one's a lot more work to feed and *much* more difficult to convert."

"Really? Don't you just have to bite them?"

Caden chuckled, shaking his head. "It's the same process as converting a human—with venom—but grizzlies fight back and they're vicious. More than likely, the animal will rip you to shreds before you can pump enough venom into him. You'll heal, of course, but...It took Bishop three tries. You should have seen him." Caden released another chuckle. "He was practically naked when he stumbled into the cave, his clothing bloody and shredded to pieces."

My eyes went wide. "Well, why would he do it, then?"

Caden paused, choosing his words. "Cougars and wolves make fierce allies. They're quick, fierce, and follow command like a programmed soldier. They usually travel in packs, making it easier to take down a vampire if they have to. Their teeth are strong enough to tear him or her apart and then carry the heart to us so we can burn it." He stopped talking, a funny smirk on his face. "You're looking at me like I have two heads," he commented.

"I'm sorry...heart?"

He grinned. "Yes, we still do have hearts in here." He thumped a fist against his chest. "All of our organs are still there. I guess they're basically ornaments now, though. Useless. Except our heart."

"Don't forget to tell her about that other organ that still serves a useful purpose," Bishop boomed. "You know, our—"

Fiona cut him off with a swift whack across the chest. "You're a regular Casanova," she muttered, shaking her head. Behind her, Amelie was giggling.

"So, your heart still works?" I blurted, getting flustered as I realized what Bishop was about to say.

Caden was shaking his head, eyes downcast, smiling to himself. I wasn't sure if it was at my loss of composure or at Bishop's brazenness. "*Our heart*," he began again, glancing over at Bishop, who was grinning like the Cheshire cat, "still beats and pumps blood through our veins. As long as our heart remains within our bodies, we can regenerate. And it's strong. Piercing it with a wooden stake or a sword won't kill us, unless the weapon is on fire. That's the only definite way to kill one of us—burn our heart, either with our body or on its own. If you can get it out of us, that is."

"Once," Amelie spoke up, "I saw a vampire's head get cut off and thrown aside. A few minutes later, the body stumbled around, looking for it. When it picked it up and 'plugged' it back in, all the flesh mended itself. Good as new."

"Oh, come on!" I looked skeptically at her.

"Honest. Scout's honor!" She held up two fingers.

I glanced at the others, expecting to see a hidden smirk or the crook of a smile.

"Well, don't say I didn't warn you!" Amelie chirped.

"Always burn them," Fiona said in a serious tone. "That way, you know they can't come back and hunt you down—because, believe me, they'll be pissed."

"As if any human would get a chance in the first place," Bishop muttered sarcastically.

Caden nodded in concession. "Back to Big Brown. A pack of cats or wolves can't match the ferocity of one grizzly. Having an animal *that* powerful at your command, especially in a situation like this, where we need all the protection we can get—that's why Bishop did it. One of those things will rip a heart right out of a chest cavity and eat it...good luck trying to get that back."

I glanced over at Bishop, lying precariously on a bed of rocks, flicking Fiona's ear. He still looked like that easygoing, sometimes obtuse cool kid from high school. Not exactly someone who ever paid an ounce of attention to me, let alone willingly battled a two ton animal three times for my protection.

My heart swelled.

As the shadows lengthened and the dappled sunshine faded, the first pangs of hunger rumbled in my stomach. I was sure it was a mistake—I hadn't been here that long, had I? It rumbled again, this time loud enough to attract Caden's attention. He looked down at my stomach, then up at my face, concern sweeping over his. "Time to go!" he announced. "The human is hungry."

I shrugged it off, not wanting to disrupt their fun. "I'm okay."

"No you're not. Come on!" He hopped to his feet, whistling.

"What am I, a pet?" I quipped.

Caden threw an arm around my shoulders and pulled me close to his chest, scratching behind my ear.

"Ha–ha," I said sarcastically, hazarding a peek up to find those beautiful jade eyes gazing back, an inexplicable look in them. *You are so unbelievably hot.* My heart began thumping wildly in my chest. *Thank God the pendant masks that.*

"Ready to go?" Caden asked, chuckling.

I nodded dumbly. *Anywhere. I'll go anywhere with you.*

઒

"Looks like chicken feed," Bishop commented dryly, his nose scrunching up in disgust as I inhaled three nature bars. They had found me some figs and berries to snack on but the exertion of walking up the mountain drove my hunger to levels of starvation.

I good– humoredly elbowed him in the stomach, wincing as my funny bone cracked against his rock hard muscles. He bellowed laughter, earning an eye roll from Fiona.

"What a mess!" Amelie announced as she surveyed the stuff scattered all over the cave, though her childlike face wore an eager expression. Suddenly she shrieked, diving down to grab something small and black. She held it up. A bathing suit.

I frowned. *Why would Sofie—that's right.* I had mentioned the oasis. I didn't think she was paying attention though.

Amelie frantically rooted around until she found one for each of us.

Trunks in hand, Bishop and Caden bolted, Caden covering his eyes dramatically to hide his view of his sister, who had already begun shamelessly peeling off her clothes.

Fiona handed me a black bikini. I swallowed, holding up the two–piece, trying to figure out top from bottom. There was more string than covering. "Is there something in there a little more...modest?"

"Oh, don't be silly, Evangeline," Fiona murmured, already adjusting her own skimpy hot pink bikini over her supermodel–like curves.

"Okay," I grumbled, changing quietly, dreading standing next to these two. When I was done I felt naked, even though all my vitals were covered. The cold air wasn't helping.

"What are you looking for?" Amelie asked, seeing my eyes darting over the piles of clothing.

"There was a big, fuzzy red blanket somewhere here."

"Come on!" Fiona looped her arm through mine and dragged me down the tunnel, picking up speed until we were jogging. Amelie ran ahead of us, giggling hysterically, holding a giant flashlight that had come in the mountain bag.

I forced them to slow to a walk, out of breath. "So...when do you think Rachel will be back?" I asked casually.

"When the Council gets bored of watching vampires bludgeon each other nearly to death, only to heal and do it over again," Fiona answered. I cringed in horror as she elaborated: "A gladiator tournament."

"She's a Council member and, as such, must keep up appearances," Amelie added in a haughty voice in snide imitation of Rachel.

"Where did she go?"

"To New Shore. It was the capital city when this was a country. Most of it has crumbled and grown over now. She wouldn't have gone if she had known you would be here—you're so early! She won't be back for another week, at least," Fiona answered.

I exhaled loudly, earning a laugh from them. "She's not the nicest person I've ever met," I said, wrinkling my nose.

Fiona snorted. "Evangeline, you're too polite. She's a cold–hearted, vicious bitch!" Her violet eyes flashed with anger.

I looked at her, not prepared for the blatant loathing in her normally serene voice. "Yes, well, she is also drop–dead gorgeous. I guess all guys are the same."

"What?" Amelie asked, her face twisting with confusion. "Ohhh, you mean Caden. Believe me, their 'relationship'—and I use that term loosely—has *nothing* to do with her looks," Amelie said. "But she is madly in love with him—crazy, fanatical, psychopath love."

"But he doesn't love her?" A spark of hope—a glimmer of the impossible—ignited within me.

Fiona held her finger up to her lips as we rounded the corner and entered the oasis, ending the conversation before I could get an answer.

"Wow," I mumbled, taking in the scene. Steam rose from the water, swirling in the chilly mountain air that stirred the countless flames around the cavern to create a beautiful, dreamlike mist.

We found Bishop and Caden relaxing in a small, circular alcove. The water lapped just below their chests, the precise height to adequately show off Caden's strong shoulders and neck. He had the perfect curves and ridges around his frame, the perfect amount of flesh and muscle to make him look neither beefy nor lanky. *Perfect.* I heard myself groan wistfully before I could control myself.

They stopped talking and turned, Caden's eyes immediately landing on me. My shoulders hunched inward as I instinctively wanted to hide, wishing I could cocoon myself in that red blanket. *Maybe the mist will blur his vision,* I hoped. *Highly doubtful.* I wrapped my arms around my chest, trying to cover my entire upper body—a justifiable action, considering the chill in the air.

Fiona trotted over and slithered in beside Bishop, wrapping her arms around him before resting her head on his broad shoulder. Amelie was no less confident about her body as she jumped in beside Fiona, taking enough space for herself that I was forced to squeeze in beside Caden.

Next to those two, I probably resembled a rodent, scurrying to the edge and gracelessly clambering down, half tumbling in my hurry to find concealment in the water. Caden offered his hand and I took it, knowing I would likely end up falling on top of him otherwise. I didn't know what was wrong with me lately. I wasn't so physically inept anywhere else but near them and their superpowers.

When the warm water covered my flesh, I was able to relax and breathe again.

"Ah, the good old days: hot tubs, girls in bikinis …" Bishop reminisced, leaning back with his arms stretched lazily to either side of him, displaying his muscular biceps. "Eve—next time back, surfboards and a keg, 'kay?" He waited for my giggle and nod of assent before his head fell back and he closed his eyes, resting peacefully.

"So, you all *used* to be human, right? Do you forget all of your skills when you...convert?" I asked cautiously. "I mean, why couldn't you pick up where humans left off, with all the manufacturing, electricity—all that stuff?"

"Sounds so simple, doesn't it?" Caden laughed without mirth. "Because we're narcissistic, selfish creatures who want all the luxuries with none of the hard work behind it." He paused. "Think of Viggo and Mortimer. The 'good vampires.'" I caught the sarcasm. "Where do they get their money? Do you see them working? Earning a living?" Caden's Adam's apple protruded as he dropped his head back against the rock ledge. I had the urge to run my finger along it, but I resisted. He chuckled. "They rob their victims. They go after the ones whose wallets are thick, and whose illicit activities make their death unsurprising and welcomed. I'd bet my life on it. It's what I used to do."

I shuddered at his blunt admission. But was he right? I had wondered where they earned their money.

Caden continued. "You'll be hard–pressed to find a vampire fixing toilets or serving drinks, unless they have an ulterior motive."

"Sofie serves coffee," I answered, challenging him.

Caden's head rolled to face me. "I wonder why …" His voice was soft, protective. A gentle warning.

"You're right. I have to question everything, don't I?"

He nodded, a small smile touching his lips before he sat up again.

My eyes drifted around the alcove, landing on each vampire for a brief moment, listening to them chatter and laugh happily. *That means I'm sup-*

posed to question all of you? The idea distressed me. I didn't want to question them.

Every fiber of my body was keenly aware of Caden's presence, so close to me. Now and again his arm would bump against mine as he laughed. I'm sure it was accidental, but each one of those nudges sent electric ripples through my body. I managed to steal several glances at him, pacing myself so I didn't get caught ogling. Soft–looking masculine fuzz had started to grow in the center of his chest. Hairy chests had never appealed to me before. Now, though …

"Bishop?" Fiona's low, worried voice cut into my fantasies. I glanced over to see the male vampire no longer languishing in the tub but sitting rigid, scowling and shushing her with his hand while he listened for something. The group sat tense for a moment, aware of something I was blind to.

Finally he shook his head, then grinned at Caden. "Nothing. Big Brown took care of it."

He had been communicating telepathically with his pet. About what, though? "More vampires?" I guessed, a shiver running down my back.

"Not anymore," Caden answered, turning to smile reassuringly at me. "We're good."

"Told you he was worth the battle." Bishop smirked arrogantly at Fiona, then threw a wink in my direction. He leaned back again, closing his eyes.

More vampires. Lurking in the mountains—the mountains I had hoped would be impenetrable—on their way here to torture me when they found me. I swallowed a lump. "Are they ever going to stop?" I whispered. "One of them may get past—"

"They won't." Caden's voice was soothing. "Don't worry." Underwater, an invisible hand landed on my knee and squeezed gently before sliding away again. A thrill rippled from the point of contact to the rest of my body. I swallowed. If he was trying to distract me, he was doing a fantastic job.

"You wanna go stretch? I need to stretch," Amelie announced, grabbing my hand and effortlessly pulling me to the connecting pool, no doubt to further distract me from the talk of vampires in the jungle.

"Sure," I mumbled, glancing back at Caden. He was watching me. Always watching.

When I learned that "stretching" meant doing a swan dive off a twenty foot–high boulder into a shallow part of the pool where jagged rocks peppered the bottom, I politely declined. I instead dove under, swimming toward the center of the lake.

Something brushed lightly against my leg. I turned to see Caden beside me, giving me an open–mouth grin, reminding me that I was the only one who had to resurface for air. We both surfaced.

"Follow me. I want to show you something," he said. I nodded eagerly, willing to follow him into the pits of hell. "Big breath, okay?"

I nodded again. We dove under and Caden grabbed my hand and began towing me, swimming effortlessly. Down, down we descended, flying through the water at high speed. As the lake floor dropped beneath us, swallowing us whole, I began to think the pits of hell was exactly where we were headed. Soon I couldn't even see my arms in the darkness enveloping me. Caden must have sensed my agitation because he drew me closer, one of his arms wrapping around my waist to pull my back against his chest. Now I had two things to freak out over—the paralyzing darkness and Caden's proximity.

I sensed a directional change. And then we finally surfaced. Spent air burst from my mouth and I inhaled loudly. Luckily I had been so focused on his hand against my ribcage that I forgot about panicking over my need for air.

"Too bad the pendant can't breathe for you," he said into my ear, still holding me tightly.

"Yeah, that'd be helpful." My voice broke. "Where are we?" I looked up at moonlight shining down through a circle of night sky—a gaping hole, I realized—to illuminate the placid lake and a powerful waterfall maybe thirty feet high, far down on the other side of this particular spot.

"We're on the other side of the mountain, near the ocean."

Caden's arms slid from my body. I turned to see him already out of the water, standing on a rock ledge that extended the full length of the cave wall. The black and gray swim trunks that Sofie had chosen for him sat low on his hips, revealing the defined, muscular shape of his abdomen and pelvic bones. A fine line of hair crept all the way down his stomach, disappearing under the waistband of his trunks …

"Evangeline?" The sound of my name snapped me from my blatant gawking. I turned away quickly, heat crawling up my neck. *You're such a pervert, Evangeline.* It took a moment to regain my composure. When I finally felt brave enough to look back, Caden was grinning at me, not the least bit uncomfortable. He offered his hand. "Here."

I took it, and he effortlessly yanked me out into icy air. My body tensed with the cold. I briefly considered jumping back into the water but Caden's grip on my hand tightened. "Come on." Caden began walking briskly along the ledge, tugging me along.

"Where are we going?" I asked.

"I want to show you something."

We walked to the other side of the cave and stopped by the ferocious waterfall, the sound of its rushing water reminding me of Viggo and Mortimer's jet engine. Caden turned and said something.

"Pardon?" I yelled.

He leaned in close, his mouth next to my ear. "You need to hold on tight." I nodded, squeezing his hand. Chuckling with amusement, he yanked me toward him until our chests were touching. My heart started pounding. I heard myself suck in air as he again moved his mouth next to my ear. "Close your eyes and put your face against my chest." The vibrations from his words tickled my skin, making my heart pound harder. "You feeling okay?" His voice was innocent enough.

"Yup," I said, annoyed with the telltale thumping in my chest. *How can he not know?* Could this vampire be *that* oblivious? Maybe he could be, thanks to my necklace.

"Are you sure?"

More vibrations causing more tickling causing more pounding. My breathing became raspy. Unable to speak, I instead nodded and buried my face in his chest, expecting to pass out.

His body shook. Was he laughing? He leaned in to speak to me again.

"Wrap your arms around me."

I locked my arms around his back, feeling his smooth skin and rigid muscles. His strong arms lifted my body, squeezing tightly. The ground suddenly disappeared from beneath us. And at that moment I realized Caden's intention. We were jumping *through* that giant, ferocious waterfall.

The torrent of water hit us, beating down on every muscle in my shoulders and back and effortlessly driving my hands apart. Thankfully my bare feet were touching hard ground before I had a chance to panic.

"You can come out now," Caden whispered.

I pulled my face away from the comfortable nook I had located in his chest.

"I figured it was best not to tell you what we were doing," he explained, looking sheepish.

"Good call," I muttered, allowing only a fleeting scowl. *I can't be mad at you.*

He smiled—such a sweet, genuine smile—then nodded to something behind us. I turned. And squinted at a sea of silver, thousands of metallic, ropelike vertical strands glowing brilliantly in the darkness of a wide tunnel. They swayed gracefully back and forth as if being coerced by a gentle breeze that never touched my skin. They had to be at least three feet high, growing in round clumps right out of the bedrock.

Stepping forward, awe slowing my feet, I reached out to touch one of the strands. It was soft and pliable, like yarn. My eyes widened. I knew what it was.

15. Sea of Merth

"This is how Merth grows?" I whispered, turning to Caden.

He shrugged. "Guess so. None of us have ever seen it like this before. It's next to impossible to find. The Council's been hunting for it since the war. We knew Jethro had some, but didn't know where he got it from. It's why he was so territorial about this place. I'll bet there are groves of this stuff in these mountains."

The mention of the Council reminded me of Rachel. "So...will Rachel tell the Council about it?" *And about me?*

Caden sighed loudly. "We're not telling her about this." He closed the gap between us, his expression serious. He reached up to delicately touch my cheek. The gesture made my heart begin hammering erratically in my chest. "She's not going to tell them about you. I'm making sure of that." I caught the sudden twitch in his cheek, like he was trying not to wince.

"What's wrong?"

He dropped his hand, moving away from me. "Being around this much Merth is painful. But I wanted to show you. If we can figure out a way to get some out, you should take it back with you...for protection."

I suddenly remembered. "Sofie asked me to bring back as much as I can. I don't know why," I added when I saw his questioning look.

His jaw tightened. "What is that witch not telling you?"

Probably as much as I'm not telling you, I thought guiltily. Watching him wince in pain just so he could show me a way to shield myself from him and his kind, my need for secrecy and protection vanished instantly. "I can bring you back with me," I blurted.

Caden's eyes widened in alarm. "What? You said—"

"I lied! But I'm telling you now. There is a way to take you back."

"How do you know?"

"Sofie told me."

Caden sneered, his doubt obvious. But then he must have had a thought, because his face turned grim. "Take who back, exactly?"

They really don't miss anything, do they. I swallowed. "Well, that's the problem; I don't know how or who I can bring back—"

Caden cut me off. "Don't say a word to the others about this."

"Because I may not be able to bring them back with me?"

"Yes, exactly. It wouldn't be fair."

"But if I can figure out how, then you can come back with me."

"No!" Horror made it a shout. I jumped back, and he softened his tone. "I mean, it doesn't matter if one of us goes or all of us go ... " He chewed his lip as if deliberating what to say. "We haven't been exposed to human blood in over seven hundred years," he began, then paused to clear his throat, which had turned hoarse. "That necklace disguises what you are here, right?" I nodded. "But you said that, in your world, it's useless. These vampire friends of yours can smell your blood, sense your emotions, all that."

Again, I nodded and his jade eyes locked with mine, turning hard as he spoke again, slowly and deliberately. "What do you think will happen when one of us is exposed to the scent of human blood—a scent that drives us to kill with more intensity than you could ever possibly imagine—for the first time in seven hundred years?"

I pursed my lips, beginning to understand where the conversation was going.

He didn't stop there, though. "And which human will be in close proximity?" His left eyebrow arched, and I swallowed. "You wouldn't stand a chance. You'd be dead before you knew what was going on."

Caden grimaced.

"But you could control yourself, couldn't you?"

"No, Evangeline." Caden shook his head, dismissing my faith in him. "You don't understand how powerful this need for blood is." He stepped away from me and began pacing. "When Amelie was still human, she had a boyfriend. They'd been dating for three years. She loved the guy. He was a bit of a wanker in my opinion, but...I'm her older brother so I'm supposed to be hard on boyfriends. Anyway, when she was turned, she made the mistake of going to see him. I don't know what she was thinking. Well, I do. She wanted to see him. She *had* to see him."

"What happened? Was he scared off?" I asked.

"No...Well, he might have been if she ever had the chance to tell him. Between her thirst for his blood and her overwhelming desire for him, she couldn't control herself." Caden looked down at his hands. "She killed him. Drained him of every last drop of blood."

I gasped. "Poor Amelie!"

Caden barked laughter, shaking his head at me. "Poor Amelie? What about poor wanker?" He sighed, stopping in front of me. "Amelie lives with that guilt every day, as strong now as it was seven hundred years ago. I couldn't live with myself if I did that to you." His fingertip brushed my cheek, raw pain momentarily flashing in his eyes.

I swallowed and—I don't know where the bravery came from—timidly moved my fingertips up to touch his, where they rested on my cheek. Or tried to, anyway. My hand was trembling enough to mimic a Parkinson's patient.

He abruptly grabbed my hand, panic marring his gorgeous features. "Oh God! You're freezing! Why didn't you say anything?"

I *was* freezing, I realized—but that wasn't why I was trembling. Either way, I wasn't going to admit it.

"Let's go." He tugged me after him, his jaw taut.

"Go" meant jumping through the waterfall again, something I didn't exactly enjoy, but I was easily mollified by burying my face in Caden's chest again. Once through, he swung me up into his arms with ease, cradling me like a small child. "There's another way," he murmured and began running down an unseen tunnel—completely dark—at warp speed.

It took only minutes to get back to the others, but my teeth were chattering uncontrollably by the time we arrived. Caden leapt into the natural hot tub where we had started, me still snug in his arms. At first the shock of the heat felt like a million tiny prickles against my skin, and I winced with the sting. When I saw Caden's pained expression, though, I fought hard to smooth my face.

Caden refused to let go, holding me tightly as he apologized repeatedly, "I didn't realize how cold the air was for you. I forgot about—I'm an idiot!"

"It's ok–k–kay, I'm warming up–p now," I said between chattering teeth, trying to ease his conscience.

"No, it's not okay! You're stiff as a board!" he exclaimed.

A burst of laughter escaped before I sucked it in. It was the feel of his bare, muscular abs against my ribcage and *something else* against my hip that was preventing my body from relaxing.

"I should have known better," he continued. "It's bad enough that you have to worry about being attacked by vampires, now you may die of hypothermia." His hand furiously rubbed his brow.

"Thanks for showing me th–the Merth. It's b–beautiful, even though it's d–dangerous to you," I continued, attempting to distract him.

He heaved a huge sigh, then frowned at me. "You're allowed to get angry."

"It won't accomplish anything," I answered, smiling at him. "B–besides, it was fun." I averted my gaze shyly.

"Which part, being pulled down a pitch black, underwater rabbit hole, or being pummeled by a waterfall?" he retorted sarcastically.

The truth was, I had already forgotten about those minor distractions; my mind still reeled from the feel of his body against my back as he pulled me through the murky abyss and his strong arms as they held me tightly, protecting me. I wasn't about to tell him that, though. "All of it," I answered instead.

He muttered something incoherent, rolled his eyes, and shook his head at me.

My rigid muscles finally started to unlock.

"Good God, Caden. Her lips are blue!" Amelie had stealthily swum up. Her normally raspy voice sounded condemning, and she glared at her brother in disapproval.

I defended him. "It's okay! I'm fine."

Amelie rolled doubtful eyes. "Did he show you the Merth, at least?"

I nodded, another surge of guilt souring my stomach at the thought that I was keeping my secret from her when she was so willing to share theirs.

"Cool, huh?" Amelie threw a mysterious glance at Caden, then dove under the water and swam away.

I sighed, wishing I could read them like Sofie could read me. My teeth had finally stopped chattering, but my fingertips, when I reached up to scratch my nose, were shriveled. "I need to get out." I held my wrinkly hand up in front of Caden's face, scrunching my nose in disgust.

"Wait right here."

Caden's arms slid out from around me. I watched his chiseled body as he leapt out of the water and disappeared down the tunnel. He returned thirty seconds later with the plush red blanket under one arm and several large chunks of wood tucked under the other. He had a vibrant fire blazing in seconds. Hoisting me out of the water, he wrapped me in the blanket and led me over to sit next to the flames. He slid in directly behind me, his legs stretched out on either side, and began rubbing my arms and back.

Although I didn't mind the doting, I knew I was taking advantage of his unwarranted guilt. "Thanks. I'm good now." He ignored me, continuing to half dry, half warm me. "Really. I'm fine. Don't worry about me."

"We should change those bandages on your hand, too," he murmured.

"Oh, to be invisible …" I mused sarcastically.

He pulled me back toward him until I was close enough that his inner thighs touched my hips and his chin hovered over my shoulder. I was sure I felt warm breath tickling against the nape of my neck. *But he doesn't need to breathe, does he?*

"Are you still cold? You're trembling," Caden murmured.

"Nope, I'm good," I muttered, heat crawling up my cheeks. *The opposite, actually.* I squeezed my eyes shut and focused on my breathing.

I heard a lid pop and opened my eyes to see Caden rifling through a medical kit. It was enough to distract me from Caden's inadvertent torture for the moment. I raised a querying eyebrow.

"I found this earlier in my bag, along with a note. Courtesy of your maternal vampire, I gather?" He grinned.

"Seriously?" I frowned. "What'd the note say?"

"That I should keep an eye on your stitches because you'd be preoccupied. She didn't say with what."

You. I'm preoccupied with you, dummy.

Caden gently unwound the bandages. It had been three days since the attack. I think. It was getting hard to keep track of time. The cut was healing nicely, the old woman's stitch work impeccable. Caden held my hand tenderly in his, inspecting the wound from several angles. Then, ever so lightly, he drew a circle around it with his index finger. "Does that hurt at all?" He turned his face slightly so his mouth was next to my cheek.

"No," I squeaked. *How can he not know what he's doing to me!*

Sighing, he began wrapping my hand up in new bandages.

"Cannon ball!" Bishop yelled in warning. I looked up in time to see him plummeting from atop one of the highest boulders. He splashed into the lake, sending an enormous wave radiating outward. Luckily we were out of range.

I gasped. "The rocks!"

Caden's body began to shake. He was laughing at me. When I remembered why, I started giggling as well. Of course Bishop would be fine—the jagged rocks might not be. "I keep forgetting. You all seem so...normal," I said, turning slightly to steal a glimpse at Caden's face, which could never in a million years be described as *normal*.

Amelie leapt off the same boulder, landing on Bishop's back and tackling him underwater.

"They're close, those two. Amelie reminds him of his own little sister. She didn't survive the war," Caden explained, tossing the old bandages into the fire.

A movement to my left caught my attention. Fiona slyly darted from a hidden alcove to tackle Bishop the second he emerged from the water. Amelie popped up then and tag–teamed against him.

"And Amelie and Fiona...I think those two share a brain," Caden added.

I laughed. "Have they always been so close?"

"Instantly. Just like how they've attached themselves to you."

That same guilty pain twisted my stomach again with the knowledge that I would choose Caden over them, if I had to. But I so desperately didn't want to. Why couldn't I bring all four back? Why did I have to choose? *Because anything else would be too easy, Evangeline. And nothing comes easy for you.*

I leaned against Caden's chest, my eyelids drooping, suddenly exhausted. Not pendant–cooling, universe–changing exhausted, just plain tired from the day's excitement. I couldn't remember the last time I'd actually slept. But I didn't want to sleep. I didn't want to leave them. Ever.

Unfortunately, my yawn didn't escape their notice.

"Come." Fiona beckoned to Bishop as she hopped lithely from the water. "Let's see if we can blow up that air mattress."

Bishop jumped out of the water and, slapping Fiona's butt playfully, tore down the tunnel. Fiona chased after him, howling with laughter.

When I turned back, Amelie was out of the water as well. "I'm going to help Fiona, otherwise Bishop's liable to distract her," she said cheerily, leaning down to give me a quick hug before turning to skip down the tunnel and out of sight.

I smiled, wondering what they'd be like if they were surrounded by humans, their primal hunger tested daily. Would Bishop be a loveable, obnoxious goof? Would Fiona be so laid–back? Would Amelie still leap around like a silly girl, throwing her arms around me in affection? And Caden, would he still vanish into the woods to pick me flowers?

Would they feed off humans?

I wondered if we would be friends. That was what they were— friends. My first friends in years, and they were a bunch of vampires. The first guy I couldn't be near without going weak in the knees, and he was a vampire. And I didn't care. Right down to my core, I knew there was no part of me that was bothered by that. I wanted to be with them forever.

But could they be lying about everything? Pretending?

"Go to sleep," Caden whispered, sliding back so I was lying down, my head resting against his lap.

"I'm not tired," I said through another yawn, fighting heavy eyelids.

He smiled down at me, his green eyes twinkling. If only it meant something more than general friendliness.

A delirious giggle escaped me.

"What?" he asked, his brow knitted.

"Nothing," I murmured.

I felt his fingertip trace my upper, then my lower lip. *This can't be innocent. He can't be this oblivious to my feelings. Would he act so flirtatious, knowing?* I started playing the day through in my head—the flowers, the doting, the gentle nudges and touches. Maybe he did have feelings for me?

With every ounce of energy, I held Caden's gaze, trying to read those impenetrable pools of jade. But the pools finally blurred as I lost the battle with my eyelids. I let them rest, reveling under his touch.

☙

I was certain my eyes had closed for only a minute. But when they opened again, daylight peeked in from the cave entrance. A pit full of ash from a night's worth of logs sat beside me, the flames barely flickering anymore. I inhaled and grimaced, the mixture of chill air and stale smoke unpleasant.

I was still on Ratheus. Lying on a mattress. In a sleeping bag.

"It's high quality. The label says 'Good to minus twenty–five degrees Fahrenheit,' so you should be toasty."

I rolled over. Caden lay on his back beside me, one arm supporting his head, *The War of the Worlds* open in his other hand; he still wore the sky blue shirt and jeans he had on earlier. "Imagine, humans being exterminated, their blood devoured, the end of the world. How ridiculous." He smirked.

My heart skipped a few beats. He was lying *so close* to me. Only a hundred layers of flannel, fluff, and a Gortex–like exterior stood in our way. And clothes. My hands roamed my body, feeling flannel and sweats. "Where's my bathing suit?" I asked, feeling my cheeks heat.

"Amelie changed you. Bishop and I were nowhere around," Caden confirmed quickly, his face solemn.

A small sigh of relief. "I'm still here," I said, half question, half statement.

"Yes. Is that a bad thing?" He put the book down and reached over to twist a strand of my hair between his fingers.

"No ..." I smiled shyly.

His finger slipped down my cheekbone to my lips then, that mysterious smile on his face. "No," he repeated, leaning in to press his forehead against mine.

I think my heart stopped beating altogether. Such intensity in his eyes, so tempting...I leaned forward and kissed him. Just like that—no warning, no invitation.

For a second I was sure he was responding, but then he pulled away. "Evangeline, no," he murmured softly. "I didn't mean for that to happen."

Oh God. Oh no! My stomach constricted, nausea swelling through me as I felt the blood drain from my face. I swallowed repeatedly, sure I was going to be sick, the crushing realization that I had misunderstood him overwhelming. Of course he didn't like me *that way*. How could I ever entertain such a ludicrous idea? And now I had ruined it, made everything between us unbearably awkward.

I had to get away.

I started wriggling furiously, trying to work myself out of my sleeping bag. Thanks to a secure zipper pulled to the top, I was trapped. With a little focus and maneuvering, I managed to free my arms, only to have Caden grab them.

"No, don't," he pleaded softly. I struggled in vain to break free of his grasp. He finally pinned me down onto my back and leaned over me so our faces were level.

"I'm sorry, that was stupid. I don't know why I did it." I averted my gaze, fighting the tears that threatened to spill from my eyes.

"No, it's my fault," he whispered.

"No. *I'm* the idiot who misread everything."

"You're not an idiot and you didn't *misread* anything," Caden said through clenched teeth.

I frowned. *I didn't? Does that mean...*Hope stirred. I looked up at him, questioning.

That hope was instantly trampled with his next words. "Listen to me carefully," he began with cold, determined resolve in his eyes now. He spoke slowly and clearly. "It can't happen. You and I *can't* happen. We will *never* happen."

A hard, agonized lump filled my throat. I squeezed my eyes shut and concentrated on breathing. A single tear slipped out and ran down my cheek. Then another. And another. I took a deep breath. When I was sure I'd suppressed any other tears, I opened my eyes. Caden's were now shut tightly, his jaw clenched and his lips pressed together as if fighting an inner demon. He hadn't moved from his position; he still hovered over me, pinning my arms down.

I tried to make sense of what he was saying, but I couldn't. *You didn't misread anything.* So did he feel something for me? But his next words were so definite, so uncompromising: *We will never happen.* I didn't understand. "Why?" I heard myself croak, not intending to ask that out loud. I knew the answer already. *Because you're a plain little girl.*

Caden leaned in, his lips grazing mine, so lightly that it couldn't be intentional. *He didn't mean to do that. It had to be an accident. His eyes were still closed. He couldn't see anything.*

When his eyes finally fluttered open again, I saw the distance in them. "We are two different species, living in two different worlds. It's impossible," he said. With a heavy sigh of resignation, he let go of my wrists and flopped back down beside me to stare vacantly up at the ceiling.

"I'll figure out a way to bring you back," I declared.

"Just me?"

"No...I'll figure out a way to bring you all back. There has to be away."

"Yes, but it'll be too dangerous for you to stand in the same room with me, let alone...anything else."

A strange sensation rippled through me when he said that. Be *with* him, he meant.

Caden sighed, pressing his hand against his forehead.

"Is it Rachel?" I asked quietly, then bit my lower lip.

He began laughing, then groaned. "How could I forget about *her*?" he muttered to himself. He groaned loudly again, running a hand through his hair, sending it into disarray. His face went disturbingly calm as he fell deep into thought for a moment. Finally he turned to looked at me. "Yes, it's Rachel. As long as she and I are together, you and I can't be."

I nodded slowly, rolling onto my back to stare up at the cave ceiling, wanting to be anywhere but there so he wouldn't see me cry. As if hearing my silent pleas, the constant burn of the pendant faded. "I'm leaving now," I announced, my voice hollow. *Back to a house of devious vampires and a back–stabbing dog.*

My head rolled toward Caden for one more look into those beautiful jade eyes. I saw anguish. And then I was gone.

ᘓ

My eyes snapped open. The pain of Caden's rejection still burned hot through my body. That pain was quickly quashed, though, by the sight of my balcony doors hanging haphazardly from their hinges, the glass shattered. I sat up to find the corpse of a large black animal, too mutilated to identify but most certainly dead, lying on the floor, its blood splattering the walls and floor of my perfect white and silver bedroom. The creature had obviously gained entry from the balcony, though I had no idea how, given we were five storeys up and it had no wings.

A deep growl sounded behind me. I turned to see Max facing my bedroom door, hackles raised.

Someone—or something—was on the other side of that door, and it wanted in.

Hide! a deep male voice ordered.

I leapt out of bed and whirled, looking for the source. There was no one in the room but Max and me.

Under the bed!

My eyes darted suspiciously to the curtains, half expecting a tiny old man to pop out from behind them and introduce himself as the Wizard of Oz.

Now! the voice shouted.

It no longer mattered where it was coming from. The warning shot through my paralyzed legs like a lightning bolt, forcing them to move of their own accord before my brain could instruct them. I dove under the bed a split second before the door exploded, splinters of wood flying in every direction.

Ferocious snarling intermingled with the ghastly sounds of tearing flesh and bones snapping like twigs. I heard countless yelps of pain but I couldn't identify the owners. I clenched my fists and gritted my teeth, my fear for Max outweighing that for myself. Even with his betrayal—spying on me for Mortimer—I didn't want him hurt in doing his job to guard me.

From my vantage point, I could only see feet. There were so many of them—gigantic, hairy, black paws with talon–like claws. Max was outnumbered.

A final yelp, then my room fell to dead silence. I remained in my hiding spot, gripped by fear, watching as a set of black paws limped toward me. They stopped at the end of the bed. A big black nose sniffed under the bed. I recoiled as far back as possible.

You're safe now, that male voice—the one who had warned me to hide—whispered. He was obviously in great pain.

The animal by the bed keeled over, its yellow eyes coming level with mine as its chin settled on the floor.

"Max!" I slid out from my hiding place. Five more heaps of flesh and gore like the one that had greeted me lay nearby. I gasped as I saw Max's torn and punctured body; a pool of blood was rapidly forming underneath him. I crumpled to the floor, resting my forehead on his, and wept.

Don't worry. I just need rest, the voice whispered.

I gasped.

16. Telepathy

Yes, it's me you hear.

My eyes bulged. "How?"

Before Max could answer, a commotion erupted in the atrium. Max lifted his head, struggling to stand.

"Stay," I ordered gently as I crept out onto the balcony, the broken glass from the doors crunching beneath my sneakers.

Sofie was shouting at someone. "Why would you do this?"

Leaning over the railing, I spotted the top of Sofie's fiery red head as she squared off against another woman.

"The perfect revenge requires a fair amount of risk," the woman answered coldly. A wave of recognition hit me. I'd heard that bitterness before. It was the young woman from the park. *I thought she was dead!*

"Revenge for what?" Sofie's bewilderment seemed authentic.

"For the worst betrayal," the woman replied acidly.

There was a long pause as Sofie no doubt worked hard to recall where their paths had crossed.

"You're not the only witch who has found a form of immortality," the woman hinted.

Another long pause. Suddenly Sofie gasped in recognition. "Ursula?"

The woman cackled viciously. "You'd be surprised what you can do with host bodies. I've gone through dozens now. It's exhilarating, like shopping for fine furniture. I've tried out every ethnicity...always beautiful, though. And young. Those are my prerequisites. It's a lot of work, but worth it. I've been able to remain alive, year after year, studying you, waiting for the perfect opportunity to punish you. I can't believe I missed the connection between you and the girl all these years. That bloody dog was constantly in the way so I could never get too close."

Old news, Ursula. I knew she was spying on me. Tell me something I don't know. Like how Sofie betrayed you too.

"All of this because of Nathan? I think both he and I were sufficiently punished, don't you?" Grief filled Sofie's voice.

"Nathan was mine and you murdered him!" Ursula ear–piercing shriek startled me.

A chill ran down my spine. With everything else, Sofie was capable of murder.

"He never loved you," Sofie calmly answered, pronouncing every word with slow precision.

"Oh please, save your lies." Ursula turned her head slightly, the only indication that she was aware of Viggo and Mortimer's presence in the shadows. "Those two imbeciles of yours hired me to watch over you five years ago. They wanted to know what kind of magic you were playing with. Of course they didn't know who I really was."

Sofie gasped. "I knew it!" she screeched, her finger pointing accusingly at Viggo.

"I think you've divulged enough information, Ursula," Viggo said, sidestepping to close in on her, Mortimer on the other side.

"Did Sofie tell you that the pendant is a key?" Ursula asked, avoiding Viggo's outstretched hand.

Sofie lunged for Ursula's neck but Mortimer intercepted, holding her back.

"What do you mean?" Viggo said, a sharp undercurrent in his calm voice.

"It's a key. Plug it into the right lock or portal and you'll get whatever you need with it. It's obvious to anyone looking at it, including Sofie."

Mortimer whirled on Sofie, hurling her back to smash through a ground–level French door with the power of his wrath. "What else have you been keeping from us?" he thundered.

Ursula's speckled green eyes darted up to lock with mine for a split second before moving on. The others didn't notice. "I did some digging after I met your girl at the park," she said to the others. "It was interesting...The police report for her mother's death was in your handwriting, Viggo. If you were going to kill her, why didn't you just bite her?"

In one fluid motion, Viggo reached up and snapped Ursula's neck. Her body dropped to the ground, its life extinguished, her last words ringing in my ears as I collapsed to the floor.

17. Murderer

Max limped out to rub his wet nose against my cheek. It barely registered. "Is it true, Max?" I choked out.

Silence.

"Don't go mute now. What do you know?" Max blinked, averting guilty yellow eyes. *He knows something.* "That woman's crazy, right? Viggo never would have killed my mother. There's no way, right?" I pressed, on the verge of hysteria.

I tried to stop it, Max finally answered.

"What?"

Max closed his eyes and sighed—an odd reaction from a dog—and a peculiar thing happened. Images flashed through my mind. At first they were fuzzy and faint, but the clarity strengthened until it was like a movie trailer was playing inside my head.

It was night. Someone walked along a dimly lit sidewalk on a quiet street in drizzling rain, though the person had no umbrella, just a jacket hood. The camera angle in my head shifted to show car lights approaching. There was nothing unusual about it until the car's engine revved. The person's head turned, the headlights illuminating a female face. The face of my mother, as young and beautiful as I remembered her.

The driver suddenly gunned it and swerved, sending the car up onto the sidewalk. I caught the fleeting look of confusion on my mother's face a second before the car struck her.

She didn't have a chance.

I gasped, my hands flying to my throat. So many times I had recreated the accident in my head, but this was a thousand times worse.

And it didn't end there. The car stopped after hitting her. The door opened and the driver stepped out. I couldn't make out a face in the shadows but I recognized that it was a man. He took several long, casual strides over to my mother's motionless body. When he stooped over her lifeless body to dip his fingers in her blood and the headlights shone across his face, I saw a blonde man with piercing blue eyes. And I knew who it was.

Viggo murdered my mother.

I cried out as wounds that had closed but never healed tore open as surely as if it were happening all over again. Only this time the wounds gaped wider than ever before. *But why? Why would they kill my mother? What did Viggo gain?*

The vision blurred, then disappeared altogether. I scrambled to my feet and swayed, barely able to stand upright, then bolted into my room, intent on escaping this prison. Instead I found myself face to face with my mother's murderer.

"Thank goodness you're okay. You were gone four days this time. We were beginning to worry," Viggo said, stepping forward. I recoiled. He chuckled. "Oh, you heard that nonsense? She was a delusional witch. Pay no attention."

"Why?" I quavered. "Why would you—" I couldn't say the words—couldn't get them to form in my head, let alone my mouth. "I saw!" I finally whispered. Mortimer and Sofie had stepped into the room behind him, but I kept my eyes on...the murderer.

"What do you mean, you saw?" Viggo's eyes narrowed, their typical calm morphing into something altogether unfamiliar.

I nodded toward the giant dog, now standing at my side.

"What?" Mortimer's whisper was harsh, and his eyes bulged. "How is that possible?" He turned to Sofie. "How is this possible? Did you do this?"

Sofie's head fell back as she laughed hysterically. "No, but it makes me so happy!"

Mortimer glared at the dog. "You disappeared from my mind, but I thought you were just angry with me! I didn't think you had traded allegiances."

"It doesn't matter," I interjected, forcing bravery. "Why? Why would you do something so …" My eyes burned but no tears came. Even my eye ducts were in shock.

"Monstrous?" A smile flickered over Viggo's lips. "Well, at least we can give up this silly charade. It was becoming quite taxing." His voice, once placid and soothing, had a sinister edge now. Maybe it had always been there, but I'd been deaf to it until now. "I need to move somewhere less...cluttered." Viggo's eyes skimmed over the corpses and destruction in the room. "Sofie, why don't you explain why I felt the need to kill Evangeline's mother? And make sure you explain your part in it."

Sofie was part of this? Of course she was. She's a murderer. Ursula confirmed it. My stomach twisted, all the same.

"Do I tell her the truth, or your version of it?" Sofie retorted bitterly.

Viggo responded with a wicked chuckle. "Do you even remember what the truth is anymore?" With that, he vanished, Mortimer in tow.

"Let's get out of here," Sofie said quietly.

I nodded, not because I wanted to go anywhere with Sofie, but I needed to get away from this death zone. I zeroed in on the hallway beyond the door, not allowing my eyes to wander for even a second as we maneuvered around the blood and gore.

We went to the library. "Where to begin," Sofie said, settling on the leather couch. She folded her hands in her lap and stared at them, lost in thought.

"How about explaining why you've been watching me my entire life," I snapped, drawing her emotionless, pale green stare to my face, "and why you cursed me. And about my mother's death." Once the questions began, they spilled out like an overturned jar of beans, scattering uncontrollably. "This crazy Ursula woman, who was she? And Nathan, the guy you murdered?"

My last question sparked a reaction. Sofie's pale eyes displayed raw pain. I had struck a cord.

"Nathan is the vampire who turned me," she answered quietly, then exhaled as if to compose herself before launching into a long explanation. But then she was up and pacing around the room, nervously chewing on her thumbnail. I wasn't used to this side of Sofie—anxious, uncertain. I watched in silence, intrigued.

"Nathan and I were desperately, madly, irrevocably in love," she began, running one of her slender hands through her silky red hair, a waver in her voice. "You should have seen him, Evangeline. He was the inspiration behind the tall, dark, and handsome cliché. Gorgeous. I remember the moment I first laid eyes on him. It was 1887. I was sure my chest would swallow itself whole." She dropped her hand to her side. "Anyway, Nathan was a vampire and I was a witch and our kinds abhor one another, which made our relationship tricky, to say the least. Like the Montague and the Capulet families in *Romeo and Juliet*."

So now you're trying to compare yourself to the greatest love story of all time? I wanted to snort.

Sofie smirked. "Maybe not as enchanting, but definitely as heart–wrenchingly impossible."

Ugh, I forgot—she could read me like an open book.

"We wanted to spend the rest of our lives together and, for Nathan, that meant eternity. Now, that was trickier. You see, witches, if exposed to a vampire's venom, will simply die. Every single time. We can't survive the transition. I don't know why; it's in the genes, I suppose. Anyway, naïve and ambitious as I was, I was bound and determined to figure out a spell around this certain death. I knew I was a uniquely gifted sorceress and I was arrogant enough to believe I could solve what others had been unable to. I *did* solve it …" Her eyes sparkled with excitement that was extinguished almost instantly. "Or I thought I did. Never once did I imagine such terrible consequences."

Sofie paused long enough to sit down in the leather chair. "Nathan was such a fool. He fully trusted me. I told him to bite me, to inject me with venom, and he did. When I woke up, I was immortal. I knew it instantly. I could feel the overwhelming power coursing through my veins. It was exhilarating." Sofie sighed sadly. When she continued, her voice was thick with torment. "I found Nathan's lifeless body lying beside me. The spell had reversed the consequences. It killed *him*. *I* killed him."

She'd cast the spell for love. Not for selfish, foolish gains, as Mortimer had said. He had lied as well.

"I killed my soul mate, Evangeline. And I would have jumped into a flaming pit, had it not been for Veronique." Sofie was out of her chair again and standing in front of the mantel in the blink of an eye, smiling adoringly at the painting of the dark–haired beauty. "Veronique was my younger sister." Her voice fell, grew distant. "She was normal...Not a witch, I mean. The sorceress's gene skipped her. She was always so supportive of my love for Nathan, for a vampire. The *only* supportive one. That's because she understood implicitly. She was madly in love with not one, but two of them—one named Mortimer and the other named Viggo."

I thought my eyes were going to pop out of their sockets.

Sofie turned to me and chuckled. "Yes, my silly, sweet sister saw something in both of them. Outrageous, isn't it? Veronique was waiting to decide between the two before transforming to spend eternity with them." She swallowed hard, looking down at the floor. "When I cast my spell, it destroyed that possibility for her. Mortimer felt the change immediately. He described it as the only life force within him, drained. Later we learned that every vampire felt something strange happen. They soon discovered that their venom was rendered useless. It was an unexpected outcome of the spell. Things like that can happen.

"In my attempt at eternal love and life, I destroyed any chance Veronique had of the same. As inconsolable as I was after Nathan's death, I couldn't leave my sister like that, to suffer and die alone. And no other witch would ever dream of helping her, even if they could."

Intrigue overshadowed my anger with Sofie for the moment. "But you said that was a hundred and twenty years ago. So...Veronique died?"

Sofie shook her head. "I knew it could take years to fix my error and there was no way to reverse it because of the nature of the spell. As I told you before, once these types of spells are cast, they can't be undone. Veronique didn't want to get old and gray, waiting, so we decided to 'preserve' her and place her somewhere where she could safely wait."

"Where?" I whispered, picturing an underground tomb or coffin of sorts, dark and dusty and morbid.

"You've passed her many times, even admired her." Sofie smiled secretively. She watched intently as I tried to decipher her riddle. When I frowned, shrugging in a sign of concession, she prompted, "In the atrium...?"

The atrium...I gasped. "The statue! You turned your sister into stone?"

"No!" Sofie laughed. "She's *inside* it. Entombed—like a mummy, only without all the white gauze."

I shuddered involuntarily, shocked at the realization that an actual person was trapped inside. But it suddenly made sense. "That's why Mortimer and Viggo spend so much time there."

She snorted. "It's not for their love of fine art, believe me."

"So she's alive in there?" I whispered.

"Sort of. She's basically frozen, her mind in a coma, her body not aging. Once you bring a vampire back with you, I can release her and she can be transformed and live happily ever after with whichever of those two urchins she sees fit to choose."

"Which one will she choose?" I wondered aloud.

"Good question." Sofie leaned back in her chair. "It'll spell disaster for the other one, surely. I want to be as far away from them as possible when that happens."

"They're not your friends, are they? Viggo and Mortimer, I mean. The fighting...it isn't an act."

Sofie smiled. "We tolerated each other until five years ago. The night Viggo killed your mother."

"Why did he—" I couldn't finish the sentence. Renewed agony stabbed through my heart.

She cringed, sensing my pain. "Because I kept you secret," Sofie admitted reluctantly, shutting her eyes. "I cast that Causal Enchantment one hundred and twenty years ago, Evangeline. We waited for the fates to respond, to provide us with the solution. Then one day, eighteen years ago, the answer flooded into my mind. The spell had affixed itself to a newborn baby." Her eyes popped open. "You."

A cold chill slid through my body.

"The spell had set all kinds of rules and boundaries, specific things that couldn't happen or the spell would corrupt itself. You couldn't know about the existence of vampires before the night of your eighteenth birthday; you couldn't be compelled—ever. And you had to wear that necklace and touch the statue of your own free will. All kinds of stupid rules."

She spread her arms, the movement like an unconscious plea. "I never chose a human to bear the brunt of this, Evangeline. Believe me. Your name, your birth date, where you lived...it was all decided already. Please believe me, I didn't intend any of this for you...Anyway, I kept it from Viggo and Mortimer. For years, they didn't know the fates had responded, that the spell was finished. Max kept you secret too." Sofie turned to gaze adoringly at Max, all signs of hatred gone.

"When I suddenly moved to Portland—not exactly the mecca for urban life—Mortimer sent Max there to *protect* me." Sofie rolled her eyes, snorting. "I wasn't stupid. I knew why he was there. It was a cover, of course; he was to keep tabs on me and report back. But I discovered he was feeding lies to Mortimer about basic things that I was doing. It was his way of telling me he was on my side. It's shocking, really, that a werebeast would disobey its master like that. I didn't know why, but I thanked the heavens every day. Eventually I revealed you to Max and we watched over you, trying to protect you while you grew up normally. While I tried to break the spell."

"What happened, then?"

Sofie paused, swallowing. "They found out...Mortimer somehow forced an answer out of Max and they learned of you. Viggo swooped in, ready to kidnap and imprison you. Exactly what I expected would happen.

So I explained why he couldn't—all of the rules. Viggo was furious that I had kept you secret for thirteen years, but he wasn't willing to risk breaking the spell; he decided it was best you had no bonds in the human world. So he killed your mother."

I flinched at her words; they may as well have been a solid punch to my stomach.

"And then he promised that anyone else who got close to you would die. He wasn't bluffing. So I spent the next five years compelling everyone to stay away—your foster families, your friends, the boys at school—everyone. I didn't want you surrounded by death."

"Is that why ..." My whisper faded to nothing. *It wasn't me after all?*

"There's nothing wrong with you, Evangeline," Sofie confirmed, her expression sorrowful.

My whole life had been staged, controlled by vampire puppet–masters on a quest to fulfill their love for their entombed one hundred and twenty–year– old girlfriend and sister. "Why keep this story of Veronique a secret?" I asked, adding bitterly, "Viggo could have told me the other night, while he was painting himself as a martyr."

She sighed. "Because Viggo thinks you'll default to trusting him if you hate me. Plus they've sworn me to secrecy in all things Veronique–related, on penalty of injury to you."

"But...*why*?" I was beginning to sound like a broken record.

"They're terrified of someone finding out about her who could cause her harm."

"She's encased in marble and magic!" I exclaimed.

Sofie chuckled. "When you're madly in love, you don't act rationally. Like Ursula."

I had forgotten about her until now. "How is she involved in all this? She was at the park, you know."

"Besides being the witch that those two twits hired to spy on me? They don't trust me." Smiling sheepishly, she added, "With good reason, I guess." She began massaging her temple with her hand. "Ursula is the classic example of a woman scorned, only she's a witch so the fury is tenfold. She fell in love with Nathan and ensnared him in a love spell to ensure his mutual affection. She's not pleasant, in case you hadn't noticed. Well, sorceress spells don't work well on vampires. Nathan realized what was going on, in effect rendering the spell obsolete. He would have killed her if she hadn't been so pathetic. He had a compassionate streak in him." She smiled wistfully. "One of the reasons I loved him so. Anyway, not long after that, he and I met. It was love at first sight. Ursula was bitter, believing that, if I had not 'moved in on her territory,' he would have forgiven her and fallen madly in love of his own accord."

"But that was over a hundred years ago. Are witches immortal too?" I asked, recalling her mentioning something about host bodies but not understanding this hocus–pocus stuff.

Sofie shook her head. "It appears she found a way to jump from one human to the next, taking possession of them for her own form of immortality. She's clever. That's why I didn't recognize her. When Viggo and Mortimer discovered Max's betrayal, it seems they decided to hire a spy as another source of intel. I had sensed a witch from time to time near me but I never put the two together." She smirked contemptuously. "I just thought I had a fan."

My head was spinning by now, trying to keep track of all the different ways they had deceived each other. There was small comfort in the fact that I wasn't the only victim. "But Ursula's dead now, right? Viggo killed her?"

Sofie shook her head. "I'm afraid that's not the last we'll see of Ursula in one form or another. I'm not exactly sure how she possesses her host bodies, but it must use up a lot of her powers. Don't worry. She won't get through these gates a second time, now that those two half–wits know not to invite her and her conjured leopards in."

I nodded, working to digest everything. "Is there anything else you need to tell me?" I asked, my eyes studying Sofie's eyes for any signs of a lie.

She met my gaze steadily. "Everything I've told you is the truth. I swear it. On Nathan's grave."

Does that mean anything, considering she killed him? I wondered. It didn't matter. I decided she was now the least harmful snake in the pit of vipers.

Her and Max.

We sat in silence for awhile. Max came over and hunkered down, resting his chin on my lap to look up at me with soulful golden eyes. I looked from him to Sofie. "How am I hearing Max?"

Sofie shrugged. "I don't know, but...you have no idea how pleased I am!" A goofy grin overwhelmed her face.

"Mortimer said something about him lying to him?"

"Yup! He's been making up things and leaving out details since you've come here. And after you snuck off to the park, he just stopped talking to Mortimer altogether." The broad smile was still plastered on her face. "I guess all those years of spying on you made him fall in love."

She talks too much, Max interrupted inside my head, his irritation evident.

I couldn't help giggling, even given the bizarre method of communication. I hadn't been wrong about Max's friendship, after all. *One* genuine thing around here, at least. Patting Max's head once, I stood up and walked over to Veronique's picture to study the catalyst of my curse. Gazing up at those olive green eyes, I searched my feelings for resentment, but found none. Rationally, I knew this was no more her fault than being cursed was mine. Or even Sofie's.

"What a devastatingly beautiful woman," a relaxed male voice suddenly said from beside me. Viggo, sliding in unseen like a ghost, as casual as ever. As if he hadn't murdered my mother.

I instinctively assumed a defensive stance, my hands balling up into tight fists. A soft, wicked chuckle escaped him, one that sent a shiver down my back. My anger morphed instantly into fear. He was a monster.

"I met Veronique at the Emperor's Royal Ball. I watched her glide down the O'Hara staircase with the purity of an angel, wearing this very dress. I knew I had to have her."

"And she settled for you until she found something better," Mortimer chimed in, appearing from a corner, an edge of competitiveness in his voice.

I stood quietly, wondering what their new angle was.

Viggo rolled his eyes. "One evening, Veronique was traveling to meet

Sofie in the next city when a group of bandits attacked her carriage. They would have raped and killed her, if not for the aid of Mortimer here, who happened to be hunting in the nearby woods. I owed Mortimer for saving my true love and, so confident in her love for me, I never thought my lovely angel would fall prey to this rugged brute's wiles. Alas, Mortimer and Veronique grew close and, before I knew it, she was professing her love to both of us. We became bitter enemies, ready to tear each other apart, except that it would cause pain to Veronique for one of us to die. So we waited, impatiently, for her to choose—me, of course—so I could transform her and have her forever. But then her witch of a sister had to go and mess things up!" Viggo said lightheartedly.

"Why are you telling me this?" I asked bitterly. "You didn't want to tell me anything before and now you're just brimming with true–life stories."

"To show you that we're just like you!"

My mouth dropped open in shock. "You murdered my mother and destroyed my life. You probably snack on newborn babies! You're nothing like me! And you're trying to win me over with epic love stories, thinking I'm going to help you?" I trembled with rage now.

He quirked a brow. "Are you saying you're not?"

"Help my mother's murderer spend eternity with his true love? Hmm, let me see ..." Uncharacteristic bravery was yanking words from my mouth before my brain could process them. But I didn't care. I couldn't hurt Viggo's feelings if I tried.

"Well, then...there's no reason to keep you anymore, is there?" Viggo's eyes had turned cold, his smile menacing.

All four dogs leapt forward to form a wall around me, but not before Viggo had my pendant within his grasp. "You may tear my heart out, Max, but not before I rip this pendant from Evangeline's neck," he said, his eyes locked with mine.

18. Choices

"Viggo," Mortimer warned, a wary eye on the dogs. He still seemed flabbergasted by Max's new allegiance to me.

Viggo ignored him, standing fast with my pendant in his hand, hysteria twitching on his face. "You are going to help us because you want to help yourself. You're going to bring these friends of yours back, right?"

I stood frozen. *Caden. Amelie. Fiona. Bishop.* Their faces flashed in my mind.

"You're going to go out and look for this portal for the pendant," he continued. "Check every rock, every cave, every city."

"The place is crawling with vampires. I'm dead if they get hold of me," I replied warily.

"You're dead if I get hold of you." Viggo's lips curled into a hideous smile.

A chorus of deep, menacing growls sounded but no one paid any heed.

"How many vampires are left on this Ratheus, anyway?" Mortimer interjected.

"I don't know. I don't think there's been a census done lately," I answered sullenly, my eyes glued to Viggo. *Murderer.*

"My, someone's finally found her tongue. When did you become so grating?" Viggo asked with an infuriating smirk.

"When I found out you murdered my mother."

"Didn't you explain, Sofie?" Viggo's eyebrows lifted, but his focus remained on me. "That was Sofie's fault. She deceived me." The gleam in his eye turned my blood ice cold. "Don't ever deceive me."

"You want to be free of us, don't you?" Mortimer added, a hint of desperation in his voice.

I faltered. "And will I? Be free of you once I bring them back?"

"Absolutely."

I don't believe you. But it didn't matter. Either I refused and Viggo wrenched the necklace off me right here, right now, leaving Caden and the others in Ratheus for eternity, forever beyond my sight, or I risked dying by going along with this. Highly probable risk but just a risk, all the same.

"So you want me to just wander around until the necklace starts talking to me? What if I get caught? So far, the two run-ins I've had with the vampires of that world haven't exactly ended well. Remember? I almost died both times."

"But that was before. You are so much wiser now, and the necklace has properly adjusted. I'm sure you'll do just fine," Viggo assured me, smiling. He stepped away, releasing the pendant. "So it's settled?"

If I release Veronique and she chooses Mortimer, then this will be worth it. "I'm glad you're feeling good about this plan, given you're not the one who's going to die," I grumbled. "And if I die then this whole plan is finished and you have no hope of ever turning Veronique."

Mortimer raised an eyebrow at Sofie.

She sighed. "If the lapse in time continues as it's been going, with you staying longer and longer away from here...I'm afraid you'll one day—soon—simply not return. Then it won't matter. You can't survive long in a place like that."

"That's why I was hungry...and tired," I thought aloud. It also explained all the supplies for me that Sofie had packed. *She had known it would happen. That or she took the 'be-prepared' Girl Scout Motto to a whole new level.* "So every time I go over now, I'll be there for longer and longer and eventually I'll stay there forever?"

Sofie nodded.

Would that be so bad? I wouldn't have to help my mother's murderer find true love. And I could stay with Caden, Amelie, Fiona, and Bishop. In a cave, with no electricity, no running water, no food.

Four vampires and one human, living together in harmony. No, five vampires. Ugh. Unless this Rachel thing ended and she went back to whatever crypt she belonged in. Who was I fooling? She wouldn't go anywhere. Not before she tore the flesh right from my bones as I watched, screaming.

There would always be the constant threat of death. No, not threat. *Inevitability.* Even if I evaded death by Rachel or some other vampire, it would catch up to me eventually with age. A vivid image popped into my head then—a wrinkled old woman in a black string bikini struggling to shuffle into a hot spring lake, watched with disgust and pity by four young, beautiful vampires. It made me shudder. That'd be worse than dying.

Unless …

"What would happen to the necklace if I stayed there forever? Would it keep protecting me? Like, from their venom?" I asked Sofie. *Could I be...turned?* The very idea made my skin crawl, but I had to know.

Her eyes flashed knowingly. "It could keep working, not realizing that you can't return to Earth anymore. That, or kill you. Which one it will be...it's a toss–up."

Old or dead. I sighed. Well, that ended that idea. I could handle the caveman life if it meant spending it young and with Caden, but the alternatives—old and wrinkly or with Rachel—were unthinkable.

So that left me helping the vampire who'd murdered my mother or letting him kill me. *Could I get away? Could I bring them all over then escape?* Hope sparked for only a millisecond; he'd hunt me down. I'd spend the rest of my life being the prey of a desperate two thousand–year–old vampire. "The rest of my life" would prove much shorter than expected.

I swallowed the painful lump in my throat. "Okay."

"Okay?" Viggo's brow rose incredulously.

I nodded.

"Fabulous!" That deceptively charming smile was back. I saw through it now, though.

"Is there anything you need?" Sofie asked softly, sadness in her eyes. "I can go pick up some supplies."

I hesitated. "A wet suit." Viggo and Mortimer looked at me suspiciously. "In case this portal is underwater," I quickly added. Or in the cave with the Merth, which was exactly where I was headed. I was going to bring back as much Merth as possible so I could wrap myself in it.

CR

Hello, Max's deep voice boomed clearly in my head.

My eyes widened.

Still not ready?

"No, I'm not ready to hear voices in my head. I'll never be ready to hear voices. But that won't change anything, will it?" I muttered bitterly, turning onto my back in bed to stare up at the ceiling. So I was having a conversation with a dog. So what? Plenty of people talk to animals.

Leo had moved my things—whatever hadn't been damaged—into another suite. The furnishings were similar here to those in my previous room, but the magical vibe was gone. *The Bloody Quarters,* I mused, my eyes scanning the rich red walls and fabrics. If those giant leopards had been massacred in here, the carnage would have blended in nicely.

I reached over and touched one of Max's massive paws. "How can I hear you?"

Because you're my master now.

"What does that even mean? How am I your master?"

I don't know. It just happened. Mortimer used to be my master and now you are.

"And how do I talk to you in my head? You know, telepathically?"

You can't. I don't know why, but it's only one-way communication.

I nodded, somehow disappointed with the limitation. "Sofie said you watched over me?"

Yes.

I brightened with an idea. "You need to show me what you saw, Max," I urged. "You have to if I'm your master and I order you, right?"

I heard a loud groan of annoyance. *You're sounding like Mortimer already.*

"Oh...sorry Max." I smiled sheepishly. "But it's important."

What would you like to see?

I thought for a moment. "My mother? Before ..." *Before she was murdered.* "I need to get that image out of my head. Please Max."

That picture show began in my head again. This time I was looking through a window at a girl of maybe five, her long blond pigtails tied with peacock blue satin bows, sitting on a stool in a small kitchen. She was savoring a batter–covered beater as if chocolate was the most heavenly taste ever created. A blonde woman, her back to the girl, was loading a tray of cupcakes into the oven to bake. She turned, offering a dimpled smile and a laugh to the little girl.

My mother.

Warmth warred with stabbing pain in my chest. My memory hadn't done her justice. I had forgotten how beautiful she was, with her shoulder–length, sandy blonde hair and infectious smile. Even at a young age, I'd noticed how she turned heads. But it wasn't just her looks. She also had that charismatic, clever personality that won people over in seconds. The room would light up when she walked in. At least for me, it always did.

Images began flashing in my mind again. Faces...faces I recognized as those in the foster homes I had moved through in my youth. Mrs. Boulding, the Avon lady. Mr. Billsbury, the drunk. Mrs. Clairmont, the evangelical loon. The Darlings. They had been relatively normal ...

The images went on and on, a candid viewing of my transient life until it stopped with the image of me stumbling in front of Newt's Brew. Watching the scene from Max's point of view, I saw Sofie's pricey lantern fall over and smash without ever coming into contact with my leg.

Magic. It had all been staged. A chill swept over me.

But that wasn't the most unsettling discovery in all of this. "How did I not see you?"

I didn't want to be seen, Max said matter–of–factly.

Of course. A three hundred pound dog lurking in my apartment and prowling the streets after me, and my Spidey–senses never kicked in. But Eddie, the crazy homeless guy, had seen him.

"How often were you watching me?"

There was a long pause. *You were never alone.*

The sudden urge to vomit hit me like a tidal wave. I bolted to the washroom. After several minutes of staring at the white porcelain toilet bowl—nothing was coming up, it was just my nerves—I gave up and stumbled back with the awful knowledge that there had been a pair of eyes on me for my *entire life*, and I had never suspected it.

"Max, show me everything you remember," I demanded.

I remember everything.

"Okay, the important things."

I lay down on the bed, my eyes staring at the ceiling without seeing it, getting a play–by–play of my childhood through the eyes of a dog. Some memories were specific, like the Halloween I dressed in a penguin costume—my mother's favorite animal—and waddled out the front door, only to fall flat on my face and give myself a bloody nose because the costume bound my feet together too tightly. Other images were vague—me, sitting in my room, crying quietly as I clutched a framed picture of my mother. I had done that often in the early days.

Max showed me another flash then, one that didn't require a replay for me to remember every second. I had just turned thirteen and was at home watching reruns on television, what I normally did while waiting for my mom to get home from work. The doorbell rang. *Is your father home?* a policeman asked when I opened the door. I shook my head. *Do you have any family you can call?* I shook my head, frowning, wondering what was going on. The female police officer smiled gently and asked me to wait a second while she called someone on her radio. Child Services showed up not long after, sending me to my room to pack a bag of things.

That was the night Viggo murdered my mother.

The images stopped.

"How are you doing this?" I asked Max.

I just can.

"Show me more, then. Show me everything."

He obliged.

Me, studying alone in the library for hours. Me, alone and leaning against a chain link fence after school, reading a book as all the other kids hung out together. Me, alone in a park, swinging so high that I looked ready to sail off. Me, always alone.

Bitterness swelled. Of course I was alone. Viggo had made sure of it. What would my life have been like without this blasted curse?

◌

I stared vacantly at Sofie as she walked into the room, another mountain bag slung over one shoulder as if it were filled with cotton balls.

She has your best interests at heart, Max said.

"How do you know that?" I answered.

Sofie looked up at me, frowning. I shook my head dismissively. "Oh." She smiled, glancing over at the dog sprawled on the king–sized bed. "Ready to go? It's time to strap you in."

With everything that had transpired—the attack, learning the devastating truth about my mother and my life—I hadn't had a second to think about Ratheus...about Caden's rejection. It seemed so trivial now, yet my stomach tightened all the same, a wave of nausea draining my face of blood.

But, in the end, it wasn't trivial. Hope that Caden might feel something for me, that I could save him and the others from their isolation, was all I had left. I had lost everything else because of this curse. Something good had to come of it.

Was there *something* more than friendship there? His words had been so contradictory. Was I reading too much into them, hearing what I wanted to hear—what I needed to hear? There *had* to be some twisted reason that had brought him—a sweet, kind, gorgeous, down–to–earth creature—together with the anti–Christ, Rachel.

I dragged myself off the bed to sit in front of the bag.

"Great," Sofie said cheerfully, affixing the straps.

I frowned at her. She was way too cheery.

Viggo's listening, Max said. *They think she's keeping secrets from them. They don't trust her.*

"Wonder why," I grumbled. Sofie glanced up, shushing me with her finger.

Sofie wants me to tell you to stay put. Don't go looking for the portal.

"But what if—" Sofie's hand clamped over my mouth, accompanied by a severe glare of caution.

You'll never find it and you'll just be putting yourself in danger. It will find you.

My mouth opened to speak but snapped shut when Sofie's mint eyes flashed with another stern warning. Did that mean she knew where it was? I nodded once, my eyes darting suspiciously between the two of them. Did Sofie ask Max to relay the message earlier, or could they also communicate? I was dying to ask, but I couldn't. I'd ask Max later. I had something more important to ask.

"Sofie?" I said, hesitant. "Do you think there's any way I can bring more than one of them back?"

"I wish I could say yes or no," she murmured. "There's a chance, though...There. One done." Her hands moved to the next strap. "You've really taken to them, haven't you?"

"No," I lied. Viggo didn't need another way to hurt me. I caught Sofie's knowing smile. "It just seems cruel to bring one back and leave the rest there."

"Yes. It would be," she agreed. "Let's hope you don't have to make that choice. Either way, I wouldn't mention that part to them. For your sake."

I listened to the clock ticking as Sofie finished buckling me in.

Sofie opened her mouth to speak, then hesitated. "I know they're your friends," she began, "but please be careful. You're such a trusting girl, Evangeline."

Desperately gullible. That's what I was.

CR

Fiona had a torch burning within seconds of my arrival. "Let me help you with that!" She started on the straps of my backpack.

"It's so good to see you," I exclaimed, smiling with genuine happiness.

It vanished the second I saw jet black hair in my peripheral vision. My body went rigid, a prickly sensation filling my lungs. Rachel was back. And wearing an outfit Sofie had purchased for her. "Hi Rachel." I held my breath and forced a smile, hoping it looked authentic.

She looked at me like a snake studying a mouse it was seriously considering for dinner. *Did Caden mention to her that I threw myself at him? No, I'd already be dead.*

I heard myself exhale, all fear of Rachel vanishing as Caden walked in. My heart practically leapt out of my chest and a big, dumb grin that I couldn't control stretched my face. I was filled with a volatile mixture of anxiety and excitement. All I needed was that returning smile, a glint in his intense jade eyes that would tell me all was okay. That *we* were okay.

His eyes skimmed over my face—no smile, no wink, no sign that he even recognized me—before he strolled over to Rachel. He wrapped his arms adoringly around her, nuzzling into her thick mane of black hair, whatever aversion to public affection he had before clearly gone.

My smile slid off my face.

"What did you bring us?" Rachel asked, her cool lemon eyes passing over me, giving me chills.

"I...Stuff," I mumbled.

"You're back!" Amelie exclaimed, suddenly appearing to skip over and give me a big hug.

I nodded, unable to form words.

"Did you bring blood?" Rachel's eyebrow arched severely.

"Are you nuts? No! She's not bringing us human blood," Fiona snapped, her normally placid face showing rare annoyance. She untied the strings and knots and began pulling items out of the bag.

"Boots!" Amelie cried in delight, hoisting a pair of brown leather riding boots. Fiona had a matching pair. There was a third set for Rachel. I wanted to burn those.

"Mine!" Bishop shouted, startling me, as an acoustic guitar appeared. I had barely noticed him stroll in, even when he stopped to ruffle my hair. Seeing his genuine pleasure, I felt a tiny ball of warmth swell in the pit of my twisting stomach. Sofie had listened to every word I'd ever said about them.

"Check it out!" Bishop tossed the instrument to Caden, who caught it with one hand. Letting go of Rachel, he strummed the first few notes of some song.

"You play too?" I asked, giving him a chance to acknowledge me.

"Of course I do." His voice was detached and cool, his expression remote, his eyes not leaving the guitar strings as he spoke. He may as well have smashed me over the head with the instrument.

"Stupid girl," Rachel mocked, laughing at my wounded expression.

"Show us how to turn this on." Fiona shoved a portable DVD player in my face, forcing my attention to her. It gave me a chance to hide the pain on my face. She grabbed my hand and squeezed it. Sympathy. Caden must have told them.

"Oh, this...for movies," I stammered. "There's a bunch of battery packs as well, to keep it running."

"Are any of them good?" Amelie interjected, holding up a collection of DVDs.

They were trying to distract me, to keep my mind preoccupied. A very considerate, if useless, act. "Um, yeah. I mean, no. I mean—" I couldn't think straight. "I don't know."

"Has she always been so stupid, or is this new?" Rachel said to Caden, loud enough for me to hear.

"I know. The witch could have looked a little harder," Caden responded, reaching out to grab her hand and pull her into an affectionate embrace.

It was a razor-sharp verbal stab. I dropped my gaze to my hands, salty tears welling in my eyes. I couldn't take much more of this.

Fiona's hand grasped mine again and squeezed as Rachel giggled wickedly, likely pitying me. I dared one more glance at Caden, one more gaze at that beautiful face before I accepted the instant and horrible demise of my fantasy and moved my focus to the dark reality of my situation: my death if I didn't find the secret of this spell.

My eyes crawled up along Rachel's back, over Caden's arms, still wrapped lovingly around her, to his perfect face. To see his eyes glued to me, a strange look in them. *What is that look...pity? No, pleading. But for what, exactly?*

Rachel's hand massaged Caden's chest and abdomen seductively, her fingers curling into claws that raked over him hard enough to leave impressions in his shirt. I shut my eyes, a mixture of revulsion and anger flaring, though I knew I had no right. He wasn't mine. He was Rachel's, as ghastly a proposition as that was. She could do whatever she wanted with him—to him. But telling myself that did nothing to ease the pain of the knife being twisted in my heart.

I opened my eyes. Rachel's face was now burrowed in Caden's neck, her attention otherwise occupied. I glanced up at Caden's face again to see that same pleading look, only more intense. *I'm sorry,* he mouthed slowly.

My eyes went wide in surprise. Sorry for what? For morphing from sweet and affectionate to exhibitionist asshole?

Amelie loudly cleared her throat. I turned to look at her. She stared hard at me, as if sending me a message telepathically. *I'm not your pet, Amelie! I don't know what you're trying to tell me!*

Something very strange was happening here and I hated it. I wanted the last trip back, with its laughter, its ease. Its time with Caden. No Rachel. If only there was some way to make her go away again …

"Sofie says I can bring you back with me," I suddenly blurted without thinking.

Everyone's eyes bugged out, Caden's in horror.

A plan was forming in my head. My own web of deceit. The very idea of lying to Amelie, Fiona, and Bishop made me ill but I had no other choice. I needed Rachel gone. I'd explain afterward. "Sofie thinks the answer is somewhere out there and someone needs to go looking for it," I continued, my voice trembling.

"What the hell does *that* mean?" Rachel's face screwed up.

"Well …" *Think fast, Evangeline, or she's going to see right through your sloppy efforts!* "You know how the statue just appeared, out of nowhere? Sofie's spell put it there. To create a point of origin. But something else also appeared. A portal for my necklace. It will tell me how to bring you back with me." *Not you though, Rachel.*

"She's lying to you," Caden said, throwing a panicked glare in my direction.

I ignored him. "It could be a scroll, a book, another statue. Whatever it is, you'll know. It won't look seven hundred years old."

"Where do we start?" Amelie leapt onto her feet, her typically animated personality in overdrive.

Rachel was more wary. "It could take years to find it, if at all!"

"No. It wants to be found." *By you, Rachel. Go fetch.* "Sofie thinks it's either in the mountains or in a city. Somewhere still inhabited, where someone who was familiar with the city could find it." *Like you.*

"The only city left is New Shore," Fiona began.

"Hey, isn't that where you went, Rachel?" I asked innocently. "You know it really well, don't you?"

"Yes, but there's nothing like what you're talking about there." She bit her lower lip. "I'll have to do some searching …"

I have her.

"Maybe I'll go look around during my trip there next week."

No, it has to be today. This instant! I silently screamed, my thumbs squeezed so tightly within my fists that I thought I might break them. "That's a problem …" I said, pausing to formulate my next lie. "Sofie said that we're running out of time. I only have a few more trips before the spell wears off."

"Oh my God! We better start looking!" Amelie exclaimed. "Come on! Let's go! I'll take the north mountain, you take the south, Fiona," she rambled.

"We can go to New Shore," Rachel said, her arm around Caden.

No, not 'we'! Just you! I reached over to grab Fiona's hand, squeezing hard, wishing I could take a time–out and explain everything.

"What about using Scout and the others to search?" Fiona said. She hadn't picked up on my panic. I wanted to cry.

"Of course! Great idea, babe!" Bishop cried, kissing Fiona.

No, no, no! This plan wasn't going how I wanted it.

"Of course Caden is connected to half of our guard around here, so he needs to be here to communicate," Fiona said slowly.

My panic escaped through my mouth in a long sigh. I glanced over at Fiona, who winked at me. She understood. I fought the urge to hug her, silently begging her forgiveness for lying.

"But, I just got back!" Rachel scoffed, a horrified expression on her face. "We've barely seen each other!"

"Fiona's right," Caden said, taking Rachel's hands in his and staring into her eyes. If he was indeed feigning great disappointment at the idea of being apart, his acting skills were impressive. Rachel began shaking her head in response. "We need all the help we can get in these mountains and the valleys." He cupped her chin. "Plus, as long as Evangeline is here, we should have as many of us as possible around for protection. You know New Shore best, out of anyone. And you'll have no problems searching it, being part of the Council. No one will question you."

Rachel's bottom lip curved down in a childish pout.

"Think of this new world...human blood," he whispered.

I could see the uncontainable lust flash in her eyes with the mention of human blood. Her dangling carrot. That Caden had previously renounced the act of killing humans didn't phase her. "Fine. I'll be back as soon as I can." With one obscenely long, mauling kiss for Caden—one that I didn't watch, instead locking eyes with Fiona—Rachel vanished.

I exhaled slowly, covering my overjoyed smile within folded hands in the small chance that it may be inappropriate. The ball of anxiety over Caden still sat prominently in my stomach but at least now I'd have a chance to find out what the hell was going on.

"Let's do this!" Bishop announced.

"Wait." Fiona's eyes narrowed, communicating silently with him, nodding toward the cave entrance. With a slight frown of concern, he nodded and walked over to stand by the entrance, staring out into nothingness—listening or smelling, I assumed.

We sat silently, waiting for Bishop's sanction. My eyes flitted over to Caden to catch him staring at me, expressionless. His eyes dropped.

"And she's gone! Crossed over the first mountain," Bishop announced in a booming voice.

I had to figure out how to do that with Max, I promised myself.

"Okay Evangeline, what's going on?" Fiona asked.

At the same time Caden yelled, "I told you not to say anything!"

"Don't get mad, everyone," I said, my hands out in a sign of peace. I had just lied to a group of vampires about the one thing they desperately wanted. The gravity of that began to sink in.

Amelie, Bishop, and Fiona's eyes darted between Caden and me. "You knew about this?" Amelie's raspy voice was full of shock.

I took a deep breath. "I lied," I began. She turned, her angelic face crestfallen, the brightness in her eyes fading. "Not about taking you back!" I quickly added. "Before, when I told you that I couldn't take you back, I lied."

"So you can?" Amelie's emerald eyes began glowing eagerly again.

"Sort of …" My eyes darted to Caden, looking for help. He turned away, jaw clenched and eyes closed.

"Well, which is it?" Amelie cried in frustration.

"That's the tricky part. I don't know exactly how to do it."

"So all that stuff about the portal was a lie?" Bishop said slowly and evenly.

"No! That was true! Sofie said there's no use in looking for it, though. We'll never find it that way, she said. But...there's more." I paused, dreading this part. "I don't know how many of you I can bring back. That's why I didn't tell you."

"But...there's hope?" Amelie began pacing. "Maybe you can bring us all back?"

"Yes! Maybe. I mean, Sofie thinks I can." A lie. A little white lie but a lie all the same. One I prayed would never be proven wrong.

"Bring us all back so we can kill you when we get there?" Caden leaned against the cave wall, his expression blank, his voice flat.

"We won't kill her, Caden!" Amelie glared at her brother.

"My sister, the eternal optimist," Caden sneered. "And if she's wrong, you're the one who pays." He pushed himself off the wall and turned, his back to me now like a slap to my face.

My eyes roamed the group, studying expressions full of optimism, shock, angst, and horror as they silently played the situation through in their heads. There was a long pause, then chaos erupted. Amelie and Fiona began giggling and hopping around like sugar–high children, hugging each other. Bishop grabbed me and repeatedly tossed me into the air until I was sure I would puke.

I looked over to where Caden stood calmly, seemingly apathetic to the prospect of leaving Ratheus. *Or leaving with me,* that paranoid part of me whispered.

"So what's the plan?" Amelie asked when she and Fiona took a break from bounding around.

I shrugged. "Sofie said to wait and, when the time was right, we would find the portal. It needs to be soon, though."

"Why?" Caden quickly asked.

I explained the curse's warped sense of time.

"Are you saying that if we don't figure this problem out soon, you'll die?" Caden asked, his voice still unnaturally calm, that unreadable expression on his face.

I nodded. He averted his gaze to the floor again.

"Is there any chance that the portal is out there in the woods?" Bishop asked.

I shrugged again. "Sofie doesn't think so, but I guess it wouldn't hurt to search, right?"

"We'll have some of our pets check things out," Bishop agreed. "It wouldn't take them long. It will stretch our perimeter guard, but we should be okay."

"Okay, so what do we do in the meantime?" Amelie asked.

I turned to Caden. "Can you take me to the place where the Merth grows again?" I asked softly. "Sofie needs it."

"Sure. Anything for Sofie." The sarcasm was impossible to miss. He disappeared down the tunnel, carefully avoiding my eyes.

Sending Rachel away hadn't changed anything, I thought bitterly.

CR

"We can't go in there. It's too painful for us weak little girls," Amelie explained with an apologetic smile. She and Fiona stood on the ledge by the waterfall.

"And you'll have to pick it yourself. Merth only has to touch us to make us flop like rag dolls," Bishop added, squeezing my shoulder.

"That's okay." I smiled, glancing over to see Caden approaching us. He had vanished for a brief time while we were gathering the mountain bags and I was changing into my wet suit.

He stopped in front of me. "Let's get this over with. I hate being near this wretched stuff." He picked me up as he had the other day. I buried my face in his chest again, only this time the awkwardness was unbearable.

We were through the waterfall and standing beside the sea of Merth in seconds. I looked up at Caden and Bishop's faces. As much as they tried to disguise it, they couldn't hide the pain in their eyes. They each trailed behind me with a canvas bag, careful not to make contact with the swaying cords as I hastily yanked the delicate strands of Merth and stuffed them in the bags.

"These are too pretty to pull out," I murmured.

"Pretty enough to sedate an army of vampires," Bishop responded wryly.

There're only three vampires I want to sedate, I thought as I worked. Funny; Sofie didn't make that list. Maybe I was crazy after all.

Both bags—the one I'd brought tonight and the one from before—were filled in no time. There was still a sea of silver growing. Enough to fill a hundred of these bags if I needed to …

A shout from Bishop made me turn in time to see Caden crumpling into a patch of Merth. I gasped, recalling his description as I realized one of the strands had grazed his leg: *A thousand razors cutting into his flesh.* I ran to him and grabbed hold of his arm, pulling with every ounce of strength I had. Somehow I got him out.

Dropping to my knees, I cradled his head in my lap. "Are you okay?" I asked, pleading.

His eyelids flickered open. He gazed up at me.

"Caden?"

Silence followed—seconds that felt like hours—then I felt a hand on the back of my head. Caden pulled me down to kiss me.

And then he abruptly broke off, murmuring, "Sorry." He was on his feet and moving away from me in a flash. "I got caught up in the moment. I didn't mean to do it."

"No, of course," I said, scrambling to my feet. I glanced around for Bishop. He had vanished. I looked back to Caden, and my heart went cold. His jaw was taut, his full lips pressed tightly together, and torture was alive in his eyes. "It's okay. I know! You just want to be friends. Go ahead! Say it!" I fought tears but they escaped anyway. I furiously rubbed them away.

Unexpected amusement flashed in his brilliant green eyes. "You want me to lie to you?"

19. The Cover, Uncovered

I frowned, confused by his answer. *Why would he be …*

Caden suddenly appeared in front of me, wrapping his arms around my body, pulling me toward him, his chin resting on my head. "It's been hell, waiting for you all week," he murmured, easing his grip enough that he could lean down and press his forehead against mine. "I hated leaving things that way. I wanted to explain …"

I couldn't breathe, even when I consciously reminded myself that I needed to. The Caden from before was back, the Caden I didn't ever want to be apart from again. *But what did he mean?* "Can you explain now?" I heard myself ask, grudgingly pulling far enough away to look up at him. "I mean, why were you...like that earlier?"

Caden laughed. Cupping my face with his hands, he sighed. "Because of you," he said.

I stared hard at him, my brow furrowing. "I don't get it."

He kept staring intensely at me. "That's why I'm with Rachel...because of you." Caden chuckled. "You're looking at me like I have two heads again," he murmured, pulling me close to him, his sculpted chest against my cheek.

"That makes no sense," I mumbled, genuinely confused.

"Amelie was right. You are oblivious."

I scowled.

Caden exhaled noisily, pushing me away so I could look into his eyes again. They searched my face, touching on every detail, memorizing every line. "That first night you arrived here, on Ratheus, I had just come back from New Shore for the first time in hundreds of years. I was going to report Jethro for having Merth. I'm no rat, but it was either that or start a war with him, one that would surely cause death on both sides. I couldn't risk losing any of these three, especially my sister.

"The Council hears grievances on occasion, as their way of governing society—it's a circus show, really. Entertainment. Anyway, it was at the Council meeting that I first met Rachel. They would have laughed me out of there, possibly killed me, if she hadn't spoken up, saying she would personally investigate the matter. I believed her. Stupid, right? So I led her back to that small cave we were in that first night.

"It wasn't until we were sitting in our cave that she told me I was her soul mate and she had to have me." He shuddered. "The feelings weren't mutual, believe me. I was looking for a diplomatic way to let her down when Amelie showed up, you in her arms. It all happened so fast. Rachel saw you and, realizing what you were, demanded we take you back to the Council. She's ancient—I don't even know how old—and therefore impossibly strong. We could have fought her, maybe killed her, but one of us would have died in the struggle. Or she could have escaped, running back to the Council to tell them before we had the chance to catch her. She's even faster than Bishop, and he's the fastest of us."

Caden paused to Rachel's eyed narrowed push a strand of hair away from my face. "So I did the only thing I could think of to stop her. I pretended to love her and used that to my advantage." He shuddered again. "I convinced her that we needed to hide you. It worked like a charm...except for one small problem," he murmured, softly running the back of his hand along my cheek. "The only thing more deadly than a hungry vampire is a jealous vampire. Rachel is a narcissist. She wouldn't even consider the idea that I'm deceiving her—that in truth I'm disgusted by her. But she's also terribly suspicious. If she even suspected for a second that my thoughts and feelings were with someone else ..."

I felt the nervous flutter in my stomach as I heard him say those words but I quickly reprimanded myself, sure that I was reading too much into it. He had to be talking about someone else. I remained silent.

"That night you were bitten...if she had ever found out what had happened, she would have torn through me to get to you."

"But you had no other choice," I said defensively.

He chuckled to himself. "I suppose not," he whispered, looking at me strangely. "That's why I was so cold to you today. It's getting so much harder to pretend. I was afraid she'd see right through me." He pushed my hair away from my face then, those gorgeous jade eyes gazing adoringly at me. "I knew...the moment I laid eyes on you, I knew." His hands slid down my arms to twine his fingers with mine. He pulled my hands behind my back, forcing me closer to him.

Butterflies the size of bats began madly flapping around in my stomach, flying at warp speed. *Am I imagining things?* I swallowed. *Is this impossibly beautiful man telling me what I think he is?* "So that means you're not with Rachel, right? You don't love her, after all," I whispered, needing to hear him say it.

"No, not her. I don't love her." He buried his face in my neck, inhaling deeply. "I thought you would have figured it out by now. I promised myself I wouldn't tell you anything, for your sake. It's safer to keep you in the dark, given Rachel, with you being human, with you being from another world ..." he went on, naming all the obvious obstacles. "But that's not possible anymore," he said, pulling away to gaze down at me again, his face solemn, "with you attacking me that morning and all."

"I didn't attack you," I stammered, embarrassed.

The corners of Caden's mouth twitched. *He's teasing.* "I don't know what came over me," I admitted sheepishly.

"And I thought you were reserved," he quipped.

We stood there, silently staring at each other. The urge to lean forward and "attack" him again became unbearable. But I wasn't going to initiate it this time. So I stood there, trembling in anticipation.

He let out a loud sigh and dropped my hands to slowly back away from me. "I shouldn't be doing this." He dipped his head to study the ground. When it lifted again, his face had gone stony. "I meant what I said about you and I being impossible, but I wanted you to understand why."

My mind was reeling with the sudden change in direction. "What...what does that mean?"

Caden heaved another resigned sigh and leaned against the cave wall. "It means we continue doing what we've been doing, pretending this conversation didn't happen. That these feelings don't exist."

"Why? What do you mean? I can't sit around and watch you being pawed by that she–devil!" I said, my eyes narrowed with incredulity. How could he even suggest such a thing?

"Don't worry about me. I can handle it."

"I bet," I grumbled, suddenly realizing that a beautiful seductress throwing herself at a guy, willing to do God–knows–what, wasn't exactly the worst punishment in the world.

His eyes flickered with recognition at my insinuation. "Hey, if you have a better idea, I'm all ears," he snapped. But he quickly apologized, adding, "The only way any of that is bearable is because I'm imagining you."

I felt myself blush furiously, a strange sensation stirring within me. "So what now?"

"Now we get out of this cave," Caden said softly, wincing.

It hit me then. "Merth!"

"Yeah, it hurts."

"No! I mean, we can bind her in it."

"No, 'we' can't because 'we' can't touch it," he explained patiently.

"I can, though," I began, but he was already shaking his head furiously.

"Not a chance. It's too dangerous."

"But I could—"

"No!" Caden yelled, then clenched his jaw tightly again.

I shrank back.

"I'm sorry. I didn't mean that. This was what I was worried about— why I didn't tell you how I felt in the first place. It's going to be hard enough to ignore each other. I can't be worrying about you pulling any insane stunts with her. What you did today, lying to her like that—it was stupid. Impressive, but stupid. She's the most dangerous, wicked creature you will ever face in your life, and I'd like that to be a long life."

My anger flared. "Then maybe you shouldn't have run off into the woods to pick flowers, and been so damn flirtatious!" I snapped back at him.

He smirked. "I thought getting angry was pointless." That only infuriated me more. "I've never seen you angry. It's endearing." He smiled adoringly at me. The smile only lasted a second, though, fading as he stepped in closer to me. "I know...I shouldn't have. But I couldn't help myself. I'm not much better than any other vampire out there."

"No, you're different," I whispered with stoic conviction.

"That's because this pendant is protecting you, Evangeline," Caden lectured softly, reaching up to run his finger along the silver chain, grazing my collarbone and sending shivers through my body. "Believe me, things would be different otherwise."

"You'd be fine," I said firmly, closing the gap between us. I slowly reached up to touch the tips of my fingers to his chiseled jawline.

"Evangeline, please, don't make this harder than it already is," he pleaded, but then he leaned in, letting his lips tenderly fall onto mine. My knees buckled, but Caden's arms were there to grip me firmly. I wasn't going anywhere.

It wasn't until he pulled away that I managed a breathe again. He rested his forehead against mine, closing his eyes.

"What if we find another hiding place? Move the statue there? Rachel won't know where we went," I suggested.

"You're brimming with ideas today, aren't you?" he retorted sarcastically. "Then there'd be no incentive to keep Rachel quiet. Besides, it wouldn't take long for the Council to track us down." He stepped away from me again, a sad smile on his face. "Come on. We should get back to the others."

CR

We stepped into the main cave as Bishop made a loud crashing sound, evidently enjoying a board game Sofie had included in the bag. And seriously annoying Fiona, based on her irritated frown.

"Battleship?" I asked. "Sorry. A bit lame." *What was Sofie thinking?*

"You're kidding, right? This is awesome!" Bishop countered. "If you haven't figured it out yet, things get boring around here."

"I hadn't noticed," I murmured, stealing a glance at Caden.

"Stay awhile," Fiona muttered absently, concentrating on the game.

"How long have I been here now, anyway?" I suddenly remembered that I didn't have much control over that.

"Not sure, but it was morning when you came and it's dark now," Amelie responded. "Tired? Hungry?" She tapped the top of the cooler that Sofie had packed for me, full of bottled drinks and food. Scattered untidily about the cave was everything I had ever brought for them. The portable speakers were perched on one of the benches, playing music softly in the background. My mattress and sleeping bag were laid out. The two giant Merth-stuffed mountain bags rested on the far side of it, as far away from the group as possible without being out of sight.

Now that Amelie mentioned it, I realized I was both starving and exhausted from the day's events. Rooting through the cooler, I grabbed a chicken salad and sat down on the bench beside Amelie. "Is the Merth bothering you?"

Her curls bobbed as she shook her head. "I can't sense it at all. Must be the canvas liner." Suddenly she hugged me. "I *so* wanted to tell you, but I was sworn to secrecy!"

"You knew?" I whispered.

Amelie rolled her eyes in response. "Of course we knew."

"How could you keep that a secret?" I asked, mildly irritated.

"Oh, I'm the one keeping secrets?" she retorted dryly, and I averted sheepish eyes. "Because Caden was right—you were better off not knowing," Amelie answered, showing no sign of remorse.

Caden sat down beside me, cutting our private conversation short.

"Rachel should reach New Shore by noon tomorrow if she runs," Amelie said, fiddling with a digital camera. She hopped to her feet.

"Smile!" The flash went off as the camera captured a picture of me with my mouth full of food. "I wonder how long before she gives up and comes running back to her 'Smoopy Woopy,'" she teased. Caden glared at her. I didn't find the reminder too amusing either. "Oh, come on. I'm your baby sis. I'm supposed to be a constant thorn in your side," she said matter-of-factly, then snapped another picture.

The giant cave reverberated with another of Bishop's obnoxious explosion sound effects. Fiona jumped up and whipped the small plastic boat at his face. "Have fun playing with yourself!" she announced, adding in a spiteful tone, "In *every* way."

"Oh, come on, Fee! It's not my fault I'm just better than you at everything," he responded in mock innocence.

His cockiness infuriated her more. Fiona marched over and sat down on the bench across from me, arms crossed and brow knitted as she glowered at the fire.

"Those two should be banned from competing against each other," Caden observed, smirking. "It's the only time you'll see Fiona angry. I'm afraid she'll claw his eyes out one day."

"What's the point? They'd just grow back," Fiona grumbled.

"Cheese!" Amelie called cheerfully, snapping a picture of Fiona, Caden, and I together. Likely not a flattering snapshot.

"Pictures usually turn out much better when your subjects aren't eating or brooding," I said casually.

"I figured you'd want some pictures of us to admire when you're home," Amelie said, then promptly stuck out her tongue at me.

Caden laughed as he rose to go and join Bishop.

It was my chance to pick up on the previous conversation. "Then you also know that we're apparently 'impossible' and he wants me to pretend I don't care when Rachel is climbing all over him," I whispered harshly.

"Yup!" Amelie chirped. "Don't worry, though. It will all work out."

"Well...what am I supposed to do until then?" I asked the two female vampires.

"Convince him otherwise," Fiona responded in that sultry voice.

"What do you—" Her impish smile silenced me. Instantly grasping her meaning, I felt myself flush.

"Ew...That's my brother you're talking about," Amelie moaned, feigning disgust. But then she winked at me.

Fiona leaned back on the bench, her dour mood giving way to uncharacteristic giddiness. "I'm still having a hard time believing this is all happening. Where will we go? What will we do?"

Panic set in. *What if I can't bring them all back?* No, I wouldn't even consider that. It was too painful. I brushed my fears aside. "Well, I'm sure you can stay at Viggo and Mortimer's. They're quite accommodating when they need something from you," I said wryly. The mention of Viggo reminded me of my mother—of her death.

"What's wrong?" Amelie asked.

Caden was sitting beside me in a flash, a concerned look on his face.

"Well, I learned a few more things while I was back ..." I started filling them in on Ursula's attack, Sofie's confession, and Max being able to talk to me. I ended with how Viggo murdered my mother. The cave fell to silence then. "So I guess Sofie will release her sister, one of you can bite her, and then everyone lives happily ever after." I smiled sadly.

"Not a chance in hell!" Bishop erupted.

"There's no way we're helping Viggo after what he's done to you," Fiona agreed, her voice ominous.

I was already shaking my head. "I just want to be done with all of this. With them."

"And you will be," Caden's low voice was menacing.

I glanced at him. "I don't want to help Viggo, but—"

"Then we don't help him!" Amelie announced firmly.

"And what, be hunted? I've already got that lunatic witch after me. I don't need two vampires hunting me too," I said. "I thought the same, but it won't change anything."

"He can't hunt you if he's dead," Caden said with icy determination.

"No! I'm not risking it. I'm not going through all of this only to have one of you killed when we get there." I was almost screaming now, desperate for them to understand how serious this was.

"Okay, okay." Caden's arm went around me.

"I just want to be done with all this," I mumbled, feeling tears welling in my eyes.

"And will they be done with you, after all this?" Fiona asked quietly.

I shrugged. "I mean, what else could they want with me? They've already murdered my mother and ruined my life."

"And Sofie? You don't seem to be too angry with her anymore,"

A sad smile pulled at my lips. "I'm not sure, but I think she's been played in this mess as much as I have."

"I don't know, Evangeline," Caden said softly. "Sometimes I think you're—"

"Too trusting. I know." I smiled. "Sofie said the same thing."

He nodded. His hand slid tenderly down to the small of my back, where his thumb drew tiny circles. My appetite for food instantly vanished, shifting to desire for something entirely different. I gave my head a slight shake. When had I turned into such a hormonal maniac?

The camera flashed as Amelie snapped another picture, lifting the somber cloud I had dropped over them. "Do you think I could pass for a high school student?" she asked innocently. "I had so much fun in high school."

"That's because you spent your days seducing the football team and making their girlfriends jealous," Caden joked.

Amelie smiled smugly at him. "Well, I *am* going to do some stage theater. It's more discrete than film. I'll likely have to travel around the world so I don't have to take fifty-year breaks. And I'll wear wigs and contacts so I'm not recognized," Amelie said confidently. "You can come with me, Fiona, be the voice behind my lip synching."

"Gee, that sounds like loads of fun for me," Fiona drawled with exaggerated annoyance, but she was smiling.

Bishop walked over to sit beside his girlfriend, draping his arm affectionately around her shoulders. "She's not going anywhere without me, and I'm sticking to the mountains and the ocean for at least a hundred years, showing up all those humans with my mad skills," he announced. Fiona leaned over to rest her head on his shoulder, all signs of anger gone.

"What about you?" I asked Caden timidly, hoping his answer would be "I'll be wherever you are."

He smiled wistfully. "Something productive."

"And what about your...diet?" I asked quietly. *Your desire to murder humans.*

He and the others shared glances. "It's going to be hard at first," Amelie said. "But we'll manage."

"Right. You'll feed off animals, right?"

"Right," Fiona said confidently.

I exhaled in relief. "So you'll be fine."

Caden chuckled wryly. "Not quite." My brow creased with worry, and he sighed. "Imagine the smell of ground beef frying in a pan on the stove. It's edible enough, right? You can survive off it fine. You may even convince yourself that you *like* it."

I did like it, actually, but I decided now wasn't the time to divulge that.

"Now, imagine walking down the street on the first warm day of spring, only to catch the aroma of a big, fat, juicy steak grilling on a barbeque."

"Oh," I moaned, recalling the countless times I had been tortured with that exact mouth–watering situation.

"Now multiply that by about a million," Caden added, not a hint of exaggeration in his voice.

"How are you going to fight that?" I whispered.

"That's what I've been trying to tell you, Evangeline," he said softly.

"Rachel!" Bishop hissed, flying off the bench.

I blinked, startled by the sudden change of topic.

"How?" Fiona asked, shock in her eyes.

Caden's hand moved from my back a second before I caught sight of raven black hair flying into the cave.

Rachel was back.

20. Immobilized

"You've found something already?" Amelie said, feigning enthusiasm. She'd make a great actress.

Rachel ignored Amelie, her shrewd eyes surveying the room, taking in everything. "You look like you're getting settled in," she said slowly, her steely yellow gaze falling on me and, more importantly, my close proximity to Caden.

I swallowed the lump forming in my throat. That gaze made me want to shrivel up and die.

Rachel's eyes darted to the sleeping bag. "Planning on napping while we run around, looking for this portal?"

"Oh, that...Sofie likes to prepare for every possibility. She's a worry wart." I rolled my eyes dramatically, trying my hand at acting as well. I was sure any average five–year–old could have outperformed me, but I had to keep her distracted. I didn't want her noticing the two giant bags of Merth. "Did you find anything?"

She ignored the question again, instead turning a sickly sweet smile toward Bishop. "What's wrong? Big Brown didn't tell you I was on my way?"

"No, he's busy searching the forest. Like Eve told us to," Bishop responded slowly.

Her lips twisted in an unflattering, pensive expression. "Partway there, I asked myself what would happen if you found this portal in the woods. Would you wait for me?" She stalked slowly toward me. No one moved. Worried glances flitted between them.

She stopped in front of me, taking a relaxed stance. I forced my eyes up to meet hers, my terror likely shining like bright neon lights within them.

Suddenly she was forcing herself onto Caden's lap, straddling him as if ready to perform a private show while managing to shove me off the bench at the same time. Luckily Amelie caught me before I hit the ground and made room beside her for me, wrapping her arm protectively around my shoulder. My eyes dropped to where the camera had been lying. It had vanished.

"Of course Caden would never do such a horrible thing as leave me. But the rest of you," she threw a hateful look at Amelie and Fiona, then a withering one in my direction, "I don't trust."

"Of course we'd wait for you," Caden insisted. I sensed the nervousness in his voice. He was having a hard time hiding his shock at her return.

Rachel snuggled against him, her voice turning sultry. "I couldn't risk it."

My stomach constricted into a painful knot at the sight.

"But what about searching New Shore? It's important that we find this artifact, and soon," Caden said calmly.

"It's taken care of. I met up with two Council members on my way and sent them back to search."

"What did you tell them, Rachel?" Caden asked, his voice slow and even, but I saw the flash of alarm in his eyes.

"Oh, nothing important. They're not smart enough to put two and two together. Like they'd ever figure *this* out."

Caden exhaled, visibly trying to control his anger.

"They were on their way here!" she added quickly, a rare hint of desperation in her voice. "You should be happy I've deterred them."

Caden reached up to brush her hair from her face. "Of course, yes. Good thinking."

Don't touch her with those hands! I screamed in my head.

A relieved smile stretched across her face. "I'll head back to New Shore in a week or so to double–check. They're getting eight others to help. You can come with me then, of course. Your scouts will have covered these mountains."

"You shouldn't have done that, Rachel," Amelie growled.

Rachel waved her hand dismissively in Amelie's direction. "We don't care what you think. Do we, Hon?" she purred into Caden's ear, her arms wrapping tightly around him.

He smiled lovingly at her.

I clenched my teeth as I felt another spasm in my stomach. *Caden was right. This is worse. Way worse.*

Amelie's arm squeezed my shoulders.

"We'll have to test that comfortable bed out later," Rachel said, giggling seductively, discretion obviously not part of her DNA. "Should be much more comfortable than the last time …" She turned to appraise the bed Caden and I had shared the previous night. Then her gaze fell on the mountain bags.

My stomach—already battered from watching her maul Caden— dropped to my feet.

"What did you fill those bags with, Evangeline?" her voice had turned sickly sweet. Rachel only addressed me directly when she was torturing me about my feelings for Caden, or if she wanted the truth. She likely assumed that I couldn't lie credibly. An accurate assumption, I'd say.

"Bags?" I fought panic.

"Yes. The bags. You've emptied them of their contents, based on what I see here, and yet they're full again."

"Oh, yeah," I stammered, feeling Amelie's arm squeezing me ever so slightly.

Fiona's eyed narrowed, indicating she hadn't missed Amelie's gesture.

Would it be that bad if she found out? Yes, it would. It meant the Council would have fields of Merth to inflict more pain. It would mean I couldn't bring it back for Sofie. And most important, it would prove we've been keeping secrets from Rachel. That would be disastrous. But what else could I tell her?

"Flowers," Fiona answered in her usual placid tone, saving me.

"Flowers?" Rachel's face screwed up in skepticism.

"And plants!" I exclaimed before adjusting my tone to sound calm. "You may have things that we don't have on Earth, and Sofie wants to study them, see if she can use them for some of her witchy spell–casting. Hocus–pocus stuff. I don't get it." I rolled my eyes. I knew my voice was trembling and probably unconvincing, but I couldn't help but be impressed with how easily that lie had popped into my head. Maybe I was getting better at this.

"That much?" Rachel said her eyes narrowing further in disbelief.

I shrugged. "She asked for any plant I didn't recognize. I'm not a botanist."

"Hmmm. Right." She pursed her lips, then turned her attention back to Caden, tracing his collarbone with her index finger.

My shoulders, rigid with anxiety, began to relax. My quick–thinking deception had worked.

"Show me, Evangeline," she demanded in a crisp voice, not looking away from Caden.

I froze.

"You wanna see a bunch of half–dead weeds?" Bishop scoffed.

Her left eyebrow arched severely. "Show me," she repeated.

"Um, sure," I managed in a hoarse whisper, my eyes darting to Caden. He didn't dare look away from her.

Rising slowly, I walked over to one of the bags on shaky legs. I took my time, now in extreme panic mode and condemning my cleverness. I started fumbling with the strings, trying to think of some way out of this impending disaster.

"Here, let me help you. The knots are tight," Bishop called, suddenly appearing in front of me to help unfasten one of the bags. From the corner of my eye, I saw Rachel slide off Caden's lap and take a step toward us.

Caden was right behind her, though, grabbing her waist playfully and kissing the side of her neck as a means of distraction. It partially worked.

She stayed there to revel in his affections but her snake eyes never left us.

I was too worried about being murdered at this point to be upset by Caden's actions. I watched nervously as Bishop unraveled the knot. I frowned as he continued fumbling with the strings, as if there was still a knot to be untied. *What's he doing?*

"Here, put your hand on that loop and pull," he instructed. I frowned. There was no loop. "Right here!" he said impatiently, holding his hand out, palm up. I mechanically reached over, and Bishop grabbed my hand and guided it into the bag. From where Rachel stood, she wasn't able to see what we were doing.

I understood. "Merth only has to touch us for a second to make us flop like rag dolls," Bishop had said. Just the briefest of moments, and Rachel would be controlled; restrained; no longer a dangerous problem. But I couldn't screw up. If I did, someone would likely die. It could be me, or worse, it could be one of the others. Would it work, though? Would she fall for it? We had no other choice. Committing myself entirely to the unspoken plan, I twined my fingers around one of the strands.

"Damn knot," Bishop cursed, gripping my forearm tightly enough that it began to hurt.

"You idiot!" Rachel sneered, wriggling free of Caden.

As she strolled toward us, I noticed Amelie and Fiona stealthily slide in behind her, grim determination in their eyes. Caden moved forward as well, his jaw tight with anxiety, his head shaking, warning us. Warning me not to risk it. It was too late, though.

Rachel's hand reached toward the bag.

Bishop, still holding my forearm, whipped my hand out toward her with lightning speed. Somehow I managed to grab hold of her wrist, pressing the Merth tightly against her skin.

In the next instant, four pairs of hands were securing her. She let out one high–pitched shriek and then her body went limp.

Amelie lifted her other arm up. I wound the cord around both wrists and tied a knot, my hands trembling violently the entire time.

"Her legs too," Caden instructed, his voice now devoid of all emotion.

I reached in for two more cords and went to work binding her legs at the knees and the ankles. *Will more Merth mean more pain?* I wondered sympathetically. *Will the thousand razor blade cuts turn into a million?* I gave my head a shake. *You're too soft, Evangeline. She'd do it to you in a heartbeat.*

When we finished, the previously deadly vampire lay immobilized on the ground, all bound up like a pig ready for a spit.

It was over. We were safe.

My knees buckled. I would have collapsed if Caden hadn't been there to catch me, scooping me into his arms and swiftly gliding away from Rachel.

"Are you okay?" he whispered breathlessly as he placed me on the ground, deep concern in his eyes.

I nodded, unable to speak.

He sighed heavily, leaning forward to press his lips against my forehead, his hands squeezing my shoulders. I closed my eyes, reveling under his touch. I could have stayed like that for hours, but he pulled away. "Are you insane?" he yelled at Bishop, his voice thundering in the cave.

"Hey, it worked, didn't it?" Bishop's responding yell—his display of anger such a rare sight—matched Caden's.

Caden bit his lip, thinking. When he spoke again, it was at a normal level. "Can she hear us?" he asked Amelie.

She nodded.

He strolled over to crouch beside Rachel's head. "It feels so good to be rid of you. To not have to pretend anymore," he hissed into her face. I saw confusion in her eyes. "Every time you touched me," he continued, shuddering, "I pictured Evangeline's face. It was the only way I could handle it. Enjoy knowing that." He straightened and was standing beside me again in an instant, wrapping his arms tenderly around me.

I couldn't help feeling a tinge of guilt for my part in the trap. That was until I glanced down at Rachel to see the raw fury in her eyes as she realized she had been deceived for far longer than just today. That searing gaze burned across my entire body. *Likely imagining tearing my limbs from me and bashing my brains in with them,* I realized. I stepped back into Caden's embrace and squeezed my eyes shut as I buried my face against his chest, but it was a long while before the afterimage of those devil eyes faded from my mind's eye. The feel of Caden's body against mine and his wonderfully natural scent seemed to help.

"What should we do, toss her into the fire?" I heard Amelie ask dispassionately.

"Sounds good to me," Bishop sneered. He reached down to grab her legs.

"Wait—she's not going anywhere, and who knows if we'll need her for something still," Caden said thoughtfully, still holding me.

"I don't know, Caden," Amelie answered warily. "It's better if we rid ourselves of this problem for good, here and now."

Caden looked down at me. "What do you think? She's the biggest threat to you."

I glanced at Rachel's motionless body. "We could wait until we're sure. We can always get rid of her later." As the callous words left my mouth, a wave of revulsion hit me. *I could be like Viggo. A monster.*

"Okay. Well, I don't know about the rest of you, but I definitely can't spend another second looking at her," Bishop muttered, grabbing her feet and unceremoniously dragging her down a tunnel like an awkward piece of garbage, out of our sight.

"I can't believe I just did that," I mumbled, the rush of adrenaline fading to allow bitter nausea. I almost fell onto a bench.

"No, that shade of green isn't flattering," Fiona mumbled, coming over to rub my back. I turned to see Caden staring at me, an unreadable expression on his face.

Bishop strolled back in then, dusting his hands off as if they were covered in dirt. "Try not to attract anymore lunatics, okay?" he directed at Caden before winking at me.

Caden's eyes didn't even flicker from my face as he gave Bishop the finger.

"So that *is* a universal gesture," I noted, earning a laugh from Bishop. Not even a twitch from Caden.

"All this excitement! I need to go hunt," Amelie exclaimed. "Something feisty...Oh, I don't know, a wild cat, maybe?" She grinned.

"You guys in?" her question was directed at Bishop and Fiona, her eyebrow raised suggestively.

"See you two later," Bishop called as they vanished out the cave entrance.

"One obstacle down," I said lightly. "See? Not so hard." *Except for the bound, sedated, psychotic vampire hidden somewhere in the tunnels,* I reminded myself, glancing warily down the tunnel Bishop had dragged Rachel into.

Caden took a seat beside me on the bench. "You could have been killed, Evangeline," he admonished me.

"Well, it's not like I had much choice," I retorted.

He exhaled noisily. "Yes, you did. You could have just shown it to her and let us handle it."

"I like my solution better."

"Your solution almost got you killed!"

"Okay, I'm sorry!" I cried, a tear escaping. "But it didn't and now we don't have to worry about her. Now we can focus on getting you home with me."

Caden squeezed his eyes shut. "The sooner we leave here with you, the sooner I become a danger to you; the sooner I likely can't be in the same room as you," he said miserably. "You and I are still impossible."

"No. We are not," I growled impatiently. "Maybe a tad *complex* for the moment, but not impossible."

Finally a flicker of something like amusement crossed Caden's face. "When did you become so stubborn?" He sighed. "It seems like that right here, right now, but in your world...impossible," he countered, sadness in his voice.

I gazed upon that intoxicatingly beautiful face that I was so wildly in love with and my jaw set with determination. I wouldn't give up on us and I certainly wouldn't let him. An irrepressible urge suddenly gripped me. Sliding closer, I reached over to gently cup his cheek and pull his face toward me. His eyes remained closed. "Well, then I guess we better not waste anymore of this valuable time," I murmured brazenly, reaching up with my other hand to touch his chest, the ripple of his muscles under my fingertips making me tremble.

I didn't think it would work, my novice attempt at seducing him. I assumed he'd push my hand aside, listing—yet again—all the reasons why we were impossible. Maybe he'd even laugh at my ridiculousness. But when he opened his eyes, when I saw the intensity burning within them, I knew I was far off in my assumption. I heard the low, feral groan in his throat and he closed the distance between us, responding whole–heartedly.

CR

I had no idea what time it was and I didn't care. I only cared that I would have to leave Caden at some point and I dreaded that reality.

We had spent all night on that blow–up mattress. Things had gone out of control shockingly fast and I hadn't minded one bit, abandoning all my anxiety and self–consciousness the second his lips touched mine. But, with clothing torn off and bodies tangled, Caden must have realized where we were headed because he stealthily bound me up within the sleeping bag.

"To keep us out of too much trouble" Caden had whispered.

"No. I want trouble," I'd pleaded shyly.

"I don't," he responded resolutely, his jaw set. "No, no, you don't understand," he quickly added when he saw my wounded expression. "No, that's not it. I'm...afraid."

"What? Like virgin–afraid? Same here!" My eyes widened, relief flooding me at the revelation that I wasn't the only one.

He chuckled. "No …"

Drat. My face flushed.

"But later, if...*when* you bring us to your planet, you're going to see what I turn into." Something like shame flitted across his face. "I don't want you to have regrets," he added in a whisper.

"There's no way I'll regret any of—"

He stifled my argument with an intensely passionate kiss and I forgot what I wanted to say. I may have forgotten how to speak altogether.

The sleeping bag remained a frustrating but effective barrier between us for the rest of the night. I tried to wriggle out countless times but he kept me pinned tightly underneath it until I was too exhausted to fight him.

At some point in the wee hours of the morning, when I could see the faint arrival of early dawn outside, I dozed off. It wasn't something I had planned, but with my face nestled euphorically against Caden's chest, enveloped within his strong arms, his hand therapeutically drawing circles over my back, sleep was inevitable.

"Aren't you hungry? Or thirsty? Or whatever it is you call it," I asked, peering at Caden.

"I'm okay until you leave." He nuzzled his cool nose against my neck, causing another stirring deep within me.

I slid over to rest my head on his chest, my hand creeping to glide down the ripples of his stomach muscles.

"They'll be back soon." Caden's hand clamped over mine, holding it in place.

I groaned in frustration but stayed my hand. "They've been gone awhile," I suddenly realized. "How many animals can they possibly kill in one night?"

"It's the hunt as much as the kill," Caden answered, chuckling. "As a human, Amelie condemned flyswatters as cruel. Once, when she was seventeen, she was driving along the road when a chipmunk darted in front of her. She swerved to avoid it, slamming into a giant oak."

I gasped, but he shook his head dismissively. "Oh, she was fine, surprisingly. Only a couple bumps and bruises...She was driving one of the big pickups that we used to transport horses. The truck and the tree were goners, though."

"Was the chipmunk okay?" I heard myself ask with grave concern.

Caden laughed, the deep vibrations tickling my eardrum. "Yes, I believe he made it. Amelie swore the rodent waved at her from a tree."

I giggled. "I don't doubt she did."

"She explained it all to my parents later. I thought my dad was going to wring her neck." He chuckled again.

I raised my head and propped myself up on my elbows so I could see Caden's face. "Do you still miss them after all these years?"

The seconds ticked by before he had an answer. "Being what we are, it's easy to lose yourself in the moment, in your immediate desires, as overpowering as they become. But there's always downtime, when that hunger is satiated and you have time to think. Maybe minutes, maybe hours. Or years. And in that time, your memories—which are never–fading and vivid enough that you could relive them just by closing your eyes—can overpower you. If you let them." He rolled over to press his lips against my folded hands. "I wish I could get that last image of my father out of my head. But every time I think of him, that one shows up. Like a parasite attached to my brain." He began playing with my fingertips.

"Well, hopefully we can fill your head with lots of new memories—ones without wars and jungles and mountains."

He turned to look at me with a grim expression. "There are so many things that can go wrong with this—with us. I want you to understand them all before this goes any further."

"Like what?" I asked warily, though inside, my heart was doing a full acrobatics show because he said "with us." It sounded positive, as if he was finally coming around, as if he might stop using the word "impossible."

"Like, *if* we figure out how to get back to your world with you and *if* none of us attack you—those are already two massive obstacles—I'll be focused with fighting the urge to feed off humans, regardless of whether it's what I want. We all will be."

"That's okay," I murmured.

He snorted, shaking his head. "No, you don't understand what that means. *We won't be the same, Evangeline.* This isn't a minor inconvenience, a slight discomfort. It could take years—decades, even—before you see Amelie waving her pom–poms around. Fighting that lust, that urge—it's all–consuming. It takes all of our energy and focus. You could be ninety years old before we resemble who we are today. You could be *dead.*"

That image of the wrinkled old lady in the string bikini burned in my head again. I shook my head, frantically trying to drive it out.

Caden propped himself up on one elbow. "And none of that will be an issue if one of us kills you the second we smell your blood." His face contorted with horror. "I will throw myself into a flaming pit if that happens."

"Well, maybe …" I grasped for some hope as the picture Caden painted turned grimmer by the second "… maybe Sofie can do something to extend the power of this necklace?"

Caden's eyes dropped to the pendant dangling from my neck. "Maybe…Otherwise, you and I can't be anywhere near each other. It was hard enough not killing every human that crossed my path for the first fifty years after I was converted. But you—the feelings I have for you make the urge that much more impossible to resist. Hugging you could turn deadly."

Those giant bat butterflies began thumping around in my stomach again. I took a deep breath. "You're focusing on worst–case scenarios. I'd prefer taking a page out of Amelie's book of optimism. It's much more pleasant."

"Amelie also killed her boyfriend, whom she was madly in love with," he reminded me in a flat voice.

"Good point," I muttered, sighing noisily and rolling onto my back.

Caden took that as his cue to sit up. He reached for his pants, lying in a tangled heap next to everything else I had ripped off him. "I'm more concerned about you not lasting long enough for us to find this portal." He stood up to dress himself.

"That makes two of us." I averted my eyes, heat creeping up my neck. Would this be my last trip here? Was hope for solving this curse's riddle fading as I lay here, enjoying Caden's company, oblivious to how close the end was? How could Sofie ask me to just sit around and wait for the portal to grace us with its presence?

I couldn't.

Scrabbling for my clothes, I dressed in record time—crossing my fingers that Caden wasn't watching me.

"Where do you think you're going?" he called, an amused look on his face as I headed toward the cave entrance.

"Oh, right!" I ran back and grabbed one of the mountain bag straps.

I yanked as hard as I could, with little result. "Help me!" I cried.

"Okay, okay," Caden said calmly, grabbing both bags and slinging them over his shoulder. They were so big that, as strong as he was, they were awkward to carry. "Can you tell me where we're going, at least?"

"To find this damn portal!" I announced, running out the cave entrance.

A torrential downpour greeted me, soaking my clothes in seconds.

"You can't go out in this, Evangeline," Caden said softly, placing his hand on my shoulder and pulling me back to cover.

"But I have to! We have to find this thing, and now!" Tears mingled with the rain on my cheeks as I sobbed freely. "I don't want to go back there without you."

He wrapped his arms around me and kissed the top of my head. "We'll figure this out. I promise."

"Are we allowed to come back now?" Bishop called as he appeared out of nowhere, his hair and clothing drenched. Fiona and Amelie were behind him, watching me with worried expressions.

I nodded and offered a small, reassuring smile but otherwise said nothing. The five of us stood in silence, looking out over the storm.

Caden, whose hands rested near my pendant, felt the waver of heat before I did. Within seconds I was on the ground, Bishop fastening one mountain bag to my back while Caden strapped the other to my legs. "Done!" they announced in unison as if racing to beat one another.

Caden, kneeling beside me, gripped my face and gave me a peck on the lips. "I love you," he whispered.

〇冬

I regained consciousness in my king–sized bed, surrounded by canvas. I was lying on my side, facing the balcony doors, and I couldn't move. "Max?" I whispered.

A giant wet nose suddenly smeared affection across my forehead.

"Can you please go get Sofie? Try to do it without the others noticing," I requested quietly. I had every intention of winding Merth around my body the second Sofie unbound me.

Right–oh, he murmured inside my head and I heard him trot away, his sharp claws clicking against the tile in the hallway.

Sofie's melodious voice sang out minutes later. Unfortunately it was followed by one that I had hoped to avoid.

21. Making Plans

"It's been two weeks!" Mortimer growled.

"It's not her fault, Mortimer," Sofie snapped in response.

Mortimer didn't seem to hear her. "What have you found out? And why are you trussed up like a packhorse?"

"Do you think you could untie me before the interrogation begins?" I asked, not even attempting to hide my irritation. Could I still get to the Merth in time to protect myself?

Within seconds, I was unbound. I wiggled away from the straps and sat up, only to have Mortimer swoop in to loom over me. I automatically shrunk back. My chance was gone.

I glanced over in time to see Sofie reaching into an opened mountain bag. "No!" I lunged forward to grab her hand.

She pulled out a cord of Merth.

Mortimer gasped in horror. "Why would you bring that stuff back here?"

I barely heard him, still in shock over Sofie's immunity. "It doesn't work on you?"

"Stings," she said, cringing. "But no. Because I'm a sorceress." She dangled the cord from her fingers, examining it closely. "Here, Mortimer. Let's see if it's as strong as our stuff."

Our stuff?

"If you come near me with that, I'll tear your heart out," he growled, taking two large strides backward.

I heard a loud, exasperated sigh inside my head. *Here, try it on me,* Max said, ambling toward Sofie.

"Max is offering guinea pig services," I said, adding, "There's Merth here?"

"Not until now," Viggo called out, entering the room. "We spend over two hundred years ridding the world of it, and look...you show up with two giant bagfuls!"

"Take it off him immediately afterward, though. Please," I said as Sofie moved toward Max. I didn't want Max going through any more pain than necessary.

"Of course, of course," Sofie murmured. "Thank goodness *you're* not a coward, Max," she added, her eyes flicking to Mortimer, her tone thick with implication. Viggo howled with laughter at Sofie's snip as Mortimer glared venomously at the red–haired vampire–witch.

She placed the cord on Max's back. His giant black body wavered slightly, then slumped to the floor. He mumbled incoherently in my head. As promised, Sofie immediately pulled the cord off Max.

Yes, it's the same, Max confirmed.

I relayed the message.

"Why would you bring this back, Evangeline?" Viggo asked me suspiciously, stepping forward to examine the bags.

"To bind you." The catty response flew out without warning.

Viggo grinned. "Cute."

"Did you know about this?" Mortimer asked Sofie, one eyebrow raised.

"How would I know? I was here!" she spat. "But I can use it. Smart thinking, Evangeline."

Viggo swept his hand across the open bag, allowing the tip of his finger to graze a strand. He swayed as if suddenly lightheaded. "This wretched stuff …"

"Leonardo, lock these bags in the vault," Mortimer instructed.

"I'm going to take a few strands for some testing," Sofie announced, reaching for the bag.

"So you can trap me when I'm distracted? Not a chance, witch," Mortimer snapped.

"You fool!" she snapped back, unleashing a torrent of anger. "Have you given any thought, even for a second, to what will happen when one of these vampires—who haven't been exposed to human blood for *seven hundred years*—shows up under this roof? They could kill Evangeline, they could wipe out your staff, they could break free of this building and start a New York City massacre. I appreciate that you've waited a hundred and twenty years to see Veronique, but show some common sense, you idiot."

Mortimer rolled his eyes. "Oh, stop being so dramatic. All of those possibilities are highly unlikely."

"It's not worth risking! You don't know what can happen, who these vampires are. These kinds of spells are known to have unforeseen outcomes, some of them disastrous. I shouldn't have to explain that to you …" her voice drifted.

My back hit something hard. I turned, saw the headboard, and realized I had been slowly inching backward, trying to get away from the approaching brawl. I was now cowering, knees drawn up, within a mound of pillows.

"Children, children," Viggo said softly. "Let's play nicely, now."

"He started it," Sofie muttered indignantly.

"How do you propose you'll use this Merth to solve the possibilities you've described, Sofie?" Viggo calmly asked, taking on his usual role of mediator between those two. "Is there yet another trick up your sleeve we're unaware of?"

"I need to link the power of it to this building, to form a barrier. To keep them within these walls," she answered in a more conciliatory voice. "It should be a fairly easy spell."

"Them? How many do you think are coming over, anyway?"

Three pairs of brilliantly colored vampire eyes turned to me. "Four," I said from my hiding place, adding under my breath, "I hope."

"Didn't there used to be five?" Mortimer asked, his eyes narrowing.

"Yes, but she's no longer an issue," I answered flatly, hoping to avoid any more questions about the event in which I'd been an accomplice. It likely wouldn't shine a positive light on Caden and the others, in Viggo and Mortimer's eyes, anyway.

Luckily, he turned his attention back to Sofie. "And how do you suppose we get out for food? Of course, *you* can get out; it doesn't hold *you* back...Are you trying to weaken us?"

"Don't think I don't know about that blood bank in the cellar. That could tide you over for *years*, if necessary," she shot back at him.

"And how will any of this protect the humans? They'll still be within these walls when the vampires get here," Mortimer asked smugly, thinking he had found a weakness in Sofie's plan.

"I'm working on a way to mask their blood, a talisman of sorts that they can wear. I should have it ready shortly," she answered with twice the smugness.

I breathed a sigh of relief. So she had thought of it. I would be protected. Caden wouldn't have to worry about hurting me. I couldn't wait to tell him.

"You had better not be tampering with Veronique's necklace ..." he growled apprehensively.

"Why on earth would I do something so dangerous?"

I felt like I was watching a ping pong match, my head bobbing back and forth as the two of them squared off against each other, Mortimer lobbying challenges and Sofie successfully launching back counterarguments.

Viggo spoke as if passing a ruling. "Okay then, it's settled. It looks like Sofie has it all figured out and I'm sure she has no intention of harming either of us, Mortimer. After all, Veronique would not be happy about that."

"Yes. However, I'm wondering where the witch's allegiances now lie," Mortimer grumbled with disdain.

Viggo ignored him. "Leonardo, if you would be so kind as to take both of these bags—minus whatever Sofie needs—to the vault."

Sofie grabbed an armful of Merth, wincing from the shock it produced, and threw a daring smirk at Mortimer, taunting him to come near her. Mortimer snarled in response but didn't make a move.

Leo grabbed hold of the straps and began dragging the bags out of the room. I wanted to chase after him, help him in some way. But I had a feeling I wouldn't be allowed out without further interrogation. I was right.

"Now that that's settled, have you been to the city to look for this portal?" Viggo calmly asked me.

"Not exactly."

"So where did you search during that time?" Mortimer pressed, taking a few steps toward me.

Max released a low, threatening rumble and all four dogs shifted to form a protective circle around the bed.

"Oh, shut up!" Mortimer snapped but he heeded their warning, sidling back.

"Patience, Mortimer," Viggo chastised, patting his shoulder gently. He turned back to look at me, those piercing blue eyes dissecting me.

What could I say? *No, I didn't go out. Sofie told me not to. But you don't know that, do you? Yes, she's deceiving you...Instead, I bound a vampire with that stuff you hate, Mortimer, and then I rolled around in the sack for hours.*

Viggo cleared his throat, a sign that I was learning meant he was deeply irritated. If he could read my mood, I wondered what he was getting right now?

There wasn't much I could tell them. Bishop did send the animals out in a half–ass attempt to search the vast jungle and Rachel did recruit some Council members...An idea struck me. I took a deep breath. "There are ten vampires searching the capital city and a small army of adept scouts searching the mountainside. By the time I get back, they will have reported back on whether anything of interest has been found. I figured that was a much safer, faster way to the truth," I said, taking full credit for the wild goose chase Rachel had sent those Council vampires on. "I think we're getting close," I added for embellishment.

The room was eerily quiet, so much so that I began to think I'd been too confident in my cleverness.

"That's great news, Evangeline!" Sofie exclaimed, genuinely happy. "And it keeps you out of harm's way."

"Yes...that is rather intelligent," Mortimer mumbled, adding, "thank you."

I stared wide-eyed at him. Those words were the last ones I expected to come from him, the grump. And they sounded genuine.

Mortimer looked at me thoughtfully. "We will owe you, won't we? Though I'm not sure how we could ever repay you."

By leaving me and my friends alone? By never asking me to do anything again? By letting us live our lives in peace while you sit quietly in your palace? Or ... "Money," I blurted, another idea popping into my head. Caden was right; I was brimming with ideas.

An extremely rare expression of surprise flashed across the vampire's face. He hadn't expected an answer to his rhetorical question, but he was obviously intrigued. "Do tell?"

"This should be interesting," Viggo mused, a smug grin on his face.

"Well, it's Caden, Fiona, Bishop, and Amelie," I began, stammering, suddenly uncomfortable. "They'll have nothing—no home, no money, no clothes."

"Well, of course they can stay here until they've settled in," Viggo offered smoothly.

Settled in. So that's what Viggo calls sucking the life out of people and robbing them of their possessions. "Well, that's just it," I said aloud. "They're not planning on adapting the usual way. They won't be killing humans."

Viggo and Mortimer bellowed out laughter. "They said that, did they?" Mortimer murmured, a knowing smirk on his face. "And you believed them, of course."

I bristled. "Yes, they did. And yes, I do."

"Okay, go on, Evangeline." Viggo waved his hand, still chuckling softly.

"Anyway...considering they're doing you a favor...I was hoping you could—I don't know, set up a trust fund for them or something. So they'll have some money to help them start out." *So we don't have to live with you two goblins.*

The roar of laughter that erupted from Mortimer shook the glass in the balcony doors. "So they're okay with blood money as long as they don't do the actual killing."

I shrugged, realizing my logic was flawed.

A curious expression stretched across Mortimer's face, then he smiled strangely. "Okay. How much do you think they will need?"

"I don't know...maybe ..." I began fidgeting. I had never asked for money before. It felt awkward. But it wasn't for me. *How much would they need, anyway? I guess enough for a condo somewhere, and a car, and some clothes.* I did some quick mental calculations. *Five hundred thousand. That should be enough to start out. It would be a small condo, cozy for the five of us, but...*I couldn't believe I was about to ask someone for *five hundred thousand dollars!*

Viggo spoke up before I had a chance. "Does ten million sound about right?" he offered, his face displaying nothing but complete seriousness.

I began choking violently, sure that I had swallowed my tongue as I sucked in a mouthful of air.

"Twenty. For each of them," Sofie piped up. She had remained quiet up until now. "So that's four of them and Evangeline. One hundred million, in an account that I will set up. Only Evangeline will have access to it. It needs to be done by this afternoon."

A small strangled sound escaped my mouth.

Viggo raised an eyebrow at Sofie, but said nothing.

"That's an awful lot of money. I'm not sure we can gather that much today." Mortimer looked as if he were about to explode.

"Oh, please," Sofie scoffed, rolling her eyes as she called his bluff. "That's nothing more than a library fine for billionaires like you, but it will give Evangeline and her friends a healthy start."

A hundred million. A hundred million dollars and twenty of that would be mine. I grasped the back of the headboard to steady myself before I keeled right off the side of the bed.

"Is this necessary?" I heard Viggo ask Sofie through gritted teeth.

"They need to be taken care of or they won't help us when they get here," Sofie said with the conviction of a priest asked if he believed in God.

"This is extortion," Mortimer growled.

Viggo turned his gaze toward me. "Is this true, Evangeline? They won't help us unless they have a *hundred million dollars* in an account?" There was that obscene number again.

I swallowed the lump in my throat, remembering that icy cold warning he had delivered previously. *Don't ever deceive me.* "Yes. They said they wouldn't help you." That part was true, but it had nothing to do with the money. Hopefully my fear would mask any telltale emotions I may be emitting.

The screech of bending metal shot through the room as Mortimer's white-knuckled grip distorted the bedpost. "How stupid are you? They're lying to you! Whatever they've told you, whatever they've done, it's all lies, you stupid little girl!"

"No, they're not ..." I stammered, his words dislodging a deeply buried fear that had been brewing but hidden inside me. I jumped off the bed and ran out of the room, Max on my heels.

CR

It was my first time in the atrium since finding out that the grand marble statue encased an even grander secret. I stood there now, gawking at it, envisioning the dark-haired sleeping beauty entombed within. The atrium's tranquil, inviting atmosphere had altered for me with this knowledge, replaced by a disquieting eeriness, as if unseen eyes were peering out at me.

"I hear her voice sometimes in the dead of night, whispering to me."

I turned to see Mortimer standing beside me, his attention fixated on the marble face. I hadn't heard him approach. A glimmer of what could be adoration revealed itself in his eyes before they glazed over with their typical ice. I wasn't sure how to respond to Mortimer's admission so I kept quiet, turning my attention back to the statue.

Max stood quietly on my other side, unconcerned by his previous master's presence. That told me Mortimer wasn't likely there to harm me. Not physically, anyway.

"Viggo had this atrium built as a replica of a villa he and Veronique visited. It was one of her favorite places. She adored the flowers and the balconies. So he decided it should be the first thing she sees when she's released."

"Makes sense," I murmured. Mortimer was acting uncharacteristically *nice*.

"It's not fair, what has happened to you, what we've asked of you. I realize that," he continued, still not looking at me.

Is he trying to apologize?

"But sometimes, when someone means everything to you—when the only reason you're alive is to see their face again—you'll accept all consequences that go along with that chance. Even if it means someone else will suffer."

Not a good apology, I concluded bitterly. "Well, as long as *you're* comfortable with me being cursed."

Mortimer smirked. "Maybe you'll understand one day."

I decided what I wanted to say. "How can you be so selfish? How can you look someone in the eye, knowing what you're doing to them?"

He turned to gaze at me with that blank, emotionless stare of his. "You don't. You don't let yourself see them. You don't let yourself feel anything for them. You look right through them. Understand?" He turned away again, his face stone.

Is that what he's doing now? Looking through me? It suddenly dawned on me that Mortimer may have a thick, impenetrable mask of his own, that he was hiding behind an illusion as Viggo had before. Only for Mortimer, it was a mask of necessary disconnect. There was a different Mortimer underneath it. Who he was—that was a mystery. But it was likely the man Veronique had fallen madly in love with.

"No. I don't understand," I replied. "But maybe it's because I'm human. We can't be so single-minded and callous."

Mortimer barked laughter. "You'd be surprised how single-minded and callous a human can be. Nine hundred years is an awfully long time to witness human nature, Evangeline. I've seen some things that would haunt your dreams every night for decades." He paused. "It's also a long time to witness what vampires are capable of—the deceit, the treachery, the games. Remember when you believed we were drugging you and dropping you in Central Park to amuse ourselves?" he asked.

I nodded, smiling wistfully. It felt like years ago. How much easier life might be if that had been true.

"If there was need to do that, we would have. Just as, if there was a need to pretend to love someone, any vampire would."

There he was, implying what I dreaded: that everything was staged. That the caresses, the kisses, the whispers of "I love you" were all an act to acquire my complete trust.

"Your money will be in an account by the end of today." With that, he was off, leaving me in a quiet atrium, wallowing in misery.

He couldn't be right. But if he was...that was my breaking point. I'd welcome death with open arms.

22. The Beards

I was still standing in front of the statue, considering the awful possibility that Caden was playing me like the stupid, gullible human girl that I was, when the garage door slowly creaked open and a jet black Bentley pulled in.

"Who's that?" I asked Max.

The Foreros, he answered, rolling his Rs dramatically to emphasize their Spanish ethnicity.

I frowned, trying in vain to recall mention of them. "And who are they?" I asked as a middle–aged man and woman stepped out of the car, followed by a younger male and female version of them. They looked about my age. All four had exotic, dark features—black hair and olive complexions.

My eyes widened." They're human!"

Yes. Though some would call them "dinner."

"So now you're a comic," I muttered, scowling. I heard that strange snorting that was Max's laughter.

The older man nodded once at Leo, then continued into the building as if he owned it, an air of confidence swirling around him. The others followed closely behind him, the young male and female peering around the atrium in awe, as if it was their first time here. The girl suddenly stum-

K.A. Tucker

bled. I shuddered as I watched her fall facedown to the cobblestones in the exact place where Ursula had met her demise, like it was some sort of reenactment.

"Klutz," the guy—presumably her brother—muttered, though he stopped to wait for her. When she didn't get up, he quickly crouched and placed his hand on her shoulder. "Valentina?" She didn't respond. "Valentina?"

I was already running toward them. By the time I reached her, the girl was conscious and sitting up on her knees, her big, brown, doe–like eyes darting around, curiously surveying the space as if disoriented.

"Are you okay?" I asked.

"Yes...I think so. I just got lightheaded for a moment. Must have been the flight." She had a high–pitched, childlike voice. Glancing up at me, she smiled shyly. With her brother's help, she got to her feet, brushing off her pant legs.

"Learn how to walk," the guy grumbled, stalking off.

She flushed. Turning to me, she said, "I'm Valentina." She offered me a flimsy hand.

I took it. "Evangeline. And don't worry. That was nothing. I'm the queen of pass–out lately. It's pretty embarrassing, actually."

She giggled sweetly. "Nice to meet you."

"Valentina!" a woman's thick Spanish voice called from inside.

"Coming, Mama!" She nodded once at me, then tore down the path and sprinted up the stairs, disappearing within seconds.

I walked back toward where Max stood watching two servants empty the trunk of several suitcases. "Do they live here?" I whispered to Max.

On and off.

"Seriously? Who are they?"

Carlos, Camila, Julian, and Valentina Forero. Viggo and Mortimer's 'beard' family, Max replied. I could tell he found the entire matter amusing.

"What do you mean, 'beard'—like a disguise?"

Yes; sometimes they find it useful to employ legitimate families, to hide assets and such.

My face screwed up in shock. "Do these people know who they're living with? Who they're covering for?"

Sometimes they compel the families, but it's less work when they can find one that only needs promises of an easy, lavish lifestyle in order to comply.

"So this family doesn't know?" There was no way that sweet girl was frolicking into a house of vampires by choice.

Oh, they know.

I did a double–take, my eyes growing wide with shock, earning another deep grunt from Max. *And my stellar intuition strikes out again,* I thought bitterly. "They must be charming," I muttered sarcastically. *A real bunch of philanthropists.* But, whatever. They weren't my problem. I had enough problems.

I found a relatively hidden spot in the garden beside a giant broad–leafed plant. *Not that I can hide from vampires and sorceresses,* I mused. *But, still...*I sat down on the low concrete retaining wall to replay those three amazing words Caden had whispered to me before I disappeared. *Had I heard them right? And were they real?*

Everything was happening so quickly. Just days ago I was desperate to be in the same room as Caden and now he was telling me that he loved me. And I could lose him forever if I didn't solve this curse. That awful feeling of dread flared up again. I wrapped my arms around my body, hugging myself tightly. My elbow rubbed against something bulky in my pocket. I reached in and pulled out the digital camera. Amelie must have snuck it in!

Butterflies stirred in my stomach. I hit the power button and began flipping through the files. There were hundreds. Amelie had filled the super–sized memory card. Their beautiful faces were there, smiling and excited over the prospect of being rescued from their hell. I scrolled to an image of Caden and my heart started racing. He was as gorgeous as ever. I ran my finger over his image.

"Is that Caden?" Sofie's voice murmured in my ear.

I let out a small squeal and the camera fumbled from my hands. Luckily Sofie, with catlike reflexes, caught it in mid–air before it could smash against the cobblestones.

"Sorry." She took a seat next to me. "Here. Delivery from Martha."

She produced a heaping plate of waffles under an even bigger mountain of whip cream, along with a bowl of fresh raspberries.

"Isn't there a fairytale about a witch who fattens up children in order to eat them?" I mused dryly.

"These raspberries are especially juicy. Eat up, Gretel...I mean, Evangeline," she said, followed by an exaggerated cackle. Despite my foul mood, I smirked.

While I ate my waffles—a bizarre meal to have in the late evening—Sofie flipped through the pictures, snorting and laughing frequently. A large part of me wanted to wrench the camera away to protect my friends' identities, but I restrained myself. I was starving.

"They seem like a fun group." I nodded. "Who's this?" Sofie held the camera out to show me someone tethered and tucked into a corner. The image was dark but I could see the glow of hatred in the yellow eyes as if they were still watching me.

I gasped and started choking on a piece of waffle. When I had cleared my throat, I managed to croak, "Rachel." Amelie must have snuck back and taken a picture at some point. "Erase it. Please." I shuddered.

Sofie studied it for a moment longer. "Deleting." She pressed a few buttons and the horrible image was gone.

I let go of the breath I had been holding but that dreadful feeling in the pit of my stomach was still there. I was still afraid. *We should have burned her.*

There was a moment of awkward silence. "I'm sure she deserved it," Sofie finally said.

"She did! We couldn't have her coming here. She's a murderer." *And she was hampering my time with Caden,* I added silently.

"No, you're right. We don't want an ancient blood–crazy vampire here," she said, adding under her breath, "We already have two of them under this roof."

A few more minutes of silence passed and then I asked what I had been dreading. "They can do it, can't they? Not live off humans?"

Sofie's hands dropped to her lap. It was a moment before she spoke. "Some of our kind fight the urge right from the beginning, isolating themselves from humans and feeding only off four–legged animals. They convince themselves that this makes them good and moral, not monsters. But all it does is make them that much more uncontrollable once they've tasted human blood. Somewhere along the way, every vampire will lose the battle. It's inevitable. And when they do...Evangeline, you've only ever seen highly controlled vampires. Viggo...Mortimer...me. We're experienced. But the new ones...they're...something else. It's a horrifying sight that will etch itself in your memory forever," she warned quietly, her jaw tensing. "It may seem contradictory but the best way to control your urge for human blood is to, at first, succumb to it. Then, if the resolve is strong enough, you'll learn to manage the craving. The downside is that the euphoria from feeding off fresh human blood has a funny way of diminishing that resolve. Like I said, it's a vicious circle. That's why there are few vampires like me out there. Human blood is addictive."

My eyes widened with concern. *Did they realize all this?* "Well, what about *my* vampires?" I asked possessively.

Sofie shook her head slowly. "I don't know, Evangeline. It's hard to say. I think their age and previous experience will help, but," she hesitated, "it would be safer if they submit to it at first. If their resolve is strong enough, maybe they'll gain control quickly."

"And if it's not strong enough?" I asked, afraid of the answer.

Sofie smiled sadly. Very slowly, very hesitantly, her hand slid over to pat mine. It stayed like that, resting on top of mine, almost holding but not quite.

I didn't pull away, finding the gesture oddly comforting. "So they should kill humans again, whether they want to or not, because it'll be safer for everyone in the long run," I said flatly. I breathed in deeply and exhaled, waiting for myself to truly comprehend this, to feel the revulsion and heartache.

It didn't come. Something else was there. It felt like...acceptance? Was that it? Was I so quick to accept the idea of feeding off humans because I cared about these vampires, because I was in love with one of them?

I heard footsteps and looked over to see Viggo strolling down the path, arm–in–arm with Valentina. Sofie's hand instantly slid away from mine.

"Lovely evening, isn't it, ladies?" he called with his typical false charm. "I'm just showing dear Valentina here the grounds."

Valentina giggled in response, unable to peel her eyes off of Viggo's face long enough to acknowledge our presence. I couldn't blame the silly girl for being completely enamored with him. I had been that stupid fawn and bought the Academy award–winning act not long ago.

"See you later! Well, maybe ..." Viggo winked knowingly at Sofie before leading Valentina away.

Sofie muttered something under her breath before saying, "That is Valentina Forero. She's—"

"Part of Viggo and Mortimer's beard family. I know," I finished.

My knowledge caught Sofie by surprise. "How do you—oh yes, of course," she muttered, glancing at Max. "You have a tour guide."

Max snorted. *Hola!*

"Yes, it's nice not to be left in the dark sometimes," I said sardonically.

"I didn't think it was worth mentioning," Sofie retorted. "But if you're eager to know, Viggo and Mortimer imported Carlos and Camila from Columbia about twenty–five years ago. They come from old money—lots of it—so it wasn't too difficult to convince people they could afford a square block in Manhattan. Mortimer has been using them as a cover, but they've outlived their purpose."

I frowned. "So what happens with them now?"

Her eyes flashed toward me, the look revealing. "Dinner...or perhaps breakfast. Or several snacks. Whenever the mood strikes them next, I would suspect. Oh, don't feel too sorry for them," Sofie added when she saw the horror on my face. "Dear Mr. Forero comes from a long line of Columbian drug lords—what a stereotype, right?" She chuckled wryly. "He wouldn't think twice about having you disposed of because you glanced at him disrespectfully."

I pictured the arrogant man who had strolled past me earlier. *Okay, but* ... 'Well, what about his wife and his children?"

"They're not much better. Camila has a stake in a diamond mining operation—a family inheritance—that employs children as young as eight. Viggo said the working conditions are atrocious, at best."

"Maybe she doesn't know?" I offered.

"Oh, Evangeline …" Sofie chuckled. "She visits the mines regularly."

"Well, his kids can't be that bad. They're still young enough, right?"

"Julian is twenty–one and Valentina is your age," she confirmed. "I suppose I wouldn't call them *evil* yet. Julian hasn't done anything too horrendous. They may have had a chance if they'd been separated from their parents, but look at their role models! As close–minded as it may sound, they're doomed to go down the same path as their parents. It's too bad, though. Julian is handsome."

I had to agree, recalling the young man's Latin good looks, his thick, dark hair and ebony eyes. He was ordinary next to Caden, but still definitely handsome by human standards.

"Well. Can't they kill the parents and set the kids free? Give them that chance?" I wondered.

Sofie turned to stare at me in surprise. "They could—but they won't."

"Well, can't you say something?"

A noncommittal shrug, then a contemplative expression flitted across Sofie's face.

I glanced at my watch. *Getting close...*Excitement stirred in my stomach; I'd see Caden again soon! But that was followed by the sickly dread that my time with him—with all of them—could be drawing to an end.

"Evangeline," Sofie said, suddenly serious, "what if you can't have everything you want, all at once?"

"What do you mean?"

She hesitated, her eyes darting to the balcony windows. When she spoke again, her voice was barely audible. "What if getting Caden and your friends here means you couldn't see them for awhile because it's not safe...for a long while. Would it still be worth it?"

"Of course. Yes. Absolutely. Without a doubt," I answered with grim resolution, though the idea of being away from Caden for any length of time tore at my insides. But at least they'd be on the same planet and this curse would be over.

"You should think about that for a moment before you answer, Evangeline," Sofie warned.

"No. I'm certain. Things can't be much worse than they are right now. He's living in another *universe*. If I can get him here, everything will work out. But you're working on that talisman, right?"

Sofie nodded. She remained quiet for a moment, her eyes focused on the cobblestone path. "I'm going to tell you something but you absolutely *must* promise me, first, that you'll do as I ask, okay?"

"Yeah, sure, I guess."

"Promise. Pinky swear." She held out her slender pinky finger.

I hesitated. The pinky swear was ironclad and uncompromising, an unbreakable pledge. It had been a tradition between my mother and me—one I wouldn't tarnish frivolously. But my gut—as blind as it was—told me this wasn't such a case. "Swear," I agreed, hooking my finger around hers, a wave of warm and fuzzy running through me.

Sofie nodded, then said, "When you get to Ratheus tonight, take a closer look at the statue. At the woman's hand. I have a feeling...Well, anyway, take a look."

"Okay," I said, frowning. "That's what I had to pinky swear to?"

"No." She shook her head. "You have to promise you won't do anything yet."

My eyes widened. Did she think that was the portal? "But—"

"No," she quickly interrupted. "I'm not ready to release Veronique yet."

I frowned. "I don't get it. I thought that spell was already cast and you just had to complete it."

"In theory, yes. However, there is one...complication that I'm still figuring out. Hocus–pocus stuff," she said, waving her hand dismissively.

My frown deepened. "But what if I run out of time and I can't come back or I die, like you said?"

"You've got some more time," she answered, winking.

"But what if—"

"No! You promised," Sofie reminded me sternly.

I nodded, grimacing. I looked around for Viggo and Mortimer again before whispering, "Sofie, they think I'm coming back with vampires next time. What happens when I don't?"

"You let me worry about that." She patted my knee gently.

CR

That night, I wasn't traveling to Ratheus with a giant bag of supplies strapped to my body. I wasn't traveling there with fear of Rachel. I was traveling there for Caden, to see his smiling face, to cling to him tightly, and to tell him that I loved him.

CR

Complete darkness met me. I waited quietly. Someone always came to meet me within seconds. Not this time, though.

"Caden?" I called out. Silence. "Caden? Amelie?" I called again, louder, my voice unsteady. *Maybe they're all out hunting.* I took a few cautious steps forward, my hands groping the obscurity in search of a cave wall.

My fingertips grazed something solid. It wasn't stone. I poked and prodded it. It had some give. Like hard, muscular flesh.

My hand recoiled. "Guys? This isn't funny. Come on, please light a torch," I called, my voice shaky. "Or bring me my flashlight."

Soft laughter. Someone was trying hard and failing to contain glee. More snickers and titters joined the first.

"Caden?" I whispered, my eyes darting about the dark in vain. I heard flint striking rock and a flame erupting behind me. A wave of relief washed over me. I turned.

Rachel stood five feet away from me, Merth free, her sadistic, lemon–yellow eyes dancing with excitement.

23. The Council

I stared in horror as Rachel's lips pulled back in a heinous smile, revealing perfectly symmetrical white fangs.

"I've been waiting for you," she purred, casually taking a step forward.

Every muscle in my body went cold and rigid as terror gripped me. My mouth dropped open to scream but only a pathetic, strangled gasp escaped.

Cackling viciously, Rachel took another step to stop within arm's reach. With wide eyes, I watched as her arm extended slowly and she gripped my chin in her hand, her thumb and forefinger clenching either side of my jaw. With no visible sign of exertion, she lifted me up off the ground. Her hold tightened, eventually bringing tears to my eyes. Still she squeezed, ready to crumble my bones to dust.

"Alright, that's enough," a male voice softly chided.

After a long pause and a low growl of displeasure, Rachel released her grip. I dropped to the vine–covered ground.

An army of torches lit the area around us then, the warm glow revealing a hollow, decaying room at least three stories high. There were gaping holes where windows and a ceiling likely once existed; the stone walls had crumbling heaps of stone at their bases. Thick roots heaved the concrete floor, and assorted vines and weeds had found homes within the fissures.

At one end sat a large, rectangular stone on a raised dais. An altar, per-haps.

I barely noticed any of this, though, my attention riveted on the group of alluring onlookers surrounding me. Vampires.

Somehow feeling returned to my legs and my feet started sliding back-ward, trying in vain to get away from Rachel's poisonous gaze, even though I knew it was pointless. I backed into something. Or someone. Holding my breath, I slowly turned.

Piercing white irises gazed back at me.

This time when my mouth opened, an earsplitting shriek escaped.

"Calm down," the vampire mutant requested, cringing. It was too late for that, though. I was shaking uncontrollably. My eyes darted to his long, skeletal fingers as they reached for my shoulder. I flinched under the bone–chilling temperature of his skin, so unlike Caden's warmth. He retracted it, instead raising both hands up in front of him, palms out, in a gesture of peace. "We won't hurt you. Look! Over there—your friends are right over there."

It took some effort to peel my focus away from his gaunt face, but I willed my eyes to follow his spindly finger. Slumped on the floor next to my statue, bound with Merth, was Caden. Amelie, Fiona, and Bishop were on either side of him, all in the same hopeless predicament.

"No!" I cried, locking eyes with Caden, watching his eyes shift from inconsolable grief as they fell on me to the worst rage conceivable as his gaze flicked to Rachel. I did breathe a sigh of relief to know they were still alive. For now.

A diminutive female vampire with Asian features stepped forward. "It's a pleasure to meet you, Evangeline," she said in a soothing, mother-ly voice. She didn't look much older than me, though I knew better. With her long, poker–straight ebony hair, black almond eyes, snow–white skin, and blood–red lips—the contrast as striking as it was sinister—she looked like a Geisha. But I knew none of it was makeup. She smiled warmly as I regarded her—a seemingly genuine smile, unlike one of Rachel's toothy sneers.

"Hello." My voice was unsteady and I was shaking violently, but I couldn't seem to stop myself.

"I imagine seeing Rachel was a bit of a shock to you, having disposed of her so effectively the last time you were here."

My eyes darted over to Rachel to see her seething, intent on freezing the blood coursing through my veins. *I think she may succeed.*

"You should have killed her then. She's quite angry." The vampiress chuckled.

I hazarded another glance at Rachel in time to see her top lip curl back in a truly atrocious smile. *That mouth touched Caden once.* I wanted to gag. She wasn't beautiful. She was a venomous snake.

"No harm will come to you under our protection, though," the vampiress assured me, her voice as smooth as fresh–churned butter. "My name is Mage. This," she rested her hand on the white–eyed vampire's forearm, "is Jonah."

I glanced at him but quickly averted my gaze, my skin crawling with repulsion.

"Not to worry. We understand it will take some time to become accustomed to his face. It can be frightening. Especially after your previous experience with that lunatic, Jethro." Mage glided closer to me. "You should have come to us sooner, Evangeline. This—" she gestured around the giant, roofless room "—is the Council."

My eyes trailed her hand, taking in the group. There were sixteen vampires in total counting Rachel, Mage, and Jonah; eight females and eight males of various races, including two more of the white–eyed mutants. And they had helped themselves to the clothing I brought over for Caden and the others.

I squirmed as sixteen pairs of brilliantly colored eyes studied me, the first human to stand before them for so many centuries. *Are they wondering what my blood tastes like? Are they picturing how to best torture me to get the answer out of me that even I don't know?*

"You're probably wondering what happened while you were away, correct?" Mage raised a pencil–thin eyebrow. Her mannerisms reminded me of a grade school teacher I once had—benevolence but with a hint of severity. It had been impossible to judge that teacher's mood accurately.

Mage didn't wait for my response before speaking again. "You see, we caught wind of this intriguing treasure hunt Rachel had sent some of our Council members on. It sounded...interesting, but a tad bit suspicious. We've been hearing whispers of strange things happening in the mountains—disappearances, fires, werebeasts. As the governing body, we became...*concerned.* So we decided to get the truth right from the horse's mouth, so to speak." Mage chuckled as if she had made a joke. "We knew Rachel was up in Jethro's mountain," her firm gaze slid over to Caden, and she smiled sarcastically, "with her 'soul mate.'"

I cringed.

"After some initial confusion, and a rather abrasive bear that I needed to deal with, we sorted everything out."

"Big Brown?" I whispered, my eyes bulging.

"Yes, what a waste." Disappointment flashed across her delicate features. "He was quite the fighter. Took three of my Council members out." *My Council members. So Mage is the leader.* That meant she had to be powerful. "Luckily I got there to deal with him before any more perished," she added casually. My eyes widened, understanding her meaning. *Very powerful.*

"Anyhow, your friends seem to have this gross misconception of us and our values. Just a misunderstanding, really. Right, everyone?" she asked, smiling sweetly, her eyes zeroing in on Caden. She couldn't possibly expect an answer from them, of course. They were bound and being tortured.

"Why are they bound, then?" I asked meekly.

"Oh, that! Well, we didn't want them doing anything rash when you arrived, before you had a chance to meet us and see that we are friends." She paused for effect. "Would you like them untied?"

My head moved mechanically up and down.

Mage nodded once toward Jonah. He strolled over to them and, hooking his finger under their bindings, effortlessly pulled them off.

That's right. The mutants are immune to Merth.

All four were on their feet immediately. I took a step forward but faltered, glancing first at Rachel, who looked ready to pounce, then at Mage.

"Go ahead!" Mage prompted, ushering me with both hands.

I didn't waste another second in hesitation. I bolted forward to throw myself at Caden's chest. He immediately wrapped his arms around me. "I'm so sorry," he whispered, planting a tender kiss on my forehead.

I heard a loud hiss and shouts and then the world spun as Caden whipped my body around, burying my face in his chest to shield me from whatever was happening behind us. He held me like that until the commotion died down. When his arms loosened their grip, I resurfaced to find Amelie, Bishop, and Rachel forming a protective ring around me. I peeked over Caden's shoulder. Rachel had been forced to her knees, four Council members restraining her. She glared at us like a feral animal, her pupils so prominent that her eyes looked completely black.

"Now, Rachel, we discussed this. If you can't behave, we will have to assist you," Jonah calmly warned, dangling a cord of Merth dangerously close to her nose.

"Of course, Jonah," she said through gritted teeth. It took a few seconds but she managed to compose herself, even producing a semi–genuine smile. The bodyguards released her with doubtful expressions on their faces.

"Go on now, Caden. Please tell Evangeline the truth, as we discussed. She needs to know that she's safe," Mage instructed in an even voice.

I looked up at Caden's face to see him staring defiantly at the vampiress, his jaw taut. They remained like that, the silence growing more awkward as the seconds dragged on, until Amelie's raspy voice spoke up.

"We're all fine, Evangeline."

"And of course they wouldn't hurt you. You're much too valuable," Fiona added excitedly—too excitedly for Fiona's normally level demeanor. She sounded hysterical.

I caught Jonah's white eyes touching hers. There may have been a hint of warning there, but it was impossible to tell. It was impossible to read anything in those dreadful eyes.

Bishop remained quiet, his eyes focused on the ground ahead of him, his arms hugging his chest tightly as if he was restraining himself. So far, if they were trying to convince me, they weren't doing a good job.

I returned my focus to Caden, looking up at him questioningly. Those beautiful jade irises gazed down at me adoringly. His face softened. "Yes, of course. We were being too protective of you. We weren't thinking rationally. You're safe with the Council. You shouldn't be afraid." He smiled tenderly, pushing a strand of hair from my face. "You *trust me*, right?"

My stomach plummeted. There it was. That word. The word he had warned me of before. He was sending me a message. It meant that I was in terrible danger. "Yes, I *trust* you," I said slowly, emphasizing that deceptive word, offering him a small smile and, I hoped, an indication that I understood him loud and clear.

He stroked my hair softly as Mage spoke. "Your friends here were very cooperative in filling the Council in," she said, again smiling at the four of them.

How cooperative? What does the Council know? And how did they get that information? Eyes wide with concern, I glanced up at Caden to see him staring straight ahead now, his face expressionless. The others held the same blank, incomprehensible gaze. Had they been tortured?

"We understand you're looking for a way to bring your friends back with you—a portal of some sort, like this statue," Jonah said.

I nodded reluctantly. Rachel could have told them.

"That's so gallant of you," Mage crooned, smiling. She was trying to win me over with kindness and flattery. She walked toward me, her hand outstretched, beckoning me to come forward. She stopped halfway, forcing me to peel myself from Caden's side, something I dreaded doing, but I knew I had no choice.

"And this necklace will tell you how, right?" Mage reached up to the collar of my shirt, her fingertips grazing my skin. I fought hard against the urge to cringe. Her long nail hooked the chain. She pulled at it until my pendant slid out. "Beautiful," she murmured, gazing at the bright orange swirls. She let go, the pendant landing softly on the outside of my shirt, visible to all.

"Your friends told us about these vampires on the other side. How they're using you." She made a tutting sound. "It's just awful, how that witch deceived and cursed you. You can't protect yourself against them. What do they have planned for you once you get there?"

"I've made arrangements to be adequately taken care of afterward," I answered vaguely.

Mage gave me a doubtful smile. "And you trust them?" She took a casual step forward. "We could help you. Protect you. This group of us around you—" she motioned to the group of vampire onlookers "—are extremely powerful. Much more powerful than those three. Even the witch. After all, we would forever be in your debt. You could have anything you wanted. *Absolutely anything.*"

So that was it. That was their angle. Nurture distrust in Sofie, offer their allegiance and protection—my own personal bloodsucking bodyguard—and all the riches imaginable. All I had to do was bring them home with me. To infest Earth. To start another war, annihilating another world of humans. *Clever vampire, but I'm on to you and this won't work.* Thank God the pendant masked my skepticism. "That would be great," I said slowly, forcing what I hoped looked like a genuine smile. "I hope I can figure out where the portal is."

"Oh, so do we! For your friends' sake, you must!"

I frowned. "I don't understand. I thought you said we were all safe here."

"Oh, yes, you are. But, you see, there's a throng of vampires outside this rubble. *Hundreds* of them. They saw us carrying this statue here, and your friends, bound with Merth. The Council is powerful, but there are only sixteen of us. We can only hold them back for a few days. Then, when they break through and find out...well, if they found out that your friends were planning an exodus without even considering them...your friends would not last long," she explained soberly. "After that, when you return...well, that group is not nearly as civilized as we are."

And who would tell them about our plan? I wondered bitterly. It was as plain as day, the threat Mage was laying before me. *Transport us now or we throw your friends to the horde. Then, when you come back, you get to die a horrifying death too.*

I glanced back at Caden and the others. They seemed so far away. I swallowed the painful lump forming in my throat, feeling the unbearable weight of the situation pushing down on my shoulders. "Well then, we need to get everyone out of here before that happens."

Mage beamed, pleased with herself.

"The scamp is lying," Rachel growled.

Mage chuckled softly. "She would never risk doing something like that—give us such expectations, only to try deceiving us. Especially when we'd see it coming and have to react accordingly," she added, smiling as she delivered another silent but clear, equally deadly threat.

What a silver-tongued vampire.

"Don't be an idiot," Rachel scoffed with an arrogant smirk. It was promptly knocked off as Jonah lashed out, striking her cheek and sending her flying. Rachel was on her feet instantly, wiping a drop of blood from her lip. She was seething with rage.

"I warned you, Rachel," Mage calmly said, glancing at Jonah. Another strand of Merth magically appeared in his hand.

Rachel growled. Her eyes darted to me, sizing up the distance between us. I knew what she was thinking. Could she get to me before Jonah or Mage intercepted? No. She decided she couldn't.

With a deranged shriek, she lunged for the next best way to tear my heart out of my body without needing to lay a finger on me.

Caden.

It was like witnessing a horrific car crash in slow motion, though I knew they were moving at warp speed, fast enough that I shouldn't have been able to discern any of it.

Thankfully, Caden outmaneuvered Rachel's flying, clawing hands before she could grab hold of him. She plowed into the statue with enough force to make it teeter several times before finally toppling. The ground shook with the crash.

"Now look what you've done, Rachel!" Mage scolded. "You're lucky it didn't break. Evangeline may not have been able to come back!"

Rachel had no opportunity to reply, though, as Jonah threw a cord of Merth around her neck. She dropped to the ground like a sack of potatoes, immobilized but facing me, her icy glare still boring into my body.

The statue's new horizontal position gave me a clear view of the woman's hand. I had never seen it so close before. *The statue's hand.* Sofie's request. My return into the clutches of the Council and Rachel had banished Sofie's suggestion from my thoughts—until now.

I crouched to peer closely at the hand. Her fingers were contorted into an unnatural, uncomfortable pose, as if to hold something small and awkwardly shaped. Like...a heart.

My pendant.

I yelped in pain as a jolt of electricity shocked me at the same time that an eye–popping burst of blue light exploded from my pendant.

24. The Portal

My eyes widened in alarm.

"What is it?" Mage exclaimed, clapping her hands. She was a female version of Viggo. Likely just as devious. *They'd get along well.*

"I don't know," I answered, puzzled. I touched hesitant fingertips to the glowing blue heart. It was icy cold. What did it mean? *Is this blue light how the pendant communicates? Have I stumbled upon the portal?*

Another brilliant flash of blue light and painful shock answered.

My mouth dropped open. It was answering me.

"It's the statue, isn't it? That's the portal?" Mage whispered, her eyes wild with anticipation.

My mouth clamped shut as I clenched my teeth together. *Stupid perceptive vampire.*

A murmur of anticipation hummed through the decaying room, the first indication that the other Council members were capable of speaking.

"I'm not sure yet," I answered honestly, gazing down at the statue's hand again, studying it more closely without making my focal point obvious. *So, all I have to do is place my heart into it?* I asked the pendant. The pendant glowed and shocked me again in response.

It was answering my questions!

But I couldn't take the pendant off or I'd die...*Maybe I don't have to take it off in order for the spell to work?*

Another glow, another shock.

How was this working? I quickly tested it. *If I'm right, you'll shock me?* I asked. I felt the responding shock. *If I'm wrong, will you shock me?* Nothing. So a shock and blue light meant an affirmation. I eagerly began rhyming off questions in my head. *Can I bring more than one vampire back?* Yes, it told me.

How will it know to bring Caden, Fiona, Amelie, and Bishop? I waited for about five seconds but there was no shock or glow of acknowledgement. But maybe that question was too open–ended. *Do I need to be touching them?* No reaction. So the answer was no. *Is there something else they need to do?* Yes, it told me. What, though? Again, an open–ended question that the pendant couldn't answer.

I sat quietly, biting my bottom lip, staring at the statue, pondering possibilities.

Anger flared deep within me. The portal had been in front of us the whole time and I was too stupid to look. It should have been the first place I looked—it was so obvious! I could have finished this blasted curse and freed us long ago.

So they don't have to touch me...Do they have to touch the statue? Yes, it told me.

So...if they're touching the statue when I put the pendant in her hand, they'll come home with me? The last shock and glow of affirmation made me gasp loudly.

I had figured it out! I knew how to bring them home with me! My grin surely stretched from ear to ear.

"What is it?" Jonah hissed impatiently.

The smile immediately collapsed. I had been so wrapped up with the discovery that I forgot the dilemma we were in. The ring of ancient, powerful, desperate vampires still encircled me, scrutinizing my every move. *How am I going to do this?*

"Well?" Mage prodded.

My eyes scanned the Council, not settling on any individual but seeing them all perfectly. Yes, they were all watching intently, growing more agitated by the second, like hounds around a barrel of meat, waiting patiently for the only answer they'd be willing to hear.

"I'm not sure what it's telling me yet," I murmured, assuming my best look of confusion. I sat down in front of the statue, legs crossed and hands against my temples as if concentrating deeply. It was good cover for hiding my panicked expression. I had to figure a way out of this mess.

I silently weighed my options. If I did nothing, we were all dead. Not an option. I didn't want to die. I couldn't let the others die. But how could I embed my necklace into the statue's hand *and* get Caden, Amelie, Fiona, and Bishop to touch the statue, all while a ring of vampires hovered around us? Vampires, I reminded myself, who could move lightning fast and tear my body apart in the blink of an eye. Who *would* tear me apart if they suspected I was attempting to leave them. And I'd be a fool to think I could outsmart these ageless monsters.

I had only one option. No alternatives. I had to bring them back with me.

All of them.

There weren't *that* many, really, I convinced myself, mentally conducting a head count. Viggo and Mortimer had more than enough space and money to house them. Sofie would have successfully wired the place with the Merth I harvested so they'd be trapped, unable to wreak havoc on New York. And Sofie would have that talisman she was talking about so the humans would be safe from the vampires' ravenous thirst.

I had pinky sworn, though …

The current circumstances had to warrant an exception. Sofie wouldn't want me dying here tonight. I had to believe that. So whatever her complication was with Veronique's tomb spell, Mortimer and Viggo would have to wait a little longer to reunite with their mummy bride. At least they'd have plenty of venomous vampires at their disposal when the time came.

The more I thought about this plan, the more comfortable I became with it and the easier it was to convince myself that I was right. Viggo, Mortimer, and Sofie could deal with this lot. After all, why should I die— along with Caden, Amelie, Fiona, and Bishop—doing what they asked me to? What they cursed me to do. They wanted one infectious vampire. Well, they were getting twenty.

Wait, not twenty. Nineteen.

I stood and turned to face Mage, fear making my movements robotic. Swallowing the giant lump in my throat, I took a deep breath. "I know how to do it. I know how to bring us all back."

"No! Don't! They're monsters! They'll destroy your world!" Amelie screamed.

In the next instant I saw her folding over as Jonah's knee delivered a powerful blow to her stomach. Caden lunged at the mutant, growling deeply. Jonah was ready for him, though, easily sidestepping the attack and countering with a thrust of his own, sending Caden flying backward into the throng of Council members. Eyes lit with malicious pleasure, and seven sets of hands reached for him.

"Stop right now or none of you will ever leave this place," someone warned in a steady voice. As nineteen pairs of eyes turned to regard me, I realized that *I* had spoken, drawing the courage to do so from somewhere deep within myself.

The threat worked. They shifted away from Caden, giving him plenty of space.

I turned back to Mage. "On one condition, though, and it's non–negotiable," I stipulated, mustering as much courage as possible, praying she couldn't see past the mask of bravado to the human who was about to pee her pants in terror. Making demands on vampires was likely a fatal proposition, but I had little to lose.

Mage's eyes narrowed. "Continue," she ordered through a tight–lipped smile.

"The only way I'll do this is without Rachel."

Mage's relaxed laughter echoed through the barren room. "Is that all? Of course. She's more trouble than she's worth." She held out her hand and I shook it, feeling the comfortable warmth of her delicate skin and wondering if making a deal with the devil felt like this.

I glanced over at the motionless lump that was Rachel, expecting to see her icy, penetrating glare still boring into me. But she had turned her focus on Mage, her eyes filled with hurt and shock. I guess she had never expected to be cast aside so easily.

So it was settled ...

I looked at Caden and the others then, and saw eyes filled with trepidation. *It'll be okay,* I tried to convey with my expression.

"So, how do you do it?" Jonah asked.

I opened my mouth to explain and promptly shut it. No, I wasn't going to give them any more information than necessary. That was one request Sofie made that I would listen to, at least.

"Everyone step forward and place a hand on the statue," I instructed.

All fifteen Council members instantly appeared around the statue, eagerness shining in their vibrant eyes. Only my four vampires dragged their feet as they moved grudgingly toward us.

"Hurry up, or we'll be going without you!" Jonah snapped.

"No, we won't," I answered smoothly. *Where is this nerve coming from?*

His cold white eyes darted to me and I saw surprise flicker in his face before it smoothed over. With a slight nod and a wink, he turned his eyes back to his hand on the statue. Unease stirred in me, and not just because of his hideous face. There was meaning in that wink. He probably wanted to kill me, but he couldn't. That knowledge brought me little comfort.

My four vampires finally reached the statue, Jonah considerately shifting to make room for Caden beside me. I reached out and grabbed hold of his arm, the need to be connected with him uncontrollable. He leaned in. "Is there no other way?"

I shook my head. "It'll be okay," I whispered back. "Sofie's prepared."

"I don't think she's prepared for this ..." he muttered, his apprehensive eyes flitting over the crowd around the statue.

"Don't worry," I offered feebly, desperate to be done with all of this. I raised my voice again. "Okay now, everyone just...stay right where you are," I instructed, my eyes on my four vampires to ensure they heard me. "Don't move." I didn't know if not moving was a requirement, but I wasn't taking any chances.

Nineteen vampires leaned closer toward the statue, their palms splayed on the statue. They must have been thinking the same thing. I could feel their anxiety and excitement lying over me like a heavy blanket. After seven hundred years, they would be in a world of humans again. My heart started pounding against my chest as hysteria briefly overwhelmed me. *I can't believe I'm doing this. I can't believe I'm unleashing this on my world!*

"You okay?" Caden asked. I glanced over, finding calm in those spectacular jade eyes.

Everything would be fine. It had to be done. With a nod and a smile, I knelt and inched the pendant I gripped in my trembling hand toward the statue's stone hand. Toward the portal.

As it approached its intended resting place, the heart of the pendant began shimmering a dazzling bluish–green, like sunlight cast over tropical waters. Like Caden's eyes. The icy cold faded to a perfectly comfortable temperature. I fumbled as I struggled to fit the pendant within the statue's fingertips. It didn't want to fit. Maybe I had misunderstood somehow? Maybe—

I heard a click.

"Now what?" Mage asked in a whisper, her eyes wide.

Frozen in a crouch so I wouldn't dislodge the pendant, I murmured, "Now we wait." *Please let this work,* I prayed. *Don't let there be any more pieces to this puzzle.* This group didn't seem like a patient lot. They'd be peeling the skin off my arms soon if this didn't work.

The seconds dragged on and my agitation increased. I was all but convinced I had misinterpreted the pendant's message when a wave of fatigue hit me. Recognizing the call back to Earth, I glanced at Caden, then at Amelie, Bishop, and Fiona. I could see it in their eyes—they felt it! Glancing around at the Council, I saw their confusion and panic; they'd gone too many years without experiencing weariness. "It's working!" I whispered breathlessly.

Looking up at Caden, I saw his eyes fixed adoringly on me. His lips moved as he mouthed, *I love you.*

Despite the current circumstances, my heart skipped a few beats. I opened my mouth to return the sentiment—

And watched in horror as he flew backward to crash into the rubble a hundred feet from me, hurled away from the statue by a still smugly grinning Jonah. Hurled away from salvation. Away from me.

"No!" I shrieked as Amelie dashed to her brother.

They weren't going to make it back in time. Within every fiber of my being, I knew this. None of this was worth it if I didn't have them.

I groped frantically for my pendant, intent on yanking it out—

CR

A cloudless blue sky hung beyond the glass ceiling above me. I was lying on the cobblestone path in the atrium, beside Veronique's tomb, the dreadful image of Caden flying away and Amelie chasing after him still vivid in my mind. I clambered to my feet, needing to see those two faces. Knowing I'd want to die if I didn't.

I found Viggo and Mortimer first. They were sitting at their bistro table, motionless, their eyes round with panic. Sofie was standing beside them, her pale, minty eyes darting about wildly. I followed her gaze.

There were bodies everywhere.

I had wanted four. I had expected nineteen. But there were more. So many more. Creamy pale, beautiful faces lay in repose on the cobblestone paths and in the flower gardens. There had to be a hundred, at least, and none of them were moving. Yet.

"What have you gone and done?" Mortimer whispered slowly, clearly in shock.

"It wasn't supposed to be like this," I stammered, shaking my head shaking back and forth in vigorous denial.

"I warned you two about unexpected outcomes, didn't I?" Sofie muttered, her tone surprisingly calm, given the disastrous situation. The four of us were standing in a minefield of comatose vampires.

The sound of shattering glass drew my attention upward in time to see a sleek black body sailing through the air from a fifth–floor balcony. Max landed beside me with the agility of a cat. The other dogs tore out the door of the mansion and surrounded me in seconds. Leo rushed out close behind them.

"I'm not sure how much help you're going to be, Maximus," Mortimer murmured.

So many vampires. So many vampires who might go ballistic as soon as they caught a whiff of my blood.

"Sofie, the talisman?" I reminded her in a sharp, desperate whisper.

She faltered, anguish in her eyes. "You weren't supposed to be back yet," she whispered. "I'm so sorry, Evangeline."

My jaw dropped.

"Evangeline, come here—now," Viggo hissed, his voice revealing fright for the first time ever.

"No! Don't move. Not an inch," Sofie immediately countered, her hand held out to stay me, her eyes riveted on a stirring body.

Bodies began to twitch and jerk then, gradually rising like corpses coming to life in a cheesy horror flick. Their vivid eyes darted wildly about—surveying; orienting themselves.

A low murmur rose from Sofie. A chant.

"What are you doing?" Mortimer hissed, frowning.

She ignored him.

Someone else joined in, amplifying the low chant—a male voice, from somewhere behind me. I turned to see who it was but a body lying bound by silvery cords on the cobblestones distracted me. Rachel. How did she get here? She hadn't been anywhere near the statue! If *she* made it ...

My heart started racing as I scanned the crowd.

I found Caden and Amelie ten feet away—the two faces I feared I would never see again. Fiona and Bishop were close by as well. I cried out, and tears of joy began streaking down my face. They had made it! Caden and my three dear friends had been rescued from their hell. At that moment, I didn't care about the other hundred vampires. Viggo and Mortimer could deal with them.

I heard the sudden rush of flames as a ring of fire erupted around Veronique's statue. Sofie must have started it. I didn't care. They could deal with that too.

I watched Caden's eyes hopefully, waiting impatiently for him to fully comprehend where he was. They were wild with confusion at first, but then I saw the glimmer of comprehension. He smiled as his eyes fell on mine. His smile grew wider. I exhaled heavily, relief flooding my body. I wanted to run toward him, to leap into his arms, to feel his body pressed against mine again.

His nostrils flared as he inhaled deeply.

An inkling of fear stirred …

I watched as his lips curled back in a snarl, then his face contorted into a horrific mixture of pleasure and anguish. He was gritting his teeth tightly, as if fighting an unbearable urge. He squeezed his eyes tightly shut. When they opened, his beautiful jade eyes were gone, swallowed by fully dilated pupils, with only a narrow rim of jade around those giant black circles. The whites of his eyes had turned crimson, the tiny white veins in them pulsating. They were the eyes of a thirsty vampire.

Max's responding growl raised the short hairs on my neck.

Caden didn't even acknowledge the threat of the dog. Those demonic eyes locked on me. He took a faltering step—and then he lunged.

Max intercepted, leaping for Caden's chest at the same time that I screamed, "No!"

25. Exiled

My earsplitting scream faded to a dull moan as I glanced around, bewildered by my new surroundings. I was sitting in a large, comfortable chair in front of a bay window. Everything outside was white and green—snow and trees. Towering snow–capped mountains and an endless ocean of evergreens. No atrium. No friends. No pit of vampires, ready to tear me into a million pieces.

No Caden.

"Not again, Sofie!" I wailed, flopping back into the chair. I felt my forehead crease and I squeezed my eyes tightly shut, but the tears still found a way out, rolling down my cheeks in a steady stream. *Another world, another twist to this never–ending curse. Is this another one of Sofie's unexpected outcomes?*

"Is everything alright, Evangeline?"

I bolted out of my chair, startled by the male voice—the tone familiar but the accent, a thick Irish brogue, new. Whirling, I found myself opposite a wall of faces. Leo stood closest to me. Behind him were eight other people that I recognized as Viggo and Mortimer's staff, as well as Julian and Valentina Forero. In the far corner stood two men with enough facial hair that they could be mistaken for a pair of mountain yetis. *One of them must be the Irishman. But why did the man speak to me as if he knows me?*

Save for Leo and the yetis, everyone looked as confused as I felt.

Max came trotting in from the hallway to stop at my side, followed by his pack mates. "Max?" I croaked with relief, throwing my arms around him. He responded with an affectionate nuzzle against my cheek.

The Irish voice spoke again. "No doubt you're all confused right now…"

I gasped when I saw whose lips were moving: Leo. His grandfatherly demeanor and distinguished British accent had vanished, replaced by a leprechaun–like Irishman. "I'll explain everything later, but know it was either this or death. Darlene?" He addressed one of the older maids who stood in a daze, dripping yellow latex gloves on her hands. "There's a clipboard on the table out there in the hall, with instructions."

Darlene stared at him for a moment longer, bewildered. Obviously I wasn't the only one shocked by Leo's dual personality. That, or she was still trying to wrap her head around the fact that she had been scrubbing a toilet only a few seconds before and was now in a log cabin in the mountains. Finally she nodded and, slowly peeling off her gloves, shuffled out of the room. The other seven staff members trailed close behind her.

That left me, the dogs, the Forero kids, the two yetis, and the man who looked like Leo standing in the large room. "Valentina, Julian, please see Darlene about your accommodations," Leo said to them. "You'll need to share a room."

"Where the hell are we, butler? And where are our parents?" Julian snapped.

Leo strolled over to stand in front of the future drug lord, a triumphant smile on his face. "I'm not the butler here, Julian. Here, in these mountains, I'm God. Piss me off once and you'll be tossed to the wolves faster than you can blink. Your parents are vampire fodder. The only reason you're not is because of Evangeline's naivety. Understand?"

My eyes bulged, listening to Leo deliver the threat. *Where did the sweet, old grandfatherly butler go?*

Julian and Valentina disappeared in seconds, the message clear. Satisfied, Leo turned to the two yetis, addressing them in some odd language that I had never heard before. The yetis grunted in unison and left out a side door.

I was now alone with Leo, wary of what other surprises he had in store for me. I watched him calmly walk over to one of the bookshelves. He pulled down a book and began fanning through the pages until a thick envelope popped out. Plucking it from the pages, he placed the book back in its rightful place, then walked over to me. "Here." He handed the envelope to me. My name, written in Sofie's floral scrawl, adorned the front. "This should make a few things clearer."

I stared dumbly at him. He ignored my dumbstruck expression and continued. "I'll be getting settled in. If you need anything, just holler." He gave one of the dogs—Remington, I recognized by the dark blue collar— a scratch under the chin, then strolled away, a knowing smirk on his face.

When he was gone, I turned to Max. "Who is that?" I whispered.

Max emitted a burst of snuffling laughter. *That's Leo. Long story. He'll explain later.*

"Do you know what's going on?"

Read the letter.

I grunted, annoyed. I couldn't tell if it was fear of misrepresenting the facts or pure laziness on the giant werebeast's part that drove Max to such useless answers. I looked for a place to sit, taking in my surroundings for the first time. The place reminded me of a ski chalet, with its cathedral ceiling and stone fireplace. The furniture was all made of wood and plush, casual fabrics stuffed comfortably enough to sink into. Overall, a pleasant atmosphere.

I ended up sitting back down in the chair by the window, clutching the stiff, thick envelope in my trembling hands. *What will I find in here?* Was it going to tell me that Sofie had been lying all this time? Or that Caden and my friends were dead? There was only one way to find out. I exhaled heavily. "Like pulling off a Band–Aid, Max," I murmured as I tore the envelope open, adding, "one that's crazy–glued to my armpit."

Inside were several pages of lined paper and a stack of photographs. Flipping through the pictures first, I saw they were the ones Amelie had taken during my last visit to the caves. Sofie had printed them for me.

My stomach dropped when I glimpsed a candid picture of Caden leaning up against a cave wall like a model in a designer jeans ad. He was smiling at something unseen in the distance, his jade eyes twinkling with pleasure. My heart ached at the sight of that smile; I needed so badly to see it again—see it so I could erase the murderous look now etched in my memory, the look on his face when he realized how much he wanted to kill me. He likely would have, had I not been wrenched out of there.

He had been right all along.

Agony tore my heart. I set aside the pictures for the time being and unfolded the letter to see Sofie's elegant script.

Take a deep breath. First of all, let me assure you this is not another spell that will have you running on a wild goose chase to another world. I promise you that. You are still here, two feet firmly planted on Earth. I just won't tell you where you are— for everyone's safety.

If you are reading this, it's because you have succeeded in bringing a vampire back with you—hopefully four, including your Caden. Now that you have, you will be relieved to know that the necklace will no longer transport you to Ratheus every night. But do not take it off. It has bound itself to you, to your heart. Without it on, your heart will stop beating.

You're probably wondering why I have sent you to this snowy cabin in the woods. Do you remember me mentioning that there was a "complication" in unlocking Veronique's tomb and that your necklace was needed to get her out? I feel I should explain the whole truth now …

Of course she hadn't told me everything!

When I was casting the Causal Enchantment, I was full of raw angst and self-pity over the loss of Nathan, love for Veronique, and the intense need to one day find love again. All of those emotions melded together and resulted in the solution to our venom issue, but also an exceptionally cruel trick. The enchantment gave me the gift of love—a different sort of love, but just as compelling—when it bound itself to you.

Anyway, this was a gift with a condition. I would one day be forced to choose between you and Veronique. How, you ask? Well, when I first entombed Veronique within that statue, I basically encapsulated her heart within her pendant. Not physically, of course, but the life force of her heart. Releasing her was supposed to be simple enough. I just had to place the pendant within the statue's outstretched hand.

I suspected this was what needed to be done to bring the vampires back with you all along. The similarities were too noticeable to ignore. However, I didn't mention it to you until today because I was trying to buy myself time. Time to find a way around the awful predicament I was in. You see, the enchantment "decided" that it would bind your heart to the pendant as well, thus entwining your life with my sister's. Once that necklace is placed within the hands of her tomb, Veronique's life force will shift back to her, pulling yours along with it and killing you.

I will never allow that to happen, I promise you that. However, Mortimer and Viggo make keeping that promise fairly tricky. They don't trust me. I expect that the moment you step foot on Earth with your friends, Mortimer and Viggo will get hold of you to ensure I complete the spell, by any means necessary. They will not wait.

If you are...where you are...that means the clock has run out. It means you could not wait any longer. You have held up your end of the bargain in bringing us the solution to our curse, and yet I haven't found a way to save you from yours.

So I have sent you far away, where Mortimer and Viggo will never find you. As far as they know, you may be on Earth or you may be on another world. The house you will be residing in, indefinitely, is the result of a dream Nathan and I shared. I had it built—unbeknownst to Viggo and Mortimer—as a safe haven for you.

I promised you that I would keep you safe. Sending you away was the only way I could do that effectively. You will be safe there until your friends learn to control their lust for human blood and I find a loophole to untangle your heart from Veronique's. I know, I know, I said there were no loopholes. But I'm determined to prove the Laws of Magic wrong. As much as I love and miss my sister dearly, I will not allow your death to be the cost of regaining her. She will remain frozen in time until I resolve this.

I doubt Viggo and Mortimer saw this coming. They will be shocked, to say the least, when you disappear, along with the dogs and their entire wait staff. I even threw in Julian and Valentina based on your sympathies. If they get to be a nuisance, just tell Leo and he'll dispose of them.

Mortimer and Viggo will be angry enough to kill me. They may do it. You may be reading the farewell words of a recently deceased vampire. One whose love for you could easily rival that of any mother for her own child. However, with me gone, they *have no hope of ever seeing Veronique again. I hope they're smarter than that. We will see.*

My hands were shaking as they fell into my lap, still holding the letter. Sofie could be...dead? The very idea sparked a great sense of loss in me, one I had not expected. I picked up the letter again.

I'm sorry that you have moved from one prison to another one. Don't try to run. You will not get far and you will make Leo's life stressful. I have entrusted you to his care, something I should have done many years ago.

I have had to hide my feelings for you until now, in fear of what Viggo may do if he realized how vested I was in your survival. I no longer have to hide.

I love you. Please believe that I live now only for your happiness. I hope we'll see each other again soon. I will take care of your friends as best I can.

S

P.S. If it's any consolation, there's an account containing an obscene amount of money with your name on it. When it's safe, it's all yours to do with as you wish.

Tears flowed freely from my eyes now, giant droplets that splattered on the pages, smearing the ink. I frantically wiped them away, not wanting to lose her words in case they were her last. *She must have written this the day I left for the last time.*

Before I returned with an entire army of vampires.

Sofie truly cared for me. Loved me, even. I had a maternal vampire and I had never known. All because she had to hide the truth from Viggo and Mortimer.

And the curse wasn't over yet. It would never be over until I was dead.

ᆻ

I must have read that letter over fifty times. When I finally looked up, dusk was settling over the snowy landscape. I was still alone, aside from the dogs. No one had once ventured into the great room. *Likely cowering, still in shock,* I thought.

I folded the letter and stuffed it into my back pocket until I could lock it away for safe–keeping in my room. Once I knew where my room was.

As if on cue, Leo strolled in with a plate. "You must be hungry," he said in that bizarre new accent. He motioned me toward a solid wood dining table, dimly lit by a chandelier made of deer antlers. I stood and followed him over in a daze, mechanically sitting down in the chair he offered. "You okay?"

I hesitated, not knowing how to answer. "I'm still in shock, I think. There's been a few big...surprises of late," I said, eyeing him as I poked the mysterious–looking stew with my fork. I had no appetite.

"Okay, go ahead," he prompted, smirking.

"Why British?" I finally asked.

He chuckled, thoroughly amused.

A heavy wooden side door burst open then, and one of the yetis stepped through, bringing an icy gust of wind and a dusting of snow in with him. I shivered responsively.

"Cold?" Leo asked. He flicked his hand toward the rustic stone fireplace across from us, and flames instantly erupted among the logs.

I frowned. It wasn't a gas fireplace. There were no remote controls that could do that.

Leo winked at me.

Realization hit me. I gasped. "You were the voice I heard chanting with Sofie," I whispered, my eyes bulging. "You're a witch?"

"I prefer warlock or sorcerer. I'm not in the least bit feminine," Leo answered casually.

"How …" I croaked, my voice barely audible.

"Oh, there'll be plenty of time to get into the 'hows' while we're exiled here; tonight is not the time for that. I may have been pretending to be the perfect gentleman's man but I wasn't faking being old. These bones of mine need a good rest after the exertion of transporting us here. Especially those four horses." He nodded in Max's direction.

I looked at Max with narrowed eyes. "Did you know?" Max found that question funny for some reason, making that odd half grunt, half snort that was supposed to be laughter. *He knew!* I scowled at him. "Do Viggo and Mortimer know?"

"No, no, no...They *didn't*." Leo shook his head. "They do now, though. Our Sofie—she's a cunning one. She surreptitiously planted me in their service about fifteen years ago."

"You pretended to be a British butler for fifteen years?" I said incredulously.

Leo took a seat by the fireplace and pulled out a pipe. "Viggo is particular about his butlers. They have to be 'authentic.' It was the only way."

"I thought your kind despised vampires," I murmured, recalling Sofie referring to witches and vampires as the Montagues and the Capulets.

"That's true. But my allegiance will always be with Sofie." He smiled mysteriously, reminiscing fondly about something.

"How" was about to leave my mouth again but he waved it off before I could utter a sound. "Another time, please," he said, puffing on his pipe, now lit.

I nodded, biting my bottom lip in frustration. "Can I at least ask where we are?"

He bellowed laughter. "You can ask a thousand times and I won't tell you."

My eyes narrowed. I glanced at Max.

"And he won't tell you either," Leo warned, eyeing my guard dog. "So don't pester him to death."

"I could order him. I'm his master," I responded haughtily.

"And he'll ignore you, on grounds that he is protecting you best by leaving you in the dark," Leo answered, equally smug.

It's true, I heard Max say. *I've learned the loopholes.*

I sighed. What was the point of being a master if my subordinate was keeping secrets and obeying only when convenient? Another set of pressing questions popped into my head. "Do you know what happened back there? Is Sofie alive? Are my friends alive?"

"Sofie is still alive. We are linked through magic. I would have felt it, otherwise. As for the others, all I can say is that Sofie successfully wired the building with Merth. No vampire is getting in or out of there."

"So they're all going to live in there?" I asked, screwing my face up as I pictured over a hundred vampires—most of them likely homicidal, blood–crazed maniacs right now—touring around the place.

"Yup! One big, bloodsucking kibbutz. That is, if they don't all kill each other." He quickly added as my eyes widened in fear, "Don't worry, I'm sure they'll all be full of love and joy, now that they have human blood again." I noted the sarcasm in his voice. "Besides, they have enough blood in there to supply the whole lot of them for a few months, and Sofie can get more. They *should* be able to manage."

I nodded. "So how long am I a prisoner here?" My eyes roamed the dimly lit, rustic room. Though much simpler in taste than Viggo and Mortimer's place, my second prison appeared equally comfortable.

Leo sighed. "I'm not sure how many years it will be yet. It all depends on Sofie."

"Years?" I shrieked.

"Calm down," he said, patting the air. "Let me explain. You see, we're in quite the pickle now. If Sofie and I hadn't brought you here, I can guarantee that you would already be dead. If not by the hands of Mortimer and Viggo—they're proficient in getting what they want—then by the fangs of a hundred or so vampires you inadvertently brought back with you. They're not stable right now. Not even your friends. You saw that, firsthand." He paused to puff on his pipe again.

I shuddered as the vision of Caden's veiny red eyes flashed through my mind.

"It would be like covering yourself in pink frosting and sitting down with a group of three–year–olds," he added.

"I still don't understand what happened," I muttered. "There were only supposed to be nineteen and that was because I had no other choice! The pendant told me they had to be touching the statue and then ..." My voice drifted off as understanding dawned. I gasped. "They've all touched the statue at some point! They didn't have to be touching it right at that moment, though. I misunderstood!"

"Not surprising. Those spells are tricky buggers to figure out," Leo muttered around the pipe in his mouth. "You were likely too excited to distinguish the details of the pendant's hints. Your biggest worry right now is Mortimer and Viggo. They'll stop at nothing to free Veronique.

They don't have all the details but they do know they need that pendant. By now they'll likely have figured out the rest. But they're not your only worry. This Rachel character...Believe me, she won't forget about you. Killing you is about as important to her as human blood. Revenge—it's an ugly thing for these creatures. From what Sofie has told me, you did a number on her." Leo chuckled.

"You don't know the half of it," I grumbled, realizing my deal with Mage to leave her behind hadn't won me any brownie points. "I hope Sofie kills her." I silently prayed that she had thrown Rachel into that massive pyre that erupted around the statue. Otherwise Caden would never be safe with her around.

Leo took another long draw on his pipe. "Listen to you—vampire–slayer." He chuckled through a swirl of smoke. "And then let's not forget about the elusive Ursula, whom we can't track because she's hopping through human host bodies like she's riding a public transit system. You are the ultimate means of torturing Sofie, a goal that drives her entire existence.

"So you see, as much as you would like to go see Sofie and these friends of yours—I'm sure this Caden fellow would be pleasant under different circumstances—it's simply not an option. And as much as we would all like to see you happy, seeing you alive is more important. We will remain here until Sofie has figured out a way to get that blasted necklace off your neck safely, and no amount of begging and pleading will do you any good. So don't bother, kiddo."

I swallowed. This imprisonment was even worse than before. At least before, I could escape every night to see Caden. Now, in this winter abyss, I had no means of contact, no way of making sure they were okay, nothing to remind me of them except my memories and a stack of four–by–sixes. "When my friends get over this whole blood–crazed thing...can they come here?"

Leo got up and strolled over to place his hand on my shoulder. He squeezed lightly. "It's not something that happens overnight, Evangeline. You know that by now. We're not sure how well they'll adjust. They could be like baby vampires and, well, they usually spend the first twenty or so years lurking in shadows before they have some level of control."

"So what are you saying? I can't see them for the next twenty years? I'll be...old! You may as well have let Mortimer and Viggo kill me!" I cried. A new flood of tears overwhelmed me.

"No, no, I'm not saying that at all. Don't get all wound up," Leo shushed me. "But...do you even want to see them after Caden tried...after that?" his voice had turned gentle.

"I...I don't know," I answered truthfully. "No, wait! Of course. It wasn't his fault! He had warned me."

"Evangeline!" Leo shook his head in exasperation, but then began chuckling. "I see what Sofie meant ..." he said to himself. "You've changed, but you haven't changed ..." He dropped his hand. "Your friends will come looking for you when the time is right and Mortimer and Viggo can't track them. We just hope that, when they do find you, they can control themselves. Otherwise the dogs and I will have to kill them, no question about it."

I looked down at my stew, then set my fork down and pushed the plate away. I buried my face in my arms. Leo's hand settled on my head, patting me gently. It was a small comfort, but he was trying. I turned and looked up at the old man, my appointed guardian, wiping away tears. "What am I supposed to do, Leo?"

He smiled. That smile, at least, I recognized as his. "Trust us."

Excerpt from Asylum

Chapter 1

"Forgive me," I whispered, knowing my words never reached her ears. She was already gone. Safe. Safely away from this deadly atrium. Safe from Mortimer and Viggo. Safe from me.

Now for damage control …

I scanned the crowd of a hundred–odd depraved vampires, their eyes wild with varying degrees of bewilderment and crazed bloodlust after the briefest scent of a human. There! Four familiar faces; the four who needed to survive. Relief washed over me. *Thank God for those pictures.*

I closed my eyes, searching for the one last thread of energy I needed to cast another spell. *Ah…*I grasped a miniscule, glowing purple helix coil, much like a DNA strand, floating beside my heart, and yanked with my mental hand. It immediately shot up to my fingertips. Armed with magic, I raised my hand toward Veronique's tomb within the brightly burning pyre. With a thought, embers leaped out to soar toward my fingertips as if magnetized.

And then I struck.

The sparks shot from my fingers and erupted into six foot–high circles of flame, forming a formidable barrier of protection around Evangeline's friends—large enough not to ignite them but tight enough to keep them from leaping out and making a run for it.

"Sofie?" Mortimer hollered uncertainly.

I turned toward him. His face a mask of shock, he stood next to Viggo, both frozen like ice sculptures, both struggling to grasp the events of the past ten seconds. I knew that confusion would quickly give way to understanding, and retaliation would follow.

I'll deal with them later. For my sister's sake, they needed to survive. And for my sake, in an indirect fashion. With another flick of my hand, three flaming circles formed—one around each of them and the last around myself. *There. That should hold them until I'm finished.*

Now, elimination.

From the corner of my eye, I caught the telltale silvery white hair and hideous features of a mutant. I shuddered, finding their very existence repulsive but worse, knowing the Merth–laced building couldn't confine them. The last thing we needed were those monsters running loose in New York, especially with the People's Sentinel watching us.

Flames shot out from my fingertips and struck the hideous creature, igniting his body as if it were made from tissue paper. His one short scream—the shrill sound of death—echoed through the atrium, sending a chill down my spine. I didn't let it distract me from my focus, though. Spotting two more mutants, I quickly dispatched them as well.

Heads started to turn as the screams attracted the attention of the other vampires. Soon enough, they'd figure out the fate I had in store for them. Then I'd have mass hysteria and vampires hiding in every nook and cranny in this place. I didn't have time to hunt them all down individually.

Fiery sparks flew freely from my fingertips, landing on any vampire in sight. Within seconds, dozens of flaming bodies were thrashing on the ground, scorching the leaves and petals of the atrium's plants and engulfing any vampires caught too near. But I knew there were more vampires out there in Viggo's urban jungle, out of my view.

There was only one thing left to do. I had to torch the entire atrium, then hope I could control the fire enough that the entire building didn't go up in flames. Inhaling deeply, reconciled to the plan, I raised both hands.

A body lying on the ground, bound by Merth, distracted me. A vampire with jet black hair and yellow eyes—Rachel. My jaw clenched as I imagined slowly tearing the flesh off her body as she screamed, only to allow it to grow back so I could do it again...But there was no time for that. Sighing with disappointment, I raised a finger toward her, preparing to rid everyone of the viper once and for all.

"Caden. No!"

The desperate scream stilled the spark poised in my hand. My eyes swept over in time to see Caden, a lost, vacant expression on his face, taking a step toward the flames. I gasped. He was going to kill himself.

With the last bit of magic I possessed after executing Evangeline's complicated transportation spell, I instantly extinguished every flame in the atrium before he could succeed.

Caden stared back at me, unharmed, resentment marring his stunning face. *That's okay. You can hate me. You're safe.*

A powerful hand grabbed me by the neck and hoisted me into the air. "Where is she?" Viggo growled, rage blazing in his eyes.

Despite everything, I laughed.